Drama...Another Man's Girl

A Sydney Lyttle Novel

Drama...Another Man's Girl
A Novel

Cover Concept by: Sydney Lyttle
Cover lay out and graphic design by: www.mariondesigns.com
Cover Models: Tasheen (Ty) McCall and Candice Bell

ISBN - 13: 978-1-4536-3919-1
ISBN - 10: 1-4536-3919-5

Create Space www.createspace.com/3462244
1200 12th Avenue South
Suite 1200
Seattle, WA 98144

In Loving Memory

My heart is saddened now that you're gone
I pray your soul has found some peace,
Although I'll miss you from this day on
I take comfort in the memories.

R.I.P. Tiffany C. Montgomery-Mason
November 2, 1979 – April 28, 2009

You will <u>always</u> be remembered, <u>never</u> be forgotten.

Acknowledgements

It is 5:03 a.m. just minutes before day break and I can't sleep. Figured since I was up I might as well do something constructive with my time like getting these acknowledgements done. I'm sitting here thinking what a journey this has been. I have to admit I never imagined that I would actually become a published author, but here I am. The pen and the pad—what a dangerous combination when in the right hands!!! First and foremost I would like to thank **God** for whom all of this is possible. He instilled the gift of words in me and guided me as those words turned into chapters and those chapters turned into novels. With him by my side—failure is not an option.

My three beautiful children **Ty, Tia & Taniah** you are the absolute best part of me. Every time I look at each one you I realize just how amazing God is. Your love has had a tremendous impact on my life. My son, **Ty**, whom I admire and respect for growing up to be the man I've always known you were destined to become. You make me prouder every day that I live. Mother's Day 2009 was my best one ever—a bachelors degree! You go boy! To my daughters **Tia** and **Taniah** the light that reflects back at me every time I look into your eyes is one that I pray will never go dim. I love you both more than words could ever express.

My husband **Craig** almost two decades!!! WOW! Where does the time go? Thank you for being there for me whenever I need you. I know I have not always made it easy, but you stuck it out. You have to have an incredible amount of patience to be married to me, and you certainly have more than your share. You are a wonderful man and I am truly blessed to share my life with you. I love you!

My **mother** who has always had my back, thank you for being there cheering me on from the sidelines and in the front row when they would let you get that close. I love you Ma. Thanks to my **father** for always believing that I could do anything I set my mind to. You have incredibly high standards that would intimidate most, but I welcome the challenge. You are the reason I aim high. You showed me that nothing is out of my reach if I want it bad enough. You have influenced my life in ways that you couldn't even begin to imagine. I love you Dad.

Sandy, **Theresa** and **Elsie**, you three are my "other mother's" and have contributed in shaping me into the person I am today. How fortunate for me that there are three of you—a triple blessing for sure. How did I get so lucky?

Mrs. Shelton AKA "Nana" thank you for not only believing in my potential, but my son's as well. You are an incredible woman and I am so lucky to have you in my life. **Mr. Shelton** I can't thank you enough for your undying faith in me. You never stopped believing in me. I will always love you for that.

i

My sister **Joy** who is without a doubt one of my favorite people in this world hands down. You have always, always, always been there for me. You have never let me down—not once. I thank you from the bottom of my heart for everything you did in helping to make my dream a reality. I love you! My big sis **Tricia**, thank you for being that positive role model in my life when role models were few and far between. I remember back when I was struggling to find where it was that I fit in and always trying to compete and getting frustrated when I felt like I wouldn't measure up. You were the one who never let me forget that it's about reaching my level—not theirs. I will always love you for that. My sister **Wendy**, thank you for all of your feedback in the early stages of the book. Much appreciated girl love ya! My sister **Stephanie**, thank you for spreading the word that my book was coming out. With all the people you know it must have taken months for you to tell everyone. Thanks a million Steph! Love ya chicka!

To my lil' big brother **Jason**, you are an exceptional human being and I am extremely blessed to be your sister. Thank you for all of your support. I love you. My other lil' big brother **James** thanks for being that fun and loving 'Unc James' that my girls adore. As you are preparing to take that next step in your life, I wish you all the best. Love ya!

My dearest **Gail**, the things that I've learned from you over the years have helped to strengthen my talent in ways that even you'd be surprised. You've always let me know that I was born to do great things and I pray that I do not disappoint you. I love you!

My cousin **Lisa**, you recognized that this was in me even before I did. Remember how it all started? Back when we were kids. At eight and nine years old when other kids were copying song lyrics—I was writing my own and you were singing them. I'll never forget those days. I'm happy that you were there to share that time with me. Love you girl! To my cuz **Tony**! You've been down for me long before stocking caps and waves even hit the scene. Your continued support through the years has meant so much to me. Thanks for everything cuz! I love you Tone!

Darshell, you were that voice in the back of my head telling me to keep going every time I felt like giving up. You never hesitated to let me know that I was wasting my time doing anything other than writing. I cannot count how many times you lent me your ear, or how often you advised me to follow my heart that you always knew were the pen and the pad. Your fierce determination is the thing I love most about you. Don't ever lose that!

My girl **Paula**, I don't even know where to begin to thank you girl. You are so many things to me. The word friend doesn't even begin to define our bond. Thank you for your continued support through the years. Thank you for allowing me to bounce ideas off of you while staying on the phone until daybreak talking about these characters as if they were people that we knew instead of figments of my imagination. I will never forget those late night conversations that kept us up waaaayyyy past our bedtime on work nights. The book is published girl. Get some sleep. My ace **Reina,** you mean more to me than I can say. You are really something special chick. I hope reading all those chapters didn't get you in trouble when you were supposed to be working. Thanks for all your input. Love you girl. My girls for *life*...**Gina, Keiah, Lorraine, Jacinda, Dawn, Tonia, Christina** and **Lucreshia**...All of you chicks are the freaking bomb! I can't even begin to express how much I appreciate all of your love and support through the years. I love all of you to pieces!

Dreana, you have not only been a great support for me, but you are a major contributor to my son's success as well. I can never thank you enough for everything you've done and all the positive feedback you have given me countless times while I was writing this book. Thanks for just being you girl because that is plenty! I love you Drea! **Queen Goddess**, thank you for all of the advice, the contact information, and especially the lectures. I really needed to hear it. Most of all; thanks for the love, support, and encouragement. It really went a long way. Much love girl.

Missy you are the bomb chick! Not only are you my writing partner in crime and business partner, but you also put your editors cap on just for me. Can't tell you how special that makes me feel. I'm grateful that you were there those times when I knew I was going overboard, but somehow couldn't seem to stop myself from taking that leap. You never hesitated to remind me that if I'm not part of the solution—I'm part of the problem. I have learned a lot about this literary game from you. I could not have done this without you. Just so you know...the grind doesn't stop here! This is just the beginning girl!

Matayah Winfrey, I truly appreciate everything you've done. Your talent knows no bounds. **Barbara**, your methods should be bottled and sold. You have an excellent way of bringing out the best in any writer. I can't tell you how much I appreciate all you've done.

Toya B thanks so much for joining the team in the eleventh hour and jumping right in like it was nothing. You are a trooper girl! There will be no more picking you up near the end of the trip—you will definitely be on board the next project before the train leaves the station!!!

My boy **Corey**, I bet you thought I forgot about you huh? Well it's pretty hard to forget one of the best people you have ever met. Thanks for everything over the years. Your continued support means the world to me. Keep doing your thing. I see you.

My fellow authors **Cassandra Miller-Gamble** and **Avery Goode (AG)** thanks for everything. You chicks are the bomb!!! To fellow author **Angelic Martin-Artiaga**, thank you for the countless e-mails and hour long phone conversations about the business. I appreciate you putting me in contact with some pretty amazing people. You have truly been a God's send and I am blessed to have you on my team.

A Very Special thanks to my son **Ty** and his girlfriend **Candice** for giving me such a gorgeous cover. The two of you together are FIRE!!! It's funny how I keep receiving e-mails and face book messages asking if I'm related to the guy on the cover because we look alike. I have to laugh at that. Like it's really that hard to figure out that you're my kid! Ty always remember that you helped your mother make her first book that much more special. I love you man!!! And, I can't forget **Keith** at **Marion Designs** for designing such a hot cover! You really did your thing Keith!!! The proof is in the pudding!!!

To all of the aspiring authors out there—if your mind can conceive it—you can achieve it. I am proof of that. To those of you who have read the excerpts on my website and on face book, thanks for all of the messages. I sincerely appreciate the feedback! Keeps me motivated!! And, to anyone who has purchased this book—I truly appreciate the support. I do realize that you had a choice, and you chose to purchase my book—I can't tell you how much that means to me!!! I hope you enjoy reading it as much as I've enjoyed writing it. If I have forgotten anyone, please forgive me and know that I truly appreciate anything you've done that has contributed to the release of this book.

Until my fingers meet the keyboard again,

Sydney

Follow Me:
http://twitter.com/InSydneyswords
http://facebook.com/Sydney.lyttle1
www.InSydneyswords.com

Please feel free to send your comments/inquiries to:
PO Box 359 Mount Pocono, PA 18344

Or E-Mail Me:
InSydneyswords@gmail.com

"Our deepest fear is not that we are inadequate. Our deepest fear is that we are powerful beyond measure. It is our light, not our darkness, that most frightens us."
-- Marianne Williamson --

Prelude

"Is it that hard for you to be around me Chass?" Shane asked, noticing my reluctance to look him in the eye.

Brushing off his cockiness and fighting to keep my emotions in check I replied, "I can handle it."

"Can you?" He leaned into me forcing me backwards.

"Of course I can," I replied sharply as I struggled to conceal the obvious effect he had on me.

"Convince me."

His tongue was in my mouth before I could respond. I tried to push him away, but my desire for him was much stronger than my ability to resist.

"Stop fighting me Baby. You know you missed this just as much as I have." He pulled his tongue out of my mouth long enough to get those words out.

"We shouldn't be in here Shane. EL is probably looking around the party for me as we speak."

"And," he said, like he could care less.

"I guess you forgot about the agreement we made to stay away from each other until I figure out a way to break up with EL."

He twisted his face up. "Listen to you. I'm up here puttin' my heart on the line and you still comin' at me sideways. What'chu mean figure out a way? Just tell him the truth. You need to stop handlin' that nigga like he gon' break. When you gon' leave him Chass? Let me know what's up."

"Soon Shane, I'm gonna leave him soon."

"How soon? How much longer you gon' have me waitin' Baby? A week, a month, what? Let me know somethin'. I had to pull you in here just to grab a minute alone wit'chu. All that sneakin' around shit is dead Chass. You can hang that up. Hurry up and cut that nigga off. You wastin' time that we could be together Baby."

"It's not that simple Shane." I was conflicted. As much as I wanted to be with Shane, I wasn't looking forward to hurting EL—although I knew there was no way around it.

"While you figurin' out how to soften the blow for this nigga, I'm supposed to what? Play the background. Watch from the sidelines."

"You act like this is easy for me."

"You think this shit is easy for me? You expect me to fall back and let you stay wit' that nigga when we both know you wanna be wit' me. I'm supposed to force myself to stay away from you until you find the right time to tell him what's up. Baby you buggin'. So I can't see you. I can't make love to you. This shit is torture," he said softly, while his fingers caressed the sides of my face.

"I don't like it either Shane. I just need a little more time. That's all. I will find a way to tell him about us."

"Nah Baby, fuck that. I can't do this shit no more. I'm done waitin'. Either you wanna be wit' me or you don't—simple as that. I want you to cut him off tonight," he said fed up.

"Tonight?"

"Yeah tonight," he repeated forcefully. "Stop stallin' Baby. It's time for you to let that nigga know what's up."

"What happened to giving me time and space so I could deal with this on my own? This is gonna kill EL Shane. The least you can do is not back me into a corner. Now all of a sudden you're so impatient that you can't wait no more. You never had a problem with waiting before."

"That was before I fell in love wit'chu Chass. And it's not all of a sudden. I been tellin' you this for how long now. I'm not tryin' to share you wit' that nigga no more."

"Don't do this Shane. You know I've never been good at resisting you."

"Then stop resistin' and go wit'cha feelings."

"I... I can't..." I whimpered unconvincingly as I struggled to finish my sentence.

He placed his finger against my lips signaling for me to stop talking. "I wanna make love to you Chass, and all I wanna hear you say is that you want the same thing," he ordered as he slowly removed his finger from my lips.

My body craved him. I wanted more than anything to make love to him. Then I thought about EL and how selfish we were being and I backed away.

"Why you keep pullin' away from me Baby? Are you tryin' to tell me that you don't wanna be wit' me?"

"Shane..." I hesitated.

"It's a simple question Chass. If you can look me in the eye and honestly say that you don't want me, I'll leave you alone." He lifted my chin up with his index finger forcing me to look into his eyes. "Now I'll ask you again, do you still wanna be wit' me?"

I wanted him. I couldn't deny it. I'd have a better chance trying to convince myself that my heart doesn't beat. I looked him in his gorgeous green eyes and slowly nodded 'yes'.

"Nah Chass," he shook his head. "I need to hear you say the words." His tone was seductive yet serious. His eyes spoke to me seductively increasing the speed of my heartbeat rapidly. I tried not to give into him, but it was a battle that I was clearly losing.

"Yes...I wanna be with you. I want that more than anything else in this world," I replied kissing what was left of my resistance goodbye.

"Then stop tryin' to fight it. This is a destiny type thing Baby. You can fight me, but you can't fight this." He pointed to my heart and then to his. "I want you. Right here...right now," he whispered as he softly kissed my lips. Then he unloosened my towel and it dropped to the floor.

"Damn Baby you look good." He looked at me like he was under a spell, while his dick stood like a pool stick.

He slipped his hand in-between my warm thighs causing my clit to throb like it had a heartbeat. With his index finger, he pushed the crotch of my bathing suit aside and slowly entered my warm inviting flesh. I moaned as my juices soaked his finger. He picked me up and carried me to the wide oak table that was sitting in the middle of the floor and sat me on top of it. Then he unsnapped the top of my bathing suit and it fell beneath my breast. He caressed my erect nipples with his soft lips while sliding his finger in and out of my soaking wet pussy. The temperature in the room felt like it rose at least ten degrees. My body was on fire. When he removed his delicious instrument from his swim trunks my clit went crazy.

"Put it in," I spoke softly in between our passionate kisses while my pussy was doing back flips. Just as the head of his penis began to enter me, the door opened.

Summer 2001…

1

Been There Done That

Chass

"**Why you keep calling me** with this bullshit? I got a man bitch! I don't want Trent!" I screamed into the phone.

"That's not what he told me. He said you keep trying to get him to come check you. What's that about?" asked the angry chick on the other end of the line.

I sucked my teeth. "If he told you that then he's lying to you, and you believe that shit 'cause you're just that stupid." Three minutes into the conversation and this chick was already working my damn nerves.

"There ain't a damn thing stupid about me Chass. Just back off Trent and we won't have a problem," she threatened.

Oh please... like I need her to tell me that. I couldn't get rid of Trent's ass fast enough. I thought angrily.

"Girl please, I am the last person you should be worried about. You need to check with the last three bitches that called me about Trent. He got y'all taking turns. What the fuck do I want with Trent? That crazy muthafucka is one finger short of a fist."

I was pissed that she actually thought I still wanted Trenton after all the shit he put me through. Seems like my bad judgment always comes back to bite me in the ass. I broke up with Trent over a year ago and he is still in denial. Trent was the worst mistake of my life, and believe me I've made some doozies. He was a rebound relationship, so that was part of the problem right there. I didn't take the time to see what type of person he was before I rushed into things with him. What I wouldn't give to do it all over again. I could have avoided that catastrophe. Who knew Trent would turn out to be a damn stalker? You never can tell with brothers these days. It's not like they wear a sign. My luck with men is so bad I should have become a nun.

"Yeah right. You ain't fooling nobody Chass. You know you still checking for Trent. Just be honest." This chick had the nerve to say.

I inhaled then exhaled deeply. Enraged by her stupidity I said, "Let me explain something to you...After I broke up with Trent, he went postal on me. Following me around, stepping to every dude who said so much as hi to me. Trent got issues. You need to check his ass."

"See now you making shit up."

2

"Mmmm humm yup that's right I'm making it up because I don't have a damn thing better to do than to be on the phone with you inventing shit! If you wanna be stuck on stupid that's on you. I don't have time for this. I've already entertained this conversation long enough as it is," I said, feeling my patience slip further away. I thought that only Trent had problems. I see now that both of them are in desperate need of some couch time. I guess that saying there is somebody for everybody is true. This shit here is a *classic case*.

"Like I said Chass you're lying." This chick had the nerve to try and call me out. She really believed Trent's hype.

"Girl please...who the hell are you that I gotta lie to you? Especially about some shit that you can easily find out. You should think about that before you automatically dismiss what I'm saying. Did Trent tell you about the ass-whipping he got courtesy of my cousins because he stepped to me on some bullshit in the park the other day?"

"Now I know you lying because that shit was over a dice game," she said with confidence like she really believed that.

I laughed into the phone. "Trent really got you snowed girl. He don't even play dice," I schooled her. This chick was so pathetic that I almost felt sorry for her—almost.

"I ain't you Chass! Trent ain't got no reason to lie to me!" The tone of her voice raised at least two octaves.

Oops...I must a hit a nerve.

I laughed again. "You damn straight you ain't me! Shit, you could never be me! I had enough sense to kick Trent's lying, psychotic ass to the muthafuckin' curb because I knew he was crazy. You say Trent don't lie to you...well it seems to me like he just keeps finding reasons." I laced my comment in sarcasm.

"What-eva Chass! You think all these nigga's out here want you! Ain't shit special about you Chass!"

"I never said I was special, but at least my shit is tight! That's more than I can say for you. Your dumb-ass is up here calling your man's ex-girl about some bullshit. How pathetic is that?"

"You're pathetic and that's why you ain't got a man bitch!"

"Getting a man has never been a problem for me *sweetheart*, so let's not get it twisted!"

"Why you still calling Trent then?"

Since the bitch doesn't have a clue I guess it's my duty to give her ass one. After all she asked, I thought as I prepared myself to reduce her pride to shreds.

"Ask Trent why he keeps blowing up my phone?"

She sucked her teeth. "Yeah right...what-eva Chass. Trent don't fucking call you! Now I know you buggin'."

"You wanna listen to the messages?"

"What messages?" she asked like I was speaking a foreign language.

3

"The messages that Trent left begging me to come back to him. The desperate stalker-type conversations that he had with my voice mail...you know...those messages."

"Yeah right. Trent ain't leave you no fucking messages! I keep telling you my man don't want you! Now back the fuck up off mine bitch!"

Click. She hung up.

I guess she didn't wanna hear the messages.

I placed the receiver back on the base hoping I wouldn't hear from her dumb-ass again. It is bitches like her that give chicks a bad name. Always believing some bullshit a man tells them. How gullible can you be? She had to know deep down that I wasn't lying. She was mad as hell that Trent still wanted me and there wasn't a damn thing she could do about it.

Let me see if I can explain what it is about me that cause men to pursue me like they don't have a girl while females hate on me so hard it should be illegal. I stand five foot-three inches, and fit very comfortably into a size six. I've been told that my figure replicates that of a coca-cola bottle—down to the last curve. My honey brown, naturally curly hair swings past the middle of my back. It touches my ass when I blow it out. I have a Caramel island-girl complexion, light gray eyes, and a tiny mole kissing each corner of my mouth. Topped with dimples so deep that makes for any chicks nightmare and her man's fantasies.

I can't even tell you the crazy-ass lines that a man will use to try and get my attention. It's straight up ridiculous. I've heard them all. I've heard that bathwater line so many times; I'm ready to straight up swing on the next brother who tells me that shit. One guy approached me in a bodega one day and said, "Shorty, you're so gorgeous, you're like an antique—they don't make 'em like you no more." I thought it was corny, but at least it was original.

My fine features are compliments of my parents who are the perfect blend of Black, Cherokee Indian, and Italian. My mother's beauty is stunningly breath taking. I'm told I look just like her, but quiet as it's kept—I ain't got a damn thing on my mother! She don't take no shit either. That's where my personality comes from. My father is equally attractive, and he is exactly the type of man who could pull my mother. He's masculine and strong, sharp and extremely intelligent. My father has always been prideful about his appearance. That man stayed in a gym. I remember when I was younger you couldn't pay my father to leave the gym. His body is still tight to this day.

My problems with male relationships have been an issue for me for most of my life. It started with my father. He dropped out of my life after him and my mother split up. The divorce shouldn't have been a surprise especially considering how much they argued. My father was a fireman—the best that Jersey had to offer. He was a little too good at his job if you ask my mother. She never understood how he could run into a burning building while everyone else was running out of it. She spent most of her time complaining about the 'bad

4

news' she dreaded she would one day receive. That fear crippled her and ultimately ruined their marriage. Shortly after their divorce my father retired from the Newark Fire Department. However, he and my mother never reconciled. The damage was done. After that, my relationship with my father was never the same. In fact, it was damn near non-existent. It was like he divorced me too. I guess he figured that if he made timely child support payments that meant he was doing his fatherly duty. At first his visits were kind of frequent until they weren't anymore. I was lucky if I saw my father a few times a year. Eventfully I got used to it—or I did a good job at convincing myself that I did. His absence left a huge hole in my heart.

I lost my virginity when I was twelve years old. When I look back I see how empty I was inside. I was searching for someone to fill a void in me that I didn't even realize was there. My need to feel loved made me vulnerable and landed me in one disastrous relationship after another.

Let me break it down...

First there was Quincy. Q had mommy issues. He was spoiled and selfish and looking for 'another mother and those shoes were nowhere near my size. I had to check him and unload his ass quick.

Then there was Quan...I actually thought he was a keeper. That was before I found out that he was eighteen and already had two baby mommas. Quan never even mentioned that he had a kid—let alone two—big mistake. If a brother could deny his own blood then there ain't shit he can do for me except hit the bricks.

Then Sketch...He was an advertising major from LIU interning at a record label in the city. He was ruggedly handsome and he had the swagger to go along with it. To put it mildly the brother thought he was the shit. I was happy with him for a while until reality set in and I realized that he wasn't interested in a commitment. I found phone numbers all over his place. He had women's underwear hidden under his mattress. There were pictures of naked women stashed in a box in the back of his closet. Yes, I was snooping. I didn't even bother to confront him with what I'd found. I just left his cheating-ass with no explanation. There was no way I was coming in second to the next chick. Never mind third, fourth or fifth.

Then came Trenton...I can't believe how cool Trent was at first. Until he became clingy all of a sudden. It was as if he woke up one day thinking that we were Siamese twins. Everywhere I went there he was. Trent was hawking me like he was paid to do it. If there is one thing I can't stand it's a clingy-ass man. Trent wore his insecurities like a wife beater, openly exposing himself for the world to see. He didn't have any shame in his game either. He was needy and he didn't care who knew it. That turned me off instantly. I tried to let him down easy, but dude wouldn't leave me alone. He was a psycho turned stalker that almost had to be put down like a dog.

5

I've never searched for the perfect man. I had sense enough to know that the 'perfect man' does not exist. Truthfully, I was satisfied with a man who didn't have a shit load of kids, a prison record, or a problem keeping his hands to himself. All that other shit like good credit, the size of his bank account, and what he was driving never really mattered to me. When I think about all of the qualities that chicks look for in a man, I didn't think I was asking for much. However, I learned quickly that even with very little expectations, you can still be disappointed.

My horrible luck changed when I met EL. He was handsome, successful, accomplished and extremely persistent. Because of my track record with men, I was reluctant to get involved again. The last thing I wanted was another failed relationship under my belt, but EL wouldn't take no for an answer. He would show up at my house with flowers, candy, cute little stuffed animals. The type of stuff that most guys wouldn't be caught dead buying. EL pulled out all the stops until he eventually broke me down. What I loved about EL was that he was a genuine romantic. His wining and dining included spontaneous romantic trips out of town along with lavish, expensive gifts. EL was older than all of the other guys I dated so he was much more experienced and definitely more mature. He introduced me to a different type of lifestyle. EL was a real gentleman. Not like that fake shit you see in the movies. EL was genuine. A quality in a man that I wasn't used to seeing—in the end, that's what won me over.

**   **   **   **

I met EL two years ago at the offices of Teen Sleek, which was a hip new magazine where my mother had just begun her new position as assistant editor. I stopped by the office to surprise her and take her to lunch. She had only been at the magazine a few weeks, but I knew she'd been buried in work. Settling into her new digs left little time for anything else and knowing my mother the way that I did, I had a feeling that she was neglecting her appetite.

The offices at Teen Sleek were very stylish and elegant. When I stepped off of the elevator I was greeted by the smell of fresh leather as my shoes sunk into the soft thick carpet. The hip décor that was spread throughout the halls gave the office a real sophisticated look with a splash of hip-hop flavor. As soon as I walked up to the receptionist, I caught the attention of this fine-ass brother who was sitting in the waiting area a few feet away from where I was standing. As soon as he saw me, he couldn't focus on anything else.

Is that the dude from the group Groove Theory? I asked myself trying not to stare. I glanced at him again to get a better look.

Nah, that's not Bryce.

6

The brother was sharp as a tack and just as fine as Bryce though. I blew right passed him and walked directly up to the four-eyed receptionist, who, by the way was staring at the brother so hard she was drooling.

"Hi, I'm Chassidy Fondain. Layla's ____,"

"Let me guess…Layla Fondain's daughter right?"

"That's right. How'd you know?"

She stood up with her hand held out ready to shake mine. "Well that was a pretty easy assumption. You look just like her."

I shook her hand. "Is my mother in her office?"

"Yes, she is. One moment while I let her know you're here." She took her seat and placed her finger on the extension then spoke into the phone. "Miss Fondain, your daughter's here."

"Tell her I'll be out in a few minutes," my mother's voice blared back from the intercom.

"She'll just be a few minutes. You can have a seat if you'd like."

I walked over to the waiting area and picked up the *People* magazine that was sitting on the glass table next to the soft leather chairs. It happened to be the "The 50 Most Beautiful People" issue. Those issues always pissed me off. I always wondered how they could possibly name the 50 most beautiful people in the world when they haven't even seen half the population.

"How are you doing beautiful? I'm EL…and you are?" the stunningly attractive brother asked, as he took a seat next to me.

"I'm Chass," I replied, sort of checking him out. The brother smelled good and dressed like he just stepped off the pages of *GQ* magazine. The fact that he was so easy on the eyes helped out a hell-of-a lot.

"What brings you to Teen Sleek? If you don't mind me asking," he said, easing closer toward me.

Before I could answer, my mother walked up. "Hey Chass. What are you doing here Sweetheart?"

I rose from my seat. "I came to take you to lunch Ma. I bet you didn't eat yet. I know how you are when you get busy."

"I'm sorry sweetie but I can't get away right now. I have a ton of phone calls to make, and a bunch of ads to go over. Maybe next week sometime."

I nodded. "That's fine Ma, I understand. Another time then. I'll just pick up you something because I know you must be starving."

"Ok thank you honey. I'll tell you what, why don't you stop by my assistant's desk and set something up for next week. She will make sure my schedule is clear for you." She glanced down the hall. "Let me get back in the office. I have one of the advertisers on hold. I'll see you later Ok Sweetie." She gave me a peck on the cheek before she rushed off.

He stood up. "Well since your plans with your Mom fell through how about you let me take you to lunch? My meeting shouldn't take long, if you don't mind hanging out for a bit."

"I'm sorry...I can't."

"I promise I won't bite," he said, with a smirk.

Shit...you better not.

"Thanks for the offer, but really I can't." I rushed off.

"Ok well it was a pleasure meeting you," his voice stretched down the hall.

I was stepping into the lobby with a bag of food from Sparraros on my way to bring it to my mother, when I noticed EL talking with two other gentlemen.

"Can you excuse me for a minute?" his voice stretched over their conversation. "Chass," he called out to me, catching me before I stepped into the elevator.

"What?" I said, in a not so friendly tone. I felt like saying...*get a life and leave me alone. I thought I'd made it clear earlier that I wasn't interested.*

"Can we start over?" he asked, with a flustered look on his face.

"Start what over?"

"This." he pointed to me and then back to himself. "The way you ran out on me earlier, I thought the building was on fire."

"I'm sorry. It was nothing personal," I said realizing that I was taking my frustrations out on him.

"Since lunch is out of the question now, I was hoping that you would maybe let me take you to dinner."

"I...I can't..."

"Why don't you try a slow *yes* instead of a fast *no*? It's not brain surgery. It's just dinner. You might even have a good time."

You're right. It's not. I thought to myself thinking that I may have been a little hard on him. So, I agreed to go. I figured I would have a terrible time, curse his ass out and never have to hear from him again—end of story.

EL picked me up and took me to this nice Bistro downtown. The food was good, but his conversation was even better. It was surprising how much I enjoyed his company. We dined outside so that we could enjoy the nice weather. The way the breeze felt slapping against my face put me in such a relaxed state.

"So...where are you from?" he asked, beginning the conversation.

"Queens."

"Really...which part?"

"Bayside."

"My sister lives in Springfield Gardens. Queens is nice. Not as fast-paced as The City, but it's cool. Hopefully you'll let me show you around."

"And what would you show me?" I asked kind of siked.

"Anything you want to see," he smiled at me. "You are so beautiful. I bet you hear that a lot."

I didn't respond. I didn't want to seem conceited.

"How old are you?" I curiously asked.

"How old do I look?"

"Oh, see I don't play guessing games...wouldn't wanna offend you."

He chuckled. "You wouldn't. As long as you don't come at me with senior citizen numbers, I wouldn't be offended."

"I'd say about thirty."

"Nah, not yet. I'm twenty-four."

Twenty-four?

EL looked so much older in that business suit and how clean cut and dapper he appeared to be. I would have never guessed twenty-four.

"What business do you have with the magazine? If you don't mind me asking. And, please don't tell me that you're one of those sales reps requesting that the magazine do a full page spread for your products or something like that?"

He chucked again, "Nah, Teen Sleek hired my firm, Miller, Goldstein & Brock to do some investing for them. Myself, and one of the partners had a meeting with the CEO of the magazine this morning."

"Did you say Miller, Goldstein & Brock?" I asked, slightly taken aback.

"I did."

"Miller, Goldstein & Brock is one of the largest investment firms in the country. They're always in the newspaper or on TV," I gushed clearly impressed.

He looked up from his glass wearing a cocky smile.

"I hope I'm not being too forward when I ask, but what do you do there?"

"I'm an investment banker. Graduated from Harvard a few years ago, and landed the position not long after graduation," he replied, sporting a wide grin.

Did he say Harvard? Ok now I'm really impressed.

Not only was the brother making major paper at one of the largest investment firms in the country, but within the few years that he'd been with the firm, EL made them millions of dollars. He was even featured in a couple of articles in The New York Times, and The Wall Street Journal. EL was known to his peers as the one to look out for. He was very accomplished. His shit was tight. I must admit, the brother did throw me off at first, but as I got to know him, the more interested I became.

EL was intelligent, his conversation was on point, and he carried himself in a cool professional manner. His gentlemanly qualities were very attractive and down-right irresistible; and it didn't hurt that the brother was not hard to look at either. Before I knew it I was looking forward to seeing him, even if I was playing hard-to-get. Not only was EL extremely attractive, but his body looked like that of an Olympic gold-medalist. He was really filling out those expensive suits. He had this aura about him that I was really digging. Everytime I tried to convince myself that EL would turn out to be another disaster; he would do or say something that would prove me wrong. None of the brothers I dated compared to EL. They weren't even in his league. It was like their ceiling was his floor. They were amateurs—EL was a pro. EL was on a level that none before him would ever dream of reaching. Half of the guys I dealt with didn't really have any long term goals. They didn't want much out of life. They couldn't see passed the next high or the next nut. EL was different. He was about something. He was a grown-ass man who knew how to handle his business.

EL and I had been seeing each other for a few weeks when he invited me to his place. I wasn't ready to take our relationship to where he wanted it to go, but EL was patient. He didn't pressure me. It was refreshing not to have a man hounding me for sex—that alone set EL apart from all the rest.

The high-rise was glamorous; complete with a bellboy, door man and a full security team. It was closely monitored like a jailhouse. This told me right away that the residents had major paper. Once we stepped onto the penthouse floor, I became very nervous all of a sudden. I tried to hide it so EL wouldn't notice, but he did.

"What's wrong Chass? Are you Ok?" he asked, with a great deal of concern in his voice.

Rubbing my sweaty palms I answered, "I'm fine."

"Are you sure?" he asked, removing a card from his jacket pocket.

"Mmmm humm. I'm sure."

EL slid his key card into the slot, a green light flashed, there was a click, and the door opened.

That's some real fancy shit right there. I admired, as I stepped inside.

I was immediately blown away. The high ceilings reminded me of a lobby at a grand hotel. It looked like you were stepping into a palace. The antique furnishings gave the place a royal look. It was fit for a king. The penthouse looked more like a show room than a residence. Some place that you take pictures of, but you know better than to touch anything. It reminded me of a scene from the movie *Pretty Woman*. I halfway expected to see Richard Gere and Julia Roberts stroll in at any moment.

The sweet smell of lobster smothered in a savory garlic & herb sauce with steamed vegetables and sautéed onions over natural wild rice led us into the dining room. The meal was spread across the anomalous stained glass table surrounded by candle light. In the center of the table sat a bottle of White Zinfandel and a bowl of fresh strawberries. A few feet away from the table there was a beverage buffet where a delicious-looking red velvet cake sat surrounded by very expensive bottles of wine. EL grabbed a strawberry and bit into it before taking a sip of wine. He picked up the bottle of White Zinfandel then poured me a glass.

10

"You should try it," he offered, noticing my stare. "The strawberries bring out the flavor in the wine."

"This is very nice EL, but you didn't have to do all this."

He pulled my chair out so I could sit down. "Stop that. I wanted to. It was my pleasure."

We listened to the soothing sounds of Luther Vandross' *So Amazing* while we ate. Nobody can relax you and get your juices flowing like Luther can. The combined effect of the soft music and the two glasses of wine I drank had me feeling good.

"Did you enjoy the meal?" he asked, expecting me to stroke his ego.

"Of course I did. It was delicious. That restaurant you used is excellent," I said, with a smirk.

"What are you talking about? What restaurant?" he asked, with a serious face. "I cooked this myself."

"Really? So where did all those empty food containers come from that are in your kitchen garbage? Last night's dinner?" I joked.

He grinned, "Ok, you got me. I see I can't fool you. I ordered from one of my favorite restaurants. I'm not the best cook and I really wanted to impress you."

"Well you definitely did that," I tapped his leg. "Even if you didn't cook."

He rose up from the chair. "So what do you think? Do you like it?" he asked, referring to his lovely living space.

"Like it...I love it! You stay in this huge penthouse by yourself?"

"Does that surprise you?"

"Well yeah. I mean I would be lonely living here all by myself. Knowing me, I would have half my family in here with me."

He walked back over to where I was sitting and stood in front of me then reached for my hand. "Hopefully, I won't have to worry about being lonely anymore."

EL picked up his glass of wine from the table and led me into the living room.

A white suede couch...please...Who in the hell does that?

"Not a thing is out of place. I know you don't keep it this way so, you must have a maid." I was waiting for him to tell me that some chick named Stella keeps the place so neat.

"Nope. No maid. I know how to keep a clean place. And, if I had a maid, what would there be for my wife to do?" He glanced at me to see if I caught that remark.

I gave him a phony smile.

Ok be easy nigga. Sounds like you hinting some marriage shit already. We ain't been together but a few weeks, so just chill.

11

"Tell me more about your family," he said, taking a sip of wine as he gestured for us to sit down.

I sighed. "We'll, you already know I'm an only child, but I come from a huge family. My mother has three sisters and four brothers, and I have more than my share of cousins."

"Y'all close?"

"Yeah, my cousins are like the sisters and brothers I never had. They practically live at our place. What about you? Are you and your family close?"

"My mom and I are very close and I'm pretty cool with my Dad."

"Do you have any sisters or brothers?"

"Yeah, I have three sisters. They all live out of town so I don't see them as often as I would like, but we're pretty close...and I have a brother that I haven't seen since I was fifteen."

"Why? What happened?"

His head hung down. "He had a total mental break down and, was sent to an institution years ago." EL's tone was strange. I'd never heard it before.

"I'm sorry; I didn't mean to drudge up painful memories."

"You didn't." He shook his head. "Don't worry about it."

EL rose from the sofa and walked toward the window, drew the blinds back slightly then peeked out. The bright lights of Manhattan lit up EL's living room. He changed the radio station to Hot 97 just as J. Lo was singing the chorus to *Hold You Down*, her duet with Fat Joe.

"You dance?" he asked, walking back to the sofa where I was seated.

"I do a little sump thin' sump thin'."

He reached for my hand. "Well, why you don't show me what a little sump thin' sump thin' is."

I danced erotically causing the bulge in his pants to grow with every move I made. The more I turned him on the freakier I danced. Then he snuck up behind me and eased into the steps I was doing. I could feel his breath on my neck as he danced behind me. He lifted my hair up and began kissing the back of my neck. Pulling him close, I wrapped my arms around his firm body. I ran my hands across his back and leaned the back of my head against his chest. He massaged his fingers through my hair as we danced.

"I'm loving this," he whispered, as his bottom lip tickled my earlobe. "Everything about you is so real, even your hair. All this is you," he spoke, softly while his fingers continued to massage my scalp.

Then he slowly turned me around to face him and slipped his tongue in my mouth. When I felt his hardness press against me, I pulled my head back, and broke up the passionate kiss that we were both thoroughly enjoying.

He looked at me strangely, "What's the matter? Am I hurting you?" he asked, surprised by my reaction.

"This is moving *way* too fast for me," I confessed, as I backed away from him like he was contagious. "I'm not ready for where this is going."

Judging by the expression on his face I could see that he was disappointed, but he was real cool about it. "We will only go as far as you're ready to go. Nothing will happen that you don't want to happen. I promise."

EL was the epitome of what a gentleman should be. He was patient and understanding. He made me feel like I over reacted. Throwing caution to the wind, I eased my tongue in his mouth and began kissing him passionately.

"Wait...wait...You don't have to do this if you're not ready," he said, pulling back a little.

"I am ready."

He backed me up against the wall and started taking off my top then he loosened my bra. I held onto his strong back with both arms as he carried me to the bedroom and gently laid me down on his massive king-sized bed. He pulled the wife beater over his head and stepped out of his *Polo* boxers. He slipped me out of my *Victoria Secrets* and kissed his way down my thighs.

I softly kissed his chest, circling the head of his thickness with the tip of my finger. I was ready for penetration. We were in tune. We each breathed heavy, slow, and strong breaths. I took his dick, held it like I owned it, and then slowly forced it into my tightness, soaking him in my wetness. EL's body tensed up and he let out a loud sigh like I'd just set him free. He cupped and caressed my ass then grabbed my naked hips while he guided my strokes. Our rhythm was perfect and natural. His tongue softly caressed my nipples as he grabbed a handful of my hair pulling it while he stroked hard and fast until his body started to shake.

"Ahhh," EL and I called out simultaneously as we climaxed at the same time.

2

Same Shit Different Day
Chass

While the news of R & B singer Aaliyah's death rocked the airwaves and dominated the news reports; my family and I were helping my mother pack up her duplex apartment in Bayside Queens and move into her new apartment in Harlem. My mother found an apartment in Harlem for half of what she was paying in Queens. The magazine was struggling and everyone was either being fired or taking pay cuts, so moving seemed like a wise choice. Besides in Harlem she would be closer to the Manhattan offices where the magazine was located. I had just moved into EL's penthouse a few weeks prior so of course I was convinced that my mother was just moving to Manhattan to keep an eye on me.

As Jon's B's *Don't Talk* played Sara and I were packing. I met Sara at a day camp when I was six years old, and we've been tight ever since. Sara is a down-ass Puerto Rican chick who will ride or die for me like no one else. She ain't no slouch in the looks department either. That's one of the reasons we're so tight—jealousy is not an issue. She was the closest thing I had to a sister. Sara and I were running our mouths when my cousin Day-Day (who got that nick-name because Aunt Tangy always said she never knew where he was from day to day) came stumbling into the room drunk.

"What's up cuz?" he slurred, crashing into one of the carefully packed boxes of spun glass figurines that I'd just finished praying would reach their destination in one piece.

"Day-Day get your drunk-ass outta here! You play too damn much!"

"A' –i—g—h–t!" he picked himself up off the floor. "All that yelling done made me fall!" he slurred again, trying to blame his clumsiness on me.

"Oh shut the hell up Day-Day! You been falling since you got here. I don't know why mommy asked you to come help us pack anyway. Take your drunk-ass back downstairs! We tryna get shit done up here! And, make sure you stay the fuck outta here until you got the good sense to sober your ass up! And learn how to handle your damn liquor!"

"I ain't even tryna hear that shit you talking Chass!" he managed to say as he dragged himself down the hallway.

"I bet if somebody offered your ass another drink you'd hear that shit!"

"Your moms moving all this stuff tonight?" Sara asked, walking into the room with a bowl of kettle corn and took a seat on the floor.

"I hope not, shit I'm tired as hell. As soon as EL gets here, I'm out. I've been here all day and I got three clients back to back tomorrow morning."

"What's gonna happen with all your clients now that your mother is moving uptown? She gon' let them come to her new place?"

"Yeah, she said she'll do it for now. But you know I gotta hurry up and think of something else because she hates all the mess that doing hair makes, and she can't stand all the people coming in and out. You know my mother never did like all that traffic."

"Hit her off with a couple dollars and she'll stop complaining."

"I already tried. She won't take my money."

"What about the penthouse?"

"Umm ummm!" I shook my head and started waving my hand in the air with the quickness. "EL ain't even tryna hear that! I'm not tripping though. I'm just glad that my clients are willing to travel from Queens Uptown."

"All of them?"

"Everybody except Jackie, Lanie and Heather.

"Fuck them. Those bitches don't tip anyway."

I laughed. "True."

"Remember I told you that I was thinking about moving in with my Aunt Lauren who lives in Harlem."

"Yeah I remember."

"Well, I spoke to my Aunt last night and she said whenever I'm ready, I can move in. My Aunt Lauren only lives a few minutes from where your Mother is moving."

"Does this mean that you are gonna be coming to my mother's all the time for a free do?" I laughed.

"For sure," she replied with no shame in her game.

"What did your mother say when you told her you were leaving?" I asked anxious to hear her response.

"What could she say? Shit, I'm damn near grown now."

"Funny. You know what I mean."

"Chass please...If she tries to say some shit now I'll laugh in her face. You can't put diapers on a teenager. Would you show up at your child's high school graduation with baby formula and diapers because you missed those baby years? Time don't stand still for nobody. She shoulda been saying shit back when I was only thirteen and staying out all night. It's too late for her to try to play mommy now. Me and my mother ain't like you and your mother Chass. We ain't tight like y'all. Half the time my mom's don't even know I'm around. She got so many muthafucka's running up and through there that she lost track of my ass a long time ago. Your mom's been more of a mother to me than mine ever was."

I used to think that Sara had it made. She got to do whatever she wanted and didn't have to hear no flack from her mother. Then I realized that there wasn't a damn thing good about having a mother who didn't give a shit about you. Sara was the middle child of seven. Back when we were growing up it seemed like every year her mother was pregnant. Every time she visited Puerto Rico she would come back pregnant. It was as if pregnancy was in the air over there. Since Sara's mother was hardly home that left Sara and her siblings to run wild without any supervision. To keep it real even when Sara's mother was home, she didn't give two shits about what her kids did. She didn't raise them; she just let them grow up.

$$** \quad ** \quad ** \quad **$$

The five-story building stood out from the rest of the buildings on the street. Outside of the property was a well maintained structure that had been covered with beige colored bricks surrounded by shrubbery that laced around the building. There wasn't even an ounce of graffiti anywhere on the walls; that meant the property was respected by the neighborhood graffiti artist. Floral pattern wallpaper covered the walls and the smell of potpourri dominated the halls. The staircases weren't consumed with the expected smell of urine, and the elevators weren't getting stuck on every floor—not at all what I expected.

The spare bedroom was perfect for me to set up shop. I had already envisioned where all of my equipment would go. The only thing left for me to do was put it there. I was struggling with one of the boxes trying to take it from the U-Haul truck when this guy rode his bike over to me asking if I needed any help. He looked a little like Keenan-Ivory Wayans with braids and in desperate need of a shave. He was dressed in jeans and Timberlands.

"I got it," I told him shrugging off his offer to assist me.

"Are you sure sweetheart? You look like you're having a hard time. Where I come from men do that," he persisted.

"Well, where I come from there aren't that many gentlemen around so women do everything because they don't have much choice."

He hopped off his bike and put the kickstand out. Good thing you moving here then. Gives me a chance to show you what you' was missing." I sarcastically giggled. "Oh I'm not moving here my mother is. I live down town with *my man.*"

"Oh... so you got a man," he said like he didn't believe me.

"Sure do. So I guess that means you'll be taking back your offer to help me right."

"I guess so," he shook his head and laughed. "Nah, I'm kidding." He reached for the box. "Since your man's not around, I guess I'm the chosen one. I can't just sit back and watch you kill yourself trying to get in the building."

"If you insist."

I stepped away from the box as he knelt down to pick it up. I figured the sooner I agreed to let him help me, the sooner I'd be rid of his ass. On the elevator ride I noticed the looks he was shooting me. He was so far from my type it wasn't even funny. Even if I didn't have a man his ass was dead in the water. As soon as he rode up on that bike it was a done deal—turned me off completely. A bike…you can't be serious. What are you a paperboy?

He carried the box to my door and sat it down. "If you need me to lift anything else, I'll be around," he said pressing the button for the elevator.

He stepped in the elevator, and then he immediately stepped out like he forgot something. "Oh, by the way Shorty why don't you let me get that number."

"Why would I do that?"

"In case you need me to help you with anymore boxes."

"I don't have a phone." I lied. "Even if I did, I couldn't give you my number. I just told you I got a man."

"A'ight well as soon as Verizon finishes plugging your moms in, get at me." He handed me a piece of paper with his number on it. "By the way everybody calls me Iz," he said just as the elevator doors closed.

Yeah right. Wait on it. Whatever your name is, I thought giving him a fake smile as I closed the door behind me. That piece of paper barely touched my hand before it hit the garbage. He told me his name, but just that quick I forgot it. I wasn't trying to remember it anyway.

Damn this shit is heavy. I shoulda let his ass carry this all the way inside. I thought, as I struggled with the box trying to get it down the hall of the apartment.

When I walked into the bedroom Sara was looking out of the window. "I'm moving in with my Aunt in a few days Chass. Then you can turn around and help me unpack," she laughed.

"Uh huh I know," I laughed back with her. "Both of us Uptown! We will run this shit over here! These Harlem chicks don't want it!" I spoke with so much authority in my voice; it made Sara stand up and clap.

"You muthafuckin' right Chass!" she said with authority. "But, the best part is these Harlem dudes are fine as hell girl. I'm loving it already."

"Come take a walk with me to 125th Street," I said breaking up the moment. "I need to pick up some hair products. I'm low on relaxer, deep conditioner, and spritz." I told her once we were half way down the steps.

When Sara and I stepped out of McDonald's we couldn't help but notice the pearly white BMW 645i convertible that was double parked in front of us. It looked like the driver was waiting for someone. As we started to walk pass the sparkling ride the door opened, and the driver stepped out. He quickly ran both hands across his shirt fanning away the wrinkles while he talked on his cell phone. Sara slowed down her pace trying to get his attention.

"C'mon girl." I tapped her shoulder then walked a few steps ahead of her.

17

"C'mon where girl the view is looking lovely from here." She glared at him.

The brother stood about 6'3 with a soft chocolate complexion. He had enough cologne on to win a contest. I could smell him from where I was standing, which was several feet away. I didn't recognize the fragrance, but it damn sure smelled good as it flowed effortlessly from his well built frame. He was a nice piece of eye candy and by the looks he kept shooting us, he knew he was being admired. That's probably why he got out of his ride—so we could get a better look.

"You see this nigga?" I asked Sara kind of thrown off. If there was one thing I couldn't stand it was a brother who just knew he was the shit, even if he was.

"Yeah I see his ass alright. I definitely wouldn't mind getting those digits." Sara's eyes glowed with interest.

I watched the brother overlook Sara's gaze and instead started eyeing me.

"Shorty in the halter top...let me holla at you for a minute," he called out to me with his cell phone pressed against his ear.

"I have a man," I spoke in a tone that would annoy most men. Although the brother was fine, I didn't get a good vibe from him. He looked like the type of dude that had all kinds of secrets.

"That's one lucky ma'fucka whoever that nigga is 'cause you gorgeous, Shorty," he spoke loudly watching me like a hunter eyeing his prey.

"I don't," Sara rang out interrupting his hungry glare.

He turned to Sara and inspected her from head to toe. "You don't huh?" His eyes zoomed in on her ass. "You lookin' a'ight in them jeans Ma. Come 'ere," he ordered.

Sara obligingly began walking toward him. After about ten minutes she walked back over to me with a smile on her face.

"I got his number." She pulled the torn match book cover with his number scribbled across it from her pocket.

"Ok give me the run down. How many baby mamas he got? Does he have warrants? You know the usual shit you supposed to find out."

She laughed, "You crazy as hell Chass. I didn't dig all in his shit like that girl, but I did ask the necessary shit like if he had a girl."

"And...What he say?"

"No girl. No kids. Tayari is single."

"Tayari, that's a fly-ass name."

"That's not all that's fly about him. That whip he pushing is sick. That shit could set a nigga back big time."

"Yeah. It damn sure could. Think y'all made a love connection?"

"Gimmie a minute."

18

** ** ** ** ** ** **

My mother wasn't in her new apartment for a week before she was throwing a card party. The party was for my cousin Chris who was just released from prison after doing three years for drug possession. Chris is that family member who stays locked up so much you're lucky if you see him every other leap year. Aside from his hideous prison record, Chris was cool. He always looked out for me. Chris was the oldest of Aunt Tangy's nine kids. I was closer to him than all of Aunt Tangy's kids put together. Chris and I just clicked. He was more like my brother than my cousin.

Gambling and drinking were synonyms at all family's functions. Almost every member of my family can drink and gamble like it's their chosen profession. Everybody was taking turns running to the ATM like they were giving the money away. One table was poker, the other was spades. Both tables had about five grand or more on it; dropping twenties on jokers and another fifty if all four aces walked.

Sara and I were in the room talking while my family was yelling and acting a damn fool.

"Your peoples is mad loud Chass. You would think they just hit the freaking lotto with all those screams they letting out."

"That's how they do it. You know they a hot mess."

She folded her arms across her chest. "I just can't see myself wasting my money on some damn cards. With my luck I wouldn't win shit."

I nodded. "I hear you girl. Me either. Gambling takes skill and I don't have any!"

"So, that luck doesn't extend to you then huh?" she asked, referring to the gambling gene that is in my family's blood.

"Nah, chick that shit skipped me. Besides we got more than enough gamblers in my family as it is, they don't need me adding to the mix!" We laughed. "Oh girl I didn't tell you that Trent had one of his bitches to call me again."

"Damn Chass! Another one? Shit how many does this make? Those chicks are fucking stupid. You've been with EL like two years and them bitches still calling you about Trent. Which one was it?"

"I don't know girl. I never even asked the bitch her name. All I know is that the bitch had the nerve to tell me that I still want Trent. What is she retarded?"

"Get the fuck outta here Chass no she didn't!"

"She damn sure did. All them chicks are insecure as hell and so is Trent and that's why that whole situation is gon' blow up in they face."

"Yeah well too bad we won't be around to see it 'cause we gon' be too busy getting our party on. There's a lot of money to be made over here Chass.

Chicks club all the time uptown so that means a lot of hair gon' be getting sweated out."

"Yeah well I gotta break myself in over here first."

"Girl please, the way you do hair chicks gon' be banging down your door, calling you in the middle of the night and shit. Watch what I tell you."

"Thanks girl. You always got my back," I said, beaming.

"Like you need me to tell you that you the bomb girl. You got mad skills Chass and I knew that shit back when you use to hook up Barbie's hair and all those ugly-ass dolls with those big faces that we use to get every damn year for Christmas like that shit was a tradition."

I laughed. "You a trip girl. You remember those dolls?"

"Of course I remember them. For real though Chass I used to hate those dolls, but I can't even front, your dolls hair used to stay fly!"

"You only biggin' me up 'cause I don't charge you!"

"That too." She laughed. "Now that your Moms live here and you 'bout to set up shop everybody gon' know how you get down on the hair tip. Your moms moving to Harlem is gon' turn out to be a blessing watch."

Just then the door flung open, and my cousin Chris stood in the doorway like he owned the joint.

"Hey cuz." He flashed a smile.

"Well if it ain't the man of the hour!" I smiled back at him.

"Is it safe to come in?" he asked, standing in the door way like he was waiting for an invitation to come inside.

I got up off my bed and slapped Chris upside the head with my pillow. "C'mon stupid." I said laughing.

Chris pushed me on the bed then started to tickle me. Then Sara jumped on his back and the three of us started play-fighting. Sara and I double-teamed Chris, but my cousin's skills were so tight that we didn't stand a chance against him. Not only had Chris' sharpened his skills, but so was the rest of him. All that prison bench-pressing really paid off because his body was tight. Chris is equally as attractive as he is built. He always kept himself up. Dude stayed sharp. I don't think I've ever seen Chris without a fresh haircut and a brand new pair of kicks. I always thought Chris resembled the actor Morris Chestnut. They could pass for brothers. I knew that Chris was gonna be a player even back when we were kids. Who thinks about looking fly and pulling girls when you're nine and ten years old? Chris used to tell Aunt Tangy that all those girls who flooded her apartment were coming over to study. Chris was giving those chicks sex exams and Aunt Tangy didn't have a clue. Chris hasn't changed in all these years—just his strategy.

"Now I see where you learned how to fight Chass. Chris ain't no joke!" Sara said, surprised as Chris held her in his clutches. He released Sara with a push then she jumped up to tackle him again. As he pinned her down I started punching him in his back. Then he let up on Sara and started in on me. Sara jumped on him, and since he had me penned, they were both on top of me. Chris flung Sara off, and dived back on me as I started rising up. Sara dived back on Chris and they both landed on my bed simultaneously. Then there was a loud bang and a crash that followed. It wasn't until my mother and Aunt Tangy came bursting into the room like they were the police, that we realized we had broken the bed.

"What the fuck!" My mother screamed. "Y'all asses done broke the damn bed!"

"Chris, get your grown ass up! Why you in here playing with them anyway? Yo ass, know better!" Aunt Tangy's voice carried over my mother's.

They must have bionic ears, I laughed to myself wondering how in the hell they heard the bed break over all the noise they were making.

"Ma, we were just…" I started to explain, but my mother cut me off quick.

"I don't care what you were *just* doing Chass. Look at that bed." She pointed. "Whose gonna pay for that?"

Just then Chris dug in his pocket and pulled out a roll of money that could make a giraffe a turtle neck sweater. "Here you go Aunt Layla. I got you." He peeled off a roll of hundreds then passed the money to my mother.

I wondered how Chris got his hands on that kind of bank and he'd only been home a few days. I didn't have to wonder much, it was obvious. Chris was back in the drug game. Whatever the amount, it was enough to shut my mother up. She stuffed the money in her bra, and then exited my room as quickly as she entered it, taking Aunt Tangy with her.

"You ain't gotta stay up here." I looked at Chris. "This party is for you. Everybody is gambling and getting drunk."

He smiled. "Oh nah, I'm good right here," he answered, looking at Sara. They started giving each other the eye.

Oh, I see where this is headed. Let me shut this shit down before it goes too far.

I pulled Sara into the bathroom and closed the door. "What are you doing?" I asked, a little ticked off.

"What are you talking about Chass?" she replied, with a stupid-ass grin on her face gawking at me like I was speaking Greek.

"You know the rule girl. We don't get involved with each other's family."

She chuckled. "Oh you were serious about that shit huh?"

"Nah girl, I just said that for my health." I pushed into her. "Of course I was serious."

"You buggin' Chass. That was before Chris came home. Your cuz is blazing. Guuurrrlll…I don't think I can keep that promise."

"Well, you better find a way. You know Chris got a girl."

"Is she here?" she spitefully asked, knowing damn well she wasn't.

I sucked my teeth. "Now you know she ain't here."

"Exactly. Three years Chass. Three years is a long time. I'm not saying she didn't visit Chris but unless they got married while he was locked up then she ain't give Chris no ass on them visits. So that means they haven't fucked in three years. She know he home and I'm quite sure she know about this party and you mean to tell me she ain't here yet. Girl please...If Chris was my man and he just came home after doing a three year bid—Jesus couldn't keep that dick outta me!"

"Sara, you gon' get tired of fucking with other chicks man. I'm telling you that shit is gonna come back on you."

She sucked her teeth. "What-eva Chass. Like I said, she ain't here. Besides that bitch don't mean shit to me. You a Liain fan not me. I never liked her ass anyway." She turned to reach for the door knob when I stepped in front of her.

"Sara don't go there. You gonna end up looking stupid."

"Please...did you see how Chris was sweating me?"

"Mmmm hum. I saw. But don't go getting all caught up in that shit. He just came home from jail so he tryna run up in anything right about now. Your pussy maybe talking to him now, but trust that Liain's will be singing to him later. If you push up, all you gonna do is cause unnecessary drama between you and Liain."

"Like I said, I don't give a fuck about her. That bitch don't mean shit to me Chass. She ain't my friend. You cool with her, not me. The way I see it, Chris is fair game. He's fine as hell and he ain't had sex in three years. Now tell me again why I should fall back?"

"Sara I'm just tryna prevent drama. Forget about Liain for a minute. Say you get with Chris then what? You know he ain't gonna be with you like that girl. Chris is not the settling down type. He ain't never been. So when shit goes down, and you know it will go down, me and you might have some issues behind it. I'm tryna prevent that shit Sara. The only thing on Chris' mind right now is tryna make up for all the pussy he missed while he was locked up. You're forgetting that Chris is my cousin. I know his ass like a book. Believe me when I tell you that a little dick on the side is not worth our friendship. Feel me?"

"By the looks of Chris, he ain't got *a little* of nothing, Sara replied, admiring Chris' appearance.

"Sara..."

"Ok...Ok...Damn Chass... I'ma fall back, damn."

"So we cool?" I asked, hoping not to visit the subject again. Family and friends mixing it up never worked. There was always some type of back lash behind it and I didn't want that to come between me and Sara.

"Yeah girl of course we cool. Please girl, ain't a damn thing coming between us. Now let's get back 'cause we left Chris in there by his self long enough as it is." She rushed passed me grinning.

This chick didn't hear a word I said. Hard headed-ass. Chris will show her better than I can tell her. Experience is the best teacher.

I stepped back into the room and watched as Sara and Chris flirted with each other. I didn't say a word. I just let them do them. It was a little after 3:00 in the morning when I found myself at the card table losing money that wasn't even mine. I turned to my mother.

"C'mon Ma. Let me get another twenty."

"Hell no Chass! What I look like a bank? I already gave you two hundred and you done lost that! You can't play for shit!"

You mean you gave me Chris' money that he gave you for that bed.

Day-Day laughed. "Aunt Layla knows what she talking about. You'se a scrub cuz. Stick to that hair shit you do and get from round the table."

I stood up. "Forget you Day-Day! Since y'all won all my damn money now I gotta get up huh! I shoulda never let y'all talk me into playing anyway."

"Ahhh shut up Chass and move from round the table. You making me lose count," Day-Day barked, as he dealt the cards.

I got my ass whipped. They took everything except the lent in my pockets. I'm far from a gambler and I knew that when I sat my ass down there. Still, I hated losing. On my way back upstairs I noticed Chris and Sara slipping out of one of the bedrooms. They were fixing their clothes and hanging all over each other.

Damn that girl don't listen. Maybe Liain's fist will straighten out her hearing.

Sara was one of those people who had to learn things the hard way. But still, she was my girl so I had to look out for her. I watched them wondering why they didn't just go to a hotel, especially since we were three minutes away from one—I guess when you're horny three minutes is a long time.

The door bell rang.

"I got it!" I ran to the door.

When I looked through the peep hole and saw Liain standing there my heart sank into my jeans. I was so nervous you would have thought that I just fucked Chris. All I could think was...*Oh shit!*

"What's up Chass?" She gave me a hug as soon as I opened the door.

Liain was about 5'9, and a little on the chunky side, but she carried her weight well. Her pretty face hid whatever defects her body had anyway. She and Chris had been dating on and off for years. Liain had about five years on me so I looked at her more like an older cousin than one of my girls.

"Your Moms told me that you moved in with that fine-ass banker dude from downtown. Damn dude is fine! Shit girl you better never let his ass go."

I smiled. "I don't see you no more since I moved. I miss you girl."

"I'ma be coming through. My peeps live around here. My moms stay over on 118th. Plus a couple of my home girls I went to school with live a few blocks from here. Best believe you'll be seeing me. Where your cousin at?" she asked, looking around.

"He somewhere around here," I replied, not knowing what to say. Imagine me saying...*The last time I saw Chris he had just finished fucking Sara. I don't know where he at now though.*

"I don't see him. Doesn't he usually be down here gambling?" she asked still looking around the apartment.

"I think he stepped out to get some more weed. You know them pot heads ran outta that shit a long time ago."

"Mmmm hum I know. What y'all got to drink?" She walked into the kitchen. "A bitch is mad thirsty."

I pointed her to the coolers filled with alcohol. "Good looking Chass." She picked up the bottle of Alize. "I'ma pour me some of this shit here and get nice while I wait for Chris to get his ass back from where ever the hell he went."

When Chris and Sara walked into the living room, I quickly ran over to them before Liain had a chance to see them together.

"Liain's looking for you," I announced, getting Chris' attention.

"Word. Where she at?" he asked nervously.

"She in the kitchen drinking," I answered, pointing him in her direction.

I looked at Sara with my face twisted up. "You fucked him didn't you?"

She sat down on the couch. "Did I? Damn, I ain't know Chris had it going on like that!"

"You so stupid. Don't say I ain't warn you."

"Warn me about what Chass?" she asked, with an attitude. "You so damn dramatic!"

"Yeah Ok let's see how dramatic I am when Liain beat that ass."

"Yeah right whatever!"

See look at them," I pointed, "I told you how they do."

"And?" she said, trying to get cute.

"I told you they were still together. You stay going after somebody's man. One day you gon' fuck with the wrong chick."

"Yeah, yeah, yeah. If he ain't got no ring then that ass is mine."

"Tell that to the next chick whose man you mess with. See if she agrees with you. Then get back to me on that."

Sara sucked her teeth as she watched Chris and Liain kissing. "Chris wasn't worried about her ass a few minutes ago."

"I bet he wasn't, but I bet you're worried about her right now. I told you how Chris gets down girl. That's my cousin, but he's a dog."

"So what Chass damn! Everybody can't have the good looking corporate nigga you got. Shit, everybody ain't that lucky."

"Sara it ain't about luck. You know my track record with men is fucked up. Men don't care about shit except themselves. I had to learn that the hard way."

24

Her expression softened. "I know girl. I hear you talking."

I reached my arms out to give her a hug. "Don't sweat it girl. Let Chris be Liain's problem. Let them duke it out."

Sara sat on the couch watching them with her face screwed up. I knew that she wasn't going to let it rest.

Spring 2002...

3

An Undeniable Force

Chass

Ever since EL took on an extra case load his time has been limited. As if he didn't spend enough time at the firm already. I was really beginning to hate that damn place. Sometimes it felt like I had to make an appointment just to see him. Although I understood that he was working, it still pissed me off that he spent so much time at the office. When I called the firm I expected to hear the voice of EL's assistant Mia, but when his voice was the one to greet me it caught me by surprise.

"Miller Goldstein & Brock," EL said, all so politely like he'd just been demoted to the receptionist.

"So, they got you answering phones now? Talking about some Miller, Goldstein & Brock," I repeated mocking him.

He laughed into the phone. "The receptionist left a few hours ago, and my assistant just left so there is no one else here except me and the partners. We're all taking turns with these phones. What do I owe the pleasure of this call," he flirted.

"The Bourne Identity came out today. You said you would take me to see it. I was calling to find out what show we were going to."

He exhaled deeply, "Ah man Chass. I forgot all about that. Is that the flick with Matt Damon?"

"Yeah," I quipped, almost annoyed.

"I really wanted to see that, but I have a deadline to meet so I can't tonight."

"How did I know you were gonna say that?" I asked pissed. "You knew about the deadline when you told me you would take me to the movies. Why do you even make these promises if you know you can't keep them?"

"I forgot. My bad. We can just go see the movie tomorrow night."

"No we won't EL just forget it." I sucked my teeth in disgust.

"Ok let me finish up here and I'll see what I can do. I'll call you later so we can set something up."

"Later when? It's already after six o'clock. You know what forget it EL. I'll just go by myself."

"Chass I said I'll take you. What time does the movie start?"

"7:45," I answered, reluctantly.

27

"Give me about an hour. I'll be home in time for us to catch that show. I have to get off this phone though. I have a meeting to get to and Vince and Ken are in my face because we have some reports to go over. I'll call you before I leave. Be ready by 7:15," EL said, in one breath.

By the time 7:50 rolled around I was way beyond pissed. The movie had already started and EL still wasn't home; so I called the office. This time the night service picked up. Then I called his cell. After I finished cursing out his voice mail for the second time I abruptly hung up the phone. I figured he was still at the office with his cell in his briefcase probably turned off or on vibrate so he wouldn't be disturbed. About an hour later the phone rang. Thinking it was EL I answered prepared to go off. To my disappointment it wasn't EL, but instead one of my clients begging me to touch up her weave. Her story was that she accidently pulled out a few tracks. Since I wasn't doing anything else, I figured I might as well do her hair. I made sure to let her know to ease up with all that rough sex because I don't make a habit of responding to those late night emergency 'fix me up' calls just because her and her man got a little too freaky in the bedroom.

"I'm going to have to start charging you for this room Chass," my mother said, with a slight attitude as she stood in the doorway watching me sweep up all the hair that covered the floor.

"Come on Ma. It's not like you're using this room anyway."

"Come on Ma my ass. You got these girls coming in my house at all hours of the night talking about doing some damn hair."

"That's what I do Ma."

"Yeah well you gonna have to start doing it somewhere else. I'm tired of all the traffic Chass. You never said anything about having these girls in here in the middle of the damn night. You live in a big-ass penthouse, you can do it there."

"Ma, now you know EL is not about to let me do hair at the penthouse. That is not even an option. Come on Ma. I'll start paying for the space, I don't care about that."

"You need your own shop Chass. You are too good of a stylist to be cooped up in this apartment."

"I told you I don't want my own shop Ma. It's too much of a hassle. This is much more convenient."

"And free."

I laughed, "That too."

Just then the door bell rang. My mother gave me that look. "This better not be another one of your clients Chass. It's after ten o'clock," she said, walking towards the door.

"It's not Ma. Gwen was it."

"Hey Miss Fondain." I heard Sara's voice. "Chass still here?"

"Yeah she's in there. Good thing you here. Maybe you can help her clean up that mess in there," she said walking towards the front of the apartment.

"How did you know I was here?" I asked, surprised to see her."

"I just saw Gwen and she told me that you just finished touching her up so I figured you'd still be here."

"A touch up…Please…I had to replace damn near all her tracks."

"Word? Who in the hell did she piss off that they gave her a whole new do?

"You know what my first thought was that her and her man got carried away, but when I saw her busted lip, and the way her eye was changing colors, I knew what it was."

"Mmmm humm…Her man beat that ass again huh? Damn that's fucked up. She shoulda been left his ass."

"She'll leave when she gets tired of making excuses for him—excuses only satisfy the people that make them. Everybody has limits, once she reaches hers, she'll leave him," I said, sweeping the last bits of hair into the dust pan.

"At least Gwen got you out that damn penthouse Chass. You been stuck in there like you hibernating or something. If it wasn't for your clients, you probably wouldn't even come Uptown."

I bent down to pick up a piece of plastic wrapping from the floor. "I have not been hibernating. I don't know where you get that shit from."

"Well prove it Chass. Come hang out with me. Beanie is having one of his famous parties tonight and since we have never been to one before I wanna check it out. See what all the noise is about. And, Chass before you start with the bullshit, I ain't tryna hear shit about you being tired."

"Girl I am tired. I don't even have the strength to close my eyes. I told my mother I'ma just spend the night 'cause I don't feel like going home."

"Come on Chass. It's the last Friday in the month and you know Beanie does it up big every fourth Friday."

"Girl please…I am not going nowhere except to sleep."

"Come on Chass. I've seen you do ten chicks hair back to back and still have energy to get your party on. There's supposed to be some real baller's there tonight—millionaire type dough. We should go and check it out."

"You mean *you* should go check it out." I quickly corrected her. "You're the one man hunting. I'm not tryna be around a bunch of niggas who swear they the shit just 'cause they got deep pockets."

Beanie was this big fat brother who used to be a bouncer at a nightclub in New Jersey. His infamous parties every month were all people talked about. My clients would always have a story to tell about something that went down at one of Beanie's parties. If it wasn't something they seen; it was something they heard. Drugs, sex, gambling—you name it—they do it at Beanies. I finally let

Sara talk me into going. I have to admit, all her begging and pleading had me curious.

The bouncer was turning people away left and right. They were very selective with who they let inside. It was as if you had to have a certain look just to get in. It was definitely a *Studio 54* type of vibe going on. After watching this guy and his girl get turned away along with all eight members of their entourage, I turned to Sara.

"You see that shit. I'm not waiting on this long-ass line just so that fake-ass Michael Clarke Duncan over there can tell me that I can't get in."

Sara looked over at the door. "Look, there go Izrael," she pointed to where Izrael was standing. "He's been tryna get with you since your Moms moved in his building. He looks like some type of VIP. Ask him to get us in."

"I ain't asking him for shit. Then he's gonna feel like I owe him something. Dude just recently stopped bugging me to go out with him. I ain't tryna start that back up again."

A few minutes later another guy was denied entry.

"What you 5-0 man?" The bouncer asked the guy standing in front of him wearing a security uniform.

"I'm not a cop man. I work security at Macy's."

"Nah dawg. I can't let you in man. That shit you got on gon' draw attention like a ma'fucka. Sorry, but you gotta bounce man."

"My cousin Mike is in there. He'll vouch for me man."

"You just gon' have to see him when he come out dawg. I can't let you in with that shit on man you buggin'. Go home and change or something man."

"A'ight man. I'll be back." The guy walked off the line just as Sara and I stepped up.

Izrael was standing by the entrance smoking a blunt. He looked over and noticed me standing on line. "They cool. They wit' me man," he said, before the bouncer could even open his mouth.

"Why they so strict with the guest list?" I asked, as Izrael led us into the party.

"They gotta be that way Sweetheart. You can't trust ma'fuckas these days," he replied, taking a pull of his blunt.

Once we entered the basement we were greeted by J.Lo and Ja Rule's *I'm Real Remix*. Beanie had the place decked out to look just like a club/mini casino. There was a bar, a makeshift dance floor, and a game room complete with card tables and slot machines. There were even ATM and change machines on each side of the room. The brother was prepared. It was as if Beanie knew that he would come across some folks running that 'all I got is my bank card' line.

The spot was packed. People were scattered throughout the place dancing, eating and playing the slot machines. There were even a few brothers rapping into a microphone. The atmosphere was strangely calm for it to be so crowded. I guess all those dudes playing cards needed to concentrate. There had to be at least six or seven tables lined up in the game room and each of them had a heavy card game going on. Since my family was famous for throwing gambling parties I was familiar with the concept, but these dudes were gambling big money. Each player had a few stacks of bills in front of them wrapped in rubber bands looking like stacks of bricks. One of the players even put up his diamond Rolex along with a stack of money. That's when I realized that the game was serious. It wasn't no nickel and dime bullshit.

"This is the shit down here!" Sara admired, as we walked through the busy game room.

"You like what you see too Ma?" Izrael asked, winking at me.

"It's a nice spot," I replied, looking around.

He hit us with that bragging type of smile. "You get a taste of how we get down over here. It's always good to know the baller's and shit. I don't know if you Queens Broads are accustomed to shit like this."

Izrael was cool. He just talked too damn much. I was never into the type of brothers who ran their mouths all the time. I call them bitch-ass-niggas. They gossip and run their mouths like a bitch. Izrael put us on to which chicks were skanks, and which dudes were stacking paper and which ones fronted like they were. He gave us the rundown on everybody within like five minutes: now tell me that ain't a bitch for you. For the most part Izrael was cool. Whatever was going down, he knew about it. You gotta respect a brother that stayed informed.

"Yo Iz that's you?" This dude looking to be about three hundred pounds picked his face up from his plate and asked.

"Nah nigga, she just peoples."

"Damn Iz! Who dat? Hook a nigga up!" Another dude said, taking a swig of his drink.

"Be easy my nigga. It ain't that type of party," Izrael told the guy. "Damn these niggas is mad thirsty. They act like they ain't never seen chicks before," Izrael complained, taking another pull of his blunt. "A'ight ladies I'ma get up wit' y'all later. I been waiting to get in on this one all night. You need anything holla," he announced right before he walked toward the card table where this guy was getting up. That dude looked like he just lost his whole life.

Once Sara smelled the baked macaroni and cheese, collard greens, and candied yams I couldn't keep her greedy-ass away from the kitchen. The tiny kitchen was overcrowded with mini fridges stacked on top of each other filled with so much beer that the doors wouldn't close. The steam from the boiling pots surrounded the elderly woman while she stirred them. I coughed from the weed smoke that filled the air making its way into my space. I hated weed. That shit made me sick. I had to fan the smoke away every couple minutes just so I could breathe what passed for fresh air in the crowded space.

"What's up with the tears?" Sara jokingly asked watching me wipe my eyes.

I responded with a push, "Shut up! You know weed bothers me. I can't stand that shit."

"Yeah well you ain't gotta cry about it Chass. You're a big girl," she joked pissing me off even more.

I pushed into her again, "Say something else stupid! I might just leave your ass down here with a bunch of muthafucka's you don't know."

She leaned into me like she was about to tell me a secret. "You wouldn't."

"Keep playing."

After we ate, I was thirsty for some alcohol so I walked over to the bar and ordered a Caramel Bailey's for myself and an Apple Martini for Sara. The lights were so dim that I didn't see the empty Heineken bottle that was rolling around on the floor before my feet. I tripped on the bottle and me, along with both drinks landed in the lap of one of the guy's playing cards.

Please tell me this shit did not just happen. Just let this floor open up and swallow me whole, I thought to myself as I picked my head up and proceeded to apologize.

"I am soooo sorry!" I lifted myself up off his lap then grabbed a napkin from the table, and began wiping his shirt, and his pants.

"It's a'ight gorgeous. You can fall on me anytime. Just give a nigga some notice next time tho," he said, with a smile.

Everybody at the table started laughing, embarrassing me even more.

"You can go get some more drinks and come fall on me beautiful." This charcoal-looking brother said, as he repositioned his cards.

"Hell yeah!" Another dude chuckled. "I won't complain if your pretty lil' ass fell in my lap!"

A bunch of wise asses. I wanted to curl up and die.

"I really am sorry. I'll have your clothes dry-cleaned. I don't mind," I offered, looking in the face of the guy I'd just fell on.

"Nah, gorgeous you ain't gotta do that. I'm good. Everything good," he replied, drying off his cards.

"Are you sure?"

"Of course I'm sure. This ain't nuthin' but a lil'," he sniffed his clothes, "Bailey's right?"

I smirked, "Mmmm humm."

"A'ight well, I'ma just have to be up in here smellin' like Bailey's while I finish takin' these niggas money. That's all. Don't worry 'bout it Shorty, everything good."

A phony smile crept across my face as I collected the empty cups that once held our drinks. I threw them in the garbage can that was sitting a few feet away from the table. Sara was laughing when I walked up.

"Gurrrl...you make one hell of a first impression chick! And of all places you had to land in his lap! You did that shit on purpose didn't you?" She laughed, as she glanced at the card table for the third time since I walked up.

I looked at Sara like she had three heads. "Ahhh huh I damn sure did. I fell in his lap *on purpose* and embarrassed the shit outta myself *on purpose*," I said spitefully. "I'll let that dumb shit slide since it's obvious that you done had one too many puffs of that blunt and way too much to drink."

"Ahhh be easy girl, it was just a joke."

"Well I didn't think that shit was funny."

"Oh, Chass stop bitching. They ain't even thinking about that shit no more. It was funny for like five minutes, but everybody forgot about it now." She pointed to the table where the card game had resumed leaving no evidence of my most embarrassing moment.

"Did you see that dude you fell on?" she asked, eyeing the table again. "Now, see I'd give him the pussy in a heartbeat. That muthafucka is fine as hell!"

"Girl please...I was too embarrassed to even look at his ass like that."

"I don't know how you missed that fine-ass face of his. EL can't even fuck with that!" she said, eyeing him some more.

"Damn, it's like that?" I asked, watching her stare him down.

"Hell yeah it's like that!" she responded shamelessly. "While you were in his lap did you happen to ask him if he had a girl?"

I shook my head. "Chick you stay with the jokes. I'ma go find a bathroom. My hands are mad sticky." I rang my hands and looked down at my soiled clothes.

"Try not to fall on anybody else." She laughed.

"Still the comedian huh? Remember what I said about leaving your drunk-ass down here. Don't think I won't do it."

Once inside the bathroom all I kept thinking was how I was gonna live this shit down? I washed my hands then dried them with the tiny piece of paper towel that was dangling from the cardboard as I stared into the cracked mirror thinking...*That was some real Jessica Simpson shit you just did Chass. And that dude you spilled those drinks on looked like his clothes cost more than it would take to feed everybody in here.*

I wished I was home lying across my bed watching repeat episodes of *Fresh Prince of Bel-Air* or better yet, someplace cuddled up with EL. I should have just taken my ass to sleep which is what I started to do before I let Sara talk me into coming. Now my clumsy little display cost me the good time that Izrael promised I would have. As soon as I stepped outside the bathroom door, a quick push caused me to stumble back inside.

"What the fuck! You need to watch where you going!" I yelled. Then I looked up and saw the face of the person who bumped into me.

This shit can't be happening. What the hell is this some sort of cosmic joke?

"Oh shit it's you." I was face to face with the guy I'd spilled my drinks on not even a half hour ago.

"Yo Ma we gotta stop meetin' like this," he said, with a smile.

I blushed. "You think?"

"You a'ight? Did I hurt you?" he asked, examining me with his eyes.

"I'm fine. You just scared me that's all."

"I'm sorry about that Ma. I didn't think anybody was in here 'cause the door was open."

"It's Ok. You could say you owed me one."

"Nah, I wouldn't say that. You sure you a'ight though?"

"Yeah, I'm sure. I'm real sorry about your clothes."

"Yo Ma, stop apologizin'. It's cool. It's just clothes. I can buy some more." He looked me up and down. "You never told me your name."

"It's Chass."

"Chass...is that short for somethin'?"

"Mmmm humm. It's short for Chassidy."

"Chassidy, I like that. That's hot. I never heard no shit like that before. It's *very* nice to meet you Chass." He licked his lips, "I'm Shane."

I smiled back at Shane checking him out without even realizing it. Shane was beyond attractive. There wasn't even a word that could describe how good he looked. The brother was so fine he made me nervous. Shane's complexion was a smooth caramel and he had the prettiest set of teeth I'd ever seen on a man before. He had me with his smile, and the cleft in his chin sealed the deal. His thick curly hair made me want to run my fingers through it. Shane didn't have the kind of hair that needed help to curl up—he had that good shit. And judging by his mouth watering frame—bench pressing had become a frequent hobby of his. And, his sexy-ass had the nerve to have green eyes on top of all of his other fine features. What was there not to like? I was already gone and didn't even know it yet. Shane's looks weren't the only thing attractive about him. He was extremely cocky, but he wasn't the conceited type of cocky. Shane was what I would call confidently cocky. He had this take-charge mentality about him. Shane looked like the type of brother who never had to wait for shit and always got his way. His swagger was off the charts. He wore that thug mentality like a badge of honor. Shane had this ruggedness about him that was sexy as hell.

"It's nice to meet you Shane," I said, looking him in the eye.

"No doubt the pleasure is all mines Ma." He shook my hand confirming our introduction. When Shane touched me I felt an instant spark like every nerve in my body had just woken up after being asleep for years. I couldn't help but wonder how I could feel such a strong connection to a complete stranger.

"I hope I see you around later." He winked at me and licked his lips again. Shane had that LL shit down pat.

34

"That all depends," I replied, flirting back with him forgetting that I had a man.

"On?" he leaned against the wall and asked.

"Whether or not I find something better to do."

He grinned. "Well I doubt that Ma, but by all means do you. Let me know how that works out for you."

"I'll do that." I turned to walk away leaving him staring at my ass as I walked off.

4

The Party Continues...

Chass

I thought I heard someone yelling my name, but with Eve and Alicia Keys *Gangsta Lovin'* blasting in the background, it was hard to tell. I looked to Sara for confirmation.

"Didn't it sound like somebody was calling me?"

"I don't hear shit," she replied high as hell. Sara was still feeling the blended effect of the weed and the countless number of drinks she had.

"CHASS!"

"See, there it goes again." I stopped walking then turned around in time to see a girl step out of the crowd. I recognized her right away.

"Oh shit Liain! What's up girl?" I yelled over the music as I hurried towards her to give her a hug.

As soon as Liain and Sara made eye contact, the vibe got real funky. It was obvious that there was still bad blood between them. Liain found out that Sara and Chris hooked up and she never got over it. They looked at each other, but neither of them said a word.

"I see life's been treating you well Chass," Liain admired looking me up and down.

"I can't complain."

"You shouldn't. Shit, you must be doing well. You gotta be wearing about two G's or more," she said, like she calculated everything I had on. "Either you got some nigga tricking on you crazy or you done found somebody's stash," she joked, while checking out my gear and my jewelry.

My shit was tight, I couldn't front. My shirt was low cut calling attention to the sparkling diamond heart necklace that lay beneath my firm breast. The diamond hoops that hung from my ears had all the chicks in the spot doing a double take.

"You ain't change a bit Chass. You still fly as hell girl. I knew that was you as soon as you stepped under that light." Liain nodded her head in the direction of the flashing red light across the room. "What are you doing over here?" she asked.

"My mom's live up the street remember."

"Oh that's right your moms did move around here. I forgot all about that. So much happened since the last time I saw you. You still with EL?"

"Yeah girl, we still together," I replied, nonchalantly. "What are you doing here? Last I heard you were doing it up real big in BK."

"Long story girl, but I'll give you the short version. I had my own spot in Brooklyn, but I gave it up just to move back in with my Moms. Chick pushed out another baby and she can't even take care of the five she got."

"For real. What has it been like two years?" I asked.

"Damn near."

"After you and Chris stopped dealing you was out and nobody knew where you went."

"I was going through some shit after me and Chris broke-up so I had to get up outta there. I had to get my head right. How is Chris?"

"I was wondering how long it was gonna take for you to ask about him. Why don't you take your ass to Queens and see for yourself."

"Cool beans. I think I might just do that. His ass needs to see how good I'm doing without him anyway." Liain said sharply, as she stared at Sara who was dancing and smoking another blunt.

Minutes later two chicks walked up to us increasing our circle. Liain introduced me to Lawanna and Roshawn. Lawanna looked like the female version of Mike Tyson. This chick was real rough in the face. Her features were so strong they were screaming at me demanding to be noticed. She almost scared the shit out of me under those dim-ass lights. Lawanna was about sixty pounds overweight. This chick looked like she walked into the party on a full stomach—and, she had the nerve to be eating a piece of chicken. I knew from jump that she didn't like me. I picked up on that vibe instantly. I couldn't be mad at her. I wouldn't like me either if I looked the way she did.

I've never been the type to make female friends. Chicks don't respond to me in a positive way at all. I never did care about what people thought about me, but I do get tired of having to defend my beauty. For as long as I can remember I've been hated on because of the way I look. Jealousy has been something that I've had to deal with my entire life. Females have always tried to get at me over some nonsense. From thinking that I wanted their man, to insisting that I thought I was 'all that'. It was just another way to disguise their jealousy. All it took were a few misconceptions and I inherit a gang of enemies. It never bothered me because I've never had a problem holding my own.

Roshawn's appearance wasn't much better. She looked like Dennis Rodman in drag. This chick looked like she was punched in the face every day of her life and the scars never healed. The marks on her face were in competition. Somebody should have put her onto coco butter, vitamin e—something. She had so many gashes chick looked like she'd been in a war. And, that shit she was wearing looked thrown together and cheap—like some shit you'd wear on a dare.

All I could thinks was...*How in the hell did they get in? They must be related to the dude working the door.*

The short stocky brown skinned chick kept looking me up and down, while the tall slim dark skinned chick fixated on the ring that protruded out of her tongue.

"So you're Chass?" Roshawn asked, sparking a one-on-one conversation with me. I could tell this chick didn't like me either just by the way she looked at me. She was trying to size me up with her long glares.

"Your reputation precedes you," she said, after several moments of silence. "My peoples from 40 Projects say you ain't no joke wit'cha hands."

By the way Roshawn talked, it was obvious that she had respect for my reputation even if she didn't like me.

"Oh most definitely Chass got skills," Liain chimed in. "Bitches stayed sleeping on her back in the day because she's so fuckin' pretty. I done seen Chass in action plenty of times. She beat this bitch out of her clothes once. I can definitely vouch for her thump game. Trust me, Chass goes hard."

"So...you went to August Martin huh?" Roshawn rolled her eyes and changed the subject.

"And, Hillcrest, John Adams, you know wherever they would take me."

"Damn, girl you was bouncin' like that. Your record must be crazy," Lawanna said, like she was paying me a compliment.

"It was, but I calmed down a lot. I'm not with all that rah-rah shit no more. I grew up."

Roshawn was eyeing me like she was ready to get it poppin'. She must a thought that just because I calmed down that I suddenly forgot my skills—let's not get it twisted! Spilling sarcasm all over my comment I had to let my position be known.

"Don't get me wrong though I'll get it in, in a minute if a chick brings it to me, but I do try to back away from all that fighting now. Sometimes you just outgrow shit."

Roshawn looked at me and rolled her eyes like she had on a pair of defective contact lenses.

"So you had a little accident." Lawanna had that sarcastic tone in her voice. It was something about these chicks that rubbed me the wrong way. I gazed at Lawanna for a few seconds before Liain's question broke my stare.

"Chass you know who that was you fell on right?" she asked, like it was some sort of breaking news.

"Some guy name Shane. Why is there something else?"

"I guess you don't know who Shane is then huh," Roshawn had that snobby tone in her voice.

"Nope, should I?"

"All we know is that he's fine as hell. Is he attached?" Sara asked, rejoining the conversation.

"Yup! To a different chick every night!" Liain laughed. "Shane got bitches from here to Atlanta tryna settle him, but he ain't tryna hear them."

"Well, he hasn't met me yet!" Sara took a sip of her drink. "On the real though, is he serious with anybody?" she asked, refusing to drop the subject.

Damn girl give it a rest, I thought watching Sara make a fool of herself over some guy she never even met.

"Nope. Shane don't do the commitment thing, and the chicks that deal with him don't even care," Liain replied.

"Well either he got a mean sex game or he must be tricking on them chicks like crazy because Li you know how it is where we come from," I reminded her.

"Nah, Shane don't trick his paper. It's not like he need to anyway. And, it ain't like he can't afford it. Dude is paid out the ass. Bitches are lining up to get a piece of that nigga. For real. It's that serious. Shane is a legend around here. Shit, you better recognize girl," Roshawn said, with a slick tongue.

"His middle name is money. All this is him," Liain pointed around the basement like Shane owned everything in it.

"I thought this was Beanie's spot," Sara said.

Liain looked at Sara with a frown. "Girl you better pay attention. Shane got this whole shit sewed up. He owns one of the hottest clubs downtown. That shit stay packed. I heard he got a big-ass mansion somewhere upstate and he got a whole fleet of cars. Trust me that dude don't want for a damn thing. Shane is a dream no doubt," she raved like Shane was out of reach for the average girl.

"Is he the reason the bouncer won't let nobody in? They got nigga's jumping through hoops tryna get in here," I asked.

"A lot of shit goes on down here. So if they don't know you, you ain't getting..." Liain's words were interrupted by a loud banging noise. The next thing we knew the door busted open.

"POLICE! EVERYBODY UP AGAINST THE GOD DAMN WALL!"

The police spread throughout the basement like roaches. Since getting arrested wasn't on my 'to do' list, I quickly grabbed Sara's hand and we ran through the crowd trying to find a way out of the sudden madness. Seconds later the lights went out limiting our visibility, and our only chance at escaping the chaos. The next thing I knew someone grabbed my hand leading me and Sara into a darkened maze. A strange sense of security came over me and I held on tight moving as quickly as I could, pulling Sara along with me. Our mystery guide led us into a space that we crawled through until we reached a tiny room which led to a flight of stairs, then through a door. The street lights greeted us as we stepped out from the darkness, allowing us to see the face of the person who took us away from all the chaos and ultimately avoided a trip to the police station.

Oh my God! Not him—again. Ok now I'm convinced that somebody is playing a sick joke on me.

"You again," I looked at Shane.

"Disappointed?" He smiled.

"Far from it. Grateful is more like it. Thank you for getting us out of there."

"Now what kind of person would I be if I left you down there to fend for yourself?"

"Well, I'm glad you're not that type of person." Sara nudged her arm into my side requesting an introduction.

"Shane this is my girl Sara. Sara this is Shane."

"How you doin' Ma?" He extended his hand to her.

"I'm better now that I'm not going to jail," she replied, flirting her ass off.

"I would never let that happen."

Just then three guys walked up. Shane looked at me. "One minute Ma. Don't go nowhere a'ight."

After Shane talked with them for a few minutes, he introduced Sara and me to his boys Tayari, PK and Barkim.

"You look so familiar," I said, looking Tayari in the face. "You sure we haven't met somewhere before?"

"I doubt it. I would never forget you Ma."

I looked at him for a couple more minutes and then it came back to me. "I remember now. Me and Sara met you on 125th Street a while ago. You were in a white beamer parked in front of McDonald's talking on your phone," I recalled, trying to jog his memory.

A slight smile spread across his face. "Oh yeah," he said, recalling that day. "How you been Ma? You still got a man?"

"Raise up Tay," Shane called out to Tay as he walked towards us.

"Oh this you dawg! My bad man I ain't know. Shit if she ain't, you better bag that!"

Shane took a seat beside me on the brick steps. "You know she got a man nigga stop playin'!"

"How do you know I have a man? I could be single," I said, in a flirtatious sort of way.

He hit me with a sly grin then said, "Huh, I highly doubt that Ma. Not the way you look. A nigga would have to be crazy, doped up and smokin' that chronic to let you slip through his fingers."

"Guess you lost my number huh?" Sara interrupted getting Tay's attention as she sat down on the step next to him.

"I must have. Give it to me again."

As Sara and Tay talked I could see them making a connection. I was thrilled because Sara had too much time on her hands: Time that allowed her to

40

be all up in my damn business. Hopefully Tay was about to be the answer to my prayers.

"Why they call you PK?" Sara asked, looking up from the steps at Shane's friend.

"'Cause my pops is a preacher so these niggas been tagged me with those initials since we was young."

"Oh word," Sara said thrown off guard. Frankly so was I. It was obvious that Shane and his crew were in the drug game so a nickname like Preachers Kid stood out like a sore thumb.

"I wonder what your preacher pops would think about you being in the middle of a drug raid?"

"What makes you think it's a drug raid Shorty?" PK placed his cell phone on the clip that was attached to his belt. "Just because police broke up the party don't mean shit. Those punk ma'fuckas do that shit all the time."

"You're kidding right? That's enough coke to keep it snowing all year," Sara said staring down the street.

"I bet those same cops will be in somebody's bar celebrating tonight because this bust will probably make their career," I agreed, watching the scene from the steps of the brownstone.

Several kilos of cocaine were taken from the basement and loaded into police and FBI vehicles. Meanwhile, people were being handcuffed and thrown into the back of police cars while others were lying on the ground listening to the officers standing over them yelling their rights. I watched from the steps of the brownstone at what reminded me of an episode from *Cops*.

"If I woulda known that place was a target for the police and the FBI, trust me I would have never taken my ass in there," I said, still focused on the commotion down the street.

"Then we might not have ever met and that would have been a tragedy," Shane said, flirting with me.

Every time Shane and I looked at each other I felt something. The connection was there. The attraction was so powerful it felt as though there was something intentionally pulling us together. Just being around Shane had the butterflies in my stomach doing back flips. The way Shane and I kept looking at each other I knew it was time for me to call it a night before going to jail would be the least of my worries. I stood up just as the police vans were driving away.

"It's time for me to say good-night. I've had more than enough excitement for one evening."

"You leavin' already Ma. The night is full of possibilities," Shane said, wearing that flirtatious grin of his.

"Yeah, it's time for me to go. It's late. I have an early morning tomorrow. Come on girl." I tapped Sara on the shoulder breaking up her intense conversation with Tay.

Shane leaned into me and whispered, "Damn Ma, you sexy as hell. When can I see you again?"

I shrugged my shoulders and smiled bashfully. "I don't know."

"How would a brotha go about gettin' to know you better," he pushed.

"I don't think that's a good idea. But, if I happen to see you around I'll make sure I say hi."

"Sounds exciting," he slyly said.

It's gonna have to be. If I spend another minute with you I'll be in some serious shit. I thought.

5

Business Before Pleasure
EL

"Are we all set with the Baltimore figures?" Vince poked his head in my office catching me buried in paperwork.

"Almost," I responded, looking up at him from my desk.

"What about the Smith and Freeman deals?"

"I closed those on Monday."

"Hewitt and Lansing?"

"Closed those on Wednesday." I looked at him strangely. "Damn Vince do you ever check your inbox? I had Mia file the paperwork days ago."

"Speaking of inboxes, when is the last time you checked yours?" he asked, handing me a stack of papers.

"Just put them over there." I pointed, directing him to the glass table directly across from my desk. "I'll peak at those in the morning."

"What is your schedule looking like tomorrow?" he asked, sitting the papers down on the table.

"I have a 9:00 with Tim Davis, an 11:45 with John Gable, and a 2:30 with Mr. and Mrs. Bathgate."

"I'd like to sit in on your meeting with Gable. He requested to move around a few figures and there were a couple questions he had regarding the clause in his contract."

"I may also need to go over a few figures with you for the Bathgate deal before I finalize their contract," I said just as my lovely assistant Mia knocked on the door.

"I just stopped in to remind you of your 11:30 with Douglas & Moore on Wednesday. I scheduled Reinhart & Fields for 4:00 Thursday afternoon." Handing me a piece of paper she added, "Here is the information you requested from their file."

"Thanks Mia."

"Will there be anything else before I go?" she asked, stopping at the door.

"No, thank you. That'll be all. I'll see you in the morning."

"Ok then. You gentlemen have a good evening," Mia said, as she politely exited my office.

"Good night *Miss* Mowry," Vince replied, smiling so wide it looked like his face was stuck.

"EL man, Mia is ripe and ready for picking." He complimented Mia's assets while his eyes were glued to her ass as she walked down the hall.

Vince is what I call a white man in a black man's body. He's a lot like the character that Joseph C. Phillips played in *Strictly Business*, but with a flip to it.

"Come in Vince and close the door man."

"Did you see the way she looked at me man?"

"Vince man...don't you have a woman?" He shot me a look like that didn't mean a thing to him. "Maybe you need to chill out man. You're not supposed to mix business with pleasure anyway. Aren't you the one always preaching that?"

He waved me off like I was making a big deal out of nothing. "This is a whole different animal. It doesn't have to be that way all the time. The two can come together sometimes."

"I'm sure. When it's convenient for you right?"

He grinned. "That's right. It doesn't matter anyway. I'm not the one she has her sights on. Miss Mia wouldn't give me the time of day if I was standing in the middle of Times Square butt naked."

I laughed. "Scary thought."

"I'm serious man. She can't see past you."

"Me? Nah man, get out of here."

"Ok. Keep pretending like you don't see it."

"I'm not pretending. There's nothing to see."

"I forgot. You're too distracted by that fine piece-of-ass you got. What's her name again? Cassie?"

"Chass."

"Chass...yeah man that's her. Man she is fine! Now she is what I call the complete package. So, it's understandable that you missed Mia's advances."

"Vince, you're seeing things man. I didn't miss anything because there wasn't anything to miss."

"Just watch the way she switches up her walk whenever you're around. I don't know how you missed that."

"I don't know how I did either, not that it matters Vince. I'm a one woman man."

"Of course, of course. But, when you get tired of being holier than thou Miss Mia will be right there waiting."

"Yeah, yeah, yeah was there something you wanted man?" I asked, cutting his so-called speech short.

"The fellas and I are going to grab a couple drinks to celebrate the closing of another great quarter. Why don't you join us? I'm sure you could use a break. You've been here since dawn."

"As tempting as that is Vince, I'm going to have to pass man. I have to finish this proposal for the Wesson deal and I have some things to finalize

44

before my nine o'clock tomorrow," I replied, sifting through the endless piles of paper that spread across my desk.

"And I thought I never left this place. If you spend any more time here you're going to have to start paying rent," he joked. "How much longer do you plan on staying here? It's eleven thirty."

"Eleven thirty!" My hand hit the desk with force. "Oh Shit Chass! I was supposed to take her to the movies! Damn! The time just slipped away from me."

"Well I guess you better practice your groveling seeing as you're going to have to spend the rest of the night kissing her ass."

I looked up at Vince with that *'shut the fuck up'* look on my face.

He relaxed his expression. "Don't look at me like that EL. You know I'm right man. You spend a lot of time defending your career choice."

"Why don't you and the fellas go ahead and get that drink. I'll catch up with you the next go round." I said, brushing him off.

I wasn't in the mood for one of his lectures—especially since Vince dug a hole in his marriage big enough to drive a truck through; after he was caught with his pants down—literally. His wife took him to the cleaners. When they divorced, she took everything except his job. And, she might as well have that since the judge awarded her very substantial alimony payments. That all could have been avoided if Vince would have been able to control his sexual urges around his former secretary. Vince is the last person to be handing out relationship advice. Besides, it's not like I needed it anyway. I get that Chass is a little unhappy about my work hours, but she understands that this is my job. She knows that I love her.

"Ok...Ok I can take a hint." He held his hands in the air to surrender. "I will keep my comments to myself."

"Sounds like a good idea."

"If you need some help with the Davis deal let me know. I'll see you in the a.m."

I pulled my cell from my briefcase and noticed that I missed three calls. Before I checked the messages, I already knew that at least one of those calls was from Chass.

"EL it's me. I've been calling the office and the night service is picking up. I know they don't usually answer the phones unless the office is closed. It's almost 8:00 are we still going to the movies? Call me back when you get this."

I hit delete then waited for the next message to play.

"Its 8:30 EL! Where the hell are you? I've been waiting for over two hours. Why haven't called me back yet? I don't wanna hear that you didn't have a chance to. There's a phone on your desk and one in your pocket. I won't be here when you get home. I'm going out."

After listening to her last message, I called her cell twice. She didn't answer either time. So, I left a message. Vince was right about one thing—I certainly had some explaining to do.

6

A Serious Miscalculation

Chass

The black Cadillac Escalade was double parked in the middle of 7th Avenue with the hazard lights on. The truck was rimmed up and the tints were so dark you couldn't see a thing except your reflection if you tried to look inside. Some guy was leaning against the truck talking on his cell. Just as Sara and I were about to step inside the store, a voice called out to me.

"Yo Chass!" it said, with a familiar tone to it.

I quickly turned around, "Hey Shane!" I replied, secretly happy to see him.

"Yo Ma what's good? How you been?" he asked, abruptly ending his phone conversation.

"I'm good. What are you doing over here?" I replied, staring him down. I almost forgot how damn good he looked.

"Just left my man Beanie's spot. You know how we do."

"You remember Sara?" I gestured in Sara's direction.

"Yeah, I remember her. You talk to my boy Tay right?" he asked.

"You could say that." She looked him up and down. Sara wanted Shane—bad. Ever since that night at Beanie's party she had it bad for him. I actually think Sara just settled for Tay because he was Shane's boy.

"Listen Ma, I gotta make a run. You feel like takin' a ride wit' me?" he asked, opening the passenger side door to that huge intimidating SUV.

My head was saying no, but the rest of me was screaming yes. My thoughts alone were reason for pause. Shane made me nervous. He is the type of man that you shouldn't be around if you're not single. You suddenly want to be available when you are in his company. I didn't want to give off that impression, so I declined.

Sara nudged into my back so hard I almost swung on her ass. "Girl what the hell are you doing! Of course we wanna go with him! Well, I wanna go shit fine as he is," she whispered.

Even her begging wasn't enough to persuade me to go.

Then he hit me with, "C'mon gorgeous. After you spilled that shit all over my clothes a few weeks ago takin' a ride is the least you can do for a nigga. Don't you think?"

"You had to go there huh?" I flashed back to that moment. "Damn you don't play fair."

47

"Whatever works." He winked at me with his sexy-ass.

I looked at Sara who was damn near drooling. "Are you asking me or both of us?"

"I was asking you, but if you want your girl to come, that's cool. As long as you come, I'm cool with whoever you wanna bring Ma."

"Where we going?" I asked, hopping in the front seat of the Escalade while Sara slid in the back.

"I gotta meet this kid to pick up some loot, but I'ma stop at this Jamaican spot in The Bronx first. It's right off Marble Hill. The food is on point. They 'bout to close up shop so I wanna holla at them before they shut shit down."

"Why didn't you eat at Beanies with all that food there?" Sara asked.

Shane turned up his nose, "Nah, I don't fuck wit' that shit. All they cook is swine and I don't fuck wit' swine."

"Well, that be some good-ass swine," she joked, applauding Mrs. Jerry and Miss Narine's cooking skills.

"If you like that shit that's you. To each its own Ma."

Shane sped up the Deegan Expressway doing at least 90 miles per hour. When we reached the restaurant, they were just about to pull the gate down. Shane jumped out of the Escalade and ran inside.

"That nigga is blazing girl!" Sara popped her head out from the back seat.

"He's alright I guess," I said, frontin' my ass off. Shane was *waayyy* past alright.

"Yeah Ok, alright my ass."

"It don't matter to me how he look. I got a man remember?" I tried to play it off.

"Girl you know you can't fool me. I know when you digging somebody and when you not and you are *really* digging Shane. Shit girl I ain't mad at you. What's not to like? Dude got it going on!"

"It's not like that Sara. I don't even know Shane." I turned my face towards the window looking to see if Shane was on his way back to the car.

"Mmmm humm...whatever Chass, even if I didn't know you as well as I do I have eyes. I saw those looks y'all was shooting each other, checking each other out and shit. Girl Stevie Wonder can see the sparks flying between y'all."

"Don't start. You're the one who's been throwing yourself at Shane, not me. And you're the one who wanted to take this ride."

"I have not been throwing myself at him. I was just flirting a little bit. Ain't no harm in flirting. Besides, he ain't paying attention to me anyway. He wants you Chass. I only wanted to take the ride because I was bored and so were you. Stop fronting like you ain't glad we came."

"ANYWAY," I said, changing the subject. "You never told me what happened between you and Tay. Did y'all hook-up?"

"We did."

"And…"

"And what?"

"You gave him some didn't you?" I watched the smile spread across her face.

"Damn straight! Shit, I couldn't let a hard one go to waste."

"You are too much chick. Judging by that smile I guess that man put it on you."

"Guuurrrlll…he had me talking in tongues!"

"Sounds like you got your back dug out huh girl."

"Mmmm humm…and my front too!" We both laughed.

Just then a navy blue Neon pulled up right next to us blocking the parking spot we were in. The music was so loud that I couldn't hear myself think. Although Sara and I both complained about how loud they were blasting Eminem's *Lose Yourself* once they shut the music off, I got a bad feeling.

"You see them?" Sara gestured toward the car.

"Yeah, I see 'em. Why the hell would they park like that? They know we gotta pull outta here."

What I found odd was that they parked, turned their music off, but didn't get out of the car. I looked up just as Shane was walking out of the restaurant. As soon as Shane climbed back into the truck he noticed that Sara's and my mood had changed.

"What's up? Y'all a'ight?" he asked, looking through his bag making sure all the contents he ordered were inside.

I pointed to the Neon. "Why would they block us in like that? That was stupid."

Shane looked out the window, and then back in his bag. "Be easy Ma. They'll move as soon as I turn the engine on."

But they didn't move. Instead, two of the guys got out of the car and leaned against it like they had no intentions on moving anytime soon. The expression on Shane's face changed suddenly. I could tell that he felt something wasn't right about those dudes either. He glanced in his rearview mirror looking at the two guys that were leaning against the Escalade fronting like they weren't trying to look inside.

Shane looked at me and Sara. "Look Ma, these niggas wanna play, but it's cool 'cause I don't play them games—especially not when I'm in the presence of young ladies."

I looked over at the car full of guys then back at Shane. "They wanna rob us right?"

"You catch on quick Ma," he said, impressed by my observation. "Don't worry about it 'cause it ain't even goin' down. He reached under his seat, and pulled out a gun then sat it on his lap. In that instant I knew that

Shane was not the one to mess with. "You nervous Ma?" he asked, noticing the way I was eyeing that gun.

"A little," I admitted.

"Don't be." He lifted my chin up with his index finger. "I would never let anything happen to you."

Shane and I looked at each other for a few seconds before Sara interrupted our stare. "You think they got guns?" she asked, glaring through the tinted windows.

"Don't worry 'bout it. I'll handle these niggas and whatever I can't handle this shit right here will," he said, referring to the glock that rested on his lap.

"Is the safety on?" I asked, like I knew one way or the other. When it came to guns I was clueless. The little that I did know I picked up from watching TV, and the rest I learned from Aunt Tangy who carries a 38 Special that she usually keeps in her purse unloaded—go figure.

"Glock's don't have no safety," Shane said, teaching me something else. "I told you Ma, I got this."

One of the guys walked up to the Escalade and started staring at Shane through the windshield. They stared each other down for a few seconds before the guy walked back over to that piece-of-shit Neon with the rest of his homeboys.

Shane laughed. "These niggas is fuckin' silly. Think I'm stupid. They hopin' I'll get out the truck so they'll have an advantage."

"They have an advantage. They got us outnumbered," I told him.

"They don't know what we got up in here. They tryin' to figure that shit out now."

"What are you gonna do Shane? It's a lot of them out there." I asked.

"Be easy Ma. I know it's frustratin' just sittin' here, but I know what I'm doin'. We gon' wait these niggas out."

Shane kept looking in his rearview and side mirrors trying to keep an eye on all six of those guys. Sara was in the back of the truck with her face pressed against the glass trying to hear what they were saying. I started taking my jewelry off. I figured if I wasn't a target, then I could probably help Shane.

"What'chu doin' Ma? Put your shit back on!" Shane demanded, like he was suddenly upset with me. "Do you really think I'ma let these niggas run up in here and take ya' shit? Yo Ma, it ain't even goin' down. Please believe me."

"I wanna help you with whatever you're gonna do. I don't do the victim thing. I know you're planning something. Let me help you."

"Help me huh?" He shook his head and smiled. "It's cool Ma, I got this. If you really wanna help, put your shit back on."

"Why they keep walking over there by the corner?" Sara asked, watching one of the guys make several trips to the corner store.

"They probably tryin' to set up some bullshit-ass signal. This street is too lit for them to try and do shit over here. 5-0 patrols this strip frequently. These niggas is scramblin'."

"What if I...?" I started to say, but Shane shot me down before I could even think it.

"What if you what? Do you really think I'ma let you try and take on these niggas? He exhaled deeply. "You are unbelievable you know that. Just chill a'ight. I need for you to trust me. I know what I'm doin'."

"Shane come on don't do nothing crazy. What if they start shooting?"

"Ain't shit comin' through here. These windows are bullet proof." He tapped the glass with his diamond pinky ring enforcing his point. Then he glanced at his side mirrors again. "A'ight listen they split up which means they probably sent a couple niggas to each corner to look out. A'ight y'all they 'bout to try and run up in here on us. I need both of y'all to go all the way to the back and duck your head down as low to the floor as you can..."

"LET THE FUCKIN' WINDOW DOWN!" One of the dudes yelled as he banged on the door with his gun.

My face was damn near kissing the floor so I couldn't see what was going on, but Shane must not have been moving fast enough for the guy because he started yelling some more.

"What'chu deaf nigga! I said roll the muthafuckin' window down! Or I'll break this shit!"

"A'ight man you got it...you got it," Shane spoke, in a surrenderous tone.

"Now run your muthafuckin' shit! And tell that bitch to pass me her shit too or I'll shoot your ass!"

Sara was trying to whisper something to me, but I wasn't paying attention to her because I was too busy trying to hear what was going on. I was so nervous because Shane was outnumbered at least six to one. Those odds were definitely not in our favor. Suddenly I heard a car door close and then there was a tussle. I eased from under the seat just a little to try and see what was going on. That's when I heard Shane's voice.

"Now, now, fellas...did y'all really think I was gon' let that shit go down? Come on now what I look like?" Shane's tone was very smug. That could only mean one thing; he had somehow gotten the upper hand.

"Drop that shit and kick it under the fuckin' car now or say good-bye to your boy!"

Shane had the glock deep into that dudes chin piercing his throat. That dude looked like he was shitting bricks. Shane had all of those dudes by the balls. If any of them even looked like they were about to flinch somebody would have been getting scraped off the concrete. They obliged and drop their guns and kicked them under the car just as Shane instructed.

"Now put your hands where I can see 'em!" Shane demanded, with the glock still on the guy.

"OH SHIT SHANE! Yo fall back, fall back. That's my nigga right there! Fall back!!" Some guy jumped out of the back seat of the Neon with the quickness and ran towards the truck.

"Fuck outta here! Hec?" Shane sounded surprised, as he eased the gun away from the dudes head just a little bit.

"Yeah nigga it's me! What's up man?" He reached his hand out for a pound.

"Fuck you doin' out here on the prowl for Hec?" Shane asked, slipping the gun back into the truck. "Yo' Hec man your crew was about to catch a bad one dawg. Out here tryin' to run up on a nigga."

"My bad man. I ain't recognize you dawg. You keep switching up your wheels man."

"Yo Hec man what I tell you 'bout this shit dawg? You need some dough come see me man. You know I got you nigga!"

"I know man, I know. I just can't fight the temptation man. I tried dawg, I tried. Muthafucka's be having too much shit so I gotta take it off their hands."

"Be careful who you runnin' up on Hec. You never know man."

Their hands collided again.

"Nuff said nigga, nuff said."

"A'ight man. I'ma get at'chu dawg." Shane gave Hector another pound before climbing back in the Escalade.

Hector signaled for one of his boys to move that beat-up piece-of-shit, and Shane drove off leaving Hector and his boys in the taillights.

"Wow Shane I'm glad you knew him, 'cause I was scared as hell," Sara said relieved, as she brushed her hand across her face as if she was wiping beads of sweat.

"I went to school wit' that nigga. Hec used to rob ma'fuckas back in the day too." Shane shook his head grinning. "Nigga still the same."

We made a stop before dropping Sara off. When it was time for me to get out, he parked the car then turned the engine off.

"Can you hold up a sec?" he asked, placing his hand on my thigh. I looked up at him nervously. My heart skipped a couple beats. I didn't trust myself around Shane, and that shit made me nervous as hell.

"I know it's late, but if you up for it, I want you to hang out wit' me for a minute," he asked, in a sexy-ass tone making it damn near impossible for me to decline.

I was skeptical, but I agreed. We drove around Manhattan for a while until we eventually parked.

7

I'm Really Feelin' You

Shane

The usual chicks kept blowin' me up tryin' to pinpoint my location, but I let my voice mail handle that shit. I wasn't tryin' to interrupt the flow me and Chass had goin'. We were in the Escalade talkin' for hours. The last time I remembered lookin' at my watch was a few minutes after we dropped o'l girl off. After that, the time just flew. The conversation was smooth. I wasn't all up in her business and she wasn't all up in mine. I just fell back and let her tell me what she felt comfortable talkin' about. When the conversation turned to my pops, that's when shit got deep.

"That nigga bounced when my mom's was pregnant wit' me. Some shit about him bein' married wit' a family. I guess he figured that a pregnant mistress would fuck up his whole shit, so he jetted before I was born. When my grand moms was alive she used to try to push me to look him up, but I never did. I never had respect for a man who bounces on his responsibilities leavin' his woman to hold it down alone."

"You never wanted to look for him?" she asked, like I was missin' out on somethin'.

"Nah, I ain't never had no interest in findin' him. I wouldn't give a fuck if the nigga was fallin' over wit' loot or just some bum-ass nigga on the street. I'm straight. I wouldn't spit on the ma'fucka if he was on fire. That dude is dead to me."

"That's how you want it?"

"That's how he made it when he bounced on my moms and left her to raise me by herself. He earned my disrespect before I was even born. No woman should have to raise a man alone. I had my grand pops. That nigga was the man. He was an old school playa. Everything I know about bein' a man I learned from him. How to gamble, how to hustle, how to hold it down and handle the responsibilities that come wit' bein' a man. That nigga *was* my pops. I didn't appreciate all he had to teach me back then 'cause when you young you think you know everything. It wasn't until I got older that I realized to be a man—I had to see a man. I'll never forget that nigga."

"After my mother and father split up, I grew up seeing my father a few times a year," she said like she could identify with my situation.

53

"See that's what I mean. That ain't no way for a kid to grow up. But, at least you had your pops in your life somewhat, and from what I can see you turned out a'ight."

"Well thank you." She smiled at me.

"Come on now Ma. You don't need me to tell you that you are very well put together. You gorgeous, smart and you know how to handle yourself. You're exactly the type of chick a nigga would be proud to have on his arm. I really dug the way you were ready to ride wit' me tonight—even if I didn't show it. I see you not about the bullshit Ma. I like that."

"So...are you and your mother close?" She asked, tryin' to get my attention off of her.

I looked away and gazed out of the window. "We were."

"Were?"

"My moms is dead. About ten years ago, my moms, her twin sister, and my little brother and sister was killed in a car bomb. Niggas was tryin' to get at me, so they sent a message by killin' my family."

Her mouth hung open, and she held her face in her hands. "Oh my God Shane for real? I'm soooo sorry!"

"That was a long time ago. My grand moms was my rock. She was there for me and my cousin Ced. Our mom's was twins so we grew up real close. People think me and Ced twins since we look so much alike.

"Another you?" she joked. "God wouldn't be that cruel...would he?"

"Ahhh, you got jokes huh?"

"So what brings you Uptown?" she asked.

"I got a brownstone down the street from Beanie's spot that my grand moms left me when she died. I stay there when I'm in town. Plus I own a club Downtown called X Marks The Spot. So, I'm around here a lot." I threw my head back against the headrest and grinned. "Why do you ask?"

"Just curious."

"Curious huh? Yeah a'ight. You fishin' to see if I came to see some chick. If you wanna know if I got a girl Ma just ask me."

She smirked. "Well do you?"

I waved off her question. "Nah, I ain't got no girl."

She sucked her teeth. "Yeah right. You expect me to believe that?"

"Seriously Ma, I'm single. I'm not sayin' I don't do me, but can't no chick claim me. That's my word."

By the look she gave me I knew she wasn't convinced.

"Should it matter if I got a girl?" I asked, anxious to hear her response.

"You're right it doesn't matter. I was just asking."

"You just overplayed your hand Ma. Now I know you interested," I said, with a smirk.

"What-eva Shane." She smiled at me showing off those pretty-ass dimples of hers.

In a split second the glare from the street lights hit Chass' face and she lit up like she was glowing.

"Damn Ma you pretty as hell." I stared at her for a quick minute admiring her beauty. And, it didn't escape me how sexy she was. "You sure I can't take you from that nigga?"

"I'm sure," she said, in a not so convincin' sort of way. Although Chass was tryin' to front; I could tell she wasn't happy wit' that nigga and that left an opening for me. Dude already laid the ground work by not spendin' time wit' his woman. All I had to do was spin it in my favor; finesse the situation a little. There was no question that Chass was gonna be mine. It was just a matter of time.

"Come on Ma. The nigga ain't even spendin' time wit'chu. If he was you wouldn't be out here wit' me."

"He works a lot. I don't always like it, but at least I know where he is. You're a different story. I don't even know if you can call what you're doing cheating."

"Maybe that's because I haven't found the right one yet. You know this whole search thing is a process."

She laughed. "You a trip Shane. That was a good one."

"So, listen Ma. What's good? "I mean I'm sure you figured out by now that I'm feelin' you right?" I threw at her.

"Why you say that?" she asked, like she didn't notice the attraction between us.

"C'mon now Ma, it has to be obvious to you by now that ever since you fell in my lap you had me interested."

"Really? I didn't notice." She smiled. I guess that was her cute little attempt at humor, but that comment gave me my answer. Still, I wanted to hear her say it.

"You want me Ma, just admit it."

"Ok, I'm attracted to you…Satisfied?"

"And, I'm attracted to you so what's the problem?"

"My man."

"Come on Ma, I'm not tryin' to get you caught out. I just wanna spend some time wit'chu. I'm not askin' you to leave your man. We can spend time together and he will never have to know."

She gave me a look like she was considerin' it, but still shot me down.

"That's not possible."

"Anything is possible if you want it bad enough. I'd rather have some of you than none of you."

*See my days are cold without you…*Ashanti's voice interrupted our conversation, prompting Chass to answer her cell.

By the way Chass was talkin', I knew that call had somethin' to do wit' her bein' wit' me. Probably her man. He checkin' up now, but how did he get so far off his game that he let me slip in the picture? He fucked up when he put unnecessary shit before his woman and left her wit' too much time on her hands. Of course I wasn't complainin'. Chass was rarer than an uncut diamond and twice as fine. She caught my attention the minute I laid eyes on her and she's had it ever since.

"Problem?" I asked, noticin' the difference in her body language.

"Nothing I can't handle."

"Sounds like your man finally discovered that you were missin'. Guess this means you gotta jet."

"Yeah."

"So...when can I see you again?" I asked, as my hand shadowed hers.

"Shane...come on," she said, puttin' up a little resistance. "I already told you."

"That's not the answer I was lookin' for. After all the time we spent in here together I thought we were bondin'." I joked. "I figured maybe you changed your mind."

"Well I _____"

"I tell you what," I interrupted, before she could finish shootin' me down. "Why don't you let me take you out and if I don't show you a good time, then you can go back to that borin'–ass nigga you got."

"Excuse me...boring?" She laughed. "What makes you say that?"

"If he excited you then you wouldn't be out here wit' me."

"Ok, let's say I go out with you and he finds out? Then what?"

"You worry too much Ma. You gon' fuck around and have a stroke. There are so many places I can take you where you won't have to worry about your man findin' out shit unless you tell 'em."

"I like you Shane. I won't deny that, but I won't cheat on EL."

"I wouldn't call it cheatin'."

"Oh really? What would you call it then?"

"I would call it two people gettin' to know each other and the last time I checked, that wasn't cheatin'."

She shook her head and smiled. "You are not gonna give this a rest are you?"

"Nah, not until you say yes."

"Alright I'll go out with you. Just as long as you don't think I'ma have sex with you."

"Whoah Ma! Who said anything about sex? I was just talkin' 'bout takin' you out and showin' you a good time."

"I just wanted to put it out there just in case the thought had crossed your mind. I had to let you know up front that there will be none of that." The tone in her voice was so damn sexy that shit made my dick hard.

I smiled at her. "I'm a gentleman Baby. I know how to keep my hands to myself."

8

We Can Get It In

Chass

"Ain't that the guy from the movie *The Five Heart Beats?"* I asked, as Shane and I entered Jezebels Restaurant in Manhattan. I looked over at the table where the actor Michael Wright was seated. He was engaged in what seemed to be an intense conversation with a stubby short white man; who looked to be in his late fifties early sixties.

"Yeah that's that nigga sittin 'over there. Looks like he kickin' it wit' his agent or some shit," Shane said, as he glanced at their table for confirmation.

When Michael caught me looking, I quickly hid behind my menu. Shane looked across the table at me and laughed.

"Chass that nigga ain't thinkin' 'bout yo ass," he said, making fun of me. It was just like Shane to point out how silly I was being for acting so start struck.

I was spending a lot of time with Shane which was courtesy of EL who had been leaving me with a lot of free time. EL was in Chicago on a business trip that he neglected to mention until he was damn near on the plane. I guess he figured if he waited until the last minute to tell me about the trip then I wouldn't have time to bitch about it. Even though EL wasn't around he made sure he kept tabs on me. So I had to be one step ahead of him whenever he decided to hit me with his usual borage of questions whenever I fell off the grid—which lately had been quite often. While EL was gone, I tried to stay away from Shane, but he had this knack for catching me when I was feeling neglected and lonely.

This petite little thing dressed like Erykah Badu walked up to our table. "Welcome to Jezebels. What can I get you?" she politely asked, pulling out her pen and pad from the front pocket of her sheet-like dress.

After taking our orders she picked up the menus and tucked them under her arm. "I'll be right back with your drinks."

Jezebels was a nice spot. The atmosphere was a throwback to the 1920's with an acoustic twist. The intimate dining space had antique crystal chandeliers, vintage paintings, a garden gate, wrought iron chairs, and an authentic wooden porch swing that hangs from the ceiling giving the place that Southern hospitality. The live band played jazz renditions of several hits from the early 90's such as Howard Hewitt's *Show Me*, Gerald & Eddie Levert's *Baby Hold onto Me,* and Tony Toni Toné's monster hit *Whatever You Want.*

After leaving the restaurant, Shane and I cruised along the FDR drive. I sat back comfortably in my seat, and stared out of the window admiring the lit up scenery. When we reached Columbus Avenue, I was preparing to get out when Shane put the Range in park.

"You might as well let me take you all the way home Chass."

"You know that's too risky."

"Risky how? Ain't that nigga out of town?"

"Yeah, but he still has eyes around here. The doorman is definitely one of his spies with his nosey-ass."

"Then I'll drop you off around the corner or down the street from his spot."

"That's Ok I'm good right here. All I need is for somebody to see me getting out of your car."

"Then come back to my place wit' me. I'm not ready to say goodnight Chass."

I released my hand from the door handle and looked at him. "Then don't."

"Oh word! Yo it's like that!"

Shane made a quick u-turn. About twenty minutes later, we were pulling up to the brownstone. Shane slipped me in through the side door so I wouldn't be seen. Once we were inside he offered me a drink.

"You got any Bailey's?" I asked, getting comfortable on the sofa.

"You know I do. I remembered you like that shit, so you know I gotta keep it in stock."

A couple minutes later I was ready for a second round.

"Do you mind if I pour myself another drink?" I asked, before swallowing the last bit of Baileys from the glass. The alcohol was causing my hormones to go crazy. It wasn't like I needed alcohol to get me to that point whenever I was around Shane because the sexual tension between us was bananas. Let's just say alcohol didn't help the situation—nothing did.

"Nah, ga head," he replied watching me walk to the bar. Shane walked up behind me just as I was pouring my drink. He was so close to me that I could feel his warm breath on my neck.

"I want you so bad right now I'm about to lose my mind," he whispered as he nibbled on my ear. I could feel my temperature rise. I was so turned on that I was almost ashamed of it. I was attracted to Shane something awful, but up to this point, I had been able to resist him. However, the alcohol weakened what little resistance I had. Who was I kidding? Even without alcohol I was doomed.

"I gotta be honest. I can't do the friend thing," he admitted, taking the words right out of my mouth.

"But you said…"

"I know what I said Chass, but I woulda said anything to get next to you."

With his finger, he lifted my face up then leaned in and kissed me. When he pulled his tongue out of my mouth we just stared at each other. Then he kissed me again. There was no denying how much we wanted each other. Although I tried to hide it, my desire to be with him outweighed any fears or doubts I had. Shane brushed his tongue across my earlobe then kissed his way down my neck. I popped open his shirt and allowed my hands to roam freely across his bare chest. Just the feel of his naked skin excited the hell out of me.

"Let's go upstairs," he demanded softly.

I would have been satisfied with handling our business right in the middle of the living room floor. That's how bad I wanted him.

"Tell me you need me," he whispered, tickling my cheek with his tongue.

"*I need you.*"

"Tell me you want me."

"*I want you.*"

Our passionate foreplay had my body on fire. He slipped out of his pants exposing his flawless masterpiece. As I gently ran my hand across his swollen manhood my pussy began to throb like crazy. I outlined his abs with my fingertips as I kissed his bare chest. He caressed my breast while he ran his tongue across my nipple sending chills up my spine. My body never responded to a man the way it was responding to Shane. Not even EL could bring out this much passion in me. His touch brought out pleasurable moans and cries of excitement. Shane glided his fingers over every inch of my body effortlessly. I closed my eyes and allowed him to explore every inch of me. He kissed his way around my stomach caressing my navel with his tongue. I laid back on the bed and let him do his thing. When my head hit the pillow it shifted slightly exposing a shiny piece of red fabric that was underneath. I didn't recognize it at first, but then I got a closer look—tacky red lingerie.

Oh, hell no! What the fuck is this? Some bitch left her shit here!

Just the thought of Shane being with another woman in the same bed that he was about to make love to me in made me uncomfortable. I was quickly turned off. My body tensed up and I pulled away from him.

"What's wrong Baby?" He looked at me confused.

I climbed out of the bed. I started thinking all kinds of shit like… *When was she here? Did he fuck her in this bed?*

"I can't do this."

"Wait a minute. What's wrong?" he asked, with persistence.

"I just can't do this," I replied, slipping back into my jeans.

"Come on now Chass, I didn't get that impression a minute ago. Tell me what happened to make you stop."

"I just can't do this. That's all."

"Why? You feelin' guilty?"

"Yeah….I mean no, well…maybe. I just shouldn't be here."

"Chass I need to know what's goin' on. Everything was good before you stopped. Did I do somethin'?" His tone was practically begging for an answer.

I didn't know how to tell Shane that it bothered me to know that there had been so many other women before me. All of whom I'm sure he had sex with in that bed. I don't know why, but I felt betrayed. It was odd considering I had a man. I wanted to be his number one. I would never settle for being a mistress when I can be a wife. What can I say? I felt like a mistress. At that moment I felt like I was standing in a long line of women waiting for Shane to "get around" to me. Shane never denied the other women he dealt with and since neither of us were looking for a commitment, the situation seemed ideal. I never expected that I would start to feel territorial and jealous. Even though I was the one being unfaithful, I strangely felt like I was being cheated on. I kept trying to deny that anything was wrong, but Shane saw right through me. The more I protested, the more he persisted. He sat on the edge of the bed still undressed dick hard as hell.

"What's going on Baby? Talk to me."

"It just doesn't feel right being here in this bed that I'm sure you've shared with so many other women. I feel like I'm just another one."

"Ok Baby listen to me for a minute. First of all you are not just another anything. You mean more to me than that. I understand how you feel. I don't like thinkin' 'bout you wit' that nigga either, but it is what it is. We both knew the situation goin' in."

"Maybe we should just let this go before somebody gets hurt."

"How 'bout if I don't wanna let you go."

"Shane we're both in a relationship and we shouldn't even be doing this."

"Chass I'm not in a relationship. I just have companions."

Shane was downplaying his status for my benefit, but I didn't dispute his claims because I was in no position to question his fidelity.

"We care about each other Chass. How is that wrong? Don't throw what we could be away because the timin' is messed up."

I shook my head. "This is wrong on so many levels Shane. You know it is. We can't control how we feel, but we can control what we do about it."

I glanced at the bed reminding myself of what almost happened between us. "This is so wrong Shane."

"I want you Chass. I don't care if that's wrong."

"I want you too, but I…" I hung my head down slightly then lifted it back up. "I didn't mean to lead you on, I'm sorry."

"Baby don't worry about that. When we make love it will be when you are one hundred percent ready."

"What do you mean when?" I said with a smirk.

"Did I say when, I meant *if.*" He smiled at me.

"So...you're not mad?" I asked, not totally buying his sincerity.

"Well, I won't say I'm not disappointed, but I can respect how you feel. Did you really think I would be mad because you're not ready to make love? Baby you got a lot to learn about me. I want you to be comfortable when we're together. Trust me I'm not tryin' to rush you into anything. I'll be satisfied just fallin' asleep wit'chu in my arms. If that's not too much to ask?"

"I'm not comfortable being here Shane. I'm sure this is where you entertain all of your women and I won't lie; it feels awkward to me."

"A'ight Baby check this out...I own a loft in So Ho. I use it for business sometimes, but most of the time it's empty. We can meet up there whenever we wanna be together. It's a nice lil' spot overlookin' the water and shit. It's on a dead-end street so it's kinda secluded. It's perfect Baby."

**   **   **   **

The next morning Sara called. She started grilling me as soon as I picked up the phone.

"Where you been girl? I've been calling you since last night."

"I just got in this morning."

"From where?"

"I was with Shane."

"You spent the night with him?"

"Yup."

"You know I want details. How thick, how long, 'cause I know you fucked him."

"You a mess chick."

"I know, I know. So, is his sex game as good as it's rumored to be? Let me know why these chicks bug the fuck out over this nigga."

"I couldn't tell you."

"What'chu mean? You did fuck him right?"

"No."

"Stop lying! You spent the night with him and y'all didn't fuck!"

"I'm not lying. We didn't have sex. I wanted to, but we didn't."

"Ahhh shit Chass! What happened? He got a small dick don't he? See, I knew something was wrong with his ass. Good hair, green eyes, nice-ass body, the nigga is too fucking fine for one thing. Damn girl of all the places to come up short."

As usual Sara didn't know what the hell she was talking about, but I let her go on for a little while before I shut her ass up.

"Sara." I sucked my teeth, "I didn't say anything about Shane having a small dick."

"So, what happened?"

"I found some lingerie in his bed, and I just couldn't go out like that."

"And that surprised you?" she asked, like I should have expected it.

"Hell yeah that shit surprised me."

"It couldn't have surprised you that much. You still spent the night though right?"

"Yeah, I did."

"What did y'all do all night if y'all ain't fuck?"

"We talked."

"About?"

"A little bit of everything."

"EL know you didn't come home last night?"

"No. He's still in Chicago."

"He ain't call you?"

"Yeah he called. He'll be home tomorrow morning."

"So...what are you gonna do now?"

"I don't know. I'm really feeling Shane, I can't lie. But, his ass got too many chicks sniffing around him. Every time I start to feel guilty for being with Shane, I start thinking that whenever EL goes on one of his business trips or he has to work late that he's with some bitch. When I start thinking like that it makes me wanna be with Shane even more."

"Chass stop that. You know EL's not cheating on you. You just tryna talk yourself into that shit so you can make excuses to be with Shane."

"You really think that's what I'm doing?"

"Yeah girl I recognize the signs. I did the same thing when I was with Paulie and sliding off with Kevin. You remember how well that turned out don't you? All I'm saying is watch yourself girl. This is a dangerous game you playing. You know how niggas are. They can creep, but let us do it and all hell breaks loose. They can dish it out, but they can't take it. As masculine and take charge as men are, they ain't half as strong as we are. EL is liable to hurt something if he finds out about you and Shane, Chass. I don't even wanna think about what he'll do. You need to stay the hell away from Shane, Chass."

"Stay away from him?" I repeated with a 'yeah right' tone in my voice. "I don't think that I can do that. Lord knows I tried."

"You gon' have to Chass. Look, I know I was biggin' Shane up to you at first, but that was only because I knew you wouldn't go for it. You'd be stupid to mess up what you have with EL for a man like Shane." Sara seemed to have a slight attitude, and I didn't particularly care for her tone. I also wondered why she was suddenly so concerned with EL's feelings.

"A man like Shane?" I repeated. "What's that supposed to mean Sara?"

"Girl you know what it means. You said it yourself. Shane put the "P" in player girl. Just back up off Shane and make it work with EL."

I started to feel like she was preaching to me so I got a little defensive. "Do me a favor Sara, let me worry about EL. The last time I checked I was grown. You just worry about Tay. You got your hands full with him." I was referring to the problems they had been having recently.

"Well damn Chass that wasn't necessary. I'm just looking out for you. Correct me if I'm wrong but didn't you leave Sketch after you found out about Belinda and Thalia. You always hated players and there is no bigger player than Shane." Sara had that double standard tone in her voice. I hated that shit, but damn if she wasn't right.

"I know girl. You right. I didn't mean to snap at you. This whole situation is crazy. I tried to stay away from Shane, but I just can't seem to fight the temptation. Those times when I do manage to resist the urge to be with him, EL's ass is posted up at that damn firm. You know his ass is barely home now since he got all those new clients. All his ass does now is work. I think he'd rather be at that firm than be with me."

"Now you know you don't believe that."

"Even if I did get involved with Shane it's not like he would expect me to leave EL."

"That's probably because he has his hands full with all those bitches he got on a schedule. If you didn't have a man you'd probably want more of his time too and that would throw his whole shit off. Y'all can't be on the low forever girl. What are you gonna do when EL finds out because it's not a matter of if it's a matter of when. You of all people should know that."

"Shane has a loft downtown that he rarely uses. He said we can meet up there whenever we wanna be together. I don't see how EL would find out. I am always at my mother's doing hair so EL won't suspect a thing. Plus EL's too busy closing deals and playing with people's money to worry about what I'm doing anyway."

"Yeah right Chass. No matter how much EL works he always manages to check up on you. It's not like you need me to tell you that. I'm surprised that Shane is going along with this Chass. He don't usually play the back. Shane don't share his women; although they share his ass." She paused for a minute like she had to think it over with herself before resuming her doubtful tone. "Still be careful Chass. Even though you and Shane seem to have it all figured out, you never know what can go down. I don't wanna see you caught up in some shit. Just be careful."

As badly as I wanted Shane I wasn't ready to give up on EL. I knew I was playing with fire, but I couldn't seem to put down the matches.

9

If That's Your Girlfriend She Wasn't Last Night

Chass

"I have thought about this since the minute I laid eyes on you," Shane growled in a sexy voice as he lifted my body so that my legs cupped his waist like a vice grip. He carried me to the bed and laid me down on the soft down-feathered comforter and softly sucked my lips one at a time. As much as I wanted Shane a part of me was hesitant. I knew that this moment would define our relationship from this point on. If I stop now, I'd still be faithful to EL, but if I continued, there would be no turning back. I would enter into a world of deception and betrayal, but I didn't care. I wanted Shane so bad I could taste it. I slowly began feeding him my tongue as our lips melted together. His muscular arms and rock hard abs had my mouth watering, and his nice firm ass left the impression of greatness.

I was ready to invite him into my world where it would be his to explore. I grabbed his rock hard dick and massaged it slowly in an effortless motion while he ran his tongue in circles across my neck. While one of his hands caressed my breast, he tried to unfasten my bra with the other. But, *Victoria's Secret* was giving him a hard time so he popped the clasp. He softly sucked each one of my breast until my nipples stood at attention. Gliding his tongue toward my stomach, he opened my legs slightly, so that access would be easy for him once he reached his destination. Then he slid his finger inside my moist opening. Shane worked that finger so well he had me damn near dripping. He glided his tongue across my swollen clit sending shockwaves throughout my entire body. The rhythmic flow of his tongue was intoxicating causing parts of my body to get hot while other parts caught chills. My hips gyrated in circular motions while Shane made love to me with his tongue. The way my body responded to him—there was no doubt that the brother had skills. I moaned in pure ecstasy as his tongue French kissed my pussy.

My body entered a state of sheer pleasure while he bathed his face in my juices until my clit began to pulsate. Shane stroked himself admiring my moment of ecstasy before he entered me. He massaged the inside of my vaginal walls with his deep sensual thrusts. Our bodies moved together as if we were joined at the waist. Shane made my body scream like no other man could—not even EL. Although I was a little ashamed of that fact, it didn't make it any less true. I had never been with a man like Shane before. He made love to me like I was a virgin. Handling me very delicately like I would break, yet his masculine strong hands were one of my main sources of enjoyment. Shane took his time to make sure that I was satisfied. Of course I reciprocated. I tightened my vaginal muscles savoring every inch of his hardness throwing my pussy back at him causing him to damn near lose his mind. His thrust became more urgent as his thick dick slid in and out of my tightness.

"AAAAAHHHHH DAAAAMMMMNNNN BAAAABBYYY! His body jerked as his warm semen filled the Magnum condom that encased his oversized dick. Beads of sweat laced his forehead and he collapsed on top of me exhausted. He rolled over beside me and grabbed my thigh.

"Damn Baby you really put it on a nigga. You got some good-ass pussy," he said, breathing heavily with his eyes closed.

Ummm…the way you work that dick of yours should be illegal—and, your tongue is pretty damn dangerous too, I said to myself as I bit down on my lip. My hormones had not had a chance to calm down and I was still feeling the effect of the hurting Shane had just put on my body. All this time I thought that Shane must be lacking in the bedroom because he got it going on everywhere else. I figured small dick, sex is whack, or he can't eat pussy. Boy did he prove me wrong! There should be a label attached to Shane warning chicks about the damage he can do with his hands, dick and tongue—the brothers' sex game is that wicked. No wonder he got all these chicks jumping out of shoes and socks! Shane is what I call a rare breed—they definitely don't make men like him anymore. Everytime I was with Shane it was like an adrenaline rush. The chances of being caught were always a factor which made it all the more exciting. Being wrapped up in Shane's strong arms, while he sexed the hell out of me made it all worth it. I stared at the ceiling as I laid beside him cuddled in his arms.

"I hope you not regrettin' what just happened between us," he said, noticing how quiet I'd become.

"No…I don't. I probably should, but I don't," I said, looking up from his arms.

"Look Chass I know you got a man and I'm not tryin' to get in between what y'all got goin', but I'm hopin' that this wasn't a onetime thing."

"Is that your way of saying you wanna see me again," I blushed.

"Most definitely." The tone in his voice heightened like he'd suddenly become excited. "And if that wasn't clear enough for you come here." He pulled me close to him then he slid his tongue in my mouth. Shane's tongue game was just as good as his sex game. He had me ready to hit the sheets again.

"Shane you really believe that we can be together and no one will find out?"

"If we careful."

65

"You sure you wanna play it like this?"

"I'll play it whatever way you wanna play it as long as we got a game Baby."

"Just as long as you understand that I'm not leaving my man."

"I don't expect you to. I'm good wit' what we got right here. As long as you make time for me, I don't care about your man."

"What about all those chicks you deal with?

He grinned. "Why don't you let me worry about that. You just concentrate on keepin' your man in the dark."

Just then my cell phone started ringing breaking up our conversation. I went to reach for it, but Shane grabbed it first.

"It's probably your man," he chuckled, looking at the number. "I guess he's lookin' for you. What'chu want me to tell him?" he asked, pretending to answer my phone.

"The same thing I'ma tell all your bitches when they call you. Now gimmie my phone!" I demanded, in a playful tone extending my arm for it.

"Chass I know you ain't gon' answer it." He twisted his face up showing a little bit of an attitude.

"Just give me my phone. It could be important."

When Shane finally gave the phone to me it had stopped ringing. I checked my call history: EL called three times. The calls were hours apart so that meant he had been looking for me all night. I thought it was strange because I didn't remember hearing the phone ring. I looked up at Shane from the bed. "I gotta get home it's almost midnight."

"What'chu mean you gotta get home? You'll see that nigga when you see him." He climbed back on the bed and spread my legs apart staring at me seductively through those emerald green eyes of his. Then he slid his face between my legs and his silky tongue started French kissing my pussy—again.

** ** ** **

I didn't intend on spending the night, but Shane kept me up to the wee hours of the morning. After we finished making love I was exhausted; like I had just worked two full time jobs. I slept so comfortable in Shane's arms that I didn't want to move. I woke up to the smell of peanut butter pancakes, turkey bacon and a cheese omelet which led me straight to the kitchen.

"He cooks," I gushed very impressed.

"Like a chef Baby," he bragged, greeting me with a smile.

I looked around the kitchen for proof of a food delivery.

"What are you doin' Chass?" he asked, looking at me like I was crazy.

"The take out containers, they gotta be around here somewhere."

"Ahhh man that hurt," he laughed. "I see you hard on a nigga huh Baby."

"It's not like I saw you cook."

"Oh see Baby I don't play in the kitchen. My Moms, my aunts, and my grand moms, all did their thing in the kitchen. I come from a family full of cooks."

"Yeah well I come from a family full of alcoholics and gamblers—that still doesn't make me one."

He laughed again, "Ohhhh, I see you got jokes. Yeah you real slick wit'cha tongue I'll give you that. I can tell you every single ingredient that's up in here, the way I cooked it, the whole nine," he gloated.

"Save the roll call and fix my plate."

He broke off a tiny piece of the omelet and fed it to me. It was so good I tried not to let on that he was feeding me too slow. I was ready to tear that omelet up and here he was feeding me baby bites.

As soon as I heard the horn blowing I knew it was my taxi. Shane walked me to the door. "Can I call you later?" he asked, like he suddenly needed permission to stay in touch.

"You better." I said kissing him goodbye.

**   **   **   **

When I got back to the penthouse EL was sprouted across the couch watching an episode of *The Wire*.

"Where the hell you been Chass?" He jumped off the couch and rushed to the door stopping me before I was all the way inside.

"At my mother's. I had a late client. She called me at the last minute wanting me to do her hair for a party she was going to."

"Really? I called and your mother said she hadn't seen you all night."

"That's because when I got there it was late and she was already asleep so I didn't even bother waking her up. You know how much she hates the traffic and I didn't wanna hear her mouth."

"Why didn't you answer your phone?" He followed behind me.

"You called?" I asked, pressing a few buttons pretending to look through the phone. "I never got it. Did you leave a message?"

"Yeah, two." He looked at me suspiciously.

"Well I didn't get anything. My phone has been acting up lately. I dropped it so many times I'm surprised it works at all. Half the time the phone doesn't even ring. Whenever I'm at my mother's I have to stand all the way in the corner of the room by the window just to get a signal."

"I'll stop by Verizon and get you a new one on my way to the office in the morning so this won't happen again."

I yawned, stretching both arms above my head. "I've been meaning to do that, but between my clients and stuff I never have time."

"I left the office early last night expecting to see you when I got home. Imagine my surprise when you weren't here."

"I thought you had to work late?"

"I did, but I let Vince handle the Chase account because I wanted to come home and spend some time with you. I realize I've been neglecting you lately, and I wanted to try and make up for it."

"You still can," I said, ready to drop the interrogation.

"You feel like going to see Mary? She's gonna be at the Garden tomorrow night."

I smiled real wide. "How'd you get tickets to see Mary? They sold out weeks ago."

"One of the partners at the firm gave them to me after a family emergency prevented him from being able to go."

"Yeeaaahhh buddy! You know I love me some Mary."

"What else you love?" he asked, in a seductive tone while his eyes zoomed in on my breast. He grabbed me by the waist and pulled me in for a kiss. Then he picked me up and carried me into the bedroom. Although my body was making love to EL, it was Shane who was on my mind.

10

My Man My Lover

Chass

Just as I stepped out of the shower, the phone rang. I grabbed a towel, wrapped it around my dripping wet body, and then hurried to answer it.

"Hello."

"What took you so long to answer the phone?" EL asked, like he was timing me.

"I just got outta the shower…"

"Oh you ain't decent?" he cut me off. "My day just gets better and better!" he said, making it clear that he was aroused at the thought of my naked body. "Stay like that. I'm in the elevator on my way upstairs."

I walked to the bed where my clothes were spread out and threw them on. As I was slipping into my shoes, I heard the door buzz which confirmed that EL had just slid his key card in the slot.

"Damn Chass I asked you not to get dressed yet." EL had a disappointed look on his face as he walked in our bedroom.

"The show starts in less than two hours and you told me to be ready when you got here." I reminded him, as I touched up my lip gloss.

"Well, since you spoiled the mood we might as well get going."

Once EL and I arrived at Madison Square Garden and I saw Mary's name scroll across the marquee, I was anxious for the show to start. Sitting only two rows from the stage, we were close enough for Mary to give us a private concert. When *You Remind Me* started to play the audience applauded. Mary opened the show with her classic and closed the show with her smash hit *Family Affair*.

After the concert, EL and I stopped at BBQ's for a quick bite to eat. Janet Jackson's *Son of A Gun Remix* softly played in the background as we took our seats. I ordered salmon and EL ordered sea bass along with a nice bottle of wine. The waiter popped the bottle and filled my glass. Just as I put the glass up to my mouth and took a sip, Shane walked in. He was with a tall brown-skinned model-looking chick. The sight of him caused me to cough up my drink.

"Are you Ok Chass?" EL rose up from his seat to pat my back then handed me a few napkins.

"I'm…O…k…I…just…swall…owed…too…fast," I coughed my words out as I wiped the drops of wine that spilled onto my clothes. I kept glancing over at Shane's table. I wanted him to see me without tipping off EL, but Shane never even looked in my direction. I probably should have been more concerned about being in the same place where both EL and Shane were, but instead I found myself trying to get Shane's attention. Watching Shane show that chick such a good time had me vexed. I excused myself to go to the ladies room just so I could walk by Shane's table. I took a few steps in his direction and that's when he looked up and saw me. His eyes lit up. Just by the expression on Shane's face I knew he was happy to see me. As far as I was concerned, he could go back to wining and dining his date. I got his attention. That's all I wanted. I breezed past him and his fake 'Naomi Campbell' with my head in the air. I could feel his eyes burning my back as I pushed the bathroom door open.

I touched up my lip-gloss in the full length mirror, and then ran my fingers across the top of my head trying to keep those stubborn strands of hair in place. When I stepped out of the ladies room Shane was standing outside the door.

"What's up Baby? Damn you look amazin'! That shit you got on is hard body right there," he complimented, letting me know that the *Christian Dior* design I picked out was an excellent choice.

"I'm glad you like it."

He took me by the hand and spun me around. "Oh, I like. Trust me, I like. You stay wearin' the hell out yo shit." He looked me up and down and smiled. "So...I see you here wit'cha man."

"Uh-Huh. And, you're here with your girl."

"I'm tryin' to be wit'chu tonight. Think you can make that happen?" he asked, twisting the huge diamonds that shone from each one of his ears.

"I can't tonight."

"Why not?"

"I'm gonna be with EL."

"You live wit' that nigga so you can be wit' him anytime. I'll have you back before he even misses you," he said pulling me into an embrace."

"Shane!" I pulled away from him. "EL is right over there!"

"I see that nigga sittin' over there. He ain't over here though." He pulled me into him again then he pushed his tongue in my mouth. He tasted so damn good that I didn't want him to stop. But, the last thing I needed was for EL to walk up and catch me with Shane.

"You like taking chances don't you?" I asked, kind of turned on.

"Story of my life Baby...story of my life," he boasted while he continued to fondle me. "So what's up wit' me and you? You gonna come see me tonight right?"

"I told you I can't tonight. Besides you look like you'll be busy anyway," I replied, referring to his date.

"I won't be. I'm never too busy for you. I can meet you as soon as you get rid of your man," he flirted trying to kiss me again."

"Come on now Shane what if EL walks up?"

I peaked around the corner of the restaurant just to make sure that EL was still seated. He was drinking his wine waiting for me to come back from the ladies room—which should have been at least ten minutes ago.

"Then he walks up. Like I give a fuck about that nigga. You wasn't worried about him the other night," he fired back at me.

Oh no he didn't.

I jerked my hand away from his. "See now you buggin'! You don't hear me saying fuck that bitch you with. I tell you what, why don't you worry about your girl, and let me worry about my man!"

"Yeah a'ight." He sucked his teeth. "You right. Let me get back to ol' girl. At least she ain't scared to be seen wit' a nigga in public." He walked back to his table. I waited a couple minutes then walked back to my mine. EL stood up just as I approached the table like the true gentlemen that he is.

That is what I love about this man, I thought, as I took my seat.

EL was the kind of man who still believed in pulling out a woman's chair, or laying his jacket over a puddle so she could step over it. EL had the kind of qualities that some men never see. Although, I was completely drawn to Shane there was something about EL that I couldn't let go of, and I didn't want to. Selfish I know, but I didn't give a damn. Who says you can't have your cake and eat it too? I'd be damned if I have my cake and let somebody else eat it!

"You took a while. Is everything alright?" EL asked, taking his seat.

"There was a little bit of a wait to use the ladies room. Sorry it took so long."

"I was about to head the search." He cracked a tiny smile.

Thank God you didn't.

I kept trying to ignore Shane, but it was damn near impossible, especially after he started paying so much attention to his date. Although I knew his sudden interest to faunt all over that chick was just to make me jealous, I still couldn't shake that feeling. So, I decided to fight fire with fire: Give Shane a taste of his own medicine. I moved in closer to EL, and we engaged in a more intimate conversation. Shane was pissed. I could feel his jealousy from across the restaurant.

You can dish it out, but you can't take it. That's what his ass gets for tryna be cute, I thought feeling myself a little too much. When I saw how much my little performance was getting to Shane, I really let him have it. EL received a business call and excused himself to take it. Just as he stepped away from our table my cell began to vibrate. I picked it up and viewed the text message.

Stp actn' lke u hvng a good time wit tht ngga whn u knw u wsh u was wit me.

I glanced up at Shane's table and noticed that he was sitting by himself.
`Where ur grl at? She ran out on u alrdy? LOL`

My phone vibrated again.
`Nah, she sttin at a tble wit anthr ngga frontn lke she ain't thkin bout the way my dick felt in her pussy the other nght or the way my tongue felt in her mouth a lttle whle ago.`

I replied.
`U the 1 frontn, but it's cool. 2 can ply tht gme.`

Another text came through.
`Fuck this. Meet me at the spot in a hour. I'm bout 2 b out in a min.`

Got 'em. I was definitely smiling inside. I knew that shit was getting to him. I glanced at Shane's table, just as the Naomi look-a-like was taking her seat.

`I tld u I cnt see u tnght. I hve plns.`

He replied.
`Yu'll fnd a wy to get rid of tht ngga and cme see me. U knw u wnt 2.`

I threw my phone in my bag then zipped it up. Just then, EL walked back to our table.

"Who was that?" he asked, adjusting his tie as he took his seat.

"Nobody. I was just checking my messages."

The waiter handed EL his platinum card along with the receipt. "You ready?" he asked, placing the card back in his wallet.

I grabbed my purse from the arm of the chair. Just as I was about to exit the restaurant with EL, I glanced at Shane whose lips read, *make sure you're ready for me.* I'd be lying if I said that shit didn't turn me on.

On the entire drive home all I could think about was Shane. As soon as EL and I arrived at the penthouse, I hurried into the bathroom and called Sara.

"Hey girl…Ummm I need a favor," I said, getting straight to the point.

"Name it."

"I need you to call the penthouse and pretend like you really need to speak to me. I'ma make sure that EL answers the phone so be convincing. Make up some shit if you have to."

"Why? What's up?"

"I can't get into it right now. But, I gotta leave and I don't want EL asking questions."

"What's going on Chass?"

"Just call Ok. I need an excuse so I can leave."

"This is about Shane isn't it?" she asked, without hesitation.

"Uh-huh."

"See, I knew it. This has Shane written all over it. Chass you got EL staring you in the face and you tryna sneak off to see Shane. Girl you better watch yourself before you get caught out there."

"Come on Sara just hurry up and call." I wasn't trying to hear that shit she was talking. All I wanted her to do was make a phone call. Considering she calls me several times a day anyway—it should have been a no brainer.

"Chill girl I'ma call, I'm just saying…EL ain't stupid Chass. He ain't working up at that big time firm for nothing. He's gonna put two and two together."

"After today, I won't take any more chances like this, I promise."

"Yeah right," she sucked her teeth. "Only until the next time Shane asks you to do this shit."

"Just make sure you wait a few minutes and then call," I said, not wanting to drag the conversation on any longer and at the same time not wanting EL to get suspicious.

"I'm just tryna keep it real with you, but you my girl so you know I got you."

"Thanks girl." I hung up.

When I walked back into the bedroom EL was lying on the bed watching TV in his boxers and a t-shirt.

"Come here," he motioned for me to walk over to the bed. He positioned me between his legs and proceeded to undress me. Once he was down to my bra, my cell rang.

Please let this be Sara, I thought staring at the phone.

"Don't answer that," he whispered, kissing my neck.

I was a little worried that maybe it was Shane because I told Sara to call the penthouse. I reached for the phone so I could view the number when EL pushed it away.

"Whoever it is, they'll call back," he said, as he started sucking my breasts. Just as he started to get into it, the phone rang.

"Aren't you gonna answer that?" I asked, lifting myself off the bed.

"No and neither are you."

"Didn't you say you were expecting a call?" I asked, reminding him of a client that he mentioned he'd been waiting to hear from.

"Damn! The Woodlawn project! Ummm! Don't move! Keep those legs spread!" he ordered, reaching for the phone. He handed me the phone with a disappointed look on his face. "It's for you."

I grabbed the phone. "Hello."

"Alright girl, I called just like you asked. Now what?"

"Sara, Sara, calm down girl. Just tell me what happened," I said, playing into the *fake* crisis.

Sara was laughing. "You are one crazy chick! What the hell are you talking about Chass?"

"Stop crying. It's gonna be Ok. Just stop crying. Now tell me what happened." My voice was filled with concern giving EL an Oscar worthy performance.

"Just don't say I never did shit for you alright girl," she reminded. "When I need a favor, I will make sure your ass remembers this day."

"I'm sure."

EL was mad as hell. But, I knew it wouldn't be difficult for me to convince him that Sara and Tay got into some shit and she needed me. I wasn't lying about Sara having problems with Tay, just the part about me needing to go to her house. You have to add a little bit of truth to every lie in order to make it believable.

11

Bad Timing

EL

I sat at the edge of the bed listening to Chass tell her girlfriend that she would be there in a few minutes. I glanced down at my hard-on and instantly felt my mood shift. My attitude was already in place before she even finished her conversation.

"I know you're not leaving Chass," I asked, watching her hang up the phone.

"I'll be right back," she replied hurriedly, grabbing her leather jacket from the hall closet.

My face twisted up like I'd just smelled a foul odor. "You can't be serious Chass. I know you're not leaving me like this," I complained referring to my hard on. Her friend's timing couldn't have been worse if she planned it.

"Sara is going through it. I really need to be there for her."

"What about what I need? Did you suddenly forget about my needs? You should be here taking care of me. Your girl can wait."

"No she can't. I'm telling you she's in bad shape. Tay really did a number on her this time."

"Their having problems again? Do they even know what a normal relationship is?"

She reached for her purse. "I'll be back as soon as I calm her down."

"I can't believe this Chass. You're the one who's been hounding me about not spending time with you. Now I'm here trying to spend time with you and you're rushing off to console your friend. What is this a joke? I'm getting tired of you running over there every five minutes Chass. Doesn't she have like a gazillion brothers and sisters? Why can't she call one of them?"

"Sara has never been close to her family like that. But, that is beside the point. She called me. That's my girl and if she needs me—I'm there." Her tone was combative.

"I'm not trying to sound insensitive because I feel for your girl, but her timing is real messed up. We haven't been together in weeks. I wanted it to be about us tonight. Why can't she deal with her own problems and stop dragging you into it, at least for tonight. You have your own man to take care of," I grunted showing off my disappointment.

"You didn't hear the way she sounded EL. Ever since she hooked up with Tay he's been dogging her. I know how Sara is when she gets like this. If I

75

don't talk her down who knows what she might get into. The last time they got into it Sara flattened all four of his tires and wrote all kinds of shit on his windshield."

"Sounds like she needs more help than you can give her. Just call her back and tell her you can't come Chass. Tell her we're busy. She can understand that can't she? Just talk her through whatever it is over the phone."

"I can't do that EL. I already told her I was coming. I'm not gonna leave her hanging like that. I won't be long. I'll be back before you even miss me," she said, trying to placate me.

"I doubt that Chass," I sarcastically replied.

"Can we talk about this when I get back?" she asked, dismissing me.

Deciding this was an argument that I just wasn't going to win, I backed off. "Alright Chass just hurry up and come back." My tongue was barely in her mouth when she pulled away.

"Damn Chass I was just trying to kiss you. You see how you doing me right. I want you to remember this when you start complaining about how much time I spend at the office. Just give me a little something to hold me until you get back. Don't leave me like this Chass."

She slipped her hand inside my pants and gently caressed my balls. Then suddenly, she stopped.

"What are you doing? Why'd you stop?"

"The quicker I leave, the quicker I can come back," she replied, heading for the door.

"Give me a couple minutes to throw something on and I'll take you over there," I said, pulling my shirt over my head.

"No...that's...Ok I already called a cab," she responded like she was nervous.

"Just call them back and tell them you don't need it."

As soon as we pulled on Sara's street, Chass leaned into me and planted her pillow soft lips on mine making me regret giving into her pleas to be there for her friend.

"I'll see you later." She opened the car door.

"Call me when you're ready and I'll pick you up."

She stepped out of the Jag then ducked her head in the window. "That won't be necessary. I'll just ask Sara's Aunt to bring me home."

Satisfied with watching her walk into the building, I drove away.

Winter 2003…

12
Who's That Bitch?
Chass

I lay in bed with EL staring at the ceiling. I couldn't stop thinking about Shane. I still smelled the *Jean Paul Gaultier* cologne that oozed from his skin. I still felt his touch. Whenever EL touched me, I fantasized that he was Shane and that shot my hormone level through the roof. I would sex EL like there was no tomorrow, and he didn't have a clue that Shane was the man fueling my sexual appetite. The stronger my desires were for Shane—the more EL benefited.

Ever since Shane and I first hooked-up we've been sexing non-stop. The man is incredible in the bedroom. He wears sex like a tailor made suit. EL can't even see Shane on his best performance and that says a lot because EL is a great lover—Shane is just much better at it. Shane knows how to rock my entire body. He has it down to a science. He is a guaranteed orgasm. Shane is without question the best I ever had. Thoughts of Shane kept me up half the night. I was finally starting to drift off when my cell rang.

"Hel...lo," I answered, half asleep.

"Hey Baby, what's up?" The sound of Shane's voice woke me right up. I quickly sat upright in the bed wide awake and starry-eyed.

"Hey, what's going on?" I whispered into the phone as I glanced at the digital clock on the night stand that displayed 3:45 a.m.

For him to call me at this time means I must have been on his mind just as much as he was on mine.

"You," he answered, flirtatiously. I wanna see you. Can you meet me at the loft?"

"Now?" I asked, watching EL as he snored. My heart was beating so loud, I could swear that EL heard it in his sleep.

"Yeah, now Chass. It's been a minute since we been together. I miss you Baby."

"I can't right now." I lowered my voice. "It's almost four o'clock in the morning."

"Why you can't?"

"Look what time it is. I can't just leave. What would I tell him?"

"Fuck that nigga. Tell him somethin' came up and you had to bounce. I know you can think of somethin'."

"He's not stupid. He won't believe that. If he wakes up and I'm not here he'll call around looking for me."

"So, let 'em look. He won't find you."

"I can't talk right now. Can I call you later," I whispered into the phone careful not to wake up EL.

"Call me later?" he repeated, like that was the wrong thing for me to ask.

"I need to call you back. He is asleep right next to me."

"Yeah a'ight what-eva." Click.

I could tell Shane was pissed. I sat up in the bed unable to go back to sleep. I wanted to see Shane, but I didn't know what I would tell EL when he woke up and started asking questions. I kept going over in my head what possible explanation I could come up with for leaving in the middle of the night.

A lie is more believable when it isn't rehearsed, I thought as I quietly slipped out the front door. I called Shane to tell him I was on my way, but he didn't answer his cell. I figured he was probably still pissed because I told him that I couldn't meet him. There was no question in my mind that he would quickly get over it once he saw me. So, I hopped in a cab and headed for the loft. It was a little after four o'clock when I got there. I made myself comfortable and waited for Shane thinking that as soon as he got my message, he would be there. About an hour passed and he still hadn't arrived so I called him again. Still, no answer. I jumped in a cab heading for Shane's brownstone.

Just before I got out of the cab, I threw the jacket hood over my head so I wouldn't be recognized then I knocked on the door. No answer, so I knocked again. I noticed the curtain lift slightly. I was sure that Shane saw me, but he didn't open the door.

Oh now you wanna be spiteful muthafucka! After I got out of my man's bed and came here to see you now you wanna leave me standing out here. This how you wanna play it.

I walked away pissed. Shane was gonna pay for this shit. Making me come all the way over here and his ass didn't even answer the door. I was half way down the street when I noticed Shane's Benz coupe drive up.

I quickly turned around and ran back up the street.

"What's up?" I called out catching him off guard.

"Oh...shit! What's up, Chass?" His honey caramel complexion turned white as a sheet.

Chass...what the hell happened to Baby?

"What'chu doin' here?" he asked surprised to see me.

"That should be obvious. I came to see you. Why didn't you come to the loft? Didn't you get my message?

"Nah, I never got no message. When you said you couldn't leave I went to take care of a few things."

Yeah right at six o'clock in the fucking morning. You got some bitch in your place, I thought looking at him wondering if he was gonna be honest with me.

He glanced at his front door then shifted his attention back to me. "Chass let me holla at you later. I still got a few things I need to take care of. I'll drop you off," he offered, trying to get rid of me.

"Later...why?" He wasn't saying later a few hours ago when he called asking to see me. We were just about to get in the car when the front door to the brownstone swung open, and this cute light skinned chick stepped out from the shadows. She looked a little like Keisha Spivey from Total. Chick was rocking the hell out of that Halle Berry cut. Home girl looked mad as hell though. I guess from being left alone longer than she expected.

"*Shaaaaaaaayyynnne!*" Her voice echoed throughout the quiet street.

Shane quickly turned around, "What?!"

"Can you come here for a minute?" she asked, reducing her tone a few notches.

"I'm handlin' shit right now. Go back inside."

Her eyes smallened and she shot me a piercing look like she wanted to burn a hole in my head. Then, just like that, she turned and walked back inside. I felt like a deer in headlights. I must have looked like a fucking fool coming over here anxious to see Shane and all along he had some other chick in his place.

"What part of the game is this?" My temper flared up.

"What'chu talkin' 'bout Baby? I don't play games."

"Is that right?" I sucked my teeth. "Is she the reason you were in such a hurry to get me out of here? I guess next you're gonna tell me that she just happened to stop by after I told you that I couldn't come see you. So this is you tryna pay me back for telling you that I couldn't meet you right."

"Yo Chass you need to fall back wit' that shit. What I gotta pay you back for? You said you couldn't bounce so I left it at that."

"So, you didn't call her as soon as you hung up on me?"

"Nah, I didn't 'cause she was already at my crib. I was gonna leave her here to be wit'chu, but you shot me down."

"What-eva Shane! So this is how you rotate your bitches!" My jealousy was dominating the conversation.

"Chass I wanted to chill wit'chu, but you said you couldn't leave that niggas crib. Now you wanna come at me wit' this attitude 'cause o'l girl is in my crib. You expect me to sit around waitin' on you while you laid up wit' that nigga! Nah, Baby it ain't goin' down like that."

"Fuck you nigga! Go ahead be with that bitch then!" I turned away from him. He quickly grabbed me by the arm and pulled me back.

"Don't walk away from me Chass!" he demanded with fire in his eyes. "The shit don't feel good do it?" he bellowed, as his grip on my arm got tighter.

"Get the fuck off me Shane!"

"Now you know how I feel every time you start screamin' some shit about that ma'fucka. Like I wanna hear shit about that nigga when I'm tryin' to be wit'chu. I'm not good at waitin' Chass. It ain't my thing." He stared into my eyes as he loosened his grip on me.

"Now you wanna make demands!"

"It's been weeks Chass. I ain't no monk. Shit I got needs just like the next man. You see ol' girl in my crib and you wanna flip on me. You knew what it was goin' in. Same as I did."

As much as I hated it, Shane was right. We had an understanding. He wasn't my man so I had no right to be whining about some chick.

"We a'ight?" he asked, like I was just supposed to forget about his half naked house guest.

"Shane please...you did this out of spite. You just wanted to make sure I knew how fast you could get a bitch over here. By all means go and be with your bitch! Don't let me stop you!"

"Is this how you want it to be between us Chass?"

"Why don't you worry about that bitch you got inside waiting on you to fuck her! That's why she came out here in that skimpy-ass shit. So go give her what she wants." I yelled at him as I was walking away.

"Oh it's like that?" His words hit my back as I walked further away from him.

When I got back to the penthouse thankfully EL was still asleep. I remember thinking how relieved I was. I couldn't stop thinking about Shane with that chick and how he was probably sexing her the way he should have been sexing me. Needless to say, I didn't get any sleep.

**   **   **   **

I was sitting at the table eating a bowl of Capt'n Crunch Berries when EL walked in.

"Morning," he said, reaching in the fridge for an energy drink.

"You're running late this morning," I said, glancing at the wall clock.

"Actually, I'm not going into the office until this afternoon. I have to take a drive to Long Island to look at a piece property that one of my clients is interested in purchasing. I remember you telling me that you didn't have any appointments until later today. I was hoping you would take a ride with me. Maybe we can grab something to eat afterwards."

A drive to Long Island sounded like it was exactly what I needed so I agreed to go. We were waiting to pay the toll for the Triboro Bridge when EL realized that he didn't have his EZ-PASS.

"Damn! I forgot my EZ-PASS! It kept falling off the windshield, so I took it down." He flipped his wallet open. "All I have are my credit cards and they don't take those."

I tapped my pockets. "Damn EL, I don't have any money on me either. I left my pocketbook on the bed."

I searched the car for loose change and stumbled across a few rolls of dimes in the glove compartment.

"What about these?" I reached the rolls to him.

"Oh snap I forgot about those. Mia asked me to pick them up for her when I was at the bank the other day. I must have forgotten to give them to her. You think they'll take those?" he asked, as if there was a law against paying the toll with dimes.

"They'll take it. It's money. It'll spend."

EL still felt the need to explain the situation to the toll booth clerk, and once we pulled up to the window, he started to. The rude clerk pushed the roll of dimes back at EL cutting him off in the middle of his explanation.

"I'm sorry sir, but the seal on this is broken which means I would have to count it. I don't have time for that. Look behind you," she pointed. "You see that line? If you pull over there you can fill this out and mail the money in." She handed EL a ticket and directed us to the side of the highway where several police vehicles were parked like they were on a coffee-break. EL was being way too nice and this chick was just talking over him which was pissing me off.

"Excuse me, but why should he mail the money when he can pay for the toll right now? That doesn't make any sense to me."

"It doesn't have to," she said rudely. "The bottom line is that I do not have time to count that. Sorry, I can't help you."

I took the roll of dimes out of EL's hand and threw it into the booth. "There! See how easy that was! Drive off EL! Shit, you paid the toll. Now her cranky-ass can do her damn job!"

EL had that 'I can't believe you just did that' look on his face. Before he could drive off, the clerk threw a handful of change back at me flooding EL's car with dimes.

"Oh no you didn't bitch!" Forget about being pissed, by this time I was steaming. That clerk had no idea the ass-whipping she was in for. I opened the door to get out of the car, but before I could step out EL drove off.

"What are you doing? Go back!"

"Chass its a'ight," he chuckled.

"No it's not alright! Go back EL! I'm not playing!"

"Chass calm down. Everything shouldn't be a fight. Why you always ready for war girl?" He laughed, watching me get all worked up.

I sucked my teeth and rolled my window down. After about twenty minutes of the cool brisk air I'd forgotten all about the incident and just sat back and enjoyed the ride.

The beautiful piece of property sat on more than three acres of land in Bethpage Long Island. The land was surrounded by a lake and plenty of trees.

EL walked around taking pictures while I waited in the car. Once he finished his business we stopped at Pizza Hut for a Deep Dish Supreme.

"I have something to show you," he gloated, just as we approached the exit.

My eyes grew big as saucers as soon as we pulled up in front of 112 Ocean Avenue. I recognized the famous piece of property right away. It was the Amityville Horror House.

"That shit look scary as hell," I said, half-joking. Suddenly, images of the horrific movie scenes scrolled through my head. "Why the hell did you bring me here? Something is seriously wrong with you EL."

He stood in front of the passenger side door smirking at me because I still hadn't gotten out of the car.

"I thought you loved those movies. Didn't you tell me those were your favorites?"

"You're a freaking nut EL. I like those Friday the 13th flicks too, but you will never catch my ass up at Camp Crystal Lake!"

He laughed, "Get out the car Chass and stop being so damn scary."

I hesitated, but I got out. *I'd be damned if I let him tease me with this,* I thought climbing out of the Jag.

"See look," he pointed. "Isn't that where..." Noticing the look on my face he stopped talking.

"I'll wait for you over here." I walked the three steps it took to get back to the car.

"Chass get back here," he said, playfully.

"No! Shit you crazy. A movie is one thing, but to be at the place where all that actually happened is something else entirely. I'm ready to go EL. This shit is freaking me out."

"C'mon Chass, we've only been here ten minutes." EL was snapping pictures like the house was his personal photo shoot.

"That's ten minutes too long."

He laughed. "Alright, alright one more minute, let me just get this last shot."

"Boy you crazy as hell and we just ate. Come on, I'm ready to go," I climbed back into the Jag and closed the door.

He laughed, "I didn't think there was anything that could scare big-bad-Chass."

"Ha...ha...you're so funny. You should really take this act on the road. When you're finished with the jokes, I'll be in the car."

"Calm down Chass. It's just a house."

Just a house my ass! Tell that to all those people who were killed in there, I thought, watching the scary piece of property in the side mirror as EL and I drove way.

13

Make It Do What It Do

Chass

The incident with that chick pissed me off more than I cared to admit. I was starting to get territorial over Shane and I didn't have the right to be. Shane and I had an understanding. He had his women, I had my man. However, that understanding seemed to fade more and more everytime we were together. The more I was with Shane; the more I wanted to be. I was falling hard and fast and there wasn't a damn thing I could do about it.

Shane and I were meeting Tay and Sara at The Apollo. Once we got to 125th Street, Shane circled the streets several times trying to locate a temporary residence for the Benz. We met up with Tay in the lobby where he was standing by the steps talking on his cell.

His ass stay on that damn phone, I thought wondering where Sara was; which was the first question I asked as soon as Shane and I approached him.

"She had to jet to the ladies room right quick," Tay answered, covering the mouth piece to his cell.

I noticed Izrael standing a few feet away from us signaling for me to walk over to him. After Izrael finally gave up on the idea of going out with me, we had actually become friends.

"What's up Iz?"

"Hey Chass what's good Ma? I'm 'bout to head back stage. You came to see me perform?"

"Perform?"

"Come on now Chass. Don't act like you didn't know I was performing tonight."

"I didn't know." I looked over my shoulder noticing three guys standing a few feet away from us wearing the same clothes Izrael had on.

"Oh, so it's a group thing."

"No doubt."

"What y'all singing?"

"Jagged Edge, Let's Get Married."

Awww shit Iz! That's my song! Y'all better tear it out the frame and represent!"

"Please believe me." He cracked a smile. His confidence was off the charts. Izrael had that R. Kelly type of voice. I knew he was gonna kill it. It wasn't until he started being cocky and bragging about having the contest in the bag that had me daring him to bet on his skills. I bet Izrael a hundred dollars that he would get booed, and as cocky as his ass is, he took me up on it. So, I was looking forward to collecting my dough.

"You ready to go inside?" Shane walked up to me with Sara and Tay trailing behind him. He grabbed my hand and led me into the dark theater. I was really looking forward to the show now that there was money at stake.

After the show Shane, Tay, Sara and I drove downtown to this soul food restaurant called *The Soul Café*. My mouth watered at the thought of fried chicken, baked macaroni & cheese, collard greens, potato salad and candied yams. I was thinking about what I was going to order in the car on the way to the restaurant. That's how open I was. It was open mic night, and we listened to the raw unsigned talent as they graced the stage.

"Who the fuck is that?" Shane reached for his drink. "Home girl can blow!"

The four of us watched in awe while we listened to the female undiscovered talent that was on the microphone doing her thing.

"She's good," I said, agreeing with Shane as I stuck my fork into my baked macaroni & cheese.

"Izrael did his thing tonight too Chass," Sara interjected. "He ain't win, but he ain't get booed either. You might not see that hundred," she threw in reminding me of the bet.

"Yeah I knew Iz was gonna blow it out the park. He sings all the time around the way, so of course he was gonna show out on stage. I knew I shouldn't have bet his ass, but he was just too damn cocky for me."

"How 'bout that Spanish dude singing that Maxwell shit? He tore that shit down!" Tay called out.

"Yeah that lil' nigga did a'ight," Shane nodded in agreement.

The next performer who caught our attention was some dude singing the Stevie Wonder Classic *Overjoyed*. He tore it up.

"Damn why these niggas ain't signed?" Shane asked, surprised.

"Somebody is definitely gonna snatch them up, especially home girl who went first. Trust me she'll be gettin' a deal soon." Tay said, just as the waiter walked up to our table with a second round of drinks.

Shane eased his body into mine then whispered. "I can't wait to get you outta here. Watching the way you working that ice cube got a nigga sittin' over here hard as a brick."

My body instantly became hot from his comment. I grabbed his hand and placed it on my inner thigh, "Me either Baby feel that heat. You know what that means…I want some."

"Oh word!" Shane damn near blurted out. "Baby we can bounce right now! Where the waiter at so I can pay his ass?" Shane said as he anxiously looked around the restaurant.

I stroked his thigh. "Be easy Baby. I'm not going nowhere. We don't need to rush out like that. We got all night. Can I finish my drink?" I winked at him while taking another sip of my White Russian.

"Baby don't play wit' me. You really think I'ma sit up in here after you done told me some shit like that? Nah Baby you buggin'. And, look at that dress...that damn dress is makin' a nigga go crazy over here. You knew that dress was gonna do that shit to me didn't you? You ain't slick Baby you know what you do to me." He reached his hand under my dress.

"Chill." I slapped his hand lightly.

"Chill, for what?" He leaned in and whispered in my ear. "I'ma keep fuckin' wit' chu 'til you ready to leave. You sittin' up in here lookin' good as hell in that shit and you tellin' me to chill. Baby it's takin' everything in me not to rip that shit off you right here at this table."

I was in the mood to play with Shane so I continued to flirt and feel on him under the table turning him on and pissing him off at the same time. I was turned on just watching Shane get all worked up knowing there wasn't a damn thing he could do about it in the restaurant. He handed me my pocketbook that was propped in between us.

"C'mon Chass and let me hit the waiter off so we can bounce!" he said, watching me play with the ice cubes with my tongue.

"I'm not ready to leave yet Shane. We haven't even had dessert. I really have a taste for that German Chocolate Cake."

"I see you really tryin' to make me suffer huh."

"You think that's what I'm doing?" I asked, with an innocent face.

"I *know* it is."

Tay and Shane stared talking about sports while Sara and I talked about fashion. The next thing I knew, Shane was tapping my shoulder.

"You ready to go yet?" he anxiously asked.

Shane's green eyes captivated me in the romantic setting. Continuing to resist him was becoming more and more of a challenge, especially since the more I turned him on the more he turned me on.

"Not yet. I haven't finished my drink," I teased.

"Chass stop nursing that shit and let's go!" he said like it was an order.

"Ok, Ok one minute."

"See Baby now you playin'. He looked at me with this '*you done fucked up now*' look. Then he reached his hand under the table and slid his finger in my pussy.

Shane's finger became very friendly with my soft spot making it impossible for me to concentrate. A couple seconds later I leaned into him. "You convinced me. Let's go."

"I thought you'd see it my way," he bragged, as he flagged the waiter down so he could pay the check.

I should have known better than to play the seduction game with Shane. Although, I knew exactly what to do to get him excited, he knew the same about me. Once we were in the car he spread my legs apart and slid his finger back inside me. Shane drove like a race car driver flying passed the other cars like they were standing still. The night breeze slapped against my face as Shane sped along the Harlem River Drive. I've always been a sucker for night air. It has a calm relaxing effect on me. I laid back and enjoyed the pleasure that his finger was providing while he maneuvered in and out traffic anxiously trying to get us to our destination.

In the elevator ride up to the loft Shane couldn't keep his hands off me. "Chass you gon' pay for that shit you pulled tonight," he threatened lustfully while slapping my ass seductively.

The incents that were left burning had the lingering scent of wild berries greeting us as we walked into the loft. Shane walked over to the stereo and pulled out Maxwell's CD, *Now* featuring; *This Woman's Work* and inserted it in the CD player. Then he laid me down on the leopard print rug in front of the fire place.

"Now starts the craft of the father…"

14

You Gets No Love

EL

"Not now EL I don't feel good," Chass groaned, as she declined my sexual advances.

I climbed out of the bed. "Not this again!" I said angrily. "That's the third time this week!"

"I think my period is coming because these cramps are kicking my ass and my head is pounding like crazy," she whined.

"Are you sure that's all it is?" I asked frustrated and not sure I believed her.

"Of course I'm sure. Why you say that?" she asked, looking at me like I did something wrong.

"We haven't made love all week Chass. I'm just a little cranky that's all. You've been *real* stingy with the sex lately. Every time I want to make love, you don't feel well. I don't know how much more of this I can take!"

"I'm not making excuses EL. You know I get these headaches and cramps every time my period is about to come. This happens every month like clock-work, but it will pass, it always does."

If it's not a headache, it's cramps. If it's not cramps, it's a headache. Now today it's both. Give me a fucking break.

I climbed back in the bed refusing to take no for an answer. I rubbed her stomach trying to sooth her while brushing my hard dick against her ass.

"Chass I wanna make love to you," I spoke softly into her ear while massaging her stomach hoping this time she would give in.

"Stop EL!" She pushed my hand away. "Why the hell are you rubbing my stomach?! Didn't you hear me say I have cramps?!"

"I was just trying to make you feel better."

"That's making it hurt worse."

I sat up in the bed. "When are we gonna be together Chass?" I demanded, sexually frustrated. "I'm getting real tired of this!"

"You act like I'm doing this on purpose EL."

"Are you?" I grunted.

"No, I'm not! If I say I don't feel good then I don't feel good damn!" she shot back.

"Well, it's a little hard to tell with all that complaining you're doing Chass. It's been over a week since we made love." I glanced down at the center of my boxers. "I'm hard as hell over here."

"A week ain't that long EL. You up here acting like it's been months."

"It sure feels like it. If I didn't know any better I would think you are making excuses so you won't have to make love to me. As a matter a fact I don't even remember the last time you initiated sex."

"Of course you wouldn't because you are too busy chasing your clients and closing deals. I bet you remember everything that goes on at that damn firm though don't you!"

"Not this again Chass! Why do I have to keep defending my job to you? There is no competition between you and my job Chass."

She sucked her teeth. "You're right there isn't!"

"What is that supposed to mean?"

"Nothing EL. Just forget it. I don't feel good so I'm not about to get into this with you again."

She rolled over in the bed turning away from me. I slid back into the bed and snuggled up behind her.

"I'm sorry Chass. I don't want to argue either. You know how I get when I don't get none. I know you hate the hours I put in, but I work hard to give you the life you deserve. Would you prefer if I were jobless and broke?" I asked, talking to the back of her head.

She rolled over. "Of course not. I'm just tired of this. I'm tired of arguing about it."

"I don't want to argue either. All I'm asking for is a little attention. Why is that a problem?"

"That's the thing. You never spend time with me and when you do all you wanna do is have sex."

"That's not all I want to do. Usually when I come home you're either asleep, hanging with your girlfriends or at your Mom's doing hair. I could complain about all the time that you spend with your friends, and all the nights you spend at your Moms doing hair that has you too tired to come home afterwards, but I don't."

"You don't want me doing hair here so where do you expect me to do it? And for your information I go out because I'm tired of being here by myself. You know how many nights I fall asleep waiting on you?" She huffed. "Too many."

"I know you have. It's my job Chass. It requires long hours. What do you expect me to do?"

"What about when you are home EL? You are not at that firm 24/7. You used to take me out. We used to do things together. Now, I couldn't pay you to take me to a dog fight!" She climbed out of the bed.

"Come lay back down Chass. Let me hold you." I said, trying to calm the vibe between us. "I'm sorry. I know you're trying. It might not look like it, but I'm trying too."

She eased back under the covers with me. I wrapped my arms around her and she began to relax. I kissed the back of her neck, then the side of her face, and then her neck again. When I noticed that she wasn't resisting, I took it a step further and started squeezing her breast. Still, she didn't ask me to stop so I started rubbing my dick against her ass. Then I kissed her earlobe and whispered in her ear, "I haven't been inside of you all week and I'm going through withdrawal."

"EL...I keep telling you I have cramps!" She pulled away from me again.

"Come on Chass. It's cold out here. I want to be inside of you where it's nice and warm."

"Can you grab the Midol from the medicine cabinet? My head is pounding and these cramps are getting worse," she complained.

I rose from the bed. "Anything else? Like maybe a cup of warm milk? I hear it soothes the stomach." My sarcasm was evident.

She sucked her teeth and rolled her eyes. "Oh you being funny. You know this is not that kind of stomach ache. I have menstrual cramps. Warm milk is not gonna cut it."

I walked into the bathroom mad as hell. My dick was harder than Chinese math and I didn't want to hear shit about some fucking menstrual cramps. I grabbed the bottle of Midol from the medicine cabinet, walked back into the bedroom and handed Chass the pills. I watched her take two pills then gulp down a mouthful of Poland Spring.

"Look, I'm sorry Chass. I'm just frustrated because I miss being with you."

"Can we talk about this later? My head is killing me," she said dismissing me.

I was sexually frustrated. I didn't want to spend the rest of the night arguing about the reason Chass didn't want to have sex this time. It was a little after nine o'clock so I figured I would go back to the office. If I couldn't be with Chass I definitely wasn't in the mood to listen to her whine about menstrual cramps. I threw my clothes back on, grabbed my briefcase from the floor of the closet and walked out of the bedroom.

"I'm going to the office. I'll be back in a few hours. I hope you feel better," I called out to her on my way out the door.

** ** ** **

When I arrived at the office, I turned on my computer and tried to get some work done. But, my mind kept fading. I kept thinking about the last time that Chass and I made love, and how good it was. I wanted to feel that again. I wanted my woman and since I couldn't have her my mood was foul. I couldn't concentrate. I guess you could say I was daydreaming because I didn't even hear Mia when she walked into my office.

"I thought I saw you come in Mr. Wiggins. What are you doing back here?" she asked, walking up to my desk.

Mia was my assistant. Just a year out of college, she came on as a temp. She impressed me with her efficiency and eagerness to learn. She was also a wiz at multi tasking. Needless to say, I hired her after the first week.

"What am I doing back here? What are you still doing here? I thought I told you to go home hours ago."

"You did, but I had to finish up some paperwork for the Leslie account and Vince asked me to pull up some stuff for Chase."

I stared at Mia while she talked. I don't think I ever realized how beautiful she was before today. Mia had a head full of tiny braids that she couldn't resist running her fingers through. She stood about 5 foot 4 inches and she had a body like one of those females you see in a video. She wore the hell out of that skirt suit. Whenever she stepped into a room, she captured everyone's attention. She just had that presence. In a lot of ways Mia reminded me of Chass. I think that's why I found myself suddenly so attracted to her. She really picked a fine time to come say hi.

"Did you finish up what you were doing for Vince?" I asked, with my eyes focused on her breast. They stood at attention as they stared back at me from the inside of her slightly opened blazer.

"Uh-huh. It didn't take long. I also finished this up for you while I was here." She handed me a few files. Our hands touched and her cotton like skin woke my Johnson back up.

"What are these?" I asked, rifling through the files.

"The Swanson, Bolder, and Kelmer files. They're all done. I knew you would want them as soon as possible. I was going to give them to you first thing in the morning, but when I saw you come in, I figured I'd give them to you now."

"You didn't have to stay. You could have just finished this up tomorrow."

"That's Ok Mr. Wiggins. It wasn't a problem. I didn't mind staying."

"What about your man? Does he mind all the late hours you give this firm?" I just had to ask because the curiosity was killing me.

"He probably would if I had one. I work too much so I don't really have time for a man."

"Ahhh come on. I don't work you that hard do I?"

"No you don't, but my second job does. I sing at night-clubs a few nights a week. Plus I've been spending a lot of time at the studio working on my demo."

"Really? I didn't even know you sing."

"Singing is my passion. It's all I ever really wanted to do."

"Maybe one day you can sing something for me."

"One day, shoot I can sing for you right now!" Her confidence turned me on even more than the skirt suit that she was filling out rather nicely.

I rose up from my desk and closed the door. "You got the floor. Let's hear it."

She sung Denise William's *Black Butterfly*. I loved it. When she started singing I felt the hair on the back of my neck stand up. Her voice was so incredible. It sent chills through me.

"That's a pretty powerful set of pipes you have there. Make sure you stay in the studio until that demo is done."

She smiled real wide. "Thank you Mr. Wiggins. I'm glad you think so."

"Oh I do. The music industry is a demanding business to be in. Are you sure you're up for it?" I asked, still staring at her breast.

"There is nothing else I'd rather be doing, other than working for you that is." She winked at me. Mia was definitely flirting with me. At first I thought I misread the signals, but that one was loud and clear.

"Can I ask you a personal question?" she asked, as she played with her manicured nails.

"Sure." I nodded leaning back in my chair.

"Does working all these hours affect your relationship?"

What is she trying to get at? I thought, as I prepared to answer the question.

"Sometimes."

"What do you do when it does?"

"I just try to reassure my lady that I have to work in order to take care of her."

"Does that work for you?"

"Not really," I said with a smirk.

"If my man was spending less and less time with me, and more and more time elsewhere I would question it."

"That's only because women question everything don't they?"

"Well...if my man looked as good as you do, I would have to question everything," she replied, stepping a little too close into my space.

Our eyes locked. I went for it; allowing myself to succumb to her advances. If Chass wasn't giving me the attention I needed, I didn't see the harm in getting it from Mia. The next thing I knew, my tongue was exploring her mouth while my hands carassed her toned body. Within minutes, my slacks were around my ankles, and the lovely Mia was graciously accepting my rock hard dick from behind. My desk had proven to be the perfect place to release my sexual frustration.

15

Uninvited Guest

Chass

While EL was preparing for a business trip out of town, I was preparing for my trip to Atlantic City with Shane; where he would be meeting with a few potential investors about a car dealership that he was opening. When EL flooded me with his usual borage of annoying questions, I told him that I would be spending the weekend with my cousin Asia who lived in Brooklyn. I even had him drop me off at her house just to make it more believable. As soon as EL drove off, I called Shane who wasn't too happy about having to pick me up from Brooklyn. He definitely didn't appreciate the lengths that I was prepared to go to in order to keep EL in the dark, and he made sure I knew that.

"Damn Baby you do way too much runnin' around over this nigga. How you end up in Brooklyn?"

"I didn't want him asking too many questions about where I would be or what I would be doing while he was gone so I told him I was spending the weekend at my cousin's house."

"Did you have to go all the way to Brooklyn? Now this sets me back. I have to be at the hotel in a few hours. This is gonna be cuttin' it real close."

"You can just leave me here if it's too much of an inconvenience for you," I joked.

"Nonsense. You know how much I've been lookin' forward to this weekend. Just be ready when I get there. Don't have me waitin' Baby 'cause time is tight."

A half hour later, Shane pulled up in front of my cousins' building blasting Mario Winans *I Don't Wanna Know*.

"You been here long?" I asked, as I hopped in the Range and closed the door.

"Nah, I just pulled up."

I wasn't in the car ten minutes before I drifted off. I guess all that running back and forth between two men can really wipe a sista out. When Shane hit a pot-hole in the road, it forced me awake. I repositioned myself in the seat and fought to stay awake.

He chuckled. "Go back to sleep Baby. You look mad tired."

"I was tryna stay up to keep you company."

"Don't worry 'bout me. We'll be there in a few. Just go back to sleep. You gon' need your rest," he said with a smirk.

That's why I'm sleeping now. I'm getting it out the way.

The next thing I knew Shane was taping my shoulder telling me we were there.

"Damn Baby I didn't realize you bought so much shit," he said pulling our luggage from the back of the Range. "We only gon' be here for two days, not two months." He handed me the carry-on then threw the garment bag across his shoulder and picked up the suitcase.

"You know me. I always over-pack."

"Over packing ain't the word. You won't need half this shit. Trust me. But, I love a woman who comes prepared," he said as we stepped into the lobby of the hotel.

The hotel lobby was magnificent and completely made of carved-out granite and pink marble. Gold statutes with intricate mosaic tile sparkled like diamonds in the sky. The scent of fresh lilies welcomed us to the majestic palace. The huge ten foot, five tier water fountains resembled a wedding cake, with the sound of soothing trickling water flowing into the bottom receptacle that was filled with large, orange koi fish that were slowly making their way around the circle.

"May I help you?" The polite clerk asked as Shane and I approached the desk.

"I made a reservation on line. Here is my confirmation e-mail and proof of my credit card payment."

Shane rested his arm on the marble counter and handed the clerk the sheet of paper. The clerk typed the information into the computer and then looked up at Shane.

"You're in suite 302 Sir," she said, handing Shane the key to the suite.

The bell hop placed our luggage on the trolley and Shane and I followed him as he rolled it onto the elevator. After the bellhop unloaded our luggage in the suite, Shane handed him a fifty and he went on his way. I walked over to the window and drew the drapes back. I was immediately captivated by the glorious view. The bright hotel lights reflecting off of the night sky, shone directly onto the water.

"A'ight Baby I'm 'bout to bounce," Shane announced, as he stepped out of the bathroom reading a text message. "These nigga's just text me so I'ma head over there 'cause the meetin' is 'bout to start. I'll call you as soon as it's over and we can meet up at the Casino. Tay and Sara's suite is down the hall so I know you gon' check ya' girl." He gave me a kiss on the cheek and walked out the suite.

I changed into my *Dolce & Gabbana* short fitted skirt and threw on my low cut flannel blouse that exposed a lot of cleavage. I zipped up my thigh-high boots and headed for Sara and Tay's suite. As I was approaching the door, their argument greeted me before I had a chance to knock.

94

"You must think I'm stupid huh nigga! Who the fuck you on the phone with now muthafucka!" I heard Sara yell.

Dead silence.

Your hand caught in the cookie jar type of silence. I could sense the tension from the hallway. Hearing Sara get all worked up reminded me of just how jealous she can be. Although Tay had given her plenty of reasons not to trust him, Sara usually doesn't need much of a push. Her relationships tend to bring out the desperate-needy side of her. It isn't attractive and it's a complete turn off to all the men she's ever been involved with. It's been a while since I've seen Sara in action. In her rarest form, she reminds me of the character that Glenn Close played in the movie Fatal Attraction. When it comes to her men—Sara has done everything except boil the rabbit.

"I'm waiting Tay. Who the fuck is that? I heard some Baby, Baby shit. You on the phone with some bitch huh nigga? Who the fuck is that?" she yelled again.

"Don't come up in here with all that noise?! I came here to relax." Tay spoke in a belittling tone of voice as he talked over Sara.

"Relax my ass muthafucka!" she screamed and then there was a loud noise.

I knocked on the door hurriedly. The door swung open and Sara stood in the doorway looking me up and down.

"What's up girl? You look nice," she said forcing a smile.

"What was that noise? It sounded like a crash." I walked passed her as I stepped inside. "Did something break?"

"Your girl done lost her fuckin' mind! She broke my phone!" Tay picked up what was left of his phone then laid the pieces on the bed.

"That's what your lying ass gets! Now you can't be running your fucking mouth with your bitches all day!"

"I already told you that was my boy. You tryna tell me I can't talk to my boy now."

"That wasn't your fucking boy nigga stop lying! You told me you were coming here for business and your ass ain't did shit but lay up on that fucking phone since we got here!"

"Yo Chass take her crazy-ass the fuck outta here!" Tay requested.

"Fuck you nigga! I'll leave when I'm good and god damn ready to!" Sara shot back.

"Ssshhh," I quickly interrupted. "Y'all gonna get us kicked outta here."

Tay sprawled across the bed. "Yo Chass check ya girl man. She buggin' the fuck out!"

"Learn how to tell the damn truth and we won't have a problem!" she yelled again.

"Yo Chass just take her wit'chu man. I ain't tryin' to hear all that."

Tay and Sara were eyeing each other like they were ready to go a few rounds. I knew that was my queue to get Sara out of the suite.

"Come on girl let's go. I'm ready to hit the casinos?"

I pulled Sara in my direction. She rolled her eyes at Tay and walked out of the suite with me. On the elevator ride Sara started to vent.

"I'm sick of Tay's shit. All this nigga wanna do is stay on the damn phone. Then when I ask him to take me shopping or to a Casio all of a sudden he's tired. He said he was going to sleep. So I left the suite to make him think I went somewhere. I didn't do shit except roam the lobby, but I needed to get away from his lying ass. When I came back to the suite that's when I caught his ass on the phone."

Sara didn't need to convince me. I knew that was bullshit. Tay didn't come all the way to Atlantic City to take a nap. He was playing Sara—plain and simple. I couldn't understand why she put up with his shit. I just looked at her thinking, *it couldn't be me*. I thought Sara was about to ruin our trip with that evil look she brought with her, along with the luggage she carried under her eyes. Sara looked stressed as hell. This relationship was really taking its toll on her.

"He thinks he slick. Like I don't know what the hell is going on. He thinks I'm stupid. It's cool though. I'll play the game with him and when his ass slip up, I'ma be right there."

"Look at it this way; at least he doesn't have a phone now."

"Please Chass...You think Tay woulda been that cool about me breaking his cell if he didn't have another one in his suitcase. And if he doesn't he'll just call the cell phone company and have them FedEx him another one."

"Damn it's like that?"

"Why you think he all stretched the fuck out on the bed like he home; getting all comfortable and shit. He is not worried about that damn phone. If he was trust me we woulda still been arguing. He couldn't even be bothered to take me to the Casino while we waited for you and Shane to get here. Now since we in AC he wanna show his ass. It's cool though I don't need him to have a good time."

"That's right girl and you don't need to be tied to his ass all night anyway. Now we have some time to cut up and get loose. Feel me?" I said, trying to make her feel better.

"Oh Chass please." She looked at me like I was full of shit. "You know you ain't tryna look in my face all night when you got Shane waiting on you. And, Shane definitely ain't tryna let me ruin y'all flow," she said, lighting a cigarette.

Just then a text came through my cell.

Meet me at the Borgata.

It was from Shane.

Sara and I headed for the Borgata talking about Tay's grimy-ass all the way there. As soon as we stepped into the lobby of the Casino, the overzealous security guard approached us.

"Excuse me. There is no smoking in here Miss." He pointed to the board that displayed the Casino's rules and regulations. "I don't make the rules I just enforce them. You have to put the cigarette out before I can let you inside," he ordered, watching Sara with his one good eye.

"Don't tell me you're afraid of a little smoke and ashes?" she snipped.

He rolled his eyes. "Be cute all you want Miss, but be cute from out there. As long as you have that cigarette in your mouth, you cannot enter the Casino."

"Sara just put the cigarette out so we can gamble. I know you mad at Tay, but you need to ease up girl. Don't take it out on everybody."

"Fuck him Chass! I don't feel like putting my fucking cigarette out. It's just getting good."

"Well I guess you feel like standing out here by your damn self. I came here to gamble and that's exactly what I'm gonna do. I told you about them damn cancer sticks anyway." I walked passed her and into the casino. She tossed the cigarette into the tiny tin trash can and followed me inside.

"Can I get a rum and coke?" Sara flagged down one of the waiters as soon as we took a seat in front of the slot machine.

"And, I'd like a Kaluha' with milk, whipped cream and a cherry on top. Oh and heavy on the vodka please," I added.

"Anything else ma'am?" the waiter asked, as if the drink order was incomplete.

"Yes, I'ma need you to come back in ten minutes after you bring those drinks and bring us two more," I replied, ready to get my drink on.

The alcohol availability was one of the things I loved about Atlantic City. As long as you were in the Casino, the drinks were free.

"Damn Chass what was that shit you just ordered? It sounded like an ice cream sundae," Sara joked, watching the waiter scurry off to fill our order.

"Unless the ice cream is spiked—trust me it's not a sundae."

After losing a few dollars, I wanted to try my luck at something else. As Sara and I walked passed the tables we heard the pit boss exclaim, "Place your bets! Place your bets!"

"You wanna get in on this one?" she asked, referring to the black jack table that we were standing directly in front of.

"Oh no, girl I'm good," I replied, looking at the slot machine right across from us. "I'm gonna try my luck on that one."

Then, I got lucky.

Ding...ding...ding!

"Five thousand dollars!" Sara called out like she just hit the lottery.

The quarters poured out of the machine like water. I had to use my shirt to catch them.

"Go grab me a bucket or something Sara." I said, pointing her towards the cashier.

"Need some help?" Shane asked as he crept up behind me. Shane was so close to me I could feel his breath on my back. If I would have moved even an inch there would have been a collision. He slid a bucket under the machine to catch the overflow of quarters that were pouring out and filling my shirt.

"You done with your meeting already? That was quick," I said surprised as I unrolled my shirt allowing the quarters to drop into the bucket.

"The meeting was pushed back until tomorrow morning. A couple investors didn't show up. Their flight got delayed." He looked me up and down and smiled, "I'm diggin' that shit you got on Baby. Why you change your clothes? What you had on was cool."

"You know I have to look good for you."

"You always do. Damn you got a nigga over here brick. Your man shoulda never let you outta his sight this weekend. His loss is most certainly my gain." He flirted.

My heart fluttered. To say I was turned on would be an understatement. "Why is that?" I flirted back.

"You know why." He winked at me. "I'm gonna enjoy you this weekend."

Ditto Baby.

The Casino employee grabbed our attention as he walked up and shut the machine off to refill it.

"Sorry it took me so long. This was all I could find." Sara handed me the bucket.

"I don't need it now girl. You took so long I thought I was gonna have to report you missing."

"Y'all ready to go hit the club?" Shane asked, returning my flirtatiously stares.

"Definitely. I have some energy I wanna burn off." I smiled at him.

"HELLO!" Sara snapped her fingers breaking our trance. "Where are you going with all this weight Chass?" She pointed to the buckets of quarters that sat at my feet.

Not feeling like standing on the long line waiting for a cashier, I suddenly looked at Shane like he was my only hope.

"Gimmie the buckets Chass," he said, catching the way I was eyeing him. "Don't make this a habit a'ight. I'ma grab Tay so we can hit up the club. Wait here until I come back."

Sara looked at me like I was in trouble.

"What?" I asked, wanting to know the reason for her stares.

"Girl you and Shane just need to go fuck and get that shit over with because the sexual tension between y'all is insane!"

I laughed off her comment.

"I'm serious Chass. We're in a casino and y'all damn near all over each other. Ya'll horny asses don't know shit about self control."

"What-eva," I mumbled thinking...*No self control my ass. I showed amazing self control when I didn't follow my urges to rip Shane's clothes off and fuck him right smack in the middle of all this damn gambling.*

She spun around in the swivel seat that connected to the slot machine. "Go ahead and get your fuck on. You know you want to."

"Girl please, we got all night for that." I was trying to play it off like I wasn't counting down the minutes until Shane and I were alone.

"You find Tay?" Sara asked, as Shane approached us.

"He said he gon' meet us at the club," he replied as he handed me fifty crisp one hundred dollar bills. Then he pulled his cell from his pocket. "I gotta return a phone call and I'll meet y'all at the club too."

Nelly's *My Place* was on full blast when Sara and I walked in the club. I spotted Tay sitting at a table in the corner so I walked over to him while Sara flagged down the waiter.

"Where Shane at?" I took a seat across the table from him.

Tay guzzled down the rest of his drink. "That nigga round here somewhere. So what's up Chass? You lookin' mighty tasty."

Tay had that look in his eye like he was in the mood to be disloyal to both Sara and Shane. It probably had something to do with the collection of empty shot glasses that were lined up in front of him. Still, I wasn't giving him a free pass. I was just about to check his ass when Sara walked up.

"I see the waiter Chass. You want something?"

You lucky nigga. I turned away from him and toward Sara.

"You already know."

"That ice cream sundae shit right," she laughed.

"You know it."

The waiter made several trips to our table bringing rounds and rounds of drinks. I drank like my life depended on it not giving a second thought to the hang over that would visit me in the morning. Shane took a seat next to me and started rubbing my thigh informing me of how excited he was. As soon as Usher's *Yeah*, came crashing through the speakers, Shane grabbed me by the hand and lead me to the dance floor. I stopped abruptly then shifted my weight to one side and placed my hand on my hip.

"You got a lot of nerve. Did I say I wanted to dance?" I joked.

"Did I ask you?" he replied with a snide grin letting me know that the decision wasn't mine to make.

"You know me Baby. I had to think of a reason to put my hands all over you sittin' at that table watchin' you get nice, that shit turned me the fuck on."

His swagger had my pussy dripping. Being with Shane was like an out of body experience. The man wakes up things in me that I never even knew were there. His fine-ass is enough to keep my panties wet, but when you throw in his confidence and his swagger, let's just say I had no wins.

The alcohol mixed with my high adrenaline had me horny as hell. I danced erotically while listening to Ciara brag about her *Goodies* while Petey Pablo threw his two cents in. Shane wrapped his hands around my waist and started moving my hips to his rhythm. I approved of his take-charge attitude meanwhile throwing mine back at him. I threw my leg around him, and started jerking my body to the beat. Shane began grinding into me from behind. Every grind left the impression of his hard dick on my ass. I could feel the heat from his hot hands on the small of my back. I backed my ass up against him while his hands roamed my breast. The club lights were flashing dimly heightening the intensity between us. My body tightened with intensity and my heart pounded at a fast pace with every move. His hands became very friendly with my soft spots. Shane had my pussy soaking wet and hotter than a baseball glove left in the sun.

"You see what'chu doin' to me," he whispered in my ear while we danced like we were sexing.

Do you see what you doing to me? I rubbed my erect nipples on his chest letting him know that I was just as turned on.

"Let's see if you can rock with me." I challenged as I backed myself onto the center of the dance floor and started feeling all over my breast and squeezing my ass while bending over and jerking my body to the beat. Shane was digging the shit out of my performance because the bulge in his pants grew with every move I made. Shane stopped dancing and stood there wearing a sexy-ass grin watching me as I seduced the hell out of him with my erotic moves.

"You workin' this Baby. I'ma fuck the shit outta you as soon as I get you upstairs," he moaned while his tongue caressed my earlobe turning me on like a faucet. We slowed things down a little when Alicia Keys, *You Don't Know My Name* started to play. I was horny as hell and I knew Shane was too by the way he nibbled on my earlobe giving my body a wicked chill. I couldn't wait to go upstairs. As soon as Alicia stopped singing, Shane gave me 'that look'.

"You ready Baby," he whispered in my ear as he wiped the sweat from his forehead.

There was no need for a response. The look in my eyes said what my lips didn't.

As Shane and I walked towards the exit, I paused. "Damn Baby I forgot to let Sara know I'm leaving."

Shane brushed my hand against the center of his pants in slow motion making sure I felt every inch of his hard-on.

"You feel this? You think I wanna wait for you to do that?"

Shit…neither do I. Sara will figure out I left when she don't see my ass.

Just as Shane and I were about to step into the hotel lobby, EL stepped off the elevator. My heart sank to my knees.

Oh my God! What the fuck is he doing here? I asked myself in a panic.

My nervousness instantly snapped me out of my alcohol-induced coma. The juices that were flowing so freely between my legs quickly dried up. My palms began to sweat and I suddenly developed a migraine. I looked into the magnificent hotel lobby hoping that it would magically disappear giving me the perfect excuse not to have to step into it. I backed away from Shane and hid behind the nearest wall column. At first, Shane just stood there like he wanted EL to see him. And if EL wasn't so preoccupied with his phone conversation, he probably would have. I kept hoping that whomever EL was talking to would hold his attention long enough so that he wouldn't notice me or Shane.

My heart must have been beating triple it's normal speed, I was so damn nervous. I watched EL standing a few feet away from the elevators talking on his cell like he had no intentions on moving anytime soon. I peaked from behind the wall column to see if EL had left, and he looked up just as I stuck my head out. He probably would have seen me if it wasn't for the bell hop who parked the trolley full of luggage directly in front of me securing my hiding spot. I was shaking like a leaf. I glanced over at Shane who was motioning for me to come to him. I nervously shook my head 'no' too afraid to move from where I was hiding.

"I'm goin' up to the suite. Come up as soon as you can." Shane mouthed his words slowly so that I could read his lips.

EL's back was turned when Shane walked onto the elevator so he never saw him. I stayed in my hiding place for a few more minutes praying that EL had left the lobby.

As soon as I started to ease my way from behind the trolley to see if EL was still there, a voice said, "The coast is clear."

I looked up at the bell boy who was wearing a huge smile on his face. He pushed the trolley back so I could step around it.

I looked at him strangely.

"The guy you're hiding from. The one with the cell phone glued to his ear. He left a few minutes ago."

"So you parked this trolley here on purpose?"

He smirked. "I did."

I thanked the bell boy and hurried toward the elevators. Just as I was about to step onto the elevator, EL walked back into the lobby and saw me.

16

Sex in the City

Chass

"What are you doing here Chass?" EL asked, walking up to me with his cell phone pressed against his ear. It was more like an accusation than a question, so I knew I had to think quick.

"Hey EL. What are *you* doing here? I thought you had a business meeting." I tried to deflect.

"Vince let me call you right back," he spoke into the phone before abruptly disconnecting the call.

"This is where my business meeting is Chass. Vince is here too. I thought you were spending the weekend in Brooklyn with your cousin."

"Sara's Aunt had a few VIP tickets so we decided to use them."

"Where are Sara and your cousin now?" He looked at me suspiciously.

"Sara's in the club, but my cousin couldn't come because she couldn't find a baby-sitter."

"Where were you on your way to?"

"To the suite. I won some money on the slot machine and I was just going upstairs to put it in my suitcase. You know I don't like to carry a lot of cash around."

"What floor are you on?" he asked, looking me directly in the eye.

"The eleventh."

He pressed the button for the elevator. "I'm on the ninth."

"I never knew you did business in Atlantic City. Is this something big you're working on?" I asked, trying to conceal my nervousness. EL's presence caught me completely off guard.

"It's not actually my deal. I've been over seeing it with Vince. I'm here to go over some figures before they finalize."

"You came all the way to Atlantic City to look at some numbers?"

He grinned. "It's a little more to it than that."

My phone started to vibrate. I knew the text was from Shane before I even looked at the message.

Whts takin so lng baby? U get rid of tht ngga or wht? I'm up in the ste waitn 4 u. Hrry up.

I hit delete then slipped the phone back in my purse. I told EL it was Sara wondering what was taking me so long. I was so nervous I was fumbling. Talk about a sticky situation. When EL asked to see what room I was in I searched my purse pretending that I left the room key with Sara. I told him that I needed to go back to the club to get it from her. Once EL went up to his room, I headed straight for Shane."

"'Bout time. You got rid of him right?" Shane asked, as he opened the door.

"I think so."

"What'chu mean you think so? Either you did or you didn't."

"Shane please...I need a minute to think," I said, as my head started spinning.

It can't be...It just can't be," I blurted out not realizing that my private thoughts were said aloud.

"What can't be Baby? What'chu over there talkin' to yourself about?"

"Shane was one of the guys you were meeting with tonight named Vincent Carter?"

"Yeah. Why?"

"Oh my God Shane I know Vince!"

"Word. Vince is my man. We go way back. He's one of the dealerships investors or he will be as soon as we settle on these last details and sign the contracts. He got into that investment shit straight outta college. He married one of my boy's sisters but they divorced now. I know his college peeps was probably tellin' him not to marry a black chick, but he did. Vince has always been about business. He knows how the game is played. That's one real slick white dude."

"Yeah well that real slick white dude is one of the partners at the firm where EL works. Did you know that?"

"Oh nah, I ain't know that."

"Damn Shane this shit is crazy. Vince works with EL every day. Now he's gonna be working with you when you open the dealership."

"Nah, Baby Vince is just one of my investors. The nigga won't be hands-on."

"This is crazy! EL's business trip was about your dealership!"

"Baby just calm down. You gettin' all worked up over nothin'. I told you I don't do business wit' EL."

"EL was on the phone with Vince when we saw him in the lobby Shane. When I asked him what he was doing here he told me that he was here for a business meeting. EL is here about your dealership. What else could he be here for?"

"The nigga could be here for a million reasons Baby."

"Vince and EL wouldn't be in Atlantic City for two separate meetings Shane. It has to be about your dealership. Did Vince mention if he was bringing anyone with him?"

"Nah Baby, we ain't discuss that."

"I'm telling you Shane, EL is here because of your dealership."

103

"I doubt it Baby, but I wouldn't rule it out. If EL is down then he is definitely behind the scenes. Vince is a silent partner so he coulda pulled the nigga in."

"He must have. EL is the one crunching those numbers that Vince is coming up with. If Vince was on his cell anytime during any meetings ya'll had he was talking to EL. Shane, EL is the real wiz behind that firm's success."

"I wouldn't know 'cause I don't deal wit' EL. But, I been dealin' wit' Vince for years. Don't worry Baby Vince has no idea that me and you dealin'. So he can't go back and tell EL shit. Try not to stress over it."

That's easy for you to say.

"So...EL working on this deal doesn't bother you?"

"Nah, should it?"

"Hell yeah it should! Shane me and you been messing around for a while and now you're about to go into business with one of the partners at the firm where EL works. Nothing about this is good."

"Baby you makin' too much of this on the real. Your man is here so what. It don't change nothin'."

"Are you kidding me?" I huffed. "This changes everything Shane!"

"Not for me it don't." He walked up on me and hugged me from behind. "Baby this is where things start to get interestin'," he whispered as he caressed my ear with his tongue. "I'ma put it down extra hard tonight and make you cum back to back to back just cause I know that the nigga is stayin' up in here," he bragged.

I pulled away from him. "This is too close for comfort for me Shane. I came to tell you that I can't spend the night with you especially now that I know EL is staying just two floors down."

"Nah Baby, I ain't even tryin' to hear that. I told you I wasn't lettin' that nigga get in the way of our plans."

"I'm sorry but this is just too big of a risk Shane." I opened the door.

"Yo Chass stop playin' and get back in here Baby. Fuck that nigga." He followed me into the hall.

"I can't do this Shane," I whispered, walking backwards down the hallway.

"So you just gon' leave me and go be wit' that nigga?" Shane was pissed.

I didn't know what to say. I just kept walking. Shane stood in the hall for a few minutes and then he walked back inside the suite and slammed the door. By the time I made it back to EL's suite, he was at the table, calculator in hand, and a pencil behind his ear looking like he was studying for an exam.

"You find Sara?" he asked, oblivious to my current predicament.

I took a deep breath then exhaled silently. "No, I don't know where the hell she is with my card key so I thought I'd come and chill with you until she turns up."

"I'd like that, although I probably wouldn't be much company."

"I see." I looked at all of the documents that were spread across the table. "Looks like you got your hands full. You look stressed out. Is there a problem with the deal?"

"Yes and no. There are a lot of variables and I have to make sure that we present the correct figures. There is quite a bit riding on this. I have a lot to do before I turn this over to Vince."

"Sounds like it's something big."

"It is. The meeting was postponed so that gives me a little extra time to get these numbers in order and perfect the presentation."

Postponed? See I knew EL was here for Shane's business meeting. Out of all the business meetings, EL ends up at Shane's. Just my fucking luck. Now what the hell am I gonna do?

The whole time I was with EL, I prayed that I wouldn't do or say anything that would give me away. There were too many ways that I could be caught, and as nervous as I was, I was pretty sure that it wouldn't be all that difficult for EL to catch me in a lie. I stayed in EL's suite just to curb his suspicions. I wasn't about to let his ass stumble upon the real reason I was in Atlantic City. EL was right: he wasn't much company. I should have considered myself lucky that he was so preoccupied. His ass was glued to his lap top the entire time I was there. When he finally decided to turn in for the night, I was relieved. Sleeping was pretty much out of the question for me though. I stayed up thinking about Shane. I knew he was mad at me because I didn't stay with him. Now I was regretting that decision. I felt like a hostage and to make matters worse, I was too damn horny to get any sleep. I'm surprised all my tossing and turning didn't wake EL, but his snores were proof that he was sleeping right through my hot spells. I had a feeling that Shane was in his suite just as horny as I was which had my clit going crazy. I kept trying to sleep, but it was useless. Unable to control my urges, I eased out the door hoping Shane wasn't asleep.

"I see I was on your mind just as much as you were on mine." He stood in the doorway smiling.

"You wouldn't believe me if I told you how much I tried to fight it."

"You can't fight it Baby. I'm in your blood."

He pinned me to the door forcing it closed then he slid his tongue in my mouth. Usher & Alicia Key's *My Boo* escaped the speakers helping to set the mood. Shane lifted my body in the air wrapping my legs loosely around his neck. Then he began licking the lips of my pussy gliding his tongue across my swollen clit sending shock waves through my entire body. My urgent strokes met his tongue as I pumped my ass back and forth. He softly massaged my ass while sliding his tongue in and out of my dripping wetness. He gently stroked my clit while his silky lips massaged the lips of my pussy causing my body to tremble. I moaned delightfully, as my juices creamed his mouth. I eased my way from around Shane's neck and began nibbling on his nuts until he couldn't stand up. I sucked his dick like it was a jolly rancher while he moaned in pure ecstasy.

"Ahhh shit Baby!" he called out several times while I massaged his balls and sucked his dick until his warm semen filled my mouth. His dick began to soften in my hands so I slid his balls between my fingers and gently massaged them giving him another erection.

He lifted me up and gently laid me on the bed then he entered me. I'm not sure if it was the combination of all the alcohol I'd consumed, or how well Shane just feasted on me that had my pussy talking a language I never heard it speak before. I was hornier than a dog in heat and my body had the energy to take on three men. I rolled Shane over and climbed on top of him. I worked Shane like a full time job causing him to let out moans that would put an owl to shame. He pulled out then rolled me over and entered me from behind. I thrusted backwards while Shane met each one of my pumps with the same urgency.

"Damn you got some good-ass pussy! I love the hell out this shit!" he spoke softly in between moans while he nibbled on my ear.

Our shared orgasm had us both feeling a little weak. I turned over and climbed out of the bed.

"Where you think you goin' Baby'?" he asked, watching me get dressed.

"I gotta get back to the suite before EL wakes up."

"Nah, Baby. Fuck that. You ain't come here to stay in his suite; you came to stay in mine."

"It will look odd if I don't go be with him at least for a little while. I can get away with saying that I was gambling all night, but If I don't go back to check him at some point then he will know something is up."

"Well Baby I'm not finished with you yet. So he's gonna have to wait regardless."

He picked me up and carried me back to the bed where we went at it again. I was so drained I could barely slip back into my clothes. I crept back in the room where EL was sound asleep. I climbed into bed beside him and pulled the covers over me.

That was close. I thought, as I drifted off with EL in my bed and Shane on my mind.

Summer 2006…

17

Changing the Game
Shane

I ain't never been the settlin' down type a cat. The thought of comin' home to the same woman every night used to make a nigga break out in hives. But, bein' wit' Chass changed me. My feelings for her caught me off guard and fucked up my whole game plan. I realized that I been tryin' to ignore what I was feelin' because I didn't want to admit that I was into her as deep as I was. Once I finally decided to admit how I felt, I couldn't just fall back and let her be wit' that nigga no more. It was time for me to step up. I had to put my cards on the table and let Chass know how I felt about her 'cause I definitely wasn't tryin' to see her wit' that nigga no more.

When I walked into the loft Chass was laying across the couch reading some shit called *The Coldest Winter Ever*. I laid my keys on the glass table and took a seat next to her.

"Baby I need to talk to you for a minute."

"Can it wait one second? This is good. Winter is off the hook!"

I grabbed the book and laid it on the couch between us.

"Shane! I was reading that!" She looked at me like I was crazy.

"I got somethin' I need to say to you and it can't wait."

"Sounds serious," she replied, givin' me her full attention.

"It is. Baby it's time for you to cut that nigga off," I told her gettin' straight to the point. I was never big on wastin' time.

"Cut him off…"

"I'm in love wit'chu Chass and I'm not tryin' to share you wit' another man no more."

She gave me a strange look then she turned away from me.

"Baby what's wrong? You don't feel the same way?" I asked, hopin' that wasn't the problem.

She turned back around to face me. "Shane I've been in love with you since the first time I saw you I just didn't know how to tell you. When we got involved we said no strings and I didn't want to make you feel trapped."

"I love you. You could never make me feel trapped."

"When did we get so complicated Shane?"

"We love each other. What's complicated about that?"

"You expect me to trust what you're saying and I don't know if I can do that."

108

"So you doubt my feelings for you."

"I didn't say that. I'm just not sure if you're ready for us to be more than what we've been. You're not the type of man to settle down. Are you telling me that you're willing to give up your freedom to be with me?"

"That's exactly what I'm sayin'. Chass I don't want you like this. I don't want us to be together on the side or sneak around behind closed doors. I want us to have a real relationship. I want you all to myself. I can't even think about you bein' wit' that nigga without losin' it. You have no idea how that shit makes me feel every time I think about him touchin' you. When we started dealin' I know it was supposed to be on the low, no strings, and I was cool wit' that. But, now I just ain't wit' it no more Baby. You mean more to me than this."

"Are you seriously gonna give up all your women?" she asked, not convinced of my sincerity.

"Definitely. I would have never told you how I felt if I wasn't ready to make that move. Besides no other female could ever get in the way of my feelings for you. But, I can see that you have doubts so what I gotta do to prove it to you?" I asked, hopin' that I wouldn't have to straight up humiliate myself to prove that I loved her.

"Is this really happening?" she asked, like she thought our declaration wasn't real.

"Baby I just told you I love you—it don't get no more serious than this. There ain't nothin' more important to me than you and that's on my life. I want you wit' me, and I need to know if you down for that Baby?"

"You know I wanna be with you Shane, but I don't think you're ready to make that move, and I'm not just talking about the women. There are parts of your life that you never discuss with me."

"Ask me anything Baby. I'm an open book."

"Mmmm humm...with blank pages," she said with a smirk.

I laughed. "Ooooh Ok my Baby got jokes. I know what'chu gettin' at. My business is a part of my life that I can't share wit'chu. It's no place for a woman—especially my woman. I know you skeptical, but that doesn't have to be a deal breaker for us. The next move is yours. You gonna leave him right?"

She suddenly got quiet.

"Baby you a'ight?"

"Shane..." she hesitated.

"What's up Baby talk to me."

"I think we need to chill for a while."

"Chill...Why?"

"I need some time."

"Time for what?"

"I just need a little bit of time to process all this. I never expected this. I hoped for it, I even prayed for it, but I never thought I'd get it."

"Baby come on now we just admitted how we feel about each other and already you tryin' to put distance between us."

"That's not what I'm doing Shane. I just need time to get my head together so I can figure out how to tell EL I'm leaving him. I know it's a little late in the game for me to be worried about his feelings, but I am. The least I can do is not flaunt our relationship in his face."

"You don't wanna be wit' the nigga no more so why you stallin'?"

"I'm not stalling Shane I just need some time to figure some things out."

"Baby you over thinkin' this."

"Shane, please. Can you just give me some space? I need to think and I can't do that if I'm with you."

I wasn't feelin' the whole space thing, but I agreed to it. I was basically askin' Chass to change her whole life to be wit' me. The least I could do was let her handle what she felt she needed to without gettin' in her way. Bottom line was whether I liked it or not Chass had ties to dude. They had history. I had to respect that no matter how I felt about it.

"A'ight Baby if that's what you want I'll give you some space. But don't make me wait too long."

"I won't. I promise."

18

Pool Party

Chass

Sara pranced around Petit Peton showing off the stiletto pumps she was trying on. "You like these Chass?"

I glanced towards her feet, "They alright if you like huge heels," I responded unimpressed making it clear that I didn't particularly care for the shoes. If I would have known that shopping for a pool party would bring out the tasteless side of her, I would have left her ass at home.

"What? Wait a minute...You don't like these?"

Sara had a surprised look on her face as if I just insulted her taste. I didn't like the shoes, but I didn't have to wear them so I really didn't give it much thought.

I sighed, "I thought you were looking for flats or flip flops to wear with your bathing suit. It's a pool party—not a fashion show."

"I know girl, but I'ma just have to stroll my ass up in there with these on. These shoes are hot!"

"Well, if you like 'em girl, that's all that matters."

I didn't have to convince Sara to buy those 'fuck me pumps', she snatched them up quick and we headed to Nordstrom's to finish shopping. I hadn't realized that a few hours had passed but the look on Sara's face was giving me the hint. She sat beside me on the leather bench pouting like a little kid while I tried on a pair of banging-ass sandals.

"You ready to go yet?" Sara had about three bags in her hand and was looking at me like I was an expired meter.

"What does it look like? You see me still shopping right?"

"Come on Chass you don't have to make a career out this shit. Why you always gotta take all day every time we go shopping? You bought enough shit to sink a boat. Damn girl. Let's go. I'm ready to bounce."

I released the strap, and then removed my right foot from the sandal. "Alright girl, let me pay for these, then we can go. You got what you want now you wanna rush me," I squabbled on my way to the register.

Sara and I were walking pass the Gucci store as we were leaving the mall when my attention immediately zoomed in on the mannequin that was rocking the flyest bathing suit I'd ever seen. I stopped dead in my tracks to admire it some more before running my ass in the store and straight to the bathing suit that had my name written all over it. On my way to the register I snatched up a pair of sandals and sun glasses, and I was all set.

In the cab ride home Sara took out those ugly-ass shoes again. I twisted my face up at the sight of the shoes thinking; *who ever designed those shits needs to be arrested. I used to think that we had similar taste. Clearly, nothing in life stays the same.*

I turned my face toward the window to finish our conversation. The cab dropped Sara off first, but before she got out we agreed to meet up at her place in two hours; but we both knew for me that meant three.

**   **   **   ***

Dressed like I was on my way to a Sports Illustrated Swimwear photo shoot, I had on my diamond hoop earrings, matching tennis bracelet and anklet that were all a part of my 'EL Collection'. I was very pleased with the way my 24-karat thick gold Chassidy name chain that was dripping in diamonds sat firmly between my breasts. The slit in the middle of the bathing suit showed off the flower ring that protruded from my navel. The Gucci sandals displayed my perfectly pedicured toes that had diamond accents embedded into the nail polish. When you add the shades—you couldn't tell me shit. I tossed a few things into a bag, wrapped a towel around my waist, and walked out the door. I hopped in a cab and headed straight for Sara's.

"Not Chass on time for a change," she joked, as she opened the door to let me in.

"You so funny. You ready?" I walked into her bedroom.

"Yeah I'm ready. I'm just waiting for Tay to get here," she replied, pulling her hair into a ponytail.

"Is he on his way?" I asked, taking a seat on the window ledge.

"He should be. He told me he had to meet up with Shane first."

"Oh."

"Speaking of Shane..."

"Who was speaking of Shane? I just asked when is Tay gonna be here."

"Oooooh defensive," she joked. "If you can't even hear Shane's name without blowing a gasket girl then you are worse off than I thought."

"Well..." I paused taking a deep breath then I exhaled extra hard. "It hasn't been easy I can tell you that."

"Have you thought about what you're going to say when you see him?" Sara asked, stepping into a conversation that I really didn't wanna have.

I convinced myself that putting distance between Shane and me was what I needed to do in order to clear my head so I could deal with EL. After being disloyal to EL for so long, I felt I owed him that much not to prance my relationship with Shane in his face. Maybe it was too little too late, but it was all

112

that I could do. My actions haven't really supported it, but the last thing I ever wanted to do was to hurt EL.

"I try not to think about Shane. It only distracts me. I know it should be simple for me to just cut EL off, but it's not. Every time I try to tell EL about me and Shane I can never seem to get the words out. I love Shane but, I care about EL. I don't know how I can hurt him like this."

"It's a little late for that Chass."

"I know it is. That's why this is so hard."

"Well if you gonna try to front like you ain't thinking about Shane then you are gonna have to do better than this. You've been in a funk ever since y'all stopped dealing. You need to snap out of it girl."

"Yeah I know."

"When is the last time you saw Shane?"

"Not since we agreed to stop seeing each other."

"Remind me again how you thought not seeing Shane was gonna help this situation? Y'all already did the damn thing like numerous times Chass so what's with the space?" she asked, as if she thought I made a mistake by putting distance between Shane and I.

"Because I still don't know how I'm gonna break this to EL and I didn't wanna put Shane in a position where he would feel like I was stringing him along. The last thing I need is him pressuring me to leave EL. The situation is bad enough."

"Has he been putting pressure on you?"

"A little, but I can't blame him. He's been real patient with me. The minute I realized how I felt about him, I shoulda left EL. This is on me."

Just then we heard Fantasia's *When I See You* blasting right outside the window alerting us that Tay had driven up.

As soon as Sara and I hopped in Tay's sparkling white BMW, I started thinking how anxious I was that I was about to see Shane. I was missing him something awful and I couldn't wait to see him.

"Where'd you say this place was?" Tay looked at Sara and asked after we'd been driving around Long Island a little longer than we should have been.

"Why are you asking me?" Sara cut her eyes at him. "You know damn well that I don't know shit about Long Island."

"Figures," Tay shook his head grinning. "A typical city chick—can't get outta the city."

Tay pulled out his cell and called for directions. Not even twenty minutes later we were driving up to the massive four-story bricked colonial, that had balloons pinned to the gate that screamed party over here. Tay drove around the circular driveway and the valet met us at the door of the car as the three of us got out. Tay threw his keys over the hood of the car to the blonde hair blue-eyed guy who looked like one of those guys I'd seen in a shampoo commercial. It wasn't hard to tell that this valet thing wasn't a permanent gig for him. I'd be willing to bet that in another year or so he would be the next Tom Cruise.

The sounds of water splashing and loud music filled our ears as we walked along the stoned path which led to the back of the luxurious estate. Sara and I gave each other one last look making sure our shit was tight.

"Get it girl!" we sang in unison as our hands collided. We walked through the gate and into the party. The DJ was yelling into the microphone when we walked in.

"All the ladies, all the ladies, all the ladies in the house say hooooooooo!"

"Hooooooooo...!" The girls screamed.

Then the DJ threw on Luke's *"Doo Doo Brown"*. The crowd went bananas as the explicit lyrics to the song rocked the party. All the girls danced erotically while the guys watched with their mouths damn near hitting the pavement. Sara and I danced our way over to where Aleyma and Alayna were standing with a couple of nice looking dudes. Aleyma and Alayna were identical twins who were clients of mine. As soon as we reached their table, Aleyma greeted us.

"What's good Leyma?" I looked around the party.

"Having a good time," she replied, as she placed the straw in her mouth and took a few sips of her apple martini before pointing out the food and beverage tables.

"I could use a drink." Sara sucked her teeth while she watched Tay talk on his cell. I'm sure she needed a drink just to get her mind off of whatever they were going through today.

Looking at her sweating his phone conversation, I turned her so she could face me.

"Girl it's not about him today. We came here to have a good time. Don't let him spoil it."

She shook her head in agreement. "Yeah you right Chass. I ain't gon' sweat his ass. I came here to enjoy myself. Shit, fuck him! You ready to get in the pool?" she asked, watching everyone splash around.

"Nah, I'm good. I'll have a drink though."

She sucked her teeth. "Oh so you wore that fly-ass bathing suit for nothing!"

Letting out a sarcastic giggle I replied, "Girl please, you must have forgotten who you're talking to. Trust me this bathing suit will accomplish what it was meant to. I'm just not in any rush for all hell to break loose once I drop this towel that's all," I taunted, displaying a devilish grin thinking about how pleased I was with my assets when I looked in the mirror earlier.

"Did you see Shane yet?" Sara asked, staring at me to see my reaction.

"Please...Don't even talk his ass up." It had been almost a month since the night that I asked Shane to give me some time and I never thought I could miss anybody so much. Although I was trying to play it off, I was dying inside.

Just then the DJ mixed Juelz Santana's verse on Chris Brown's Run It Remix and everybody started dancing and singing the lyrics....*We can get it in...we can get some friends...do it like the Ying Yang twins start whispering...*

I slid down to the platform, and eased my feet into the pool. Once I got nice and comfortable, Liain walked up.

"Hey girl, I see you made it." She squatted down beside me.

"Yup, we finally found it. This place is off the hook! Whose house is this?" I asked, admiring the hell out of it.

"Girl, don't get me to lying. I think some basketball player lives here. One of Shane's friends 'cause you know his ass knows everybody. This place is tight though right. You know dude got mad dough if he just letting a bunch of strangers run around in his shit like it's nothing."

"You got that right. So how long you been here?" I asked, wondering if we missed anything by arriving late.

"We been here about an hour if that," she replied as she tightened her towel.

"We who?" I asked, looking around the party trying to locate any signs of her entourage.

"Me and Jewel rode with Shane."

My face twisted up. Now that was the wrong damn thing to tell me. My mood did a complete one eighty.

"Since when do you rock with Jewel?"

Liain looked at me with a 'where the hell did that come from' sort of look. I didn't give a fuck. Any chick that dated Shane was automatically an enemy of mine.

"Since, I needed a ride to a party that her and her man was going to."
Her man huh? Yeah Ok.

Now this chick done really pissed me the fuck off. I couldn't let Liain know the real reason behind my sudden mood shift, so when she asked what my problem was with Jewel, I told her that I'd heard some shit that Jewel said about me. Hearing Liain talk about Jewel and Shane like they were a couple had my blood boiling. But, before I flew off into a fit, I figured I would see what was taking Sara so long with my drink so I could calm my ass down, meanwhile shrugging off her conversation.

I approached the mini bar with my attitude straddling closely behind me. However, that was a thing of the past once I saw Shane. The sight of him made my heart race. I couldn't stop staring at him. I tried not to be obvious although, I had to be. He was leaning up against the fence wearing a pair of navy blue swim trunks, and not much else. He held what looked like a fruity drink in his right hand. Since I knew that Shane didn't drink shit with an umbrella in it, I assumed the alcoholic beverage belonged to one of the many chicks that were swooning around his fine-ass like he was an art exhibit.

What I immediately noticed was how good Shane looked in those damn swim trunks. His perfectly cut frame was displayed for all to see. The man had a body like LL Cool J. Forget a six pack—there wasn't even a name for the abs on Shane. The swim trunks he was sporting were pulled down so low that just another inch and all of his secrets would have been exposed. His flawless caramel skin was glistering in the sunlight. The sunglasses he was rocking provided a certain mystery to him which made him that much more sexy. The man just oozes sex appeal. My pussy throbbed as I watched him thinking to myself...*Damn that nigga is blazing! There should be a law against looking that good!* He definitely had my attention. It was cool because there ain't a damn thing slouch about me. I rubbed the last of the baby oil on my inviting skin, and made a quick adjustment to my diamond Chassidy chain, that I wore the hell out of.

It's time to drop this towel, I thought looking Shane directly in the eye letting him know that this 'little show' was all for him. I adjusted my bathing suit making sure it properly complimented my assets the way it was supposed to. The most amazing thing about the bathing suit was the slit in the middle that showed off my Janet Jackson six-pack from her video *That's the Way Love Goes* which was speaking a whole other language. I knew I looked damn good, and if I needed confirmation all I had to do was look around the party because I was being watched like a motion picture. As much as Shane tried, he couldn't keep his eyes off me.

I kept trying to talk myself into not approaching him, and judging by the way Shane was eyeing me; he was having that same conversation with himself. A few tried, but no one could keep our attention long enough to hold a conversation because we kept drifting off making eye contact with each other. I wanted to go to Shane and just say fuck that promise, but I didn't. His ego was preventing him from approaching me, and my pride was winning against my urges to go to him. Although, I had been trying not to think about him, at that moment, all I wanted was his conversation and his company. I thought I could handle seeing him, but this shit was torture. Trying to ignore Shane was useless. I'd have a better chance at pushing a bus up an icy hill in a snowstorm. His presence was bold and inviting. His stares were so alluring that they dominated every urge in my body. Shane looked like he wanted to kill every single guy that approached me asking where I was from, or if I had a man. Shane had a girl in his lap, hanging all over him and whispering in his ear, but he was too busy all up in mine to pay any attention to her.

I didn't let it get to me, or at least I tried not to. I snuggled up next to my Bailey's like it was my best friend and drank until I was tipsy. After a while, my bladder was ready to burst, so I excused myself and headed for the bathroom. As I was leaving the half bathroom, to my surprise Shane was standing outside the door with his right leg propped up against the wall looking sexy as hell. Seeing him caught me off guard, and had me so nervous you would have thought I was under arrest. Assuming that he was waiting to use the bathroom, I stepped aside to let him pass when he grabbed me by both arms pinning me against the wall in a seductive motion.

"So you wasn't gon' say shit to me Chass? That's fucked up. You were really gonna treat a nigga like that?" He spoke like he was upset with me.

"You ain't say shit to me either Shane. So what did you expect me to do?"

"I expected you to acknowledge a nigga, damn. I was gon' speak to you. You know a nigga can't ignore your ass." He released his grip on me.

"Is that right? Well, you seemed to be doing a fine job to me."

"What's that shit supposed to mean?"

"You know what it means. I guess you just can't help yourself. You gotta make sure you are surrounded by a bunch of bitches at all times don't you?"

"What-eva, you see where I'm at right now don't you."

"Yeah well we both know this is a bad idea. The last thing I need is for somebody to catch me with you before I have a chance to tell EL about us."

"Don't you think I tried to stay away from you Chass? But, I couldn't stand this shit no more, so I followed you out here."

"I started to stop by your table to say hi, but it looked like you were busy so I didn't," I said half jokingly.

"Ha...Ha...Ha...You funny," he teased, patronizing me. "This is a party Chass. I can't stop females from approaching me."

"Ummm hum I bet you can't." I said trying to hide my jealousy, which was starting to take control of the conversation.

"Check you out. You got a lot of nerve. You must of had a half dozen fake-ass Usher lookin' ma'fuckas in your face all day. So, ga 'head wit' that shit."

"It's a party Shane. I can't stop dudes from approaching me." I just had to snap back on his ass with that same "it's a party" line he just ran on me.

"You stay with the jokes," he said, not finding the humor in my comment. "I was gonna snatch you up when you first walked up in here, but I fell back. I'm tryin' to respect your decision to give you some space and let you handle shit, but I ain't gon' lie, me not bein' able to be wit' you got a nigga tight."

"You sound like you don't understand why I'm doing this."

"I don't. Not really." He propped both arms against the wall as he towered over me. "You might wanna run that by me again."

His cockiness was turning me on like crazy. It's just something about his swagger. The man is just so damn smooth. Being so close to Shane brought to the surface so many emotions that I was trying so hard to hide.

117

I looked down the hallway to see if anyone was coming. "You know this isn't the place for that conversation."

"You're right. It's not." He led me into one of the unoccupied rooms and closed the door. "When we gon' be together Chass? I don't know how much more of this shit I can take."

"I just need a little more time."

"How much more time?" Shane asked, not ready to drop the subject. "You already had me waitin' long enough as it is."

"Why you throwing me attitude? You already knew the deal before you marched your ass out here. If you didn't wanna hear me tell you again, then you shoulda stayed out there with your cheerleading section."

"There you go. Yo Chass you need to stop playin'. I told you what it is. You the only woman I want. You got my heart. I only agreed to stay away from you 'cause you asked me to so you could handle shit wit' that nigga. I shoulda never let you talk me into this shit. Baby, I haven't made love to you in almost a month. That's my word I'm about to lose my fuckin' mind."

Now why did he have to say that? I asked myself, as my clitoris woke up from its nap.

"You know I'm still waitin' for you to tell me you left that nigga right?" He eased closer to me intensifying the sexual tension between us.

"EL is probably here by now and I'm sure Sara is wondering where the hell I am." I said, backing away slightly feeling my resistance breaking down.

"Is it that hard for you to be around me Chass?" Shane asked, noticing my reluctance to look him in the eye.

Brushing off his cockiness and fighting to keep my emotions in check I replied, "I can handle it."

"Can you?" He leaned into me forcing me backwards.

"Of course I can," I replied sharply as I struggled to conceal the obvious effect he had on me.

"Convince me."

His tongue was in my mouth before I could respond. I tried to push him away, but my desire for him was much stronger than my ability to resist.

"Stop fighting me Baby. You know you missed this just as much as I have." He pulled his tongue out of my mouth long enough to get those words out.

"We shouldn't be in here Shane. EL is probably looking around the party for me as we speak."

"And," he said, like he could care less.

"I guess you forgot about the agreement we made to stay away from each other until I figure out a way to break up with EL."

He twisted his face up. "Listen to you. I'm up here puttin' my heart on the line and you still comin' at me sideways. What'chu mean figure out a way?

118

Just tell him the truth. You need to stop handlin' that nigga like he gon' break. When you gon' leave him Chass? Let me know what's up."

"Soon Shane, I'm gonna leave him soon."

"How soon? How much longer you gon' have me waitin' Baby? A week, a month, what? Let me know somethin'. I had to pull you in here just to grab a minute alone wit'chu. All that sneakin' around shit is dead Chass. You can hang that up. Hurry up and cut that nigga off. You wastin' time that we could be together Baby."

"It's not that simple Shane." I was conflicted. As much as I wanted to be with Shane, I wasn't looking forward to hurting EL—although I knew there was no way around it.

"While you figurin' out how to soften the blow for this nigga, I'm supposed to what? Play the background. Watch from the sidelines."

"You act like this is easy for me."

"You think this shit is easy for me? You expect me to fall back and let you stay wit' that nigga when we both know you wanna be wit' me. I'm supposed to force myself to stay away from you until you find the right time to tell him what's up. Baby you buggin'. So I can't see you. I can't make love to you. This shit is torture," he said softly, while his fingers caressed the sides of my face.

"I don't like it either Shane. I just need a little more time. That's all. I will find a way to tell him about us."

"Nah Baby, fuck that. I can't do this shit no more. I'm done waitin'. Either you wanna be wit' me or you don't—Simple as that. I want you to cut him off tonight," he said fed up.

"Tonight?"

"Yeah tonight," he repeated forcefully. "Stop stallin' Baby. It's time for you to let that nigga know what's up."

"What happened to giving me time and space so I could deal with this on my own? This is gonna kill EL Shane. The least you can do is not back me into a corner. Now all of a sudden you're so impatient that you can't wait no more. You never had a problem with waiting before."

"That was before I fell in love wit'chu Chass. And it's not all of a sudden. I been tellin' you this for how long now. I'm not tryin' to share you wit' that nigga no more."

"Don't do this Shane. You know I've never been good at resisting you."

"Then stop resistin' and go wit'cha feelings."

"I... I can't..." I whimpered unconvincingly as I struggled to finish my sentence.

He placed his finger against my lips signaling for me to stop talking. "I wanna make love to you Chass, and all I wanna hear you say is that you want the same thing," he ordered, as he slowly removed his finger from my lips.

119

My body craved him. I wanted more than anything to make love to him. Then I thought about EL and how selfish we were being and I backed away.

"Why you keep pullin' away from me Baby? Are you tryin' to tell me that you don't wanna be wit' me?"

"Shane..." I hesitated.

"It's a simple question Chass. If you can look me in the eye and honestly say that you don't want me, I'll leave you alone." He lifted my chin up with his index finger forcing me to look into his eyes. "Now I'll ask you again, do you still wanna be wit' me?"

I wanted him. I couldn't deny it. I'd have a better chance trying to convince myself that my heart doesn't beat. I looked him in his gorgeous green eyes and slowly nodded 'yes'.

"Nah Chass," he shook his head. "I need to hear you say the words." His tone was seductive yet serious. His eyes spoke to me seductively increasing the speed of my heartbeat rapidly. I tried not to give into him, but it was a battle that I was clearly losing.

"Yes...I wanna be with you. I want that more than anything else in this world," I replied, kissing what was left of my resistance goodbye.

"Then stop tryin' to fight it. This is a destiny type thing Baby. You can fight me, but you can't fight this." He pointed to my heart and then to his. "I want you. Right here...right now," he whispered as he softly kissed my lips. Then he unloosened my towel and it dropped to the floor.

"Damn Baby you look good." He looked at me like he was under a spell, while his dick stood like a pool stick.

He slipped his hand in-between my warm thighs causing my clit to throb like it had a heartbeat. With his index finger, he pushed the crotch of my bathing suit aside and slowly entered my warm inviting flesh. I moaned as my juices soaked his finger. He picked me up and carried me to the wide oak table that was sitting in the middle of the floor and sat me on top of it. Then he unsnapped the top of my bathing suit and it fell beneath my breast. He caressed my erect nipples with his soft lips while sliding his finger in and out of my soaking wet pussy. The temperature in the room felt like it rose at least ten degrees. My body was on fire. When he removed his delicious instrument from his swim trunks my clit went crazy.

"Put it in," I spoke softly in between our passionate kisses while my pussy was doing back flips. Just as the head of his penis began to enter me, the door opened.

"What the fuck is this shit Shane!" Jewel yelled as she barged in the room. Shane and I both jumped off the table at the same time.

"So you fucking this bitch now!" She ran towards me. "I'ma fuck you up bitch!"

"You think so," I said with a laugh. "Then bring it!" I demanded.

Shane grabbed Jewel before she could get her ass whipped. That chick didn't want it. She just didn't know.

"Yo Jewels calm down man!" The base in Shane's voice increased a few notches. "Our shit is dead so you ain't got no reason to be actin' like this just chill."

"I better not see you in the street bitch!" she threatened, while still in Shane's clutches.

"You see me now! I'm right here Jewel. Bring it!" I yelled as I stepped closer to her. "Let her go Shane! Fuck that! Let that bitch go!"

All of the commotion was beginning to draw attention. A bunch of staff members who were hired to cater the pool party had the door surrounded trying to see what was going on. PK made his way through the nosey bunch and into the room.

"Everything cool in here?" PK asked.

"Take her ass home PK!" Shane ordered, releasing Jewel into PK's arms.

"I'ma see you bitch! Don't even worry about it!" Jewel struggled with PK as he tried to escort her out of the room.

"Oh bitch please...Do I look worried to you?"

Jewel was getting hostile so PK had to restrain her and carry her out of the room. PK closed the door behind them giving Shane and me a minute to get ourselves together.

I looked at Shane. "I thought you locked the door!"

"My bad Baby I thought I did."

"I bet everybody knows what happened now."

"Baby you worrying about the wrong shit. You need to be worried about cuttin' that nigga loose. Jewel ain't ya problem. She heated right now because of what she just walked in on, but she'll get over it. She ain't got no choice. In the meantime you need to tell that nigga what's up before somebody else does."

"If he's here then he probably already knows."

"Nah, I doubt it. The party is all the way in the back. They ain't hear shit. Those people that were crowdin' the door are the staff and they don't know you to say shit." He glanced over at the oak table then shook his head a couple times. "I can't believe I'm up here settlin' for this...A fuckin' hard-ass table when we could be makin' love on silk sheets in a king sized bed!"

I straightened my towel then pushed my hair back with my fingers. "You're right I have to tell EL tonight, before the rumors start spreading like wild fire." I walked back out into the yard to rejoin the party.

"Where the hell you been Chass?" Sara walked up to me and asked. When Sara saw Shane coming from the same direction I just came from, she gave me 'the look'. "Never mind, I know where you were. Girl EL's looking for you."

"Where is he?" I asked, looking around the party.

"I don't know. He was just out here. We heard all this yelling and shit a little while ago. Sounded like somebody was arguing I couldn't really make out what was being said, but whoever it was sounded like they were pissed. Maybe he went to see what happened."

God damn I sure hope not.

"Why you look like that Chass. You know who was screaming and shit like they crazy?"

"It was that bitch Jewel."

"For real? What's her problem?"

"She walked in on me and Shane."

"And she flipped like that?" She paused then gave me a weird look. "She walked in on ya'll doing what?"

"We were about to have sex."

"Oh shit! For real! Damn Chass! So what happened?"

"Basically what you heard. She was yelling and saying what she gonna do if she sees me on the street."

"Word Chass? I wouldn't sleep on her if I were you. I know you can handle yourself, but now that Jewel knows that you and Shane are seeing each other she is gonna come at you."

"Let the bitch bring it on—with both guns blazing!"

"Just watch your back girl. You know better than most what a jealous bitch is capable of." She leaned into me and whispered, "Incoming."

Just then EL walked up.

"Where'd you disappear to?" he asked, staring me down.

"Those buffalo wings don't mix well with watermelon, so I had to take a trip to the ladies room." I lied with a straight face.

He turned up his nose, "Too much information."

"You asked."

"Did you hear all that yelling a little while ago?" he asked.

"Nope, I was in the bathroom. I must have just missed it."

A few guest started spreading around the party asking if anybody wanted to play pool volleyball just in time to put an end to EL's questions.

"Nah, I'm good, I'll just watch." A few guest declined when asked to participate.

I laid across the pool chair while EL massaged sun screen on my back and my shoulders. Shane watched us from across the yard fuming. EL received a call and stepped inside the house away from all the noise to take it.

"What was that shit about Chass?" Shane walked up to me with an attitude.

"What was what about?"

"Don't play stupid wit' me Chass. It doesn't suit you. I'm talkin' 'bout the way you lettin' that nigga touch all on you. Check that nigga Chass. Don't let him be feelin' you up like that."

"Oh Shane please." I exhaled hard then sucked my teeth. "You got chicks taking turns hanging all over you and you up here talking about me."

"Just dead that shit! Don't have me hurt that nigga Chass. I'm dead ass."

"What's up Shane?" EL walked up to Shane holding his hand out for a pound.

"Sup man? How you," Shane replied, nonchalantly, and reluctantly gave EL a pound. Then he gave me that 'I'll get up with you later' look before walking away.

EL watched as Shane rejoined his boys then he gave me an odd stare. "Why the hell was he all in your face Chass?"

"He saw me sitting over here by myself and he was just making conversation. You know tryna be polite."

"He looked like he was interested in more than your conversation Chass, but you're a good looking woman so I can't expect guys not to be interested." He looked at his watch, "I gotta get out of here. One of my clients just called. Their leaving tonight for Boston and I need to pick up some proposals from them before they leave for the airport so I need to head out. You coming?"

"I guess," I replied, not really ready to leave. "Just let me grab my bag."

"Chass can I speak to you for a second," Aleyma was walking towards me.

I looked at EL, "I'll meet you at the car."

"Make it quick. I need to be in The Bronx in about an hour," EL said.

"What's going on girl?" I asked, watching EL walk away.

"Watch your back Chass. I overheard Jewel talking about doing something to you. She even got a couple other bitches talking about jumping you."

"Was that before or after she left the party?" I asked, wondering when she had time to plan an ambush.

"This was around the time that you and Shane disappeared. One of them chicks said they saw Shane follow you inside the house and the next thing I knew Jewel disappeared."

I rested my hand on her shoulder. "Thanks for looking out Leyma. I appreciate it."

"Those bitches are grimey Chass. Keep your eyes open. If anything goes down you know I got you," she said, reassuring me of her loyalty. Aleyma was cool. I liked her and her sister from day one. I always did appreciate real chicks—but, rarely did I come across any.

19

The Shit Done Hit The Fan

EL

Chass and I were on our way to the city after leaving Long Island when we found ourselves caught in a pile up. I exited I-95 at Bartow Avenue and took my chances with the street traffic. We were driving up Gun Hill Road when suddenly the skies opened up and it started to pour. There was no warning not even a sprinkle to indicate that rain was to be expected. It seemed like I blinked and it was dark outside. It was difficult to see the road when the sky was still providing some assistance, but with the darkness, visibility was almost impossible. The water splat onto the streets like it was angry with it. The rain was hitting the windshield so hard it was disturbing.

"Damn where'd this shit come from?" I asked, changing the speed of the windshield wipers. The water covered the windshield faster than the wipers could clear it. "I didn't hear anything about rain today. Did you?" I eased my foot off the gas. I couldn't see a thing so I pulled over, put my hazards on, and waited for it to let up.

"At this rate we'll never get home," Chass pouted spreading her hands across her chest as she stared out the window into the darkness.

I turned on the radio to drain out the sound of the water hitting against the windshield. I flipped the dial to *WBLS 107.5*, which rocked jams from the 90's. It seemed to be the only station with clear reception. Chass barely said a word. She suddenly seemed nervous and uncomfortable around me.

"Everything alright?" I looked over at her.

"Yeah I'm fine," she replied, her back facing me as she continued to stare out of the window.

"Are you sure? You look like something's bothering you."

She turned to face me. "Actually EL, I have something I need to tell you." Her expression turned serious.

"What is it?"

"It's about us." She sounded cryptic.

"Well, you certainly know how to get a man's attention Chass, I'm listening."

"EL...You know I care about you right?" she asked, like it was a trick question.

"Yeah I know." I was waiting to see where she was going with this.

"EL...I... I need to be by myself for a while."

124

"You need to be by yourself. Where'd that come from Chass?"

"I just don't feel like we're getting what we need from each other. It's like we're just going through the motions. You don't feel it?" She tried to flip it.

I repositioned myself in the seat as I eased back onto the road and pulled up to the traffic light.

Going through the motions...What the hell does that mean? She is really trying to play me.

"What is that Chass? You sound like some chick from a soap opera. If you have something to say just say it."

She turned her head towards the window avoiding eye contact with me.

"EL...I don't wanna be in this relationship anymore. I don't feel the same way I used to."

I raised an eyebrow, "Is that right?" I asked, with a 'yeah right' tone of voice. "How long have you been feeling this way?"

"For a while now, I just didn't know how to tell you."

And you still don't, I thought as I watched her little performance. It was clear that Chass was lying, but I didn't call her on it because I wanted to see how far she would take it.

"So, that's it? You think you can feed me that *played-out* space bullshit and expect me to believe that? Tell me the truth Chass!"

"EL...It's complicated."

"Then simplify it for me. Did I forget your birthday or some petty shit like that?" I asked, attempting to make her out to be as shallow as one of those dumb-ass blondes.

"You've always been good to me EL. It's not that."

"Then tell me the real reason why you're leaving me. After six years together and you can't do better than that."

"EL... I'm sorry...I'm not tryna hurt you. I just don't know how to tell you..."

"Just tell me who he is Chass. Who is this dude that got you stuttering and shit! Do I know this dude?"

"Why do you think it's another man? Can't I just want to be by myself for a while?"

"Come on now Chass. Do I look stupid to you? Only another man would be the reason for your sudden need for space. Stop stalling and tell me who he is!"

"EL please..."

"Chass don't you think I deserve to know the real reason you're leaving me. Respect me enough to tell me the truth. After all we've been through; you owe me at least that."

She gazed into her lap. "It's Shane."

125

"SHANE!" The hot blood flooded my brain and the veins in my forehead began to visualize. "I knew he was sniffing around you for more than your fucking conversation! How long has this been going on Chass?!"

EL listen...I know you don't believe me but I care about you. I never meant to hurt you."

"You slept with him Chass?"

"EL..."

"Tell me the truth. Did you fuck him?"

"Yes...we've had sex," she mumbled.

"What! I can't believe you fucked him! How many times did you fuck him Chass?!"

"EL please... why does that matter?"

"Because it matters to me. How many times Chass!"

"EL...I never meant for you to get hurt."

"Yeah right! You never meant for this to happen." I was madder than a seasoned ticket holder at a cancelled game. "What did you think would happen? Did you think I would just be cool with you fucking another man! Now you're suddenly concerned about my feelings! Where was your concern when you were letting that muthafucka stick his dick in you!"

"EL...please just calm down. It's pouring out here. Can you please just pay attention to the road?"

"Chass he doesn't give a fuck about you. You fucked up our relationship so you could be with a selfish-ass muthafucka like Shane! What the fuck is wrong with you! I can't believe you threw away what we had for him!" I felt like someone ripped my heart out and handed it to me.

"I know you probably don't believe me, but I never wanted this EL. I really do care about you."

The part of me that was still in love with her wanted to believe that, but the other part was tempted to throw her lying-ass out of my car and run her over.

"All this time I actually thought that we had something special. I thought you were the one. I can't believe how fucking wrong I was!"

"We did have something special EL, and for a long time. We just weren't meant to be together for longer than we were."

"Is that what you tell yourself so you can sleep at night?" I looked at her in disbelief. I couldn't believe that she could do this to me. "Answer me this Chass. How long have you been fucking Shane?"

"EL please..."

"Just answer the question!"

"About three years."

I was no longer able to control my rage—it was controlling me.

"THREE FUCKING YEARS CASS!" I couldn't believe what I was hearing. "You've been fucking Shane for three years! That's damn near half our relationship!"

"You never had time for me EL. Your work always came first."

"You ungrateful bitch! I didn't hear you complaining when I was dropping thousands on you! I don't recall you having a problem spending my money!"

"It was never about the money. I never cared about that."

"Yeah right. You never stopped me from spending though did you! And, Shane...that grimey muthafucka knew you were my girl, and he still pushed up. But, I guess I can't just blame him. It does take two doesn't it? It's not like you put up any resistance. I thought better of you Chass. You disappoint me, you really disappoint me."

"EL, please slow down! You are driving way too fast. It's pouring out here. Please slow down!"

As hurt and angry as I was, I still loved her. Chass was the only woman I ever gave my whole heart to—the only woman who would ever own it completely.

"I can't believe you could do this shit to me!" I slammed my hands against the steering wheel with a great deal of force as I hung my head down in disbelief. I looked up just in time to catch a glimpse of a large object blocking our path.

"EL WATCH OUT!"

20

The Aftermath

Chass

I didn't know where I was or how I got there. I was seeing double maybe even triple. My head was hurting so bad my brain felt like it was lifting weights. The pain was about ten times worse than a killer hangover after a night of non-stop drinking. Every time I tried to turn my head, the pain was unspeakable. I guess that's why I was sporting a neck brace. Every breath I took was like a tug of war with my lungs. The razor sharp pains felt like I was being stabbed repeatedly in the same spot. I tried to pull myself up, but my body wouldn't cooperate. I lifted my gown to see if there were any other visible injuries and noticed the huge welts across my stomach and my breast. I couldn't feel anything in my left arm. It was as if it wasn't even attached to my body. I'm not a Doctor, but it wasn't hard to figure that I had a broken arm, and my ribs were either broken or badly bruised. I still couldn't figure out what was going on with my head though. Put it this way—I was in pretty bad shape.

I removed the IV from my arm and was struggling to get out of the bed when a nurse walking passed my room saw what I was doing and rushed over to me in a panic.

"No, no, no please stay in the bed. You have several injuries. You need to stay in bed."

I asked her, "Where am I?"

She slowly helped me back in bed. Propping two pillows behind my head she replied, "You're in Montefiore Hospital." Then she swung the bed tray around placing four pills on it.

I started to panic. "Why am I here? What happened to me?"

"Please just try to stay calm Miss Fondain you were in a car accident."

"A car accident!" I repeated, hysterically trying to get out of bed again.

"Please Miss Fondain I don't want to have to restrain you." she said, reluctantly while she gently held me down. "Just try to relax you're going to be fine."

"How long have I been here?"

Inserting the needle into my arm, she replied, "About twelve hours. You've been unconscious."

"My mother…my family, did anyone call my family?"

"Yes, Miss Fondain your mother is here. She just ran to the cafeteria to grab a cup of coffee. She's been here all night."

"How bad is it?" I asked, slowly pulling my body upright in the bed.

Noticing my anticipation she replied, "Please just try to relax. It's actually much worse than it looks. You have a concussion, you suffered a few broken ribs and your left arm is sprung."

"And, the neck brace?"

"You have quite a severe case of whiplash. The doctors didn't want you trying to turn your head too quickly because it can be rather painful."

"Are you sure I'm gonna be Ok?"

"Of course you are. You just need to lie back and try to stay calm so I can take your blood pressure." She tightened the contraption around my arm and pumped the little black ball.

"The guy...the guy I was with...is he..."

"Mr. Wiggins is in a room down the hall. He's still unconscious. He's being closely monitored."

"Chassidy!" My mother ran into my hospital room with both hands covering her mouth. "Oh my baby is awake. You had me so scared. Are you Ok honey?" A worried look spread across her face as she hugged me tight.

"Please be gentle Ma'am," the nurse interrupted. "Although her injuries aren't life threatening, they are quite serious. Too much movement could be extremely painful for her."

"How long do you plan on keeping my daughter in here?"

"That's up to the doctor Ma'am."

"Where is the doctor? Can I speak with him?"

"He's with another patient at the moment. But, he will be here shortly to examine her."

"Don't worry Ma, I'll be Ok." I tried to reassure her.

"Chass honey I've never been so scared in my life. I am so relieved to see that you're awake."

"How's EL? Have you seen him?"

"I peaked in his room a couple times. He's still unconscious. I'm sure he's gonna be alright Chass. All I heard was that you had been in an accident and I was out the door before the lady on the phone could finish giving me the details. I ran out the house so fast I think I left that woman on the line," She took a moment to recall the phone conversation before continuing. "All I heard was accident and I was out the door!"

"I need to see Shane."

"He was the first person I called Chass. I left him a message. I'm sure as soon as he hears it, he'll be here."

"Ok Miss Fondain your temperature and your blood pressure are both normal. You may not have an appetite, but I really need for you to try to eat something. You need to keep your strength up. I just administered some medication. It should begin to take affect right away," the nurse said before exiting the room placing my chart in the slot on the door.

"Are you comfortable honey? Is there anything you need me to get you?"

"I'm just glad you're here Ma."

"Where else would I be? Are you sure you're Ok? You look like you're in a lot of pain Chass?"

"It's not that bad Ma. The medicine must be working."

"I just feel so helpless. I feel like I need to be doing something."

"Just you being here is enough Ma. Don't worry."

"You're my daughter. It's my job to worry about you. Now please tell me what you were doing out in the middle of a monsoon?" She pulled up a chair like she anticipated it would be a long story. I cracked a smile because my mother always had a way with words.

"We were on our way back from Long Island when we got caught in the storm."

She wiped the tears that were strolling down her cheek.

"You're lucky to be alive honey. It could have been so much worse than this. When I saw the pictures of the car I thought they were going to have to commit me."

"How'd you see pictures Ma?"

"You'd be surprised what you can find out when you're determined, especially when your child is involved."

My mother had plenty of connections. She always seemed to know someone, who knew someone. Kinda like the man, standing next to the man, standing next to the man.

Suddenly, a sharp pain shot up my back and I clinched the sheet. Catching a glimpse of the pain in my face my mother ran to get a nurse.

"It's Ok Miss Fondain just take a deep breath," the nurse instructed, as she adjusted my medication again. The higher dosage quickly took effect. My body began to relax and I started to drift off like I was under anesthesia.

"I will be back to check on her in a little while," The nurse told to my mother as she checked my IV again before marking my chart.

I woke up to find my mother asleep in the chair next to my bed. "Ma," I tapped her hand. "Wake up."

How are you feeling honey?" She repositioned herself in the seat and stretched her arms above her head.

"Better. I actually took a nap without being poked with needles. Why don't you go home and get some rest Ma. You look tired. I'm Ok, don't worry about me. It's not like I'm going anywhere, at least not for a few days."

After I finally convinced my mother to go home and get some rest, I made two phone calls. The first call was to Shane, but I ended up speaking to his voice mail. The second call was to Sara. Not even an hour later, Sara was walking into my room wearing a sneaky look on her face.

"Hey Chass. How you feeling girl?" she leaned in to give me a hug.

"Ouch…be careful. This shit hurt." I pulled back a little.

"I brought you some goodies girl," she said pulling out chips and chocolates. "I know you not eating the crap they serve here."

"No thanks girl. I'm not hungry. I just wanna go home. I hate hospitals."

"How long you gotta be in here?"

"Probably a few days."

"Shane know you in here."

"My mother said she left him a message and so did I."

"He ain't calling Chass. Knowing Shane he gon' bring his ass down here. I saw EL. He looks like he's in a coma."

My expression saddened as I looked at Sara with watery eyes.

"Why you look like that? He's gonna be alright isn't he?"

"I honestly don't know. He hasn't woken up since we been here. I feel responsible. Maybe if we weren't arguing about Shane…"

"Chass, he gon' wake up. Everything's gonna be alright."

"I hope so Sara. I would never forgive myself if anything happened to EL."

"Try not to worry Chass. EL is gonna be alright and so are you. You're a fighter girl. You always have been ever since we were kids."

Sara stayed with me until visiting hours were over. After she left I tried to get comfortable, but sharp pains began to consume me. I pressed the button to dispense the medication, and the next thing I knew I had drifted off again.

**   **   **   **

I was slowly walking out of the bathroom when I noticed a shadowy figure standing by the window.

"Hey Baby." Shane surprised me as he stepped from behind the curtain.

I smiled happy to see him. "So you got my messages?"

"Yeah I got 'em. I woulda been here sooner, but I had to run to Delaware wit' Ced. As soon as I heard what happened I jetted back here. How you feelin'?"

"Better than I was. How'd you get in here anyway? It's like two o'clock in the morning Shane. Visiting hours were over a long time ago. They strict here."

"Baby there are ways around anything. You know I was gon' find a way to see you. Nothin' was gon' stop that."

"Some chick huh?" I wanted to laugh, but I couldn't. The shit hurt too much.

He cracked a smile, "Why you say that?"

"Because I know you Shane. You might as well tell me who she is. The daughter of one of the doctors, one of those chicks from the cafeteria, or maybe even one of the nurses?"

"It's this chick I used to deal wit' from maternity. She got me up in here to see you."

"You a trip Shane. Asking one of your old girls to sneak you in here. Only you would do something like that."

He winked at me. "Drastic times and all that. So Baby what are the doctor's sayin'?"

"I have a concussion, and two of my ribs are broken. It feels like somebody dropped a truck on me."

"Somebody did," he joked.

"Shut up! You stupid!" I laughed then stopped suddenly. The pain was severely intense.

"Are you in pain Baby?" Shane asked, noticing the way I was clutching my chest.

"It hurts when I laugh and especially when I take deep breaths. And my neck is killing me. I can't even turn my head without squinching. I hate having to turn my whole body whenever I wanna to turn my head. I feel like a freaking robot! The doctors say its whiplash."

"While you in here they gonna keep givin' you heatin' pads to relax your muscles. That's what they did for me back when me and my cousin Ced was in a car accident."

"What happened?"

"Stupid nigga ran a red light and drove right into us. Ced came out of it better than I did. I was in physical therapy for almost a year behind that shit. It took even longer than that before my body felt right again. I made sure them ma'fuckas paid for keepin' me laid up all that time. Those idiots were drivin' a Hostess truck. My lawyer did her thing. She had a field day wit' the case. We sued Hostess from here to the next millennium."

"At least you and Ced wasn't hurt that bad and y'all got paid too."

Just then his eyes darted over to the table where my food tray was.

"Why you ain't eatin' Baby?" he asked, noticing that my plate of food was still in-tact.

"The food is nasty as hell in here."

"Sure you right. Want me to grab you somethin' from the spot across the street?"

"That's Ok. Sara snuck me some goodies in earlier. I don't have an appetite."

"Baby how'd this happen? Your message just said that you and EL was in an accident. Did he lose control of his car?"

I pressed the button and the bed rose slightly.

"Me and EL were arguing and the next thing I knew, this truck was in front of us. I screamed for EL to stop and everything seemed like it was moving in slow motion after that. He tried to swerve, but that's when he lost control of the car and we crashed. I hit my head and it must have knocked me out because the next thing I remember was waking up here."

"You said y'all were arguing. So that must mean you told him about us."

"Yeah, he knows."

"Baby what if this wasn't an accident? I'm startin' to think that nigga crashed his shit on purpose?"

"Why would he do that? We both could have been killed."

"Maybe that was his intention. I don't think it's a coincidence that as soon as you told him about us you end up in the hospital."

"EL could have been killed too Shane. Why would he risk his own life? This was an accident. It was raining hard and he wasn't paying attention to the road."

"You movin' up outta that niggas crib when you get outta here right?" he asked, but before I could respond the sound of keys dangling interrupted our conversation. Shane slipped behind the curtain just as the nurse walked in to take my temperature and draw some blood. Once she left Shane came out of hiding.

"You better get out of here before you get caught and that chick loses her job. We can't have that because we may need her to sneak you back in here tomorrow night."

"I'ma leave soon as I know you gon'be a'ight."

"Then I hope you brought your overnight bag."

"Nah, but I can go get it."

21

Jealousy Meets Envy

Chass

Five days in the hospital and I was being released. I still needed assistance with things like reaching into high places, and washing my back in the shower. It still hurt when I breathed. The pain was mild, but constant—like it had no intentions on going anywhere. I was getting stronger by the day. Although, I wasn't one hundred percent, at least I was going home. I hated hospitals. The food is hideous and the smell of death lingers in the halls. Not to mention, there is no cable; not even a DVD player. My bag was packed days before the Doctor even told me that I was going home.

Whenever a nurse would come into my room to take my blood pressure or change my IV bag, I would bombard them with questions. They all said the same thing: direct my questions to the doctor. The wait was torture. Five minutes seemed like five days, but in reality I only waited a couple hours. It was about ten o'clock in the morning when a Ryan Seacrest look-alike wearing doctor's scrubs walked into my hospital room. He looked too young to be a doctor; he looked more like an intern. He advised me to avoid strenuous activity until my body had time to heal. I nodded and agreed with everything he said hoping to speed up his visit so I could get the hell out of there.

I stopped by EL's room as I was leaving the hospital. He was asleep and I think I was secretly relieved that he was. I had no idea what I would say to him anyway. I asked the duty nurse about his condition before I left. I was relieved to hear that EL's condition had improved.

With Sara's help, I moved out of the penthouse and into my mother's apartment while EL was still in the hospital. I figured it was best to be out of the penthouse before EL came home. I was hoping to spare us anymore unpleasantness. Considering the last conversation we had landed both of us in the hospital—I had reason to be concerned.

** ** ** **

It was a Friday night and the apartment was packed. My mother was having another one of her gambling parties. Sara came over to keep me company while my mother entertained her guests.

"So you gonna move in with Shane now that you and EL are over?" she asked, lying across the bed doing a crossword puzzle.

134

"Shane is nowhere near ready to take that step and neither am I. Did you forget that I just moved out of the penthouse? I am not rushing into anything."

"I know you not. This shit is still bothering you I can tell. Do you even know how EL is doing since you left the hospital?"

"I called and found out that he was released a few days after me."

"I wonder what he said when he came home and saw that you moved out."

"Now that he knows about me and Shane, I'm sure he was glad to see that I was gone."

"You ready for the hair showcase in a few months or what?" she lifted her face from the book and asked.

"I been ready. The closer it gets the more nervous I get though, but the fact that all the stylist get national exposure is what I'm most excited about. I'm still thinking up styles to do on the models. It gotta be some sick shit! I'm tryna blow the competition out of the water!"

"You will!" she said, excited. "You got mad skills Chass. You can do hair like most of us breathe. These stylist out here can't fuck with you! What you have is a gift—not a talent."

"Awww…thanks chica." I leaned in and gave her a big hug.

"Just as long as when you become a famous stylist with big name clients you still do my hair for free," she joked.

"See, I should have known that those compliments came with a price," I laughed.

"Chass!" The staggering voice blaring through the apartment was Layla Fondain's after she'd had a few drinks in her. I recognized the alcohol's affect on my mother right away.

"Chass!" she called out again when she didn't get a response from me the first time.

"Yeah Ma," I answered, walking sluggishly into the kitchen where she was preparing plates of food.

"I need you to go to the liquor store and pick up a bottle of rum and Hennessy," she instructed with urgency, as she placed the lids on the pots that covered the stove. The empty bottles of liquor that filled the garbage was the reason why she was in such a hurry for the alcohol. It wasn't even midnight and everyone had already drank themselves into oblivion.

I walked back into the bedroom. "Come on girl." I tapped Sara on her leg.

"Come on where?" she asked, closing the crossword puzzle book, and lifting herself into sitting position.

"To the liquor store…where else?"

"Damn Chass they drank all that shit already. Your moms had a lil' liquor store up in there."

"Do you really have to ask? Shit girl you know how my family drinks."

"And they had to wait until I got nice and comfortable to drink everything up too didn't they?"

"Girl that bed ain't going nowhere." I tapped her leg again. "Now come on so we can hurry up and get back."

Just as Sara and I were leaving the liquor store, Jewel walked in with Roshawn and Lawanna. Jewel's face twisted up when she saw me.

"You finally came up for some air huh?" Her tone was real funky.

"Excuse me?" I quickly turned around ready to knock the shit out of her.

"How long you been fucking my man?!" she asked. But it wasn't really a question; it was more like a test.

What I really wanted to say was, *I've been fucking the shit outta Shane for years*, but I maintained and controlled my urges to blow her world sky high. Instead I took the sarcastic approach which is guaranteed to piss a bitch off.

"Well, that all depends...whose your man?" I spitefully asked knowing damn well who she was referring to.

"Damn it's like that!" Lawanna stepped in front of Jewel. "You fucking that many niggas that you have to question her man's identity before you even answer the question!"

"*Ok let's try this again.*"

"Let me see if I can dumb this down for y'all. Who I fuck is *my business*! As a matter a fact, I'ma leave the Q & A to y'all. Since y'all have all the answers anyway what you need me for?"

I walked away leaving them standing there dumbfounded. I wasn't even out of ear shot when they started talking shit.

"I can't stand cocky fucking bitches like her Jewel!" I heard Roshawn say. "You gonna let her diss you like that. First you catch the bitch fucking your man and now you gon' let her play you like that!"

"Bitches like her are the reason why chicks get they shit broke up. If it was me I woulda been brought it to her fake Amerie looking ass!" Lawanna added.

"You hear them bitches Chass!" Sara stopped walking and turned around. "They up there gassing Jewel up."

"Yeah I hear them back there. I ain't paying those bitches no mind. Jewel had all that mouth at the pool party and now that we're face-to-face she done lost all that hostility. I see her girls got enough to give her some."

I always did hate chicks that put themselves in the middle of shit that didn't concern them. No worries. Like my mother always said: There is plenty of ass whipping to go around.

"Yeah they definitely tryna get some shit started."

"Please...Those chicks can say whatever the fuck they wanna say as long as none of them put their fucking hands on me we good all day."

136

The thought of getting my ass whipped never crossed my mind. I was more pissed off that Jewel was calling herself Shane's girl rather than the fact that she approached me in the first place. As Sara and I walked further down the street we heard Lawanna and Roshawn's voices getting closer.

"Go head Jewel do that bitch!" Lawanna yelled.

"Fuck her up!" Roshawn added.

Their voices were ringing closer confirming that they were only a few steps behind me so I quickly turned around.

"Well I doubt very seriously if you can beat my ass, but you can damn sure give it a try," I bragged, daring Jewel to take me up on my offer. I was praying that chick would swing so I would have an excuse to beat the shit out of her: Approaching me talking about being Shane's girl. Giving herself a title that she didn't earn. Jewel didn't have what it took to hold onto a man like Shane, and that's why she was in my face—because she knew that I did.

Sara stepped in-between us. "Nah, fuck that Chass you ain't fighting. Shit, you just got outta the hospital." She pulled me by the arm leading me into the street. "Ya'll just gon' have to save this shit for another day."

"Why the hell you do that? I wanted that bitch to touch me," I griped reluctantly allowing her to pull me away.

"For what Chass? You don't have to fight for Shane. Shit you already got him. Jewel is just mad because Shane don't want her tired-ass no more."

"I told Shane about these fucking bitches."

"Oh shit Chass!" Sara called out.

I turned around just in time to catch the glare from a shiny object coming straight for my face. I raised my arm in time to prevent the blade from slicing into my flesh and it cut my sleeve instead.

"Fucking bitch! You tryna cut me!" I lunged at Jewel punching her in the face before she had a chance to swing the blade again.

"Get that bitch Jewel! Cut her ass! Slice and dice that bitch!" Lawanna and Roshawn instigated from the sidelines.

I grabbed Jewel's wrist and we struggled. I twisted her arm until she dropped the blade. When I bent down to pick up the blade that's when she kicked me in my side. I squinted in pain as I grabbed the blade from the ground. Jewel charged me. I swung the blade several times like I was possessed. She belted out screams that could wake the dead as she grabbed her face soaking her hands in blood.

**   **   **   **

Word spread fast about the make-over I gave Jewel. A few days after the fight a gang of girls had my mother's building surrounded. Whenever I would look out of the window I would hear them yell, "Come downstairs bitch! You gonna get fucked up as soon as you come outside!"

137

My mother was cursing like a sailor she was so mad. The final straw was when somebody threw a dirty diaper at the window. Baby shit splattered all over the glass. Since my mother's apartment was on the fifth floor all I could think was that they had some good-ass aim.

"Oh hell fucking no!" my mother yelled again. "This shit done went far enough! These little bitches think they can't get their asses whipped! Oh hell fucking no! Let me call Tangy." She picked up the cordless and dialed. "Tangy better get her ass over here before I kill one of these little bitches!"

As tempted as I was to go outside and whip on some of those chicks, I wasn't stupid. I knew I would get jumped with the quickness. Girls were coming out of the woodwork like it was a Macy's, Bloomingdales, and Saks Fifth Avenue sale all in one. They were out for blood. Although a lot of chicks were gunning for me, I wasn't intimidated. My skills had always held me down in the past, so I didn't have any reason to believe they wouldn't now.

Aunt Tangy and her clan arrived around the same time Sara did. After my mother and I filled them in on the situation, we went downstairs to confront all those chicks who couldn't wait to get a piece of me. When I noticed a few familiar faces in the crowd I pointed my family in that direction and we headed towards them waiting for the cars to pass by on the bustling 8th Avenue street. Once we reached the other side of the street, I spotted Roshawn and Lawanna right away. I didn't concern myself with who else was out there. I saw who I needed to see, and it was on.

"What's up now bitch?!" My punch extended from around the car, and landed exactly where I intended—Roshawn's nose. The blood gushed out instantly. Once she grabbed her nose, it was over for her. I beat that bitch to a pulp. She didn't have a prayer, and I was just getting warmed up.

My cousins had the crowd on lock. They made sure nobody got through. While my mother and Aunt Tangy made sure nobody jumped in.

One of the local dealers approached my mother and my Aunt.

"Can y'all take that shit back across the Avenue? I don't need this type of heat," he complained, as he openly counted a wad of money. My mother looked at him like he had three heads before she shut his ass down.

"Oh muthafucka stop bitching! You ain't seen shit! We'll make it so hot over here your ass will be scared to fart!"

"What-eva man," he mouthed, as he twisted his face up and sucked his teeth. Realizing that he didn't want any part of what was going down; he took his ass back across the street with his attitude in tow.

One little girl said something about going to get her mother and Aunt Tangy just lost it.

"Go get her! And tell your mother to hurry the fuck up, shit we ain't got all day!" The poor girl ran off in tears.

After I whipped Roshawn's ass, I looked for Lawanna who I saw in the crowd right before the fight, but she must have jetted when she saw her girl go down. Just as things started to calm down my family and I were heading back across 8th Avenue when we heard yelling coming from behind us.

"There she go! You about to get fucked up bitch!" Lawanna and a few other girls were walking towards us.

"Y'all want something?" My mother asked in an angry tone.

"Yeah, we want that bitch Chass! And we ain't leaving 'til we get her ass!" Lawanna yelled from where she stood.

"Well put your 3-D glasses on then bitch 'cause I'm coming straight at you!" I dashed off the steps and swung on Lawanna catching her on the side of her face. She stumbled back, but she didn't fall. Then she started swinging her arms in a windmill motion with her eyes closed. I looked at her in disbelief.

You gotta be kidding me. This can't be how you fight, I thought as I stood there watching Lawanna swing at nothing but air. I was real disappointed in this chick. She looked and talked like she could really throw down, but looks can be deceiving. I never did like fighting chicks that catfight and can't box.

"Let me get at this bitch Chass!" Sara jumped in front of me and immediately starting beating the hell out of Lawanna. What Sara did to that chick wasn't even legal. I almost felt sorry for her. But, Lawanna gave an open invitation to beat the shit out of her when she decided to go to sleep in the middle of a fight. Who fights with their eyes closed? What they hell was she doing praying? If her eyes were open she would have seen the switch Sara and I pulled on her non-skill-having-ass. A gang of chicks tried to rush us. It took Chris, Day-Day and Shawn to hold all those girls back. Then Aunt Tangy took her gun out of her suitcase-like pocket book and started waving it in the air.

"If y'all think y'all gonna jump my niece y'all got another thing coming! Y'all wanna fight Chass it's gonna be one-on-one!"

"Alright...alright...enough is enough!" Mr. Wayne the owner of the corner store walked up to us. Y'all messing with my business. There are better ways to deal with problems than to be out here acting like hooligans."

The look my mother shot him I knew she was about to let him have it. "Why don't you take your fake Red Foxx looking ass back in that crappy-ass store of yours, and finish selling all that expired shit you got up in there and stay out of shit that doesn't concern you!" She barked on him.

That old man turned his lip up and walked back into his store just as my mother instructed but, not before he said some slick shit first. "No damn class! Just ghetto!" He managed to say just before the glass door swung closed behind him.

My mother turned toward the angry crowd of girls that had us surrounded. "Does anybody else wanna fight or have y'all had enough?"

"I do." A familiar voice spoke, but I couldn't see their face until Liain stepped out from the crowd.

Aunt Tangy's face turned bright red. She looked at Liain like she wanted to beat her ass herself.

139

"Now Li, I know you're not standing there talking about fighting Chass. I know your ass knows better than that!"

Liain sucked her teeth while staring Aunt Tangy in the face. "Tangy who said anything about fighting Chass? I'm here to whip Sara's ass!" She responded, switching her focus onto Sara.

Liain and Sara never liked each other. It dated back years ago when Sara had a thing for Chris. But it still had me thinking that it was mighty damn convenient for Liain to pick today of all days to fight Sara after having plenty of opportunities to do it in the past. I was never comfortable with the fact that Liain was so close with all those chicks who she knew didn't like me. In my opinion she broke loyalty right then and there. I wasn't expecting her to have beef with them, but she didn't have to flaunt them around the hood like they were the latest design. She had to know that those chicks were planning to run up on me and she didn't even bother to give me a heads up. That's what I call some real crossover shit. That's what enemies do and it was obvious that I'd just acquired a new one. I wasn't about to let Liain fight Sara, so I stepped up.

"Please...Not even...You ain't fighting Sara. You might as well get that shit out your head right now. You'd have a better chance at breaking your father out of Rikers Island!"

"Fuck you Chass! Ain't nobody scared of you!" she yelled over the rowdy crowd.

"Fuck you too you phony bitch! And I don't expect you to be scared of me—just be prepared for me!"

Liain rushed towards me when Chris grabbed her. Then she started kicking her feet all wild and crazy. Like an idiot, I walked right into it trying to get to her. Seconds later, I started clutching my chest in pain. It felt like someone was cutting straight into my veins with glass.

This bitch just re-opened my fucking wound.

The pain was so intense that I started to get dizzy. Liain somehow managed to break away from Chris and was coming straight for me. She was quick but she wasn't quicker than Shane, who picked me up, threw me over his shoulder, and carried me into the building.

"What'chu doin' out here fightin' Chass?!" he angrily asked, as he carried me onto the elevator.

"Why the hell are you bringing me upstairs?! My family is still down there Shane!" I was mad as hell that he carried me off in front of everybody like I was defeated.

"You ain't got no business out there fightin' Baby. You just got outta the hospital. Just chill a'ight." He put me down gently and we slowly walked into apartment.

"I need to go back downstairs! It's too many of them out there Shane! I need to be down there!" I gasped clutching my chest.

140

"C'mon Chass. Baby you're hurt. You ain't totally healed from the accident and you out there fightin'."

He reached out to touch me when I swatted is hand away.

"Get off me Shane! All this shit is because of you! I told you to keep your fucking bitches in check! That bitch Jewel tried to cut me so I opened her fucking face up!"

"Word." He chuckled. "You a trip Baby. You cut her for real."

"From ear to ear," I replied, as a tear rolled down the side of my face. The pain was really starting to get to me.

"I'm takin' you to the ER Chass. You look like you in a lot of pain Baby."

"No Shane! I'm not going back to the hospital! I'll just take a couple pills so I can go back downstairs."

"How many times I gotta tell you? I'm not lettin' you go downstairs Baby so face it and just chill."

"Please Shane you can't stop me!"

"Ok Baby you might wanna rethink that. I said you ain't fightin' no more and you are in no position to protest so fall back. Now just calm down and let me take care of you. I can't have my woman out there fightin'. It's just not happenin' Baby. All those chicks will get checked and this shit better not happen again."

Underneath the anger, I was smiling. Shane walked up to me, in front of all of those girls, threw me over his shoulder and carried me away from all that drama leaving them standing there looking stupid.

"For real Shane," my tone was much calmer, "I need to get back downstairs."

"Yo Chass ease up. My peoples is down there makin' sure that everybody take they asses home and trust me ain't nobody else fightin'. It ain't even goin' down. Whatever my peoples can't handle your family got, so be easy Baby."

Sara walked in the room while Shane was still trying to convince me to stay put.

"What happened after I left?" I asked, struggling to get comfortable.

"Liain and a bunch of other bitches was tryna come at me and Chris and Day-Day shut them down. The next thing I knew PK fired his piece in the air and everybody scattered like roaches. You Ok?" she asked, noticing how uncomfortable I looked.

"It hurts like hell, but I'll be alright. That bitch re-opened my wound." I sucked my teeth as I rocked back and forth on the bed trying to numb the pain thinking... *The next time I see that bitch she better pray that God is taking calls that day.*

Sara leaned down to give me a hug and that's when I noticed that she was crying.

"You ain't no joke Chass. You know I woulda fought Liain, but you wasn't having it."

"You my girl so you know I always got your back." I told her as we embraced.

22

Play'd
EL

Chass moved out without saying a word. Closets cleaned out, drawers empty. No good-bye—just gone. When I came home from the hospital and noticed that she'd left, I was mad as hell. It was hard for me to believe that she could walk out on me while I was in the hospital, but that is exactly what she did. I was home for a few days when Mia stopped by to bring a stack of files from the office. Until I was cleared to return to the work, I was forced to work from home.

"What happened here?" she asked, staring at the huge spaghetti stain on the wall from where I'd thrown my plate against it.

"I don't feel like talking about it."

"Ok, we don't have to talk. I guess you don't want to hear what I heard about Chass and what's been going on with her since she moved out?"

That remark certainly got my attention. "What did you hear about Chass?" I anxiously asked.

"No, no you said you didn't feel like talking so..."

"Mia I don't have time for games. What is this about Chass?"

"I heard that there was a big fight on 147th and Chass was right in the middle of it. Apparently she cut up some girl's face and had a lot of girls wanting to fight her."

"Who told you that?"

"Everybody's talking about it."

"Since when do you listen to gossip Mia?"

"It's not gossip. I got this from somebody who was there."

"Do you know who the girl was that Chass is supposed to have cut?"

"I don't know all of the details, but I did hear that they were fighting over some guy. They said that Chass and her whole family got beat up and some guy broke up the fight and carried Chass away. The police were there, ambulance...all that."

"Get out of here! Really? You said some guy broke up the fight?"

"Yeah, some tall brown-skinned guy. Sounds a lot like the guy I saw her with the other day."

"What guy? When was this?"

"One day last week."

"Where?"

"In So Ho. They were in a Mercedes E-Class."

"What did this guy look like?"

"He was driving so I'm not really sure how tall he was, but he looked to be over six feet. He was light browned skinned and I think he had wavy or curly hair, and he was very well built."

"They were in an E-Class you said?"

"Uh-huh. A Silver one."

"Shane owns a Silver Mercedes E-Class. Where were they at in So Ho?"

"Over there by Lakeview Diner."

"The one by the Towers?"

"Not too far from there."

"And you're sure it was Chass?"

"Positive."

"Mia, when you get to the office tomorrow grab my rolodex and pull out all my real estate contacts in So Ho. Check to see if Shane has leased or purchased any property within the past few years. Call me tomorrow with whatever you find out.

**   **   **   **

"Mia just give me the address!" I demanded, sensing her reluctance.

"I just don't think it's a good idea for you to confront them." I could sense the panic in her tone.

"What are you my mother?! All I asked you to do was to give me the address!"

"Just calm down and listen to me for a minute EL. I think you are way too upset to think rationally right now. What do you think confronting them is going to accomplish? Chass is probably just going to lie anyway."

"Look Mia...I don't have time for this. Are you going to give me the address or do I have to make those phone calls and get it myself?"

I couldn't blame Mia for holding out on me. My tone wasn't exactly friendly.

"First promise me that when I give you this address, you will not try to get out of bed and go over there. You keep forgetting that you are not supposed to strain yourself. You are in no condition to be moving around."

"The address Mia..."

"Ok...Ok," she said in a surrenderus tone like she'd finally given up trying to convince me to proceed with caution. "But just listen to me for a second. I know you're upset right now, but whatever you're thinking...don't."

"You finished."

"As long as you know what's on the line then yeah...I'm finished."

"You can stop stalling now and give me the address."

144

"Ok it is…8118 Harborview Towers. It's over by the _____,"

"I'm familiar with the location. One of my associates used to own a store front over there a couple years back," I interrupted.

"EL…"

"What?"

"I don't wanna see you get into any trouble over Chass. She's not worth it."

"Trust me I know what I'm doing. Listen I need you to do me another favor."

"Anything, just ask."

I thought about how Chass was cheating on me right under my nose. Harborview Towers wasn't more than fifteen minutes away from my penthouse. She didn't even have the decency to take her cheating-ass out of town to do her dirt. I looked down at the piece of paper that I'd written the address on and just stared at it, wondering how long she had been fucking Shane and then coming home to me.

8118 Harborview Towers.

This is where Shane fucks my girl.

8118 Harborview Towers

Damn. I looked at the address again before balling up the piece of paper and throwing it across the room.

They playing me was all I could think about.

My blood was boiling. My anger was becoming harder to control. My chest sunk in and out with every breath I took.

"EL…" Mia called out, bringing me back to the conversation.

"Ok Mia, here's what I need you to do for me."

23

Can't Walk Away

Chass

"Hello," I answered sluggishly.

"Chass it's me." Sara sounded strange.

"What's up girl? Why you sound like that? What happened now?"

"Did you hear about EL?"

"EL...no... hear what?"

"He can't walk Chass. He's paralyzed!"

"Paralyzed! Get the fuck outta here! How you know?"

"My brother's baby mom's is best friends with that chick EL works with. What's her name again?"

"Who Mia?"

"Yeah that's her."

"Oh shit for real? Is it permanent?"

"Oh, girl I don't know. Our conversation didn't get that far."

"Paralyzed...Damn that's fucked up. Are you sure?"

"That's what my brother told me." She paused for a minute then asked, "You gonna go see him?"

I had to think about that for a minute. EL and I weren't together anymore. And, to make shit worse we broke up on bad terms. I was sure that I was the last person he would want to see, but still I answered, "I don't know."

"I hear you," she said, like she understood my position. "This is messed up girl. Damn...EL...paralyzed. That shit don't even sound right."

"I know girl. I do wanna go see how he's doing. I feel bad for him. But, things didn't exactly end well between us. I did leave him for Shane. I don't even know what I would say to him."

"Well you know EL better than I do. I mean if what my brother told me is true and EL really is in a wheelchair then he might be resentful toward you."

"Resentful? Oh you mean because I'm with Shane?"

"No Chass, because he's in a wheelchair. Not to downplay your injuries or anything, but you walked away from that accident with a few broken bones, but you did *walk* away from the accident—EL didn't. Get what I'm saying?"

I thought about it for a minute realizing she had a point.

"Yeah I hear you. I'm up here thinking about what went down between us, and what I should be thinking about is EL. All that other shit is petty compared to what EL must be going through now."

"You should go see him Chass. I know you're with Shane now, but it wasn't so long ago that you were with EL. Worst case scenario if EL doesn't wanna see you then leave, but at least you made an effort. I know you Chass. If you don't go see him, you will never get over it."

"You're right. I need to see how he's doing. I won't lie, I do still care about EL and I wouldn't wish this on anyone."

** ** ** **

"Is EL here?" I directed my question to the petite blonde woman who answered the door dressed in exercise gear.

She responded, "We were actually just finishing up his session."

I asked, "Can I come in?"

"I'm sorry I didn't catch your name," she said, like she was suddenly interested in it.

That's because I didn't throw it. I hate that expression.

"My name is Chass. If this is a bad time I can come back," I offered, realizing that I was interrupting something.

"Well hello Chassidy," her voice rose an octave. "Please excuse my manners. I'm Valerie, Mr. Wiggins' physical therapist. I thought you looked familiar. I recognize you from the photos Mr. Wiggins has of you on the desk in his study. Please come in," she requested gesturing for me to step into the foyer. "I will let Mr. Wiggins know you're here."

A Physical therapist...Damn EL really is paralyzed.

Valerie's presence should have been all the proof I needed of EL's condition. But, for some reason I still needed confirmation, and when EL rolled himself into the foyer—I had it.

"Hey Chass," EL said stopping his wheelchair at my feet.

I was speechless. The strong, confident man I knew had been reduced to a wheelchair. EL looked worn out; his usual athletic frame was slumped over.

"EL...how...are...you?" I was stumbling over my words, and finding it difficult to make eye contact.

"I'm as well as to be expected I guess. It's a lot to get used to. How are you?" he asked, seeming like he was really concerned.

"I'm doing Ok."

"You look good Chass. Even after a near fatal accident you still come out of it in not so worstful wear. It's hard to believe that you were even in an accident. Not even a scratch on you."

147

"Well...my ribs say otherwise," I joked, trying to throw a little humor into the situation. The fact is I was very uncomfortable seeing EL in that wheelchair. The little bit of pain that I was experiencing couldn't compare to what he was going through."

"So...What brings you here?" he asked, as he looked at me with an odd stare.

"I just heard. I wanted to come and see if there was anything I could do for you. Is there anything you need?"

"Well actually you can tell me why you moved out? I'd really love to know the answer to that Chass."

"After what happened between us I figured it was best that I move out as soon as possible. I didn't want you to come home from the hospital and have to look in my face after what went down."

"What do you mean after what went down?" He looked at me confused. "Is this because of the accident? Do you blame me for putting you in the hospital?"

"Blame you? No, EL I don't blame you. Why would you think that?"

"Wasn't I the one driving? At least that's what I was told. I thought maybe you were upset with me because I was probably on my cell or something right? Is that what happened? Was I on my cell and not paying attention to the road? I know how much you hate that."

"No, EL that's not it." I looked at him strangely. "What do you mean that's what you were told? Are you saying you don't remember?"

"Everything about that day is a blur Chass. I honestly don't remember waking up that morning. I was hoping you could help me fill in the blanks."

Just then Valerie stepped into the foyer. "Mr. Wiggins," she said, "I apologize for the interruption but, we need to get back to your session."

"Chass can you wait around for a little while? I won't be too long," EL asked, rolling himself into the gym.

I nodded. "Sure, I can wait," I said, without hesitation.

EL turned his den into a home gym. I watched while he and his therapist worked on muscle reflexes and leg exercises. After his session was over, EL didn't waste any time jumping back into our conversation.

"Ok Chass you never answered my question. Why did you move out?"

I looked down at EL realizing that he really did not remember me telling him that I was in love with Shane and no longer wanted to be with him. I found myself in the awkward position of having to break up with EL all over again. I couldn't do it. I didn't have the heart to hurt him like that again—especially in the condition he was in. My stomach started to turn from the guilt that filled it and I thought it best not to remind EL that we were no longer a couple.

"Chass?" he looked up at me waiting for a response. "What happened that made you move out? Come on now you can tell me."

"We had an argument about the firm again and things got a little heated between us right before the accident," I lied. Something I swore I would never do again.

"A little heated?"

"You know me. I always over do it. I was upset because we had to leave the party early to deal with one of your clients. I was pissed about that and you being you always trying to defend the firm so we both said some things I wish we could take back."

"Are you sure that's all?" he asked. It was almost as if he could sense that I was lying to him.

"Yeah," I replied waving off his concerns. "That's all it was. You know I can tend to be a drama queen at times."

"Don't I know it," he joked.

"What did the doctors say about your condition?" I asked, as I crossed my arms across my chest and then quickly reverted back to my original stance. I was fidgety. The situation was awkward as hell. My feelings about EL being in that wheelchair were tearing me up inside—like I needed another reason to feel guilty.

"They say I may never remember what happened that night. I've read cases where the short term memory is never recovered right before a traumatic event. I might have to get used to the fact that I may never get that block of time back. As for my legs..." He paused then glanced down at his legs and continued. "Well, the doctors aren't too optimistic."

"What? Are you saying that you could be in this wheelchair for the rest of your life?"

"That's a real possibility."

"How are you really doing EL? I mean how are you adjusting to all of this? I know it can't be easy."

I looked around the penthouse focusing in on all of the equipment, and how much the place had changed in the short time since I'd moved out.

"I'm taking this one day at a time. I have a private nurse and Valerie is here a few days a week. My mom and my sisters stop by several times a week as well. Even Mia checks in on me and brings work from the office to keep me busy."

Even now that you are confined to a wheelchair, still your first priority is that damn firm.

"You shouldn't be thinking about work right now EL. That firm can manage without you for a little while."

"If I didn't have work to focus on I would go stir crazy sitting in this penthouse all day Chass. I have to do something to try to get my mind off of this."

"Do you need anything? Is there anything that I can do for you?" I asked, feeling helpless.

"There sure is. You can move back in."

"EL…"

"Now Chass, hear me out before you say no. This is probably one of the most difficult times in my life and I need you Chass. I can't imagine how an argument could have gotten so far out of hand that it caused you to move out. But, I'm really hoping you will put that aside and help me through this. The staff is very nice, but they are strangers to me. I want *you* here with me. Just think about it."

EL was laying it on thick, but it wasn't like he needed to because the guilt was already kicking my ass. I couldn't change what happened between us, but I could be there for him now—I owed him that much.

I finally convinced Shane why I needed to move back into the penthouse, and I damn near had to sell my soul to do it. He didn't agree with my decision, but he respected what I felt I had to do. The guilt I was carrying over what happened to EL weighed me down. But, it also served as my motivating force. EL needed me and I couldn't let him down—not again.

During the next few weeks, I sat in on most of EL's therapy sessions because he seemed to work that much harder when I was around. I guess he was trying to impress me. I even worked with him outside of his regular scheduled sessions whenever he felt up to it. He was getting stronger a little more every day.

I didn't tell EL about Shane and me. I couldn't find the words. I was convinced that if I told him it might jeopardize his recovery and I just couldn't take that risk. He had enough to deal with already with the paralysis, and the memory loss, which I was sure, had already taken its toll on him. The last thing I wanted to do was to lie to him. I'd done enough of that already. I felt like I didn't have a choice. I found myself in the exact same position as before. There was this strange sense of déjà-vu that had come over me.

24

Him or Me

Chass

"Meet me at the spot."

I already knew why Shane wanted to see me without him having to say another word. It had been more than five weeks since I decided to move back into the penthouse. I was spending so much time helping EL that I rarely saw Shane. His tone of voice reminded me that he wasn't happy about it. I pressed the phone against my ear and dipped out of the gym where EL was about forty-five minutes into his vigorous work-out session. The sweat dripping from his forehead was a sure indication that he wouldn't even notice that I stepped away.

"What time?" I whispered, as I walked into the bathroom and quietly closed the door.

"How soon can you be there?"

Peaking at my watch I spoke into the phone, "five o'clock." which was more than two hours away.

"Why five o'clock Chass?" Shane sounded like he wasn't willing to wait until then. "What's wrong wit' right now?"

"I can't leave now Shane. EL's session isn't over yet."

"Don't that nigga got a physical therapist? Where she at?" he asked, with a lot of attitude.

"She's in the gym. They are in a session."

"If she there then what he need you for?"

"Shane I told you that I sit in on the sessions so I know how to help EL when he doesn't have therapy scheduled. He is real motivated to walk again so he over does it sometimes and since I can't talk him out of it the least I can do is try to make sure that he doesn't hurt himself."

"Damn Baby you ain't no physical therapist. You already doin' way too much for this nigga as it is!"

"Shane I don't wanna get into this argument again."

"Don't argue. Just meet me."

"I just heard on the radio about a pile up so I'll wait for it to die down before I leave. I don't feel like sitting in a cab in the middle of all that."

"Then I'll come get you. What time you want me to scoop you up?"

151

I cracked open the bathroom door and stuck my head out just to make sure that EL hadn't taken a break and rolled his wheel chair around the penthouse looking for me.

"You can't pick me up from here," I whispered into the phone as I ducked my head back into the bathroom and closed the door.

"Of course not Baby, I'll pick you up on Columbus."

"Ok I'll hop in a cab and be there in about a half hour."

"A'ight."

I cleared my incoming calls, and then took a deep breath while thinking about what reason I would give EL for rushing out in the middle of his session. Pretending that I used the bathroom, I flushed the toilet and walked out the door. When I stepped back into the gym EL was trying to lift himself up on the bars. Judging by the veins popping out of his forehead, I knew that he had been at it a while.

"Where's Valerie?" I asked, walking towards the equipment.

"I ended her shift early today."

"Why?"

"Because...I worked her enough for one day," he strained to say as he struggled to pull himself up off the mat.

"You need some help?"

"Just help me into my wheelchair."

Spotting my jacket hanging off the handle on the treadmill I walked over to retrieve it. "I'm gonna run a few errands. Do you need anything while I'm out?"

"Only some legs. Think you can pick me up a pair?" he said, half joking.

"EL don't play like that," I replied, helping him into his wheel chair. "I know it's frustrating, but you will get through this."

"That's easy for you to say Chass...you can walk."

"I believe you will be able to walk again EL. In fact I know it. I have seen you over come so much. You will beat this too."

"Yeah...yeah...yeah," he said, dismissing my comment. "How long will you be gone?"

"I'm not sure. I have a few errands to run. I called your mother and asked her to come over while I'm out. Will you be Ok until she gets here?"

"Yeah, I'm cool. Just help me onto the sofa." He pointed to where he wanted to sit.

"You sure you don't need anything?"

"I'm straight. Go ahead and handle your business. George is on duty tonight. If I need anything before my moms get here, I'll call him."

** ** ** **

I spotted Shane's Range Rover as soon as the cab turned the corner. "Right here!" I instructed the driver.

"Fifteen dollars," he announced. I reached into my purse and pulled out a twenty.

"Nah, Baby I got this. Put your money away." Shane was standing outside of the driver-side window handing the cab driver a fifty dollar bill.

I climbed out of the cab and embraced him. "Hey you!" My smile got real wide. "I missed you."

"Back at you Baby," he said with a kiss.

"Everything Ok?" I asked, climbing into the Range.

"Why wouldn't it be?"

"You didn't sound right on the phone."

Shane switched the gear out of park, and then removed his foot from the brake.

"I just wanted to see you Chass. We ain't been spending much time together lately."

"I know." I exhaled. "My time has been split between my clients and helping EL."

"Which leaves no room for me." The expression on his face changed suddenly and I didn't particularly care for the tone in his voice.

"That's not true Shane. I always have time for you."

"Not lately," he said with a slight attitude as he turned away from me redirecting his attention to the road. "What the hell are these niggas doin'?" Shane complained, while resting his hand on the horn for several seconds.

"I told you traffic was like this. We might be here for a while."

"No the fuck we won't be." he blew the horn again. "Stupid ma'fuckas just sittin' there! What shade of green are they waitin' for?"

"They probably waiting for blue."

He grinned, "Cute Baby...real cute."

Once we got to the loft I turned on the TV and took a seat on the couch. I was looking forward to a nice relaxing evening with Shane, but he obviously had other plans.

"Chass let me ask you somethin'." His expression turned serious. "Do you still feel somethin' for that nigga?"

I sucked my teeth but didn't answer the question.

"Come on Baby don't try to game a gamer. You wouldn't be doin' all this shit if you didn't still feel somethin' for him."

"I never said I didn't care about him Shane."

"So, you still care about him huh?" he asked, with an attitude.

"Why you looking at me like that? I don't have *those* kinds of feelings for EL anymore. But, we do have history so I will always care about him."

"Chass, one minute we were gonna be together and the next minute you back up in that nigga spot. I wanna know how he managed to suck you back in. That's what the fuck I wanna know."

"He didn't suck me back into anything Shane. He's paralyzed remember!"

"Shit yeah I remember! I also remember the night he crashed his shit. That was the same night you told him about us."

"Yeah, so."

"Baby the nigga ain't stupid. He know what he doin'."

"Are you still tryna say that he crashed on purpose?"

"It wouldn't surprise me if he did. He wouldn't be the first nigga to do some stupid shit just to hold onto a female."

"Shane please...I don't believe that for a second. Both of us could have been killed and EL is the one who ended up in a wheelchair."

"And I bet he's milkin' that shit for all it's worth. He's probably takin' his time tryin' to walk. Why rush when he got you there doin' everything for him? Shit the nigga got it made wheel chair and all!" He got up from the sofa and walked out of the living room.

"Shane you sound ridiculous!" I followed him into the bedroom.

"Do I? I don't think so Chass. This whole situation is suspect. Somethin' never felt right to me about the timin' of this whole shit anyway."

"Well, you are way off base about EL. This is crazy! EL would never do something like that. You don't know him like I do."

"Yeah Ok keep tellin' yourself that. You have seriously underestimated his feelings for you if you think that he wouldn't do whatever he had to just to keep you wit' him, and you playin' right into his hands." He sat down on the bed and started unlacing his sneakers.

"Like I said, you don't know him the way I do Shane."

"I never said this would make sense. Trust me Baby I'm a man. I know these things. I wouldn't wanna loose you to the next man either. I don't doubt he feels the same way."

I waved him off. "Shane you just have a suspicious mind."

"So you just gonna dismiss what I'm sayin' Baby all 'cause you don't wanna hear it," he huffed pissed off. "How much longer you plan on helpin' him?"

"I don't know. I haven't thought that far ahead."

"Baby you gon' have to come better than that. You sound like you makin' a career out this shit!"

I sucked my teeth. "Did you ask me here to interrogate me? Because I didn't come here for the third degree Shane."

"Baby you need to ease up wit' all that. If you think this is an interrogation I must be losin' my touch. I asked you here so we could spend some time together. You know Baby I'm startin' to think you like waitin' on that nigga hand and foot. If you didn't you woulda bounced and left his ass in that wheel chair weeks ago!"

I sucked my teeth. "You know what I'm outta here." I put my jacket back on.

"You outta here? Just like that huh? You outta here?"

"It's not just like that Shane. I see you still on some bullshit."

"Oh so now a nigga can't ask questions?"

"You tryna make it seem like something is going on between me and EL when you know damn well it isn't!"

"Did I say that?"

"No, but that's what you're getting at and I didn't come here to argue."

"Well that makes two of us." He pulled me into a kiss.

"Stop it Shane." I pulled away from him pretending to still be upset. I was pissed off by his accusations—not by his advances.
Backing me up against the wall he slyly said, "Say it again Chass, and this time make sure you mean it."

I felt myself succumb to him. My body enjoyed his touch way too much for me to contest, and my mind had no control over my urges. Playing with my emotions and turning me on at the same time he repeated, "Ga head Chass. Tell me how you want me to stop again. I'm listenin'," he taunted, as he began to undress me. His tongue caressed every inch of my mouth while his finger carassed my moistened flesh. He outlined the lips of my pussy with the tip of his finger and then eased his rock hard dick inside me. Kissing my neck softly he whispered, "This feels incredible Baby. I love the shit out this pussy."

I moaned as his sensual strokes woke up every nerve in my body. We moved together passionately and with a steady rhythm until we both reached our peak. After we finished making love, Shane sat upright in the bed and looked at me.

"Baby I need you to listen to me. I mean *really* listen to me." His tone of voice captured my attention. "I can't even front I love the shit out you but, I ain't wit' this right here. I thought about this a lot and I can't go along wit' this shit no more. I was never comfortable wit' this shit from jump. I can't just sit back and watch you play house wit' that nigga no more. I can't do it Baby. I need to know that you gon' walk away from him. You either wanna be wit' me or you don't. Simple as that."

"What are you saying?" I asked, rapping myself in the sheet.

"I'm sayin' you gotta make a choice. If you choose him, I won't lie that shit will hurt like a ma'fucka, but I will respect your decision. I'll walk away and I won't bother you again."

"You would really walk away from me? From us?"

"It's not like I want to Baby you know that. But, I ain't got no choice. This shit right here ain't me."

I couldn't believe that Shane was giving me an ultimatum. It was selfish of him to force my hand this way. Why couldn't he just understand how I felt? Why couldn't he see why I had to do this? How could he be so selfish? How could he expect me to walk out on EL again? My relationship with Shane is partly the reason why I needed to be there for EL now. Although I loved Shane more than my own life, I couldn't just walk away from EL when he needed me the most. I sunk my head into my hands and sighed realizing that no matter what choice I made, someone was gonna get hurt.

"I can't believe you're doing this. How can you be this fucking selfish!?"

"Selfish! I have been more than patient and you know it. This shit been goin' on way too long Baby. You been back in dudes crib for over a month. I'm surprised I put up wit' it this long. He got his family, private nurses, therapist and shit. Trust me he don't need you."

"Listen to me for a minute." I tried to reason with him, but he wasn't hearing me.

"Nah Chass, I'm done listenin'. Are you gonna walk away from him or what?" he asked, all the patience drained from his voice.

I loved Shane so much, but my guilt over what happened to EL was more powerful than anything else.

"I...I can't," I whimpered, as the tears flowed freely from my eyes.

"You can't or you won't?" he said, all the patience drained from him voice.

"Please try to understand that I love you with all my heart Shane, but I can't walk out on EL again. Not when he needs me the most. Please try to understand that."

"Sounds like you made your decision."

His words were cold as if there was no emotion left in him.

25

The Set Up
Shane

"You ain't new to this kid. At least that's what you told me before I put you on. You said you did this shit before so you know what needs to be done."

I was tryin' to school one of my employees on how to handle a lil' business rival.

"So, I'm just supposed to roll up on 'em and take his shit when he's five deep?"

"What'chu think nigga damn?! I gotta walk you through this shit! Do I need to hold your dick when you piss too?! The ma'fucka tryin' to set up shop in our fuckin' territory. I don't give a fuck how many niggas he got wit' 'em. Did you think he was gon' roll solo when he tryin' to shake up somebody else shit? I shouldn't have to tell you how we handle niggas that don't show us respect. I thought you knew what we do to ma'fuckas that disrespect our territory?"

"Nah man. You ain't gotta tell me."

"A'ight then. Handle it. Hit me back when you got somethin' to tell me."

"Yo Shane, but what if _____,"

"What if nothin' man! Enough wit' the questions. If you can't do the shit let me know and I'll send somebody else to do what you seem to be havin' a problem wit'."

"You ain't gotta do that man. I got it."

"A'ight then. Handle it. Show me you a soldier then nigga and do what needs be done!"

"A'ight man. I got you."

"You better have me man. I ain't in the mood for you to be fuckin' up."

I pushed my cell closed and laid it on the counter. This nigga picked the wrong day to play stupid. I pay them niggas to be out there handlin' shit. If I wanted to be called every five minutes I might as well be on them streets my damn self. My temper was flared up. I've seen niggas locked down handlin' shit better than I was. Chass got my head all fucked up. I still can't believe she chose to stay wit' that nigga rather than be wit' me. She got me sittin' up in the crib ready to flip. I feel like my whole world just blew up. My pride is bruised, and I don't know what to do with all this rage. I never wanted to settle down to avoid this shit right here. I'm not the fallin' in love type of dude. I've always avoided that shit like the plague. Once you give a woman your heart—she got you. I needed a bottle of Hennessey or maybe even the Goose. Like alcohol could fix this shit. I'm not lookin' for a temporary fix anyway. I want my woman. Bein' without Chass is like Michael Jordan without a basketball—it ain't right. But, I'm a man so I gotta maintain. I'm sittin' up in the loft of all places. This is the last place I should be. The spot is the same as the last time Chass and I were here together. Her lingerie is hangin' on the chair, bottles of her perfume are spread across the dresser, and the dirty dishes are still in the dishwasher from when she made lasagna. Her presence is all over this spot. Who am I kiddin'? It wouldn't matter where I was tho. It's not like I need any reminders of Chass. I can't stop thinkin' about her, and trust me I tried. I need to stop kiddin' myself. Like I could ever forget about Chass. She's in my blood. Chass is in my heart.

I had to get out of the loft before I remodeled the place wit' my fist. I jumped in my ride and headed straight for the FDR. I was about to spring a surprise visit on PK. I wasn't plannin' on droppin' by his crib until later, but I needed to refocus my attention somewhere else. PK had some dough for me so, he'd just become a priority.

"Speak nigga," PK's voice blared through the phone like it wasn't two o'clock in the mornin'.

"Yo what up man? What'chu doin' wide awake this early for dawg?" I really didn't care why he was up, just as long as he was so I wouldn't have to wake his ass up when I stopped by his crib unexpected.

"I was hungry so I got up to fix me somethin' to eat. What's up? Why you on the horn so early for man?"

"I'm on my way to come check you. You got that for me right?"

"Yeah I got it. We good money dawg. I just thought you wasn't comin' through 'til tomorrow."

"It's two o'clock in the mornin' nigga so it is tomorrow. I'm around your way so I figured I'd swing thru now. I'll be at your crib in a few."

A black Lexus coupe was pullin' out of a parkin' spot as soon as I turned the corner onto PK's block. I pulled right in. I walked towards the four story brick buildin' and glanced back at my ride just in time to see the light inside go off as the alarm set. As soon as the elevator reached PK's floor, the sounds from the TV met me in the hall.

He got that shit blastin'. This nigga must be deaf, I thought pounding my fist against the steel door. The door flung open and PK stood in the doorway stretchin' his neck around the corner tryin' to keep an eye on whatever he was concoctin' in the kitchen. PK couldn't cook for shit.

"Come on in man." He brushed the crumbs from his shirt and started fanning away the smoke that was makin' its way into the hallway.

"Nigga you know you broke all kinds of laws the last time you stepped into a kitchen. Why you wanna try your luck again man?"

"I was hungry. What was I supposed to do?"

"McDonald's is down the street and you got Chinese spots all up and through here."

"Man you buggin'. You know I don't fuck with that shit. One of those Chinese spots just got raided last week. They found dead cats in the freezer. Nah, man I'm good. I'll eat burned shit before I fuck with them."

"Where your girl at? Why she ain't in here cookin' for you?"

"She went out with a few of them hoes from downtown. If I wait for her ass to get back I'll starve."

"What'chu in here burnin' anyway man?" I walked toward the stove.

"A turkey and cheese omelet."

"First of all turn the fire down man. That shit is way too high. You 'bout to make this whole place go up in flames. If your girl gon' make a habit of leavin' you here to fend for yourself then you gon' have to keep the fire department on speed dial nigga."

He laughed. "It ain't supposed to be smoking like that?"

"Nah, nigga it ain't. First tell me how you fuck up a omelet man? That shit easy as hell to make." I laughed.

"I don't know man. I guess it's a good thing you came thru."

While PK finished cookin', I started thinkin' about Chass again. I did a sucka move and called my voice mail just to listen to a few of Chass' old messages that I never got around to erasin'. I sat there starin' at the phone when PK threw a duffel bag in my lap snappin' me out of it.

"Damn nigga! I called you three times! Fuck you doin' daydreaming?

Damn I'm sprung. I can't even deny it. It's only been a few days and a nigga is goin' through some serious withdrawal.

"Thinkin' 'bout Chass huh man?" PK asked, bitin' into his burned omelet.

"Nah man." I lied.

"What-eva nigga. I can see it all in your grill man. I ain't never seen you like this Shane. She got you all caught out man," he laughed.

"Shit funny to you man," I snapped at him.

"Yo Shane chill man. I'm just playin' wit'chu nigga damn fall back."

"I ain't in the mood to be playin' man." I opened the bag and started countin' the money.

"You ain't gotta check my math. You know it's all there man."

I nodded, but I still counted my stacks. PK was a wiz at math, but everybody fucks up sometime.

"Tay came by here?" I threw the last few bundles of cash in the bag then zipped it up.

"Yeah," he said with a nod. "Tay checked me yesterday, early. He ain't hit you up yet?"

I slung the duffel bag across my shoulder. "Nah, not yet. I'ma stop by there after I leave here."

"Do you gotta rush off man? Stay for a minute. You hungry? I can whip up another omelet."

"Nah, nigga I'm straight."

"You sure man? This shit good as hell," he said chewin'.

"Nah man I said I ain't hungry."

Even if I was starving you couldn't pay me to eat that shit.

This nigga really did a job on that omelet. The inside was half-cooked with yolk drippin' and shit while the outside was burned.

"Ahhh fuck!" PK called out noticin' a stain on his shirt as he got up off the couch to walk me to the door. "I love this shirt. I hope this shit don't leave a stain," he complained, tryin' to wipe the grease-filled spot.

"Wit' chu cookin' man you better hope that shit don't leave a hole!"

He laughed. "You'se a funny ma'fucka Shane!"

"A'ight man I'ma catch you later dawg." I held my hand out for a pound and then I stepped onto the elevator.

**   **   **   **

I was sittin' in the brownstone watchin' TV when the phone rang.

"Talk to me," I answered. My eyes glued to the game.

"Mr. Williamson, I have some good news. They've accepted your offer."

I put a bid on a piece of property and I was waitin' on my broker to hit me back wit' some news.

"Can you come down to my office to sign the binder?"

"Definitely."

"Excellent." How does tomorrow afternoon sound?"

"Tomorrow afternoon?"

"Is that a problem?"

"I have an appointment that I can't exactly reschedule."

"Mr. Williamson, if you don't want anyone else to grab this property then we need to meet with the sellers as soon as possible. They've already agreed to your terms, so I'd say the ball is in our court. However, they want to have an original binder in hand as good faith and your signature is required. Their attorney is preparing the binder and he is faxing it to me later today. I wanted to get a jump on this as soon as I received the paperwork."

"What time do you need me to come in tomorrow?"

"Around four o'clock."

"Damn you can't swing it no earlier than that?"

"Mr. Williamson the seller is only in town for a short period of time. They specifically requested that time."

I hesitated. "A...'ight... I'll be there," I was reluctant, but I wasn't about to pass on the chance to purchase the property.

As soon as I hung up the phone, I thought about how I was gonna swing my appointment which was at four o'clock at my brokers office in Manhattan, and the drop which was at five o'clock in Brooklyn. I was about to pick up the phone when Tay let himself in the brownstone.

"Sup man?" he said, walkin' into the livin' room.

"I need to go see my broker to sign the papers for the sale of the property for the dealership. I really don't wanna put that off and give somebody else a chance to scoop the property. If they talkin' the right amount of paper then I'm definitely baggin' it. I just don't see how I'm gonna make the drop and the meet."

"I'll take care of the drop so you can handle that." He picked up a bottle of vodka and poured his self a shot.

"You sure man? I can switch some shit around. My broker can make it happen if he wants his dough."

"I'm sure man. Just take care of that. When that dealership pop off and niggas see those rides you gon' be sellin' its gon' be one big pay day out this bitch. I gotta go to Brooklyn anyway to see my little man. I'll be killin' two birds with one stone."

"A'ight man. Just meet Barkim at the spot at five o'clock. I'll hit him up and let him know you comin' instead of me."

"Nah, I got this Shane. I'll call Kim. You just make sure all your paperwork is in order man."

"I'm a little nervous man."

"Nervous...nah man not you. I ain't never seen you nervous man. You got this."

"This ain't the drug game man. This is on a whole other level."

"Shane you gonna kill it like always. You smart as hell man. You taught me everything I know about the business—legal and otherwise. I ain't worried. I know how you get down when it comes to that paper dawg. It's your hard work that brought this whole shit together. Let other ma'fuckas worry. All you need to do is just sit back and collect your stacks!"

Our hands collided. "So you goin' to check on your lil' man? How he doin'?"

"He good. Gettin' big and bad as shit."

"A'ight well give lil' man a pound for me. Tell him "Uncle Shane" gon' stop by and see him real soon. Maybe take him to a couple basketball games. If he gon' be tall like you then we gotta get him in early. You know prepare him for his future."

"He gon' love that."

161

**   **   **   **

The location was perfect.

The math was on point.

The square footage was exactly what I was lookin' for.

I couldn't ask for a better spot for a car dealership. I walked out of the meetin' feelin' good about the deal. As soon as I hopped in the Range, I checked my phone and noticed that it didn't have a signal.

No wonder my shit ain't ring the whole time I was in that meetin'. Fuckin' cell phone companies need to step they game up.

As soon as my signal was restored I called Tay to see how the drop went.

"Leave it at the beep and I'll hit you back." His voice mail caught me off guard. I was expectin' him to answer the phone. I called Kim, but his voice mail answered the phone for him too.

Where the fuck these niggas at?

On my way back to the brownstone, I stopped at McDonald's. While I was waitin' on the drive thru, my message box lit up.

"Yo Shane I got knocked. It was a set-up. Niggas went all in man. They was at the drop waiting for us. As soon as we stepped in the warehouse they started blastin'! I caught one in the arm. Me and Tay got separated. I ain't seen him since before niggas started shootin'. I'm at Kings County Hospital out in Brooklyn. They got police posted outside my room like I'm an escaped con or some shit. They probably gon' try to pin all types of shit on us. Call me as soon as you get this. Better yet, come down to the hospital man!"

I swerved out of the drive thru and peeled out of the parkin' lot before that chick could bag my food. I was runnin' red lights and stop signs like them shits didn't apply to me. I sped through the Brooklyn Queens Expressway like the Range was on fire. I drove into the hospital parkin' lot and ran inside.

"Tayari Stewart and Barkim Brown," I called out their names to desk nurse.

"Are you a family member?"

"Yeah."

"And your relationship to the patient is..."

"They my cousins."

She picked up a piece of paper then looked up at me. "Mr. Brown was released into police custody about an hour ago and there is no record of a Mr. Stewart."

"Check again."

She looked at me wit' an apologizin' expression. "I've already checked twice Sir."

162

"Then check two more times. If Barkim was here then Tay gotta be here too."

"I'm sorry sir; there is no record of a Tayari Stewart. Perhaps he was brought to another hospital."

The sound of her screechin' voice was like nails against a chalkboard penetratin' my eardrum givin' me an instant headache. If I didn't leave when I did I woulda caught a case behind that broad.

Now I see why ma'fuckas in here is sick. If the injuries don't kill 'em her annoyin'-ass voice damn sure will.

I walked to the Range thinkin'…*if the hospital don't have no record of Tay then he must be at the precinct. Police probably tryin' to charge him wit' some bullshit.*

I called my attorney Randal Michaels. Michaels had got a call from Barkim and was already on his way to the precinct. When I pulled in front of the 71st precinct, PK was sittin' in his Lex wit' the engine still runnin'. I walked up to the car and tapped on the window wit' my car keys. PK looked at me like he was in a daze. I tapped the window again. The second time snapped him out of it because he turned the engine off and got out of the car.

"I'm glad you here man," he said, closin' the car door. I wasn't feelin' the look on PK's face.

"What's up wit' Tay and Kim? You heard anything?"

"Michaels is in the interrogation room with Barkim now."

"What about Tay? Hospital said they ain't got no record of him. He here too?"

PK looked at me like somebody just told him he was dyin'.

"What's goin' on man? Where Tay at?"

"I don't know how to tell you this man," he said, draggin' his words, unable to look me in the eye.

"Just tell me PK!"

"Tay got hit about five times man."

"Nah man. Then why the hospital ain't got no record of him?"

"Because …"

"Because what nigga! Did they take Tay to New York Methodist?"

"Shane…Tay died on the scene man."

"Get the fuck outta here! Tay ain't dead! Nah man…I ain't tryin' to hear that shit PK!"

For a minute I thought my heart stopped beatin'. It damn sure felt like it. My body went numb. All the blood circulatin' through my veins rushed to my head at once. I suddenly felt paper-thin; like a feather could knock me over. The next thing I knew PK was liftin' me up.

"Shane, you a'ight man? Can you stand?" he asked, usin' his weight to hold me up.

"Where he at PK? Where they take Tay?"

"Coroners got Tay's body."

"Who did it PK! Who the fuck killed Tay?!

"I don't know, but we gon' find out don't even worry about it man."

"I need to talk to Barkim."

"We both do man. He the only one who can tell us what went down in that warehouse."

Me and PK walked into the precinct just as my attorney, Randal Michaels, was leavin' the interrogation room. Barkim was in hand cuffs and bein' led through the squad room by a uniformed officer. While Michaels stopped off to speak with one of the detectives, I asked the officer for a couple minutes to speak to Barkim. He agreed and gave us a few minutes.

"You a'ight man?" I asked, lookin' at his arm in a sling.

"I'm a'ight. They told me Tay ain't make it. I still can't believe it man."

"Yo Kim what the fuck happened tonight?"

"Me and Tay rolled up to the drop like a half hour early and niggas was already at the spot waiting."

"Then what happened?" I pressed.

"They started shooting."

"They just started shootin' out of nowhere Kim?" I found that hard to believe.

"Yeah man. We wasn't at the spot five minutes before they started blastin'. We didn't know where the shots was comin' from because the spot was so dark."

"This shit ain't makin' no sense to me man. Nobody knew about the drop except us. Y'all niggas ain't say shit right." I looked at Kim and then at PK.

"Of course not man," PK answered.

"Come on Shane you know us better than that man," Barkim said.

"Did you see any of them nigga's faces?" I asked.

"Nah 'cause it was too dark. It was a straight professional hit though man. Whoever set this shit up is connected in a major way and got major paper dawg."

"Why you say that?" PK asked before I could.

"Because the shit was well organized man. It was a lot of niggas yo. Me and Tay was out numbered like a ma'fucka man. They had all the exits covered. They busted out all the lights so we couldn't see shit. Them niggas was making sure we had no way out man. We didn't know what was going down until it was too late."

"Brown your five minutes is up!" The uniformed officer snatched Barkim by the arm and led him out of the squad room and down the hall of the precinct before we could finish our conversation.

Fuckin' cops.

Tay's Moms walked in the station while PK and I were waitin' for Michaels.

164

"Shane!" she exhaled relieved to see me. "What's going on? What did Tay get arrested for this time?"

"Police call you?" I asked, not knowin' what to say to her.

"Yeah, they told me I needed to come down immediately. Is Tay in a lot of trouble? Is he going to jail? They wouldn't tell me anything over the phone."

A blue-eyed, blonde-hair Caucasian detective walked up just as I was about to tell her about Tay.

"Are you Mrs. Stewart?" he asked with a tight lip.

"Yes, I am."

"I need you to follow me," he cautioned.

"Mr. Williamson, Mr. Spivey." Michaels approached us. "Come with me. I need to speak with you gentlemen privately."

Michaels led us to an empty interrogation room. He opened his briefcase and removed a few papers from it.

"Ok gentlemen this is the reality of the situation...," he said, glancin' through the papers. "Mr. Brown is looking at possession of an illegal handgun, and possession of an illegal substance with the intent to sell. Both are felonies. Chewin' on the tooth pick that hung from the side of his mouth he continued. "Combined charges can equal to maximum sentences of up to twenty years in prison."

"How police find out what was goin' down?" I asked, tryin' to figure that shit out myself.

"They received an anonymous tip that a drug deal was in progress. When police responded, they found Mr. Brown attempting to flee the scene and Mr. Stewart was DOA. Several kilos of cocaine were confiscated along with a million dollars in cash."

"You can get Kim off tho right? Police can't prove that Kim is connected to the drugs or the money right?" I asked.

"We can probably get a plea deal on a lesser drug possession charge, but Mr. Brown's gun possession charge is a direct violation of his parole, so he is going to have to serve the rest of his prior sentence. Worst case scenario, he does the three years he already has hanging over his head. Mr. Stewart's murder adds the hint of a drug deal gone bad. Since Mr. Brown was caught fleeing the scene he is the number one suspect in Mr. Stewart's murder."

"Nah, Michaels! Kim ain't kill Tay! That shit is straight-up ridiculous man! These cops is fuckin' stupid! This was a set up! I can't see Kim doin' a day of time Michaels. I need you to make this go away man."

He removed the tooth pick from the right side of his mouth and looked at me. "Mr. Williamson we have a lot of money and a lot of cocaine here. Add to that a dead body. It's not going to be easy to get these charges to disappear."

"I need you to get him off Michaels. I don't give a fuck what you have to do to make that happen. You know I don't care how much it cost. I just lost one of my boys to the streets. I'm not about to lose another one to this fucked up-ass system."

Scratchin' his head he replied, "Mr. Williamson...I can't promise anything, but I will certainly do my best."

Oh I know you will. That's why I keep that ass on retainer.

Randal Michaels was a fifty-seven year old shark. He graduated at the top of his class from Yale. The nigga damn near passed the bar in his sleep. He has never lost a major case and he's been an attorney for more than thirty years. When I first heard about this nigga, the first thing I thought was we got ourselves another Johnnie Cochran out this bitch. Michaels is no doubt as hard-nosed as they come. He ain't afraid to play dirty and that's what I dug about him. He never let me down before, so I knew he wasn't about to start now.

Just as me and PK were about to leave the precinct, we heard Tay's moms screamin'.

"No! That's not my son! Don't try to tell me that's my son! Tay mama's here to get you honey. I know that's not you in there on that table baby. Where is my son? I know he's somewhere in this damn rat hole of a police station! He better not be in a damn cage or I will sue the shit out of this department!" she yelled at the officers that were tryin' to restrain her. Mrs. Stewart was carried out of the squad room and into the office of the police psychiatrist.

A lot of shit wasn't addin' up and I had more questions than answers. I turned toward PK. "How many times did you say Tay was hit?"

"About five."

"And Kim."

"Once."

"Once huh?"

"What'chu gettin' at man?" PK shot me a weird look.

"Somethin' is off about this shit PK."

"What'chu mean man?"

"Just think about it for a minute. Tay gets hit five times and Kim gets hit once. Somethin' don't seem funny about that shit to you?"

"You sayin' somebody was tryin' to kill Tay?"

"I don't know man. I'm still tryin' to piece this shit together. Judgin' by how many niggas Kim said was at the drop they was makin' sure that somebody didn't walk away from that shit. They wasn't too concerned about Kim or he woulda been layin' on a slab next to Tay."

"A professional hit?" he questioned. "We ain't had no problems in a minute man."

"This is what I'm sayin'. The shit don't make no sense PK. We have done this a million times. Now all of a sudden they knockin' off niggas in our camp now!"

"Edwardo and them niggas maybe. We did shut they shit down a few months ago man," PK threw out there.

"Nah man that shit don't fit. Edwardo and his camp is a bunch of bitch-ass niggas. They would never roll up on us—never."

"Carlos and Roberto?"

"Why would Roberto and his crew suddenly flip on us and wanna take us out? Business is boomin' like a ma'fucka. Somethin' else is goin' on PK."

"Shane it ain't like we saints man. We got mad enemies dawg. This shit can be anybody."

"All them nigga's been dealt wit' PK. Besides half of 'em ain't got the resources to come at us hard like this, and the other half ain't got the balls. We lookin' for ma'fuckas wit' a shit load of dough and nothin' to lose. There's somethin' we ain't seein'."

"Like what?"

"Somethin' just don't feel right to me man. This shit ain't addin' up. The math's funky."

26

Burying My Boy
Shane

Tay was like my brother. We grew up together. We couldn't have been any closer if we were blood related. We go all the way back to sandboxes and pro-keds. I remember back when all we did was run around gettin' high and chasin' chicks. Tay stood six feet three inches, but he was this short lil' nigga when we met. He had to step on a crate just to look me in the eye. I used to tell him, "You gon' always be my nigga, even if you don't get no bigger." Then Tay shot up to 6'3 almost overnight. He knew he was the shit then. Me bein' me I had to show him up. I couldn't have him thinkin' that he could see me in no way shape or form. I couldn't let him beat me at shit. I always had to be the winner at everything. I can count the times on one hand that I ever lost anything—and that's not including three of my fingers. Tay was cool wit' my ego. Not many other niggas were. Most are intimidated by me and my style. I always lived by all or nothing. You either come hard or stay home. Is there any other way to do it? Tay was a lot like me and that's how we became boys. We used to slap box in the street after playin' spades and drinkin' like we ain't have a liver. It feels like it was just yesterday. We were boys for over twenty five years. That's a long time. I still can't believe my nigga is gone.

The mornin' of the funeral everybody was callin' to give their condolences. Even though I knew they meant well, I wasn't tryin' to hear shit about Tay bein' in a better place. There wasn't a damn thing better about bein' in a box in the ground while the ma'fuckas who put you there was out celebratin' or onto their next hit. Somebody was gonna pay for takin' my boys life—there was no doubt about it.

R Kelly's *I Wish* popped on the radio just as I was in the bathroom shapin' my shit up. The lyrics was so on point wit' what I was feelin'. It had me reminiscin' and missin' Tay even more—especially the part about slap boxin' in the middle of the street. I was lookin' for my tie when my cell rung. I picked it up and looked at the screen.

Private.

I ain't answer it. A few minutes later the phone rang again.

Private. Again.

Persistent ma'fucka.

I wiped the shavin' cream off the right side of my face and answered the phone.

"That hit was meant for you nigga! How does it feel knowin' that your boy died in your place?"

"Who the fuck is this?!"

They ain't say shit.

"Who the fuck is this?!" The ma'fucka still ain't say shit; I heard his ass breathin' tho. "What's up wit' these junior-high school games dawg? Show yourself you punk ma'fucka! If you man enough to take a life then you man enough to own up to it!"

More breathin'.

Here this nigga go wit' this heavy breathin'? His ass done seen too many fuckin' movies.

I don't know if the heavy breathin' was supposed to intimidate me, but it didn't. If anything it had me even more heated.

"Ga head and breathe now nigga 'cause when I find out who the fuck you are—trust you won't be breathin' no more!" The muthafucka hung up.

That call was on my mind from the time I left the house until I got to the church. Not knowin' who this nigga was left me wide open and vulnerable. I hated that shit. One thing that phone call did give me and that was the missin' piece to the puzzle I had been tryin' to put together since Tay was killed—the killer thought Tay was me. Which meant somebody wanted me dead. It wouldn't be the first time when niggas got shit wrong and killed the wrong person. Now it made sense why they let Kim live. He ain't fit my description. Kim is a skimpy lil nigga. He don't weigh 130lbs soakin' wet, and he pale as shit; nowhere near my complexion. Tay was about my complexion, close to my height and close to my build. You could easily mistake Tay for me—especially in a dark spot. Five bullets—there was no question that they wanted to make sure my boy wouldn't walk out of there alive. So they killed Tay thinkin' they killed me. The question I had was how did they know about the drop?

When I got to the church a few people were standin' outside talkin'. There was no one inside. I guess nobody wanted to be alone wit' a dead body, so I was. Gave me a chance to have a minute alone wit' my boy. The silence in the church was so loud it was deafenin'. I stood over Tay's body and just stared at him. He looked like Tay; he just looked like he was sleep.

"I got you Tay. You ain't gotta worry 'bout shit my nigga. I'ma make sure you rest in peace dawg. I'm gon' catch these ma'fuckas Tay. Them niggas that did you is done. They 'bout to take their last breath dawg. That's my word on everything I love. I got you baby boy." I looked down at Tay expectin' him to get up and walk out of the church wit' me.

"I knew you'd be in here man." The voice came from behind me breakin' the awkward silence. I turned around to see my cousin Ced who'd just flown in from Georgia early this mornin' for the funeral.

"What up man? Thanks for comin' Cuz." I leaned in to give him a pat and a pound.

169

"You ain't gotta thank me man. You know Tay was my dawg. I wouldn't be no place else. I just wish I coulda been here sooner. I had some shit to take care of. Don't worry 'bout shit tho man. We gon' find the niggas that did this. You know I got you covered. I already put the word out about what happened to Tay man. My peoples is lookin' into it. As soon as I know somethin', you know somethin'."

I gave him another pound. "Thanks man. I got ears on the streets right now too so I should hear somethin' soon."

"Let's take a walk man. The service don't start for another few minutes; it will give you a minute to get your head right," he offered, noticin' how shook up I was.

"Some nigga called while I was in the crib gettin' dressed talkin' about Tay died in my place. I can't stop thinkin' 'bout that shit."

"Word yo. Now niggas is playin' on phones and shit. I got you dawg. Don't even worry about it. They gonna regret this shit once we find out who the fuck they are."

"No doubt."

As people started enterin' the church I couldn't shake the feelin' that maybe one of them could be the one who killed Tay. It coulda easily been someone we knew. Since enemies usually come with familiar faces—I was eyein' anything that looked suspicious. Me and Ced was standin' in front of the church talkin' when PK walked up.

"What up Ced?" PK held his hand out for a pound as he approached us.

"What up man?" Ced slapped his hand. "It's been a minute."

"Yeah, it has." PK looked at me. "How you holding up man?"

"They killed my nigga dawg. How you think I'm holdin' up? That's Tay in that casket man."

"I know man, I know." PK patted my back. "Police call you?"

"I ain't fuckin' wit' police. I let my answerin' machine pick that shit up. Michaels is handlin' the case. They can holla at him."

"My girl said they called the crib a couple times."

"Fuck police. Just fall back and let Michaels deal wit' them incompetent ma'fuckas. That's what the fuck I pay him for."

"Michaels tell you anything about when Barkim gettin' out?"

"Nah, not yet. I left a few messages for 'em. I'm just waitin' for him to hit me back. I went to see Kim day before yesterday."

"He straight?"

"Yeah he a'ight. I took care of everything he need while he locked down. He fucked up about Tay tho. He was the last one to see him alive so you know that's fuckin' wit' him."

Tay's baby moms rolled up in a limo wit' Tay's son in her arms. She looked like she ain't slept in months. TJ looked so much like his father in his suit and tie, that shit brought tears to my eyes. When I first met Tay, he wasn't that much older than TJ. Just as Josette and TJ walked inside the church, Chass and Sara walked up. Chass and I locked eyes for a second before she walked inside the church behind Sara.

After the service was over, I was standin' in the back of the church right next to the double doors when Chass approached me.

"I'm so sorry about Tay." She looked at me; her eyes swelled up wit' tears. "I know how close y'all were."

I wanted so bad to take her in my arms, but I refrained.

"I wanted to say something to you earlier, but I saw you talking and I didn't want to interrupt."

I picked up her hand and stroked it. "I know you came for your girl, but I appreciate you bein' here. Means a lot to me."

"I didn't just come for her. You lost Tay too." She stroked my hand back.

Just then Ced walked up.

"Shane we gettin' ready to hit the cemetery. You ready man?"

"Yeah man. I'll be right there."

I looked at Chass whose mouth hung open. No doubt she was amazed by the resemblance.

"By the way Ced, this is Chass... Chass this is my cousin Cedric."

"Nice to meet you Ma," he said, with a nod. "Too bad it's under these circumstances."

"Same here." Chass looked at me then back at Ced. "Anybody ever tell you that you and Shane look just alike."

Ced blushed "All the time Ma...all the time. A'ight Shane I'ma be in the limo. It was nice to meet you Ma," he said, before he stepped off.

"Damn Shane you wasn't lyin' when you told me how much you and Cedric look alike. Y'all could pass for twins!"

I blushed slightly. "Yeah I know."

"Ok I'ma let you go. I know you gotta get to the cemetery."

"You not comin' to the gravesite?" I asked, not ready for her to leave.

"No, I don't do cemeteries. I never have. Tay looked real good. Y'all put him away nice. That's how I wanna remember him. I can't see him being put in the ground." She looked at her watch. "I gotta get going. I'm doing a hair show in Atlanta in a few days and I have to finish packing."

"Knowin' the way you pack that's about a week's worth of work right there."

"You know me so well."

"Do I? What about your lucky keychain? Don't forget that."

"You remember that keychain?" she asked, surprised.

"I remember everything about you."

I looked into her eyes hopin' she could see how much I missed her and how much I still loved her. Death has a way of puttin' your life into perspective—especially all the important shit.

She turned away breaking eye contact. "Shane I just wanna say again how sorry I am. I know how much Tay meant to you."

"Thanks again for comin'," I leaned over and kissed her soft cheek. "You bein' here means more to me than you know."

The whole time Chass and I talked all I could think about was how much I wanted her back. But, those thoughts vanished as soon as I got in the limo. On my way to the cemetery the only thing on my mind was that ma'fucka who called lettin' me know that I was the one who was supposed to die. I couldn't shake that shit.

27

The Ultimate Betrayal

Chass

The hair showcase ended a day early due to scheduling conflicts and several stylists that didn't show up. With no reason to stay in Atlanta, I went back to the Omni, packed my bags, and headed for the Hartsfield-Jackson Airport. Tired, but I was finally on my way back to New York. I settled into my comfortable window seat and began to unwind. But, trying to relax was damn near impossible with the chatterbox that sat next to me. This chick went on about her kids and grandkids like I asked about them. When she started on her great-grandkids, I pulled out my iPod and tuned her ass out. She finally got the hint and shut up.

I thought about calling EL to let him know about the change in plans, but I figured since he wasn't expecting me until tomorrow, I'd just surprise him. As soon as the Stewardess announced that we were approaching LaGuardia Airport, I glanced out of the window for confirmation. I recognized the landmarks below which confirmed that we were approaching the runway. I peaked at my watch amazed by how quickly the hours passed. I grabbed my carry-on from the overhead compartment and sat it in my lap.

Rushing through several impatient travelers, I headed out of the airport in search of a taxi. Once the driver pulled up in front of the high-rise, I paid him, grabbed my luggage, and walked into the lobby.

"Miss Fondain?" George, the doorman announced, shock spread across his face. His greeting felt more like a question than a hello. The weird look he was wearing did little to hide the fact that he was surprised to see me.

"Hey George," I replied, as I wheeled my luggage across the sparkling marble floors and onto the elevator that opened as soon as I stepped up to it.

"How was your trip?" he asked, giving me more conversation than usual as he trailed closely behind me. George spoke with a funny accent and he always wore a ridiculous smile on his face. He reminded me of the character, Mr. Bentley from *The Jefferson's*. He definitely had that silly-ass expression down pat.

"It was good. I made a lot of contacts and gained some exposure," I answered, trying to ignore the odd expression on his face.

Once the elevator reached the penthouse, he picked up my luggage and rolled it into the hall.

"Here you are Miss Fondain," he called out rolling the suitcase at my feet. It seemed to me like George was deliberately being loud. He also seemed a bit off.

"Come on now George. What did I tell you about that Miss Fondain stuff? Please...call me Chass. My mother... now she's Miss Fondain." He cracked a tiny smile and then walked back onto the elevator.

Why in the hell was he looking at me like that? And why the fuck was he talking all loud and shit? Was he trying to wake up the whole neighborhood or what? I thought, wondering why George was acting so out of character and why he wasn't sporting his usual goofy expression that he normally takes everywhere with him.

Standing outside the penthouse, I could hear the music blaring on the other side of the door. I slid my keycard into the slot and walked inside. I called out for EL, but he didn't answer. What I couldn't figure was why the music was blasting Joe's *I wanna know* setting the mood for nothing. I picked up the remote control and turned down the volume. I figured EL must have been in a rush to one of his check-ups and forgot to turn the music off. As I wheeled my suitcase down the hall I heard strange sounds coming from EL's bedroom.

EL's here? Why didn't he answer when I called out to him? Was my first thought. My second was, *Oh my GOD he must have fell and hurt his self.* Expecting to find EL on the floor hurt or worse; I hurried to the bedroom and pushed the door open. Shock spread across my face and my mouth hung open. I'd walked in on EL and Sara having sex.

My heart beat impelled.

My hands started to shake.

My palms were sweaty.

I suddenly felt like the walls were closing in around me.

My breaths were short and sharp.

My head and my heart were at war.

My first instinct was to walk into the kitchen, grab a butcher's knife, and go Lizzie Borden on their asses. Swinging the knife until there wasn't anything left except puddles of blood. There wouldn't even be a need for a funeral when I was done because there wouldn't be any bodies to bury. Nothing left to cremate either. If I could kill both of them and get away with it there was no doubt in my mind that some old dude would be in a cemetery digging their burial plots, while I sat in a court room pleading temporary insanity. For a split second I thought about walking out of EL's bedroom, and handing them back their privacy. But, I couldn't move. My body just went numb. I was stuck in that spot, forced to face the betrayal.

My anger filled the room.

I was overpowered by rage.

Rage that was so strong it was crippling.

I knew then that I couldn't leave without confronting them. My fury wouldn't allow me to take the coward way out. No way in hell. That would have been too good for them. They were going to feel my wrath; there was no doubt about it. They were so into their pants and moans that they didn't even realize that I had entered the room. My hands balled up into tight fists as I walked toward them.

"Get up against the wall this is a bust!" I yelled over Joe's sensual voice.

"WHAT THE...OH SHIT...CHASS!" The panic spread across EL's face as he jumped off of Sara like several volts of electricity just shot through his entire body. He quickly grabbed his robe, unable to look me in the eye; his face laced with guilt.

My mouth dropped again.

Well I'd be damned! This muthafucka can walk!

"You fucking BITCH!" I lunged at Sara, but EL grabbed me before I could get to her. "How could you do this shit to me Sara?"

"Sara sucked her teeth and rolled her eyes as if my words annoyed her. "Chass please! You ain't fucking EL! You just here *playing* nurse."

"Oh really?" I struggled for EL to let me go. "Since you knew that me and EL wasn't having sex then why not come to me like a woman and tell me you wanted him. I woulda gladly stepped aside and let you have his ass! But, you thought it was better to make a fool outta me! You trifling bitch!"

"What-eva Chass. I ain't gotta explain myself to you. I don't owe you a shit." The back-stabbing bitch had the nerve to say.

"What bitch! So this is how you do me! All you care about is getting your back dug out meanwhile you helping this nigga play me for a fucking fool!" I struggled to break away from EL, but his grip on me was too tight.

"Chass can you calm down and let me talk to you?" EL was damn near begging.

"No nigga! I don't wanna hear shit you gotta say! Now get the fuck off me!"

I broke partially away from EL and dived on the bed; taking him with me. Pulling EL's weight weakened me, but my anger was my motivation. With my one free hand I aimed for Sara's throat, determined to choke the life out of her. I wasn't going to be satisfied until my hands were firmly around her neck watching her turn ten different shades while she struggled to take her last breath. Trust me I thought about how EL's ass would die too. Ripping his balls off one at a time would provide instant gratification while he belted out torturous screams before I served him with the blow that would end his life.

Sara squirmed her way out of my reach then tried to jump bad.

"Oh Chass stop all that damn whining. So what I'm fucking EL. Shit, you ain't. I don't know why you so upset. It's not like you care. You coming up in here playing the victim like you give a fuck about EL. If it wasn't for that accident you wouldn't even be here. You got your head so far up Shane's ass you can taste his breakfast!" She said, draping the oversized comforter around her naked body.

No this bitch didn't! I thought as our eyes locked briefly. Sara was surprisingly confrontational as if she had been holding onto her anger for quite some time. I was curious to hear her reasons for betraying me so I let her rant some more before I put an end to it.

"You think you're supposed to have Shane and EL? Nah Chass, it don't work like that. Coming up in here like your shit don't stink."

"Well at least it don't smell as bad as yours you fucking hoe! You gotta be the most scandalous bitch I've ever come across. You played me trick. All this time I thought you were my girl. Now look at you. Tay been dead for like five minutes and you already throwing your pussy at EL! You knew he could walk and you kept that shit from me!"

"You damn right I knew he could walk. How else could he fuck me if he was paralyzed!"

"I'ma fuck you up bitch!" I lunged for her throat again, but EL held me back.

"Get your hands off me you lying muthafucka!" I managed to get one of my hands loose and punched him in the face.

"Chass just calm down and let me talk to you. Can I talk to you?" he asked, stumbling from the blow I just dealt.

"Fuck you nigga! Now I know why George was looking at me like I was turning colors. You wasn't expecting me until tomorrow!"

"Fuck her EL! Shit, don't beg her ass. You might as well tell her the truth now. You want me to tell her," she dared like she was trying to force his hand.

Judging by the look on EL's face it was clear to me what Sara was pushing for him to tell me. I said it before he had a chance to.

"So you were never paralyzed huh?"

He hung his head in shame. "No."

"Well this shit just gets better and fucking better. What about Valerie?"

"She's a former colleague of mine."

"Is that right? And not a physical therapist."

This is some real soap opera shit here, I thought as I stood there in shock and my urge to commit murder was steadily increasing. I felt so damn stupid. I gave up everything that mattered to me just to be there for EL. What a fool I was.

"I'm guessing your memory is still in-tact too then huh?"

He didn't respond. He just stood there looking pathetic.

"I can't believe this shit. So you faked paralysis and memory loss?" I turned to Sara, "And you went along with this shit huh. Y'all trifling muthafucka's deserve each other!"

Just to look at them made me sick to my stomach. I stormed off fighting the tears that seemed determined to show themselves. EL followed me.

"Chass," he called like he wanted to begin a conversation. I kept walking without pause as if there was anything he could possibly say that would make this pill easier for me to swallow.

"Chass..." he called out again catching up to me in the guest room where I immediately started packing my shit.

"Wait a minute. Just let me talk to you."

"Wait...you can't be serious." I regained my composure then turned to face him. "Wait for what?"

"For me to explain."

"Fuck you EL! Fuck you and the horse you rode in on! You can walk *and* you remembered that I broke up with you the night of the accident!"

"Of course I remember Chass. Like I could ever forget what you did to me!"

"So this is my payback right. Using my best friend to get back at me. You are one real special son-of-a-bitch EL! I can't believe I actually felt sorry for your no-good ass! I gotta give it to you though you're good."

"I'm good," he repeated spitefully. "Chass you're the keeper of secrets," his tone dripping sarcasm as he *walked* towards me. "Who are you most mad at? Me or yourself? Think about it Chass. You set this whole situation in motion when you decided to play me for a sucka."

This muthafucka! No the fuck he didn't! He got my best friend in his bed while he's standing here butt-ass naked under that robe throwing the blame on me.

"I felt guilty because of the way I hurt you. Most of all I felt horrible about you being in that wheelchair. I blamed myself for the accident. Had I been honest with you about me and Shane from the beginning, we probably wouldn't be in this situation right now, but that's on me. You lying, pretending to be paralyzed and sleeping with my best friend is on YOU."

I felt like I'd just been thrown in the middle of a movie. I lost the man I love because I felt obligated to stand by EL. My emotions just flooded me all of a sudden and I couldn't fight it anymore. My eyes began releasing tears against my permission. I quickly turned away from EL. I wasn't about to let him see me cry. I wouldn't give his ass the satisfaction. I threw the last of my things into the suitcase and headed for the door when he grabbed my arm. I jerked it away so hard that it hit the wall.

"I thought I told you not to fucking touch me! What are you retarded!" I yelled.

"Just give me five minutes Chass. That's all I'm asking."

"Five minutes my ass. Fuck you!" I headed for the door again.

"You can at least hear me out Chass. You're no innocent." He followed behind me like I was a flight risk. "I know you're probably not going to believe me, but I didn't fake memory loss. When I woke up in the hospital, I

177

didn't remember what happened. It wasn't until later that my memories resurfaced."

I turned around. "How much later?"

"A few days after I came home from the hospital." His low tone of voice confirmed the shame he was feeling.

"A few...did you just say...a few days..."

"I was hurt Chass," he said cutting me off.

"I'm not saying I wasn't wrong EL, but no matter what I did, I never set out to purposely hurt you."

"What do you call cheating on me?"

"I call it finding a man who had time for me. A man who appreciated me and didn't take me for granted."

"You think that's what I did."

"I know it is otherwise I never would have been unfaithful to you. I tried to make it work with you EL, you know I tried. But that damn firm was more important than any chance we had. Shane was there. He had time for me. He made me feel special. Something I wasn't getting from you."

"So why not leave me? Why stay if you knew you wanted to be with him?"

"I was trying not to hurt you."

"Good job Chass. Good job." His sarcasm was evident.

"Fuck you EL! You used the one person who you knew meant the world to me. But, you couldn't have done this without me. My conscious is what made it easy for you. You knew that I still cared about you and that I would never leave you if I thought you really needed me. What better way to accomplish that than to pretend to be paralyzed. You played the only card you had left to play—the guilt card. And me losing Shane, well that was just the icing on the cake? But, I see you're not short on greed because even that wasn't enough for you. There's a special place in hell for twisted muthafucka's like you EL! Now move the fuck outta my way. I gotta get the hell outta here!" I walked towards the door again.

"Chass I made a mistake. I can admit that, but I won't lie and pretend I'm not happy that you're not with Shane."

"Of course you're happy EL. You got exactly what you wanted. Let me tell you something I may not be with Shane, but I damn sure will never be with you again! Talking about you made a mistake...Yeah right. Which one? You made so many I lost count. Was it the one when you pretended to be paralyzed to get me to feel sorry for you or the one when you tripped fell, and accidently stuck your dick in Sara! You standing here in your robe begging and tryna explain because you made a mistake. Yeah right. You're so full of shit! You and that trifling bitch deserve each other. Tell her I said thank you! She did me a favor—she took you off my hands!"

"What the hell is that supposed to mean Chass?"

178

He stood there with a stupid-ass look on his face. I just had to stick it to EL. He just looked so pitiful. So, I felt it was my duty to ease his mind, and let him know that everything was everything.

"It means...it's all good. I ain't mad." I looked him in the eye then gestured toward his bedroom. "If you like it, I love it!" I smiled as I walked out the door slamming it behind me.

This stupid muthafucka had the nerve to tell me he made a mistake. And, my dumb-ass actually stood there listening to him spew that bullshit. I honestly don't know how I stayed in that damn penthouse as long as I did without killing his ass.

As I scurried down the hall to the elevator, EL's door popped opened.

"You never told me how you got in here Chass. I thought you said you lost your access card. Did George let you in?" he asked, standing in the doorway tightening his robe.

An access card? You can't be serious. That's what you're chasing me down for? You got bigger problems than that dude. You and that bitch in there should consider yourselves lucky. Shit, I coulda been looking at double homicide, I thought as I dug in my bag and pulled out the key card.

"I thought I did lose it. Funny how I happened to find it at the bottom of my purse and apparently not a moment too soon," I sarcastically implied. I threw the card at him. "Lose my number muthafucka!"

I did a good job at hiding my feelings, but I was devastated. I couldn't believe how easy it was for Sara to betray me. She didn't show any signs of remorse. She wasn't ashamed, and she didn't seem to care that our friendship ended the minute she decided to take part in EL's revenge against me. She sat up in the bed, back leaned against the headboard, with a wicked smirk on her face like she was proud of herself. Like she didn't have a damn thing to answer for. If somebody woulda told me that Sara could do this to me, I woulda argued them down. This shit hurt me to my soul. When I looked at Sara all I saw were all the years we'd known each other. Since we were six years old we were down for each other. We invented the phrase *"ride or die"*. Sara wasn't just my best friend—she was family. Countless nights we stayed up gossiping until the wee hours of the morning about our relationships and bouncing advice back and forth between each other.

All the years we'd known each other.
All the things we'd done together.
All the places we'd been together.
All the things we'd seen together.
All that we'd meant to each other.
Every memory that I had, Sara was in it.
Everything I'd done, Sara did it with me.

I felt like somebody ripped my heart out and handed it to me. Not only was I betrayed, I was vulnerable too. I loved her. That's what made me so vulnerable. My love for Sara is what made the pain so crippling. I started to go back into EL's bedroom a bunch of times and wale on Sara; beating her ass into a coma. But, I didn't. As much as I wanted to knock her trifling-ass into next year, I couldn't do it. I couldn't bring myself to put my hands on her. As mad as I was I realized that beating Sara's ass wouldn't cancel what she did, although it would provide some satisfaction, it wouldn't make me feel any less betrayed.

EL knew how close Sara and I were, but he didn't care. She was a way to get back at me; a means to an end for him. Sara was the perfect piece to his plan. How could I have missed it? I guess I was more focused on his 'so called' injuries than his actions. I hurt him so he hurt me. Pay back really is a bitch! I probably should have expected that EL would retaliate, just not like this. But, Sara was the one whose betrayal hurt me to my soul. She was the one who threw away our friendship. It was her actions that tore me open and left me bleeding out. She betrayed me like it was nothing and she had the nerve to flaunt it in my face like she was proud of what she'd done. The worst part was that I couldn't think of a single thing I could have done to her that would justify her doing what she did to me. In the end our friendship didn't mean a damn thing to her. I guess I'll never know why Sara did me dirty, but there was only one reason why EL fought so hard to make me suffer—Shane.

28

Jail Visit

Shane

"It's good to see you dawg," Barkim said, as he took a seat directly across from me in the prison visitin' room.

"I wish I could say the same Kim."

"What'chu mean man?" He looked at me confused.

"What made you do it Kim? What made you set me up man?"

"What'chu...talkin'...'bout... man?" Nigga started stutterin'.

"I'm talkin' 'bout this nigga." I held up a copy of a bank statement showin' a deposit of a hundred thousand dollars. The deposit was made a week before the drop. The account was in the name of Belinda Brown—Barkim's moms.

"By the look on your face I'm guessin' you thought I wouldn't find out Kim."

"That's nothin' man. My mom's made a few investments and them shits paid off. That's all that is," he replied, unable to look me in the eye.

"You think I'm stupid Kim!" I rose from my chair knocking it down behind me. "This how you wanna play it man!"

I was ready to straight up bust this nigga in his head and walk out of the prison leavin' his ass sittin' there bleedin'. Loyalty wasn't optional in my camp—it was mandatory. "Keep lyin' to me Kim and you will be dead before I step into the parkin' lot!"

"Everything alright over here?" This short stubby prison guard walked up to where we were seated and asked.

"Yeah everything's cool," Barkim answered, nervous as hell.

Satisfied, the guard walked off. I picked up my chair and sat back down.

"You better start tellin' me the fuckin' truth Kim. You don't wanna lie to me right now man. You helped them ma'fuckas didn't you. I got the proof right here." I held up the piece of paper again. "You told them about the drop. That's how they knew where I would be and when. You just didn't expect Tay to go in my place. You let him walk right into an ambush Kim. I bet you ain't even warn him. You just let the shit go down."

"A'ight man listen," he pleaded. "I ain't have a choice man. These cats are well connected. Crazy paper was bein' tossed around for your life man. They threatened my family man—my family! What was I supposed to do?"

"Warn me nigga that's what! You coulda told me what was goin' down and you know I woulda made sure your family was protected. But, nah you rolled on me. You were supposed to be my boy!"

"Shane...listen to me man...they said they was gonna kill my family. I ain't have a choice man."

"Who was it Kim? Who paid you to set me up?"

"I don't know. I spoke to this one dude over the phone."

"Barkim don't fuckin' play me nigga! That shit don't even sound right!"

"I'm tellin' you the truth Shane. I don't know who it was. They gave me instructions over the phone."

"You recognize the voice?"

"Nah man."

"How'd you get the dough then?"

"It was left in an abandon building on East Tremont."

"So these niggas is from The Bronx?"

"Nah man. I ain't trust them niggas so I told them to leave the money there. I staked the place out for two days before I even went to get it."

"A'ight so who pulled the trigger?"

He shook his head. "I don't know man."

"You lyin' Kim! You was at the warehouse when the shit went down. I know you saw somethin'."

"I didn't see shit man. It was dark and everything happened so fast. I only remember seein' two big wrestlin' lookin' niggas right before me and Tay went inside the warehouse, but I can't say if they did the shootin' and I never saw their face."

"A'ight Kim I'll tell you what, as long as you locked up I won't fuck wit'chu. But, if you happen to beat these charges I can't promise how long you gon' live man."

"What'chu...sayin'... Shane?" he stuttered.

"You know what it is nigga."

"Shane...don't do this man. They threatened my family. My back was up against the wall!"

"I'm givin' you a choice Kim. Call Michaels and tell him you changin' your plea. Otherwise all bets are off."

"Changing my plea?"

"Yeah nigga what you think?"

Come on Shane...You know I can't be in no cage man. I can't be locked up. I'm claustrophobic. I can't be in no cell man."

"Your timin' is all fucked up. You shoulda thought about that shit before you rolled on me Kim. You think I give a fuck about you bein' locked up after what you did to Tay? You should be grateful you still breathin' nigga. If you was anybody else you woulda been dead before you even got processed.

182

But since we go way back I'ma let you live. I'll be satisfied wit'chu doin' a twenty year bid."

"Twenty years?" Nigga looked like he was about to piss on his self.

"Yeah man Michaels says you lookin' at twenty years 'cause you know they gon' try and pin Tay's murder on you too. That shit won't be too hard 'cause you look guilty as hell Kim. Police found you wit' a dead body, a briefcase full of dough, and another full of coke. A first year law student can make those charges stick. Drug possession...murder...that's a lot of years Kim. At first I thought these niggas must be amateurs if they let you live. Either that or they wasn't worried 'bout your punk-ass. But I knew there had to be a reason why you walked away from the hit. They needed somebody to take the fall for that shit. I already told Michaels to expect to hear from you about deadin' that not guilty plea. So don't waste your paper on a defense. It ain't worth it. Michaels is brilliant. He might fuck around and get you off and then...well you know what happens then."

"So you just gon' let me rot in here man?" he asked, like I owed him somethin'.

"It's either that or let you die. You choose 'cause I ain't got all day."

"I won't survive in here man. Once niggas find out what I did they gon' kill me man. These niggas got mad respect for you in here Shane. You like a legend to these ma'fuckas in here man. They won't think twice about takin' me out. So I ain't safe in here either."

I stood up. "Sounds like a personal problem to me man."

"So you just gon' let these niggas kill me man? You just gon' leave me in here to die!"

"You mean the way you let Tay die. Nah man I wouldn't do that to you. At least you know what's comin' so you can prepare yourself. That's more than you did for Tay nigga!"

"Shane, come on. Don't do this to me man. If I stay in here, I'ma dead man."

"You're a dead man if you get out."

I looked back at him right before I walked out of the visitin' room. That was the last time I saw Barkim. He was shanked in prison two weeks later.

29

Stuck on Chass

Shane

When I walked in X wit' Devona, I never expected to see Chass. But, there she was up in the spot; late night sittin' at a table wit' the twins. I was so nervous, I felt like a nigga wit' dirty piss at a parole appointment after findin' out that my PO was about to spring a surprise piss test on me. It was like I was caught out the way my heart was skippin' beats. Of course, I ain't have shit to be nervous about 'cause me and Chass been over for months. I knew it was a mistake to walk away from what we had, but I couldn't play the back no more. The whole time Chass and I were together I felt like I was playin' a supportin' role to that nigga's lead. That shit wasn't me. I don't do second fiddle. Chass' guilt made her feel obligated to stay wit' him, but in the end it didn't matter what her reasons were—she chose him. That shit damn near killed me, but I had to respect what she felt she had to do. I couldn't compete with Chass' guilty conscious. I had no choice but to accept it. So, I laid wit' chick after chick, just so I wouldn't have to feel shit. That only made it worse. None of them broads could make me forget about Chass. I just couldn't shake her.

As for Devona, I've been seein' her for about a week and I'm already tired of her ass. I looked her in the face real good the other night and realized that she ain't even all that fine. Now I know I'm slippin'. I feel like I traded a fox for a hound.

Chass tried to front like seein' me wasn't gettin' to her, but I saw it in her eyes every time I caught her lookin' at me—she still loved me. I tried to ignore her and pretend that I was enjoyin' Devona's company, but even I couldn't front like that. I wasn't in the club a half hour before I found myself makin' excuses to get at Chass without bein' obvious. When I peeped Chass walk outside, my heart was already behind her now my body just had to play catch up.

There goes my resistance–right out the fuckin' window.

"Order somethin'. I'll be right back," I told Devona just before I stepped away from the table. Chass was on the phone when I walked outside. I walked up behind her and tapped her shoulder.

"Long time no see."

She turned around. "Oh hi," Chass said givin' me a half smile. Then she continued with her phone conversation like I wasn't there. Chass knows that I can't stand bein' brushed off to the side and ignored. She was definitely workin' the hell out of those fingers of hers tryin' to push my buttons.

"What'chu doin' out here?" I asked, tryin' to make conversation.

Holdin' her phone in the air she snapped at me.

"I *was* talking. That is what these sleek little things are for right? To talk," she said with a tight grip on that attitude of hers while she waved her cell phone in the air.

Ignorin' her rudeness I asked, "So...how you been?"

"Minding my business," she replied, with no change in her tone.

"Yo Chass you need to chill wit' all that."

"Chill with all what?"

"I just came to check you. It's been a minute."

"You didn't have to come out here to see me Shane. You saw me as soon as you walked in the club with that trick on your arm. Not your usual flavor I might add. What happened? Getting desperate in your old age?"

Oh she got jokes. I grinned. "I ain't come out here for all that Chass. I just wanted to see how you doin'."

"That chick looks like she's getting impatient. You might wanna go see how she's doing. You need to go take care of that," she said, referring to Devona like she was some shit that I would need a prescription to get rid of. Her jealousy was eating her up and I loved every minute of it.

"Why are you out here Shane? Is there something I can do for you?" she asked, not lettin' go of that sarcastic tone of hers.

"I don't know why you comin' at me like that Chass. You know it don't have to be this way between us."

She laughed. "You're funny. You come up in the club with your girl on your arm, and then you come out here telling me how it shouldn't be between us."

"If this is how you act when you see me wit' another female then that should tell you somethin'."

"Oh really? Like what?"

"Like maybe you cut the wrong nigga off."

She sucked her teeth. "You think so?"

"You know you still want me or you wouldn't be sportin' your attitude like it's your new look. Stop tryin' to front."

"I don't have an attitude. Besides, it's not like I can go back and change things anyway."

"Like I said, it doesn't have to be this way."

"Why don't you tell me how it should be then Shane because from where I'm sitting you couldn't wait to fill your bed with the next bitch that squatted in front of you. Couldn't replace me fast enough huh?"

"Well, maybe you should stand up because shit can go over your head when you sit down."

"Is that supposed to be funny?"

"I'm just sayin' Chass; you don't know what's goin' on. I know you won't believe me, but that's not how it was."

Glancin' inside the club she said, "So...I guess that chick is posted up at your table waiting to take your order then huh?"

Chass was comin' at me hard. And although I wasn't lookin' forward to comin' up close and personal wit' her attitude, at least it was progress. I knew that if I pushed hard enough I would break down that wall she threw up between us.

"Nah, I ain't say that." I paused. "Why am I explainin' myself to you? Should it matter who I'm here wit'? I can't be wit'chu right?"

"I'm not even gonna go there with you Shane." She turned to walk away.

I reached out and grabbed her hand. "Where you goin'? Why are you always runnin' from me?"

"Who's running? I'm just going back inside."

"And away from me. Why?"

She turned her head refusing to look at me.

"See Chass somethin' is off. You been actin' real fucked up towards me since I came out here, and now you can't get away from me fast enough. What's up wit' that?"

"Nothing Shane. Just leave me alone." She tried to walk away again.

"C'mon Baby don't leave. Stay out here and talk to me."

I rubbed my fingers across her hand. The spark was still there. It was so strong. I know she felt it.

She rolled her eyes. "Baby," she repeated jerking her hand away. "I don't think you should be calling me that."

"Too many memories..."

"Something like that."

"Chass you all bent out of shape about me bein' here wit' Devona just admit it. That's why you throwin' me all this attitude."

"You're a grown man Shane. You can be with whoever you want. It's not my business who you fucking."

"Why you gotta go there? Me and Devona just cool. I used to throw her brother some work back in the day and we stayed cool. I just ran into her a couple weeks ago."

"You slept with her yet?" she asked, anticipatin' a *yes* from me.

"Come on now. I told you we just cool."

"I see you ain't answer the question."

"A'ight listen we hooked up, but it wasn't nothin'. I ain't tryin' to be wit' her like that." I was honest hopin' it would make her realize that I was bein' sincere.

"Like I said it's not my business."

"Chass just admit that you jealous because you still wanna be wit' me. No matter how much you try to front." I was feelin' myself a little. After I saw the jealousy in her eyes, I ran wit' it.

"Why would I be jealous Shane? We haven't been together in a long time. I expected you to live your life. Besides, she ain't nothing but another dumb-ass-bitch sitting up in the club waiting patiently until you come back and grace her with your presence. You got all these bitches so sprung they can't see straight. They act like you walk on water or some shit. Show me a man that can do that and I promise I won't say another word."

"Well...there was this one dude..." I said, tryin' to lighten the mood.

She smiled at me showin' off those deep dimples of hers. Then she covered her mouth like she was shy all of a sudden.

"Why you hidin' it?" I asked, starin' into her eyes.

"Hiding what?"

I reached over and moved her hand away from her mouth. "That smile. Damn, I ain't realize how much I missed it until now."

"You have?" she asked, like she was surprised.

"Of course I have Chass. Baby I can't stop thinkin' about you. I tried to get you out of my head, but it ain't happenin'. Whatever this is that I feel for you—the shit won't go away."

Chass was just as miserable without me as I was without her. She looked at me with so much love in her eyes, but before she could respond, Devona stepped in-between us.

"I got lonely in there waiting for you," she said spitefully, as she leaned in for a kiss. I moved my head before her lips could reach mine.

Yeah a'ight...Home girl think she slick. But, I got somethin' for her ass. I thought to myself fumin'.

Devona fucked up the vibe me and Chass had goin' and all the progress I made before she even opened her mouth. Chass looked like she was mad enough to chew bricks, and if she could spit fire I knew she wouldn't hesitate to burn a nigga up quick. Devona didn't know it yet, but she was gonna pay for this shit—like she had a chance in hell of keepin' me away from Chass.

I pulled Devona to the side. "Yo Vonnie I'm talkin' right now. Go back in the club a'ight. I'll be there in a minute."

"I didn't come here to watch you chase after some bitch Shane."

I tightened my jaw. "If you feel like I'm ignorin' you, I can put you in a cab so you ain't gotta worry about that no more."

She sucked her teeth and walked back inside the club. When I turned around Chass was gone. I stood outside X mad as hell wonderin' how I was gonna fix this shit. Just when I was gettin' Chass to open up to me Devona fucks up everything. I was on a mission. I needed to know if Chass still wanted to be wit' me. I saw it in her eyes, but as stubborn as Chass is, she would never admit it, at least not now. Now that I finally made some progress, I wasn't about to leave it alone. Too much was at stake for me to just say fuck it and go back to the way things were. Ironically Alicia Keys *No One* was playin' when I walked back inside X. I spotted Chass at the bar, but by the time I got there she was gone.

"What's up man?" I greeted my bartender while I looked around the club for Chass.

"What's going on Shane? What can I get you man?" he asked dryin' a glass while glancin' up at the flat screen.

"I need to know how many drinks the girl who was just sittin' here had."

"You talking about that Korean-looking chick with the mean body, gray eyes, and deep dimples."

"That's the one."

"Yo man, she's been on a binge since she got here. And, she just ordered another round before she stepped off. Since I saw her come in with her home girls I didn't say anything. I figured they would make sure she got home safe."

"Listen man if you ever see her in here throwin' 'em back like that again, call me a'ight. I don't give a fuck what time it is."

"A'ight man."

As soon as I turned to walk away Chass stepped up to the bar. "Looking for me?" she asked before she sat down.

"Why'd you leave like that?"

"Come on now Shane. You don't really expect me to answer that do you? I told you to check on your woman."

"And I told you she ain't my woman. Chass we were gettin' somewhere now you comin' at me with that attitude again."

"You mean before *your girl* interrupted." Her comment was bleedin' sarcasm.

"Here we go. I told you she ain't my girl—not even close."

She gave me the hand. "Look Shane, I refuse to be put in the middle of whatever you got going on with these bitches. I got enough problems."

"Ain't shit goin' on between me and her. If you don't believe me I will put her ass in a cab right now."

She glanced over at the table where Devona was sittin'. "She don't look like she ready to leave yet."

"I don't give a fuck about what she ready to do. Let's go some place so we can talk."

"That's not a good idea Shane. Please just go back to your table," she said almost like it hurt her to look at me. Then she looked over at Devona again. "You ain't never gonna change."

I leaned into her and whispered in her ear. "If anybody knows how much I changed it's you. It ain't over between us Chass, and you know I'm right otherwise me bein' here wit' Devona wouldn't bother you so much."

"You are really feeling yourself aren't you?" she snapped at me. Only because she knew I was speakin' the truth. She couldn't continue to deny what was between us.

"Why you keep throwin' me attitude and frontin' like you don't miss me? You up here wastin' time like we ain't done enough of that shit already. We have unfinished business between us Chass and you know it just as much as I do. I'm droppin' Devona off and I'm goin' to the brownstone. When you ready to talk call me."

When I got back to the table Devona was heated. I didn't give a fuck. The only thing I cared about was hopin' I made some type of impression on Chass. Devona could disappear and I wouldn't even notice. Chass got up from the bar and walked back to her table. Devona noticed the stares between me and Chass and tried to cop an attitude.

"Are you even gonna acknowledge my presence or are you just gonna stare at that bitch all night?"

"Get your stuff. Let's go."

She sucked her teeth, and then grabbed her purse from the arm of the chair. Devona and her attitude walked right out X wit' me before she could finish her vodka tonic. I definitely wasn't tryin' to spend the rest of the night lookin' in her face. I was in such a hurry to unload her ass that I broke at least ten traffic laws gettin' her back to her crib. When I pulled up in front of her building, she had this look on her face like she didn't recognize her spot.

"So I guess this is good night?" She looked at me like she wasn't ready to get out.

"Yeah, I got some shit to take care of."

She sucked her teeth then took her time gettin' out my ride like I had all night. Her leg was barely out the door when I sped off. Her chances of gettin' up wit' me again were dead. I headed for my crib prepared to face a night alone. Somethin' I hadn't had much practice wit' lately. As soon as I popped *Love & Basketball* in the DVD player, the phone rang.

"Yeah."

"Talk…I'm listening." It was Chass. Hearing her voice improved my mood quick.

"Not over the phone. You gon' let me come get you."

"Are you sure your girl won't mind?"

"Can I come get you or what?"

"Where you taking me?"

"Any place you wanna go?"

"How about City Island. I have a taste for sea food."

"City Island it is. Where are you?"

189

"I'm at my mother's."

"A'ight. I'll be there in ten minutes. Be downstairs."

I jetted out of the brownstone like it was one fire. I was anxious to know what the deal was wit' Chass and why she was up in X drinkin' like a fish. I got to her Moms crib in what seemed like record time, and her sexy-ass was waitin' downstairs just like I asked.

The restaurant was semi-empty, so we had our pick of tables. Chass had somethin' heavy on her mind. I could tell. After spendin' the first few minutes talkin' about nothin', I tried to get it out of her. Just as it looked like she was about to open up and tell me, the fuckin' waiter had to come to our table right then wit' the food. He started rearrangin' everything on the table to make room for our lobster and crab legs. I felt like kickin' that nigga in his fuckin' balls. That shit made me so mad I almost lost my appetite.

Chass said she was hungry, but she barely touched her food. Somethin' was up, but I knew she wasn't about to open up to me in the restaurant, which meant I was ready to go. There were too many distractions anyway. So, I took her some place quiet.

"Why did we come here?" she asked, as I opened the door to the loft. The expression on her faced changed once we stepped inside.

"Because I thought it would be a good place for us to talk. I noticed you didn't do much of that in the restaurant."

"You didn't change a thing. This place looks exactly the way it did the last time I was here."

"I didn't see any reason to. It's not like I come here."

"You don't?"

"Nah, why would I? This was our spot and without you there was no reason for me to come here."

I peeped how Chass kept lookin' around the loft. I could see in her eyes that bein' back at the place that meant so much to us was deeply affectin' her—which is exactly what I wanted to happen. I wanted her to remember how good we were together.

"I hope bein' here isn't a problem," I said, noticin' how uncomfortable she was startin' to look.

"It's not," she replied walking toward the window.

"Are you sure? Because if it's a problem for you we can go someplace else."

"Oh please Shane. I wasn't born yesterday." She looked at me like she just figured me out.

"I don't know what'chu mean."

"Come on Shane don't look at me like that. Isn't this the reaction you were hoping for? You bought me here to torture me right?"

"Torture? Nah, Baby of course not. Is it really torture for you to be here?"

"Look at you pretending like you didn't know how I would react when you knew damn well what it would do to me being back here. Just admit it. You bought me here to get a reaction out of me. Am I right?"

"Is it workin'?"

"See, I knew you bought me here to get me to reminisce on all the good times we had."

"Ooooooooh so you do remember what it was like bein' wit' me?"

"Like I could ever forget," she mumbled, thinkin' I didn't hear.

"Remember how it felt every time we were together?" I crept up behind her, my breath huggin' her neck.

Gazin' out of the window she replied, "I remember."

"Remember how good we were together?" I whispered, wrappin' my arms around her waist huggin' her from behind.

"Uh-huh."

"Remember all the times we made love right here in this spot." I pointed to the leopard rug on the floor in front of the fire place.

She turned to face me, her eyes glazed. "Of course I remember Shane. Did you think I would ever forget the happiest time in my life?"

"I just thought you might need a little remindin'."

"Well I don't!" Her attitude was back.

"Why you keep fightin' me every step of the way? I know you feel the same way I do."

She walked over to the couch and sat down. "Damn, Shane why you gotta come at me like this? I was just starting to accept that what we had is over."

"We are nowhere near over Chass. We will never be. That's what you need to accept, I have."

"So you expect us to just pick up where we left off."

"I don't see no reason why we can't. I hear you finally served that nigga his walkin' papers. There is nothin' stoppin' us from bein' together now Chass."

She placed her head in her hands and sighed. "A lot has happened since the last time I saw you."

"Talk to me. Let me know what's goin' on."

She shook her head, "It still hurts to talk about."

"Chass, I wanna know what got you lookin' like this Baby talk to me."

"I can't tell you."

"Yes you can. You know you can tell me anything."

She looked at me with so much pain in her eyes. "I caught Sara with EL."

"What'chu mean you caught Sara wit' EL?" I needed her to clarify that.

"I walked in on them having sex."

"Nah Baby don't tell me that shit. I know the nigga ain't go out on you like that and wit'cha girl!"

"He damn sure did! You shoulda heard Sara. Talking 'bout some "Tell her EL. You want me to tell her." Oooh I wanted to rip her fucking head off!"

"Damn Baby."

"Sara wanted me to find out about her and EL. Maybe not when I did, but she was definitely gearing up to spring it on me. EL was faking everything Shane; being paralyzed, memory loss, all of it just so he could keep me away from you."

"Damn the nigga went hard like that? When did all this happen?"

"A few weeks ago."

"That's fucked up Baby. I'm sorry to hear that."

"You knew something was up from the beginning didn't you? That's why you kept saying that he crashed on purpose."

"I had a feelin' that the nigga was makin' more of it than what it was, but I never thought he would do no shit like this. I definitely ain't see this comin'."

"Neither did I."

"I never did like that cat. It wasn't just because he had you. There was something about his ass that I couldn't rock wit'. I can't get over ya girl though. I knew she was fucked up behind what happened to Tay, but to go out on you like that."

"I wanted to kill her ass when I saw that shit. She actually went along with EL's lies. I've known that chick since I was six years old and I never knew she was so scandalous. I mean I knew she had it in her because I've seen her do this shit to so many other chicks but..."

"But...but what? You never thought she would do it to you?"

"It's not about EL. We weren't together like that. I was only there trying to help him. Sara was right when she said I was only there *playing* nurse."

"Damn she said that. She was really tryin' to dig into you."

"Well, she succeeded. I don't care that she was sleeping with EL. What I can't get over is her keeping his secrets. Sara knew how I felt about you and what it cost me to be there for EL. She knew he could walk and she never said a word. She watched me stick by him through therapy, rehabilitation, all of it and the whole time she knew he never needed any of it."

"Damn Baby. You didn't hurt her did you?"

"No...I couldn't. Don't get me wrong, I wanted to knock that bitch into next week, but I couldn't do it. Every time I looked at Sara, all I saw was the love I felt for her. It was fucked up that she went out on me like that, but it is what it is. I guess I got what I deserved. I did cheat on EL for years with you."

"Baby don't say that. You didn't deserve for ya' girl to do that shit to you. That was some straight fucked up shit right there. I know we did our dirt, but you never set out to hurt nobody. Why you ain't call me. You know I woulda been there for you."

"I couldn't call you. Not after what I did. I chose EL over you and I will never forgive myself for that."

I picked up her hand and slid my fingers in-between hers. "Baby I would do anything for you. Don't you know that? I ain't gon' front that shit you fucked my head up, but I never stopped lovin' you Chass."

"I'm so sorry I hurt you Shane. I will regret that for the rest of my life." She cried on my chest.

"Don't sweat it Baby. It's all good. You did what you thought was right. Your intentions were good."

She lifted her face from my chest and looked at me with watery eyes. "Yeah, well the road to hell is paved with good intentions."

"Maybe this had to happen for you to see them for who they are. As fucked up as that was somethin' good did come out of it."

She wiped her eyes. "Like what?"

"We can be together now Baby."

"Shane...I...I can't. Not after what I did to you."

I softly stroked her face as I looked into her pretty grey eyes. "I don't think you been listenin' Baby. I can't get over you. Believe me I tried to move on. Now unless I'm misreadin' signals, I thought you felt the same way."

"I can't get hurt again and I would never forgive myself if I hurt you again."

"Baby you know I would never hurt you. I would die before I hurt you." I held her face in my hands as I wiped her tears with my finger. "There ain't nothin' standin' in our way now Baby. I love you. That will never change."

"I love you too Shane. I never stopped. I couldn't even think about you with someone else. When I saw you with that chick tonight my heart sunk. I thought you moved on."

"Nah, just the opposite. I was stuck Baby. I couldn't move on. Those women ain't mean a thing to me. I mean, I cared for them, but they were just helpin' me pass the time. My head was fucked up and I didn't wanna feel nothin' so I just did whatever I had to do to get through the day."

"I have to know something," she said with an odd tone in her voice.

"A'ight. What is it?"

"Why did you make me choose between you and EL? That was the hardest decision I ever had to make."

"Baby you left me no choice. I had to. You had me in an impossible position. I knew you was never gonna let that nigga go until you worked out all the guilt you had goin' on. So I had to let you do you. I just couldn't play the back no more. I tried to front, but it fucked me up every time you left me to be by his side."

193

"I was just trying to be there for him."

"My head knew that, but my heart wasn't tryin' to hear it. My pride just wouldn't let me accept the fact that you still cared about him. Forgive me if I read too much into it, but you did walk away from me so you could be there for him."

"I know and I am soooo sorry about that. I hope you can forgive me," she said, with sadness in her voice.

"Of course I forgive you. I'm not holdin' onto that shit no more Chass. I want you wit' me. I definitely don't wanna waste no more time. I want you to move in wit' me."

She looked surprised. "You want me to what?"

"I want you to move in wit' me. Why you sound so shocked Baby?"

"Don't you think that's rushing things a little bit?"

"Nah, I don't. Not after all the time we wasted already. It's been months since we've been together Chass. It's time to do us."

"But, living together...that's a big step Shane."

"You sound like you ain't wit' it Baby."

"It's not that. I just think it's too much too soon. After seeing you with that girl tonight, I don't think you're ready to take that step."

"I know what I want, and that's you. It's always been you. Baby if I was still tryin' to live like that I wouldn't ask you to move in wit' me. I'm done wit' that lifestyle. I was done the minute I fell in love wit'chu. I wanna settle down wit'chu and I'm hopin' you want the same thing."

"I do, but..."

"Cool," I anxiously said not hearin' the but.

"Shane, you didn't let me finish."

"My bad Baby ga' head."

"I have a condition," she said, smilin' at me. I knew then that her answer was yes, but I waited for her to tell me her condition.

"A condition...Oh yeah and what's that?" I smiled back at her.

"You have to keep a full stock of Baileys at all times, and that's not negotiable. The minute you run out, I'm packing my bags," she joked.

My smile got real wide, "Done...Anything else?"

"Should there be?" she replied, with a sexy grin.

Damn, I love the shit outta this girl.

"Nah there shouldn't." I stood up. "You ready?"

"Ready for what?" she asked, lookin' up at me from where she was sittin'.

"To go get your stuff, before you change your mind."

She blushed. "You won't get rid of me that easy."

"I wasn't plannin' on it." I winked at her.

30

Upgrade U
Chass

Shane didn't waste any time moving me in. He dropped me off at my mothers so I could pack then came back a few hours later in his Escalade minus two rows of seats, and he had PK with him. They complained every minute of the three hours it took them to move my things from my mothers fifth floor apartment and into Shane's truck.

"Damn Chass, you got more clothes than a fuckin' model. What's up with this?" Shane asked, while PK was co-signing.

"That's my word. I ain't never seen no shit like this before Chass. Fuck you do, shop all day?" PK asked, hauling two boxes into the elevator.

After Shane and PK finished loading my things into the Escalade, Shane and I headed for the highway. Once we exited I-80, we drove down this long road filled with beautiful three and four-story homes. The massive stone-bricked colonials were sitting stoically on acres of land secured by iron gates showing off the immaculate landscaping. Each home with your pick of lavish cars that filled the driveways was a sight to see.

There is no way he lives over here. This must be a short cut. I thought, as I sat impatiently awaiting to arrive at our destination.

We turned into a long driveway, and then we drove up to the entrance of this magnificent estate. The lavish three-story stoned mini mansion sat beautifully behind a ten-foot high fancy iron white gate surrounded by several acres of land. Shane punched a code into the keypad, and the gate opened. The fountain centered in the middle of the circular driveway really set the place off. The house was beyond beautiful. It looked like one of the homes you'd see on The Lifestyles of the Rich and Famous—it was like that. Shane's house made EL's penthouse look like a basement apartment.

I needed a reality check. I couldn't believe a brother could live like this. The sparkling marble floors were so shiny it was like looking in a mirror. Covering the walls were the most spectacular pieces of black art that I'd ever seen. It gave the place some real flavor. To the right of the foyer was the library. The mahogany wood shelves protruding from the walls were stacked with a large selection of law books and journals. The massive two-story family room with a vaulted ceiling, commanded my attention immediately. The authentic suede cream and mocha colored sectional was beautifully crafted with matching tables. My favorite part of the room was the three hundred gallon fish tank that was custom-built into the wall giving the room a relaxed peaceful feel. I stood in front of the tank and watched as the plump greedy goldfish swam to the top of the tank every time the automatic feeder dispensed drops of food.

While Shane gave me a private tour, I calculated the cost of everything in my head. Shane was doing it big. I figured he must have spent several thousand on the art alone. Then there were the uniquely crafted custom made furnishings with the lavish accents that attributed to each rooms design which was probably another several grand. Not to mention, the house itself had to cost at least three or four million—easy.

"You thirsty," Shane asked, walking towards the bar.

"I'll take some Bailey's if you have it," I told him, as I sunk down into the soft suede sectional and got comfortable.

He grabbed the bottle of Caramel Bailey's and started to pour. Handing me my drink he said, "I hope you bought your appetite wit' you? I'm havin' somethin' special prepared since it's your first night here."

Shane led me into the gourmet kitchen, which was a chef's dream. Built in the wall was a stainless steel triple oven. The uniquely L-shaped center island was half glass half granite marble. Built in the island was a stove range, which was covered with simmering pots. The aroma seeped into the range hood that hung vertically from the ceiling directly over the island. The Red Snapper stuffed with collard greens, okra, mushrooms, carrots and onions smothered in a savory garlic and herb sauce simmering over the brown rice made my mouth water. The aroma dominated the kitchen leaving my nose paralyzed.

"How did you..."

"Before you even ask, I called Carlotta and she prepared all this," he explained just as a tiny Latin woman exited the pantry.

"Carlotta?"

"Baby this is Carlotta, Carlotta this is Chassidy. Chassidy will be livin' here now."

"Hi do chu do Ms. Chassidy. Bleasure to meet chu." The tiny woman extended her hand to me. "Mr. Chane talk about chu all tha time."

I glanced over at Shane who seemed slightly embarrassed.

"Well, I hope it wasn't anything too bad," I smiled at her.

"No, no, no bad at all. Mr. Chane adore chu Ms. Chassidy. He neva say anyting bad about chu. I work fa Mr. Chane lotta years and him neva bring woman to tha house before today," she said, walking to the oven to remove the peach cobbler. Then she reached into the refrigerator and grabbed the banana pudding.

She must be one hell of a cook because her English is horrible. I thought, as I watched the tiny woman make her way around the huge kitchen.

Shane and I dined on the patio over-looking the lovely in-ground pool surrounded by fountains, as we enjoyed the crisp calm night air. As I sat across the table from Shane there was this question that was burning my brain so I just had to ask.

"Ok Baby I give up."

Shane took a sip of his drink then put his glass down on the table and gave me a blank stare. "Give up?"

"You got me curious."

"About?"

"Why after all these years of being with me did you not only bring me to your house, but move me in."

"I had to make sure that I could trust you."

"And after three years you still wasn't sure?"

"You could say I still needed some convincin'."

"How do you feel now?"

He smirked. "Well Baby you wouldn't be here if I still had doubts. I needed to know that you wanted to be wit' me and not because of what I could buy you and how large I could have you livin'."

"Is that why you never brought any other girls here?"

"That's one of the reasons. Those broads stayed wit' dollar signs in their eyes. Those chicks were money hungry and lookin' for a come up. All they wanted was to run through my dough. I knew what they were all about from day one."

"Don't sell yourself short Shane. I'm sure it wasn't just about the money." I smiled at him.

He smiled back at me. "I'm sure it wasn't. I'm just sayin'. I can spot a trick a mile away."

"I could be a trick. How would you know?" I teased.

He laughed. "Nah, you ain't. I know everything there is to know about you Baby. Trust me. I know that you ain't in it for the dough."

"Seriously though you don't think that you are being just a little paranoid?"

He shook his head. "Not at all. I ain't never been comfortable wit' too many people knowin' where I lay my head. Especially in the business I'm in. The same shit applies to the people who work for me. They know where my brownstone is. That's good enough. And, if it wasn't it was gon' have to be."

"You must trust Carlotta otherwise she wouldn't be here."

He chuckled. "Baby if only you knew all the shit I put her through before I officially hired her. Shit, I'm surprised she stuck around. She been wit' me for about eight years. She loyal. I ain't never gotta worry about her."

After we ate we made ourselves comfortable in the family room where we watched *2 Fast 2 Furious* on the plasma that was centered directly over the stoned fire place. We got comfortable in each other's arms and fell asleep.

I was living like a rock star. I had the man of my dreams, living in a mansion on a magnificent estate, all the money I could spend, my pick of cars to drive, and Shane was blessing me every night with mind blowing sex. I never thought I could be this happy.

I was lying across the bed flipping through the pages of *In Style* magazine, when the phone rang. Glancing at the caller ID, I picked up the phone with a smile.

"Hey you," I answered, in my grown and sexy voice.

"Damn Baby, what'chu tryin' to do? Give a nigga a heart attack answerin' the phone like that!"

The sound of Shane's voice always made the butterflies in my stomach get butterflies in their stomachs. He just had that kind of effect on me.

"What'chu got on?" he asked, throwing his grown and sexy back at me turning me on like a faucet.

"Why don't you hurry your ass home and find out."

"Shit, you think I'm not. I'm gettin' off the highway right now. In the meantime why don't you give a nigga a hint?

"A hint...Ok I can do that. It's your favorite." Shane's favorite is always me butt-ass naked.

"Say word Baby you sittin' up in the crib like that and I ain't even there." I could tell he was smiling.

"Under this robe I am. So hurry up and come home. My pussy is poppin'."

"Yo Chass Baby I'm on my way. You 'bout to make a nigga go crazy thinkin' 'bout how good you must look right about now. Let me find out you tryin' to seduce me over the phone."

"Is it working?"

"Hell yeah it's workin'! My shit is hard as hell right now!"

Just as I lit the Aroma-therapy candles, I heard Snoop & Akon's *I Wanna Love You* as Shane was pulling his baby blue Bentley Coupe into the circular driveway. I ran to the window just as he was getting out of the car.

Front Door, the ADT alarm system voice indicator alerted me that he was in the house. I quickly slipped out of my robe and laid across the king-sized bed surrounding myself with pink long stem roses. I placed one of the stems in my mouth and waited for Shane to enter the bedroom. The speakers softly sang Marcus Houston's *Sex With You* when Shane walked into the room. His mouth hung open and his eyes lit up like a Christmas tree.

"Damn Baby you look amazin' layin' there like that. You almost made me crash the coupe tryin' to hurry up and get here."

He hurried out of his clothes and eased into the bed. Then he gently slid his tongue between my legs speaking directly to my clit sending me into a state of undeniable ecstasy. We made love for hours. Our numerous orgasms soaked the sheets. I squatted between his legs and slipped his dick in my mouth.

"Chill Baby," Shane said damn near out of breath.

"You soft, so I'm gonna get it back up."

"Go easy on me Baby. I can't fuck wit'chu right about now. Give a nigga a minute. Damn what'chu tryin' to do to me?"

Damn I got skills, I thought to myself as I watched my ferocious Tiger turn into a tamed pussy cat right before my eyes.

"You're not gonna need a minute by the time I'm done," I said eyeing his dick like it was a briefcase full of cash. Just thinking about how good Shane feels inside of me was motivation enough for me to put the oil back in his engine. I ignored his pleas for rest, scooted under the covers, and went to work. Within seconds his dick was standing up in my hands.

31

Cayman Islands
Chass

"Damn you sexy as hell Baby come here," Shane said, looking at me lustfully as I walked out of the bathroom in nothing more than a towel. He was sitting on the edge of the bed gesturing for me to come to him.

"I'm takin' you away for about a week. It's been a while since I spoiled you." He grabbed me by my hips and placed me in-between his legs.

"Where we going?" I asked, excited by the invitation.

"I'm surprising you. All I can tell you is you ain't gotta pack nothin'."

He rose from the bed to grab his cell that was vibrating on the dresser. After his phone conversation, he left to take care of some business. He said he would be back in a few hours and told me to be ready. I was sitting at the vanity doing my hair when the phone rang.

"You ready?" Shane asked.

"You know I am. You told me not to pack anything so all you get is me."

"Baby, that's all I need," he responded, in his usual flirtatious way.

"How long before you get here?" I asked, wondering how much longer he planned on keeping me in suspense.

"Look out the window."

I walked to the window and pulled the curtain back just as Shane was driving up. Trying to hide my surprise I said, "You're early. I guess your business didn't take as long as you expected."

"Nah, Baby we good. Now I can focus all my attention on you."

"You still not gonna tell me where you taking me."

"Nope, you just gon' have to be patient a little while longer Baby. I know its gon' be hard, but you can do it."

Once Shane and I arrived at the airport we were escorted to a private landing strip where the private jet that Shane chartered was waiting for us to board. After spotting Russell Simmons boarding a similar jet, I knew this was big business. Shane's status was off the freaking charts. Everywhere we went people treated him like a celebrity.

The jet set 2008 Series was definitely a baller's special. If you weren't holding major paper then you might as well hop your ass on a commercial flight and call it a day. This was strictly for top dogs. I knew it was some real top-notch shit when my elbow accidently pressed a button on the armrest and some chick came out with a towel and some oils talking about a massage. We were treated like the President and the First Lady.

The accommodations were beyond my expectations. The bathroom was tiled from floor to ceiling complete with Jacuzzi, full-length shower, and a lighted vanity. Even the pilot had his own private accommodations. The food and beverage bars were stacked with your pick of finger foods, fresh fruit and plenty of bottled water, and iced tea. I snacked on strawberries and whipped cream while watching Tyler Perry's *Why Did I Get Married?* on the large plasma while flipping through a bunch of hair magazines anxious to know our destination. Shane spent the majority of the flight listening to his I-POD while playing video games on his cell.

"We're almost there Baby." Shane glanced at his watch after we'd been in the air for several hours. He wrapped his hand around mine and kissed it. "You're gonna love this."

"I'm sure you went all out. You always do." I winked at him and smiled.

Once we exited the jet and I saw the sign that read Owen Roberts International Airport, Grand Cayman, I damn near lost my mind. Shane planned everything carefully making sure nothing spoiled the surprise. He even had the flight announcements suspended during the flight just to keep me in the dark. Grand Cayman was one of my favorite places in the world. I tried to contain my excitement, but I couldn't. I screamed so loud I'm surprised that Airport Security didn't ask me to leave. I jumped on Shane wrapping both legs around his back hugging him tight enough to stop his blood from circulating. Shane arranged for an Escort to show us around the island giving us a guided tour to see the main attractions which were Queen Elizabeth Park, The National Museum, and Rum Point to name a few. The staff fell all over themselves for us like we were royalty. It was some straight kiss-ass shit.

The island was beyond gorgeous surrounded by beautiful blue water and pearly white sand. The villa was made up with cluster townhouses all along the beach resembling a small village that was surrounded by palm trees. The villa consisted of two levels. On the first floor there was the kitchen, living room, dining room, half bathroom, and on the second level there were two bedrooms, which included a balcony adjacent to the master bedroom complete with a full size bathroom, Jacuzzi and a separate shower. The bathroom alone was bigger than the average apartment. Thick plush carpeting was so soft it felt like you were walking on cotton. The furniture was made up of various types of sea prints such as sea shells, sea weed, lobsters and star fish matching the look of the island. The vaulted ceilings had sky windows encased for natural sunlight. The most magnificent ceiling fans that were made of straw and shaped like flowers; hung low complimenting the rooms giving them that extra island touch. The air even smelled different. It was so fresh and clean like pollution didn't exist there. I watched as all the people splashed around in the beautiful blue water while others were running free across the pearly white sand.

This is the shit right here. This is the life.

"Are you ready to get in that water?" Shane asked, staring out at the beautiful beach as he stood beside me on the balcony.

"I think you may be forgetting something." I glanced down at my clothes. I didn't have a bathing suit or anything else to wear because Shane insisted that I not pack a thing. He even made me leave my small carry on in the car at the airport after realizing that I snuck it out of the house.

"And what would that be?" he questioned, with a smirk on his face like he knew something that I didn't.

"I just might need a bathing suit if we're going to the beach. I'm sure *Marc Jacobs* didn't design this for swimming."

"Nah, I'm sure he didn't. I think I saw a lil' shop on the tour that sells bathing suits. We can pick up one from there."

Just as we were approaching the door, Shane stopped suddenly.

"Oh shit I forgot my camera. Baby can you look in the hall closet and grab my camera bag? I definitely can't pass up an opportunity to take some pics. That body in a bathing suit...man we talkin' some serious flicks!"

As soon as I opened the closet doors bags and bags fell at my feet. There were clothes from all of my favorite designers.

"Oooooh nooooo you didn't!" I ran up to Shane and gave him a nice juicy kiss on the lips thanking him for the shopping spree that he took part in without me. He bought everything that I could possibly need and as always, he spared no expense.

He grabbed a handful of my ass then released it. "Hurry up and pick out somethin' to wear so I can show you off."

I sure hope to find some underwear in these bags, I mumbled under my breath as I felt my juices leak onto my soft silk panties. All of the excitement had me horny.

"When did you do all this?" I asked, staring at the numerous packages that were spread across the floor.

"When you were shopping, out wit'cha girls or whatever it is you chicks do when you don't want your man around."

"You just don't get enough of spoiling me do you?"

"Nah, Baby I can't help it. I love seein' the way your eyes light up whenever I buy you shit."

When I opened the *Gianni Versace* mini dress I was in love.

"That's you all day Baby," Shane watched me stare at the dress that I knew cost enough to feed a small country. "You gon' rock the shit out this!"

I held the soft fabric against my skin admiring the design.

"C'mon and pick somethin' out so we can get up outta here. I'm ready to make some Kodak moments."

My bathing suit of choice was the two-piece *Agua Bendita* bathing suit and judging by the way Shane was eyeing me—I knew I looked damn good in it. He ran his tongue across his lips and smiled.

"Ahhh that's it right there Baby. Just wait till we get back here."

"I guess that means you like huh?" I asked in a sexy tone of voice while I modeled in front of him.

"Damn straight! If you keep this up we won't make it to the beach!"

We stopped off at the restaurant that was directly in the door of the villa on the edge of the water to grab a quick bit to eat before hitting the beach. The restaurant sat under a huge canopy tent surrounded by beautiful white birds that flew low to the sand and walked very close to us. Not like the birds back home that would fly away at the first sign of movement.

I played with the soft sand in-between my toes while the calm wind blew against my skin. Shane stretched out on the sand snapping pictures of me in my sexiest poses and I made sure to catch him in all of his sexiness as well. As beautiful as our surroundings were they didn't have a damn thing on Shane. His gorgeous masculine frame surrounded by the clear blue water and pearly white sand had me mesmerized. I was eyeing his body like it was the first time I'd seen it. He looked so good with the sun beaming down on his sparkling caramel skin heightening the radiance of his emerald green eyes. Just saying that Shane is attractive doesn't do him a damn bit of justice—the man is a work of art.

We cuddled in our private canopy on the beach to block the sunset that beamed down on us while witnessing a wedding in the distance. As the sun disappeared into the clouds the lovely private beach was being overlooked by the stunning moonlight and becoming more secluded. Shane reached his hand in my bathing suit and began massaging the lips of my pussy. Then he slid his face between my legs licking his way to my goodies. Once his tongue reached my clit—it was over. He licked and sucked on my soft spot like it was his favorite piece of candy placating every nerve in my body and exploring it tremendously. I moaned fiercely as my body began to buck and my juices soaked his tongue. I gasped as he eased his thickness inside of me. I dug my lovely manicured nails into his back while enjoying his deep sensual strokes. His grunts grew louder as his strokes became more intense. As he let out pleasurable moans his warm cum shot into me like a water hose.

The moon substituted for the perfect night light while we listened to the waves as they poured against the sand allowing the Caribbean breeze to flow across our naked bodies. Once we were back at the villa I stepped onto the balcony to admire the view and lost myself in the moon light. The daytime view was stunning, but it didn't have shit on the view at night which was spectacular. The beach was calm and still. Not even a hint of what had taken place just a few hours earlier. I looked over my shoulder and noticed Shane standing in the doorway.

"Why are you standing way over there?" I asked, wondering why he hadn't walked onto the balcony to join me.

"I'm just admirin' the view."

"It is gorgeous," I agreed, as I looked over the balcony for the third time.

"Yes...*she* is." He walked up behind me and put his arms around me. I leaned my head on his chest as he spoke softly into my ear.

"I don't know what the hell you did to me, but the way I feel about you is insane. You're about to make me lose my damn mind."

"Ditto Baby," I turned to face him and slid my tongue in his mouth. We stared into each other's eyes realizing that we were both so gone.

**   **   **   **

"You ready for today?" Shane asked, just as I opened my eyes in time to catch a glimpse of his naked body right before he stepped into the shower.

"I'm almost afraid to ask," I replied, jumping out of bed and slipping into the shower behind him.

"Ok...you can come," he joked, closing the shower doors behind me.

Shane took me to a huge fish party that reminded me of a flea market except it was on the beach. The menu consisted of several different types of fish prepared any way you requested while you watched giving more of a personal feel to such a public display.

When evening hit Shane and I enjoyed the island's nightly jazz festival that was being held on the beach. The set up was simple yet elegant and stylish. The band members were dressed in silk slacks, colorful island shirts with unique seashell flip flops, earrings, necklaces, and bracelets made with seashells. As the band played the island girls danced in circles around them in their bikini top and skirts made out of straw. Shane and I danced the majority of the night while he held me close to him.

"Promise you won't ever leave me," he whispered, as he cuddled me in his arms. I followed him as he led the dance.

"I'm not going anywhere unless it's with you," I replied, softly looking up from his arms.

We welcomed the next morning on a mini yacht that was just as beautiful as the water it floated on. The boat usually consisted of about twelve people, but Shane wanted me all to himself so sharing me with twelve strangers was completely out of the question. Snorkeling was one of the island's best excursions. As soon as the boat floated into a nice little nook in between the caves and coral reefs the driver geared us up and gave us instructions. Our bodies floated in the shallow waters as we sunk our heads into the water and watched the colorful fish. Shane floated around like a pro but after a while sun bathing became more tempting to me and I ended up laying out on the deck sipping on rum punch. The views from the middle of the ocean were a sight to see. The ride was peaceful and surreal. The water was calm and still leaving no evidence of the large waves that visited earlier that day. Shane took plenty of pictures to savor every moment. We were leaned against the rail cuddled in each other's arms enjoying the night breeze.

"You feel that?" he asked, placing my hand on the center of his shorts.

"I see you brought your friend with you," I teased, as my hand found its way inside his shorts.

"Whenever you're around I can't get rid of his ass."

I caressed him until he couldn't hold out anymore.

He started unsnapping my shorts. "I want you Baby. Right here on this boat."

"What about the driver?"

"Don't worry about him. I hit that nigga off with enough dough that the only thing on his mind is what he gon' buy first. Trust that he ain't thinkin' 'bout us."

"You did all that? You must love this pussy huh?" I whispered, seductively in his ear as my hand strokes became more urgent.

"Do I! Shit, a nigga can't get enough," he anxiously replied. Then he pulled me into him ready to enter me.

"Let me take care of you," I ordered, taking control of the situation. "I want you to sit back and enjoy the ride."

"Do your thang Baby," Shane whispered, letting me know that he was at my mercy.

I squatted between his legs then I pulled his friend from his shorts and slowly licked the head of his penis allowing my tongue some playtime before I went all in. As the tip of his penis hit the back of my throat, the pre-cum oozed out creaming the back of my mouth. The taste of his sweet cum had my pussy dripping. I was so wet that I could swear I left a puddle on the floor of the boat. My jaws went into overdrive. I sucked him off like I was auditioning for a porno flick and Shane was most definitely reaping the benefits. His head was leaned back and his eyes were closed and from the expression on his face I had the shit down to a science. He squirmed as he gripped and tugged on the banister like it was running from him while he moaned in pure ecstasy.

The driver kept flashing us sideway glances while struggling to keep his attention on driving the boat. He was unable to ignore the fact that I was on my knees giving Shane the star treatment. His stares just fueled my excitement even more. Shane's body started to jerk as I sucked the shaft and caressed his balls while his cum filled my mouth. He laid me down on the floor of the boat and slid his tongue into my soaked opening devouring me like I was his favorite meal.

We crashed through the doors of the villa ripping each other's clothes off. I climbed on top of him and eased his dick inside me. He grabbed my ass and started rotating my hips as he stroked me. I opened my legs wider giving him complete access while he stroked deeper inside me.

"Wait...wait...wait...wait...I don't wanna cum yet...I don't wanna cum yet," he whimpered, as I clamped my vaginal muscles tightly around his thick dick. That shit drove Shane crazy. He squeezed my ass tighter as I rotated my hips to a hypnotic rhythm. Shane couldn't hold out any longer and exploded inside of me.

"AAAAAHHHHHH SHHHIIITTTT!" he called out as his warm semen filled my insides.

Shane took me in his arms. I rested my head on his chest listening to his heart beat like it was my favorite song.

"What'chu thinkin' about'?" he asked, watching me stare at the ceiling.

"Sometimes I feel like I'm gonna wake up and you won't be here," I admitted feeling like he was too good to be true.

"Baby, the way I feel about you, shit you ain't never gotta worry 'bout me goin' nowhere. Trust that a nigga ain't never felt like this before."

I lifted my head from his chest and looked him in the eye. "You never gave up on me Shane. You were like a dog with a bone," I said, referring to his persistence.

"I couldn't give up. I don't think you knew how deeply I felt for you, so I had to show you. Baby you are like a drug to me. Once I got a taste—I was hooked. There was no question that I had to do everything I could to get you. I ain't have a choice."

"But you even settled for things that I know a man like you would never normally do."

He grinned. "You got me on that one. I even surprised myself. But, if you want some shit you ain't never had before, you gotta do some shit you ain't never done before."

** ** ** **

I was sleeping comfortably in Shane's arms when his twists and turns woke me up. I looked up at him and noticed that he was wide-awake.

"You alright," I asked, rubbing his bare chest.

He sat up in the bed and pulled the covers across my back.

"There is something I have been wantin' to ask you, I just been waitin' for the right time."

I sat up. "What is it?" I anxiously asked, clinching the comforter nervously.

He got up from the bed and walked over to the chair where his silk robe laid and removed something from the pocket. Then he walked back over to the bed and sat down.

"Baby everything I am is in love with you. You're it for me. I wanna spend the rest of my life making you happy. You think you can let me do that?" he asked, staring into my eyes.

My heart was beating so hard and fast it felt like it was moving the sheets. I couldn't say a word. I just took a deep breath and nodded.

"Will you marry me Baby?" he asked, as he pulled out a black suede box and sat it on the bed in-between us.

"Open it," he requested, watching me stare at it.

When I opened the box and saw the ring, I thought it was the cutest little thing. The diamond was so small you would need a magnifying glass to see it. I didn't care about that. The man I loved more than anything else in this world was asking me to be his wife, I didn't give a shit about the ring or how big or small the diamond was. It was from Shane and that was all that mattered to me.

I smiled so bright it was like I was under high beams. I looked my man in his gorgeous green eyes and said, "Of course I'll marry you!"

The smile that spread across Shane's face could put clowns to shame. He rose from the bed, picked me up, and spun me around.

"Awww Baby...you just made me the happiest man in the world." He looked at me with a smirk on his face. "So you like the ring?"

"Of course I do. I love anything you give me."

Shane walked back over to the chair and came back to the bed with another black box and sat it on the bed right next to the other one.

"What's this?" I asked, puzzled.

"Open it and find out."

When I opened that box my eyes widened to the size of grapefruits. My first thought was OH MY GOD! "I love it! It is absolutely gorgeous!"

The Princess cut ten-carat solitaire diamond ring had a stunningly unique design with miniature diamonds of the same design protruding from the flawless platinum finish. I'd never seen anything like it in my life. The ring looked like it cost more than a couple Bentley's—it was that fly.

"I'm glad you like it Baby. It took my jeweler almost six months to design it."

"Like it...I love it!" I beamed. "But, I'm a little confused." I stared at both rings. "Two rings? Did you really think I needed that much convincing?" I joked.

He laughed. "Nah Baby, I just wanted to see the look on your face when you saw that small-ass diamond. I wanted to know if it mattered to you what the ring looked like. "

"As long as I'm marrying you I wouldn't care if it was a rubber band."

He smiled. "Good answer Baby, good answer."

Shane took the ring out of the box, and slipped it on my finger. The stunning piece of jewelry dominated my left hand. I just stared at it thinking of everything we'd been through to be together. How long Shane waited for me to come to my senses and realize that we belonged together and how relentless he was in his pursuit of me. He didn't let anything stand in his way, not even the fact that I had a man at the time. I was happier than I ever thought I could be.

**   **   **   **

After spending seven days in the lap of luxury, it was time to say good-bye to our lovely accommodations. We faced our final morning on the island like we did every one since we arrived—making love. I walked around the villa taking pictures of every room in my head. Flashing back on the time Shane and I spent there and how much we enjoyed each other. I came to the island with my man and left with my fiancé. I felt like I was floating. I had always loved Grand Cayman, but now it meant more to me than a beautiful vacation spot. It was a piece of paradise that Shane and I experienced together. It was the place where Shane asked me to be his wife—I would never forget it.

We'd just landed at LaGuardia airport when Shane's cell rang. He glanced at the phone. "Baby I gotta take this. I'ma be a minute so meet me at the courtesy desk. I'll grab the bags." He put the phone to his ear then stepped away from me.

I picked up a bag of peanut M&M's and a Mr. Good Bar from the concession stand and headed for the courtesy desk. That's when I spotted EL. He was leaning against the courtesy desk talking on his cell phone. Seeing him caught me off guard. The last time I spoke to EL, he called me a few days after I caught him with Sara. After I introduced his ass to the dial tone I didn't hear from him again. I walked in the opposite direction trying to avoid him, but he saw me. His face lit up like Times Square.

"Hold up a second," EL told the person he was talking to as his eyes zoomed in on me.

"Hey what's up Chass?" He walked over to where I was standing.

"Hi EL," I replied nonchalantly. I wasn't particularly happy to see EL; however, I wasn't angry about seeing him either. Although I knew that EL and I would never be friends, I didn't see the point in holding onto all that bullshit anymore. I could have easily walked away as soon as he approached me, but I entertained his conversation if nothing else, to show that I was over all that BS.

"Are you going somewhere?" he asked, but before I could respond Shane walked up.

"Fuck this nigga want!" Shane stared at EL like he was a murder suspect.

EL shot the same stare back at Shane. They both looked like they were ready to set it off right there in the airport. Hoping to avoid a scene, I tugged on Shane's arm trying to convince him to leave with me, but it was like trying to reinforce steel—he wouldn't budge.

"I don't want a damn thing from you," EL responded with a sharp tongue.

"Fuck you say to me ma'fucka!" Shane stepped in EL's face.

I pulled on Shane's arm again, but still he didn't even flinch.

Mia came out of nowhere and stepped in-between them.

"Is there a problem EL?" she asked, looking at EL then at Shane, her voice showered over by the flight announcements.

EL shook his head. "No problem. Everything's cool."

Mia looked at me then at Shane and then back at me. "I see you didn't waste any time Chass."

I shot her a fake smile then I looked at EL. "Actually I wasted damn twelve months, but whose counting."

EL didn't say shit. He just stared at me.

I tugged on Shane's arm again. "Let's go Baby. He's not worth it and she damn sure isn't."

"You right Baby. Let me get up outta here before I hurt this nigga." Shane took my hand into his and led me out of the airport.

"What did that nigga want?" Shane wasted no time asking.

"Nothing. He was just saying hello."

"The nigga is tryin' my patience. He ain't over you Chass. And the ma'fucka better raise up before I bring it to his punk-ass."

I glanced back at EL just as Shane and I approached the airport doors. Even from a distance I could see that EL was pissed. He watched us until we were no longer in his view.

If his eyes were bullets... I thought to myself as Shane and I exited the airport.

32

Club Ambiance

Chass

Shane was in our bedroom throwing bundles of cash into a duffel bag when I walked in.

"I wrapped your plate up and put it on the stove."

"I'm good Baby. I ain't hungry. I won't have time to eat anyway. My flight leaves in a couple hours. I gotta jet. I'm 'bout to head to the airport now. I'll be back tomorrow night. If you need anything hit me up on the cell."

"So you're leaving me in this big house by myself."

"Baby I gotta take care of a few things so I can hand things over to Ced. You won't be here by yourself. Carlotta gon' be here."

Like that's supposed to make me feel better. What can she do if somebody breaks in...scream...hell I can do that.

"Her room is damn near in the basement Shane. It's still gonna feel like I'm here by myself." I looked around the master bedroom with the attached loft and sighed. "Shit, Shane our bedroom alone is a damn apartment."

"You ain't got nothin' to worry 'bout Baby. Don't shit happen over here. That's why I copped this 'cause it's quiet. Them ma'fuckas from ADT looked at me like I was crazy when I had the alarm system put in. I had them install all kinds a shit. The only thing that might happen is the newspaper gettin' snatched off your lawn. And, that's only if the paperboys aim is fucked up and he don't throw it over the gate. You good Baby. The house is locked tighter than a jail. You got the codes. Just make sure you set the alarm before you turn in for the night."

I plopped down hard on the bed displaying my attitude. Shane stopped what he was doing and looked at me. "Baby if you don't wanna be in the house then go out. Call ya' girls. I know they'll be down to hang out."

"And go where? The only place I might wanna go is to the city, but I don't feel like driving for four hours to get there and back."

"Then stay at the loft if you don't wanna come back here."

"You're not worried about me getting into any trouble while you gone?" I jokingly asked as I walked over to him and gave him a bear hug from behind.

He twisted his face up and turned around to face me. "I said go out and have a good time, not get a nigga killed."

210

Shane was so damn confident it seemed like nothing could shake him—except the thought of other men around me.

I laughed him off. "You're a mess. I wish I could go with you," I pouted.

He tucked his gun in his pants. "If this trip wasn't about business Baby you know I would take you. But I gotta tie up some loose ends so I can get ready to hand things over to Ced."

"And you need your gun because…"

"Let's just say I been dealin' with these Columbians since I was twelve. It's all good as long as you lacin' their pockets, but them ma'fuckas is ruthless as hell. They would rather take you out then let you leave the business."

"Shane…" I said nervously.

"Don't worry 'bout it Baby. I got this. I'ma call you when I land."

He grabbed his duffel bag and threw it across his shoulder leaving me with a kiss. I watched as Shane jumped into the Range Rover and drove out the gate. Not even ten minutes after he left I was calling the twins. My timing was perfect because it just so happened that they had a few VIP tickets to the grand opening of a new club in the city called Ambiance. I threw on *Donna Karan*, slipped into my pumps and was out the door. I opened the door to the Mercedes E-Class and hopped in. I flipped on the radio catching the tail end of Ghost Face Killa's *Back Like that* as Ne-Yo was smashing the hook. I checked myself in the rearview mirror one last time. Satisfied with my appearance, I repositioned myself in the seat, readjusted my mirror, and pulled out of the garage heading for Interstate 80. When I arrived in front of their building and noticed that the twins weren't outside, I whipped out my cell and dialed their number.

"Oookkkkaaaayyyy Chass! We're coming," Aleyma answered the phone already anticipating hearing my mouth.

"Ahhh, come on y'all! I already got here late because of all the traffic on the GWB. Y'all had more than enough time to get ready. Chop, chop… time is money."

"You can't rush perfection," Alayna pointed out.

"Well, you better find a way. You won't have me waiting out here all night. Y'all lucky I like y'all a little bit or I woulda drove off."

"Oh be quiet Chass," Aleyma laughed. "We coming down now."

Aleyma walked out of the building with her sister trailing a few steps behind her. Aleyma was rocking some shit I coulda sworn I saw in a magazine and Alayna was wearing the hell out of one of Kimora Lee's Baby Phat designs. Both of their hair was pulled up into a high ponytail with even cut bangs looking like cute little China dolls.

Yeah these chicks can hang with me.

I glanced at them both a second time admiring their beauty.

Once we arrived at Club Ambiance, there were so many people waiting to get inside the line was down the block and around the corner. You could hear the music blaring from several blocks away. It couldn't compare to Shane's club in no way, shape or form, but it was still a pretty hot spot. When we walked inside I immediately started dancing to Beyonc'e's *Irreplaceable*. Chicks were screaming *to the left... to the left*, while trying to sing over Beyonce's powerful set of pipes. While we were walking around the club trying to find a table we noticed a group of guys sitting at the bar staring at us.

"You know them Chass?" Alayna asked, looking over my shoulder as we walked up to a table.

"Nope," I replied pulling out a chair to sit down.

Aleyma glanced up at the bar. "Damn they blazing!"

"If you like dudes that can touch the ceiling, then I guess they are blazing. Not my thing; makes me look like a midget."

A cute little hostess approached our table with a smile. "Excuse me ladies," she said getting our attention. Holding a tray of drinks she pointed towards the bar. "This is from the gentlemen sitting right over there." She placed the drinks on the table.

The three of us looked over at the bar giving the four well dressed men a 'thank you' smile.

"How did they know that I was about to order one of these?" Aleyma asked, picking up her apple martini.

I laughed. "Please Leyma anybody can guess what you drink. You look like an Apple Martini type a chick."

I picked up the Amaretto Sour that sat in front of me. "Well they were way off base on my drink because I drink Bailey's."

Alayna took a sip of her Mimosa. "Hey it's free."

A tall chocolate brother approached our table just as R. Kelly's *I'm a Flirt* began to play.

"How are you ladies doing tonight?" he asked, towering over us. This dude was so tall it was like looking at a giant—especially since we were seated.

"We're good," we responded in unison.

"I'm Raele Griffin; but you can call me Rome. I play point guard for _____."

"Hi," the twins said before dude could finish reciting his resume. I could care less who he was or what team he played for. I had this look on my face that said...*So what you're a ball player. Why don't you go dribble a ball somewhere and get the hell outta my face?* I never was a sports type a chick. Fashion and hair was my thing.

"Mind if I sit down." He gestured towards the empty seat next to me. I reluctantly agreed. Since he bought the drinks I didn't want to be rude, but I wasn't about to let the brother get the wrong idea so I made sure that my left hand was in clear view so there was no mistaking my engagement ring just in case he came over to our table expecting something other than a thank you.

"Are you enjoying your drink?" he asked, staring me down.

"I am."

"Whoa!" His eyes grew big. "Is that what I think it is?" he asked, eyeing my left hand as I put my drink up to my lips to take a sip.

I beamed. "Yes, it is."

"Whoever that dude is he's one lucky man!"

"Shane knows how lucky he is," Aleyma interrupted.

"Did you say Shane?" He looked at Aleyma.

"She did," I responded for her.

"You wouldn't happen to be talking about Shane Williamson with the green eyes from uptown would you?"

I nodded. "One in the same."

His face lit up. "Oh shit! That's my boy! My bad. I didn't mean to step on his toes. I see he finally made that move. Didn't think there was a woman alive who could make that brother settle down. But, I can certainly see why he changed his tune," he said glaring into my eyes. Then he rose from the table and looked me up and down for about the fifth time since he walked up. "Tell him Rome said congrats on the engagement. He bagged a dollar—not a dime."

"I'll tell him," I said taking another sip of my drink.

"You ladies enjoy the rest of your evening," he said, just before he stepped away from the table.

"Well damn, he was all up in your face Chass!" Alayna said, watching him walk back to the bar.

"Yeah well his breath got here *way* before he did." I twisted my face up.

Alayna took a sip of her drink and almost spit it back up. She grabbed a napkin from the table and wiped her mouth. "You crazy as hell Chass!"

"I'm serious. Dude never heard of breath mints! Damn! Plus he was laying it on way too thick anyway. It's a little early in the season for a snow job," I said with a smirk.

"You see he raised up when he heard Shane's name though. I haven't come across anybody who doesn't know who Shane is," Alayna said stirring the ice cubes in her drink.

It was like someone blew a whistle alerting the guest that there were a few basketball players in the building, because out of nowhere a fleet of chicks had the bar surrounded.

"You see how they throwing themselves at them." Alayana pointed to the bar.

"If they can get passed that damn breath…let them have him." I frowned.

213

The waitress came back to our table with another round of drinks. I pushed my glass aside.

"You ain't drinking no more girl?" Alyema asked, noticing that I hadn't touched my drink.

"No, I'm done. We had like three rounds already. I'm gonna have to hang back and let this shit wear off before I get behind the wheel. I ain't tryna have no accident. If I fuck up that Benz, Shane gon' kill me."

"Damn straight girl! You know he will. You know how niggas are about their whips. They treat their cars like dicks with wheels," Aleyma laughed.

The DJ hit his hand into the mic several times commanding everyone's attention.

"Ok everybody I'm gonna hit you with some old school flavor right now. We're about to take it way back." Then he threw on Prince's *Adore* and the club went crazy. The DJ kept blessing us with classics for the rest of the night.

The twins and I walked out of the club around 3:30 in the morning. Once we got to the parking garage, I handed the short Mexican guy my ticket along with the money and he gave me the car keys. I sped out of the garage and merged into oncoming traffic. Within minutes of exiting The Harlem River Drive I was pulling up in front of the twins building.

"Drive safe!" They yelled as I pulled off. I waved back at them right before I turned the corner.

33

Back Like That

EL

I sat in my car parked in the parking garage down the street from this new club that just opened called Club Ambiance waiting for Chass to walk out. I happen to be driving by when I saw her standing on line waiting to get in. Although I was surprised to see her, I shouldn't have been. Chass never passed up an opportunity to hang out. After hours of waiting, she finally walked into the Parking garage with the twins. She drove that muthafucka's E-Class out of the garage and flew into the street like she was being chased. I knew then that whatever it was that she consumed was still very present in her system. I followed a safe distance behind waiting for her to drop the twins off. I figured that would be the perfect time for us to talk. We had a lot of unfinished business and things to settle between us. Although it was apparent that she had moved on—I hadn't.

I discreetly followed one car behind Chass as she zipped through the streets of Manhattan like the car was on fire. When I saw the way she was weaving in and out of traffic, I flashed my high beams to let her know that she was driving recklessly. I tried to pull along side of her, but she was going at least sixty five miles per hour through the busy downtown streets and I couldn't get an opening. As soon as she stopped at a red light, I pulled up right next to her and waved for her to pull over. She hesitated at first, but finally she complied.

I got out of my car and walked up to the driver side window.

"I thought I was going to have to run you over in order to get you to stop."

"EL?" she looked at me like she didn't recognize me.

"Yeah, Chass it's me. Why are you driving like you just brought a ticket to the graveyard?! You need to slow down. These cops out here don't play. I'm sure there are some that are not on your man's payroll."

She sucked her teeth and rolled her eyes. "What do you want EL?"

"I was hoping that we could talk."

"Talk...please...about what? We said everything we had to say at the penthouse that day."

"Maybe you did, but I didn't."

"Why don't you go talk to Sara? I'm sure she'll love to hear why you're chasing me down in the middle of the night," she said drowning her comment in sarcasm.

215

"I really need to speak to you Chass. It's important."

She shook her head and let out a sigh. "I'm tired EL. I've been out all night."

"This won't take long."

She sucked her teeth again then exhaled. "Alright talk...I'm listening."

"Not out here. Come to the penthouse with me."

"Oh see now you buggin'! You can say whatever you need to say right here!"

"Come on Chass. I don't want to talk out here in the street. All I'm asking for is a few minutes."

She inhaled deeply then exhaled hard. I could tell she wanted to say no. "Alright five minutes," she said, with reluctance as she held up five fingers illustrating her point.

The penthouse was a mess. I couldn't remember the last time I cleaned. I was ashamed for Chass to see the place like that, but I couldn't worry about that now. I finally had Chass alone. I needed to take advantage of the opportunity. It wasn't likely that I'd get another one.

"Well, I'm here. What did you wanna talk to me about?" she asked, getting straight to the point.

"So...how've you been?" I asked as I pushed some clothes aside to offer her a seat.

"Good," she said coldly.

"And your Mom's...how's she doing?"

She sucked her teeth. "Look EL, I didn't come here to talk about my mother and I know that's not why you asked me here."

I could sense that being back in the penthouse had her a little uneasy. Or maybe it was being around me that was igniting her attitude. Whatever the reason Chass' body language was a clear indication that she was ready to walk out the door the minute she walked through it.

"Ok then I'll get to the point. I want you back Chass. I want us to be together again."

She looked at me like half of my head was missing. "Look, I don't have time for this EL. If this is what this conversation is gonna be about then I see I made a big mistake by coming here."

"Why is that Chass?" I asked, defensively.

"Like you really need to ask me that. You know why EL."

"No, I don't. We meant a lot to each other. I would like a chance to get back to that."

"We can't go back EL. I could never forget about all the things you did to me."

"I never said I was perfect Chass. I lost my head for a minute when I found out about you and Shane, but that's all in the past. If I can forgive you for stepping out on me then you can forgive me for my mistakes."

216

"You call faking paralysis a mistake? That shit wasn't no mistake EL. So I guess sleeping with Sara was a mistake too then huh?"

"Like I said I lost my head for a minute. I know was wrong. I never said I was perfect. And, you are not in any position to judge me. You've made mistakes too Chass, a shit load of them. If I can move past all of that then so can you. I'm still in love with you Chass and I know you still feel something for me."

"EL...I'm in love with Shane," she said like she felt sorry for me.

"You're not in love with him Chass. You can't be. You only think you are. You're in love with me. We have history. We spent years together. That has to mean something."

"All we really have between us are all of those years EL. Even if Shane wasn't in the picture, I could never be with you again. I don't even see how we can be friends after everything that happened."

I stood up. "So that's it? I'm just supposed to let you go just like that!"

I certainly wasn't grasping the concept that there was no going back for us. The more she talked about past mistakes the angrier I became. She made mistakes too. I was able to get passed hers. Why couldn't she get passed mine?

"So you're telling me that there is nothing I can do to get you back? Is that what you're telling me Chass?"

"EL...we hurt each other too much to ever go back and after everything that happened between us why would you even want to?"

"Because I love you. Isn't that reason enough?"

She rose from the sofa yawning. "Look EL I'm sorry but I gotta get home."

"Yeah I'm sure you want to hurry up and get home to Shane right!"

"Ok I'm leaving before this turns into an argument."

I grabbed her by the arm. That's when I saw the engagement ring draping from her left hand. Seeing that ring did something to me. I can't even describe the rage that came over me. I just snapped.

"What the fuck is this Chass?!" I forcefully pushed her hand back into her chest. "Shane asked you to marry him and you said yes didn't you?!"

She didn't respond which made me more upset.

"Answer the damn question Chass! Did you tell him you would marry him?!"

She took a step back. "Yes, EL I accepted his proposal," she said, as delicately as she could.

I picked up the lamp from the end table and threw it across the room.

"How the fuck could you say yes to him! How could you do that to me Chass! How! I heard that muthafucka took you to Cayman and proposed, but I didn't want to believe it. You're just going to have to tell him you can't marry him Chass. Call the whole thing off," I yelled pacing around the sofa consumed

217

with rage. There was no way in hell that I was going to let her marry another man—I'd die before I let that happen.

"What the hell is wrong with you EL? Why are you acting like this? Our relationship ended a long time ago!"

"That may be, but my feelings for you are as strong now as they were then."

I grabbed her hand again to get another look at the ring.

"I can't believe this shit! How could you do this to me? You can't possibly think that you and Shane are going to ride off into the sunset after what you did to me! You must be out of your fucking mind if you think I'm just going to sit back and let you marry another man Chass!"

34

Dr. Jekyll Mr. Hyde
Chass

EL paced the floor breathing heavily as he watched me through the corner of his eye. I had never seen EL like this so I didn't know what to expect. My instincts were screaming at me to make a run for it at the first opportunity— I had to listen to them. Judging by the way EL was acting, I knew he wasn't about to let me just walk out of there. Instead of panicking I forced myself to stay calm so I could think clearly.

"EL…remember I told you that I only had a few minutes?" My voice was starting to tremble, but I was trying my best to talk normal.

"I remember that I had to practically beg you to come here. Hell, you used to live here Chass. Now it's like brain surgery just to have a conversation with you." he angrily said as he paced around me.

"EL… It's late. I was supposed to be at my mother's a while ago. I know she's probably worried about me.

"So why were you driving in the opposite direction when I saw you?"

I tried to think of a quick lie. "Be…cause the car was on E so I was looking for a gas station."

"Your mother knows how you like to hang out Chass. I'm sure she's not worried."

"But…I…I still need to check in with her EL. Just in case." I pulled out my cell.

"You can call her when we're done." He pushed the phone back into my bag. "You never told me how you plan on getting rid of Shane. You have to break it off with him as soon as possible Chass or else he is going to be a problem for us."

I watched him nervously. I didn't know what happened to make EL totally lose his grip on reality, but he was gone. He seemed to believe that he could force me to be with him. That he could make me love him again. I knew my only way out of this madness was to play along so I played on his feelings for me. I was hoping that would soften him up and allow him to let his guard down.

"We did have some good times together. Most of them were spent right here in this penthouse." I forced a smile.

219

His eyes softened and the muscles in his jaw began to relax. "See Chass... all you have to do is just remember how good we were together and I know you'll start to feel differently about us."

"I care about you EL. I always will." I looked into his eyes searching for a glimmer of the EL I once knew.

His smile widened, "You don't know how much it means to me to hear you say that. I can make you happy Chass. I can make you happier than Shane ever could. I know I can. It won't be like before. I know I've made mistakes, but I won't make those same mistakes again. I promise. I love you more than anything. You know that right? Are you going to come back to me?" he pitifully asked.

"I need some time to think about this EL. My feelings...I'm so conflicted," I said, playing him while trying to act as normal as possible.

"I can understand that." He softly rubbed my shoulder. "That dude has you tied in knots, pressuring you, taking you out of the country and making you feel trapped. He did that so you would feel like you had to accept his proposal like you didn't have a choice. But, I'm giving you one. I don't care how long it takes. I'm not going anywhere."

Except to Bellevue—First class.

I sat beside EL on the sofa waiting for an opportunity to make a run for it.

I overestimated his sanity.

I underestimated his intentions.

He lifted my hand from my side and held it gently. I didn't resist because I knew that if I did it would trigger a negative reaction, and EL was slowly letting his guard down. I bided my time, waiting for an opportunity to make my exit.

I thought back to the day I first met EL. He was such a gentlemen. Look at him now. I hadn't realized it until this very minute, but not only was EL acting strange, he even looked different. EL was in desperate need of a haircut and his facial hair could use a little lining up as well. Although his athletic frame was still very lean, it was obvious that he'd lost weight.

As the seconds ticked away so did my patience. The more relaxed he became, the more anxious I was.

I gotta get to that damn door, I thought as I sat impatiently.

He eased closer to me. "I still haven't heard you tell me that you love me Chass," he spoke softly, breaking the few minutes of silence.

"EL...I... I'm not sure how I feel. I have a lot to work through."

"How else are we going to get married if you can't tell me you love me Chass? Don't you think I need to hear those words from you before we become husband and wife?" he asked, as he caressed the side of my face with his finger.

I started to cough. He reached over and patted my back.

"Are you Ok?" he asked, concerned.

"Can…you…get…me…a…glass…of….water?…My…throat…my…is …dry." I pretended to struggle as I coughed my words out. As soon as EL got up from the sofa and walked into the kitchen, I didn't hesitate.

I saw my chance.

I took it.

I jumped off the sofa and ran straight for the door. I didn't bother looking back. My focus was on getting to that door. When I reached my hand out to grab the knob, EL's hand came down on top of mine. With force he pushed my hand away so hard that I stumbled, and slipped on the water that spilled out of the bottle of water that he was holding. I jumped up from the floor reaching for the door again. Extending my arm around him, he swatted my hand away.

"Where do you think you're going Chass?! I'm not finished with you yet!" He flared his nostrils as he looked at me with such rage.

A wicked chill shot through my body. EL was unraveling right before my eyes. He had completely transformed from the gentleman that I stepped into the penthouse with to a deranged maniac. A sick feeling rested in the pit of my stomach. It had become clear that his appearance wasn't the only thing that had been altered. I thought about screaming, but I was pretty sure that would only infuriate him more and I had no idea to what lengths he would go to in order to keep me quiet. He stood in front of me still blocking the door.

"Nothing is going to stop me from having you Chass! Not Shane… not anybody! Not even you! You still love me. You just buried those feelings and pretended to love Shane just so you could hurt me. That was your way of paying me back because I hurt you. You know that I will never let you marry him don't you!" He grabbed me by the arm pulling me closer to him.

"EL…You're hurting me. Let me go!" I tugged on my arm until he finally let me go.

"I don't know why you're fighting me so hard. You know you want me. I know I want you. I wanna make love to you Chass." He whispered in my ear making my stomach turn.

Fuck this shit!

I jerked away from him and ran towards the door again, but he caught me before I could get to it.

"Maybe you didn't hear me! I said I wanna make love to you."

His grip on me was so tight my arm started to get numb.

"Get off me! Get the fuck off me EL!" I yelled trying to break away from him.

He pulled even harder. "I'm not asking you I'm telling you! I want some pussy Chass! Now either you can give it to me, or I can take it. But, one way or another I'm going to get what I want!" he growled.

He forced me down; my head facing the floor; his elbow clamped into my back. My heart sank as my body trembled. I screamed as I struggled to break free, but the more I struggled, the more force he put into holding me down.

"You might as well stop fighting me Chass. Don't even waste your energy. You can't win. My strength far exceeds yours and I am very motivated to get what I want and right now what I want is you." He grabbed my hair and pulled my head back then he forcibly kissed the sides of my face.

"EL... please...stop it...please! Don't do this EL please!"

"Don't make me take the pussy Chass. Just give it to me willingly. I want you to give it to me like you used to. If you just relax you might enjoy it."

"EL please stop! Please just let me go! This is rape!"

"It's not rape if you just cooperate with me. It's been a long time since I've been with you Chass. I miss you. I need you." His heavy breaths covered my back.

I struggled to break free, but he overpowered me. All the fight in me was no match for his obsession. My screams were muffled as they bounced off the floor. He forcefully ripped my pants off and my panties along with it. I tried to wiggle from under him but I couldn't because he was too strong. He had me pinned down. Then he flipped me over so I could face him.

"One last chance to give it to me willingly Chass. Don't force me to take it from you."

"EL...Please..." I cried, tears streaming from my eyes. "Don't do this. If you love me then please don't do this!"

"I do love you. I love you more than I have ever loved anyone in my life. It's killing me being without you. It's been pure torture. I need you Chass. I want you, and I'm trying to show you how much."

I thought EL might take pity on me and let me go, but he didn't. I fought as hard as I could, but my 145 lb frame was pinned beneath all 218 lbs of his. I fought hard, but he fought harder to get inside of me. It was like he was possessed. He pried my legs apart and leaned all his weight into me as he rammed his penis inside me. He continued to hold me down covering my mouth, muffling my screams.

"I miss this." he whispered in my ear as he fondled me.

He panted.

I screamed.

He grunted.

I punched.

He moaned.

I kicked.

My screams and cries were simultaneous with his grunts and moans. I screamed until I was horse, but EL was determined to have his way with me— no matter how much I protested. His body dripped sweat as he continued to plunge inside of me. I punched and kicked until my arms and legs were sore. He felt no pity for me. It was like the fight in me fueled his sick desire even more.

222

I couldn't believe that EL was violating me in such a way. I finally fought my way from under him only to be thrown back down. My head hit the floor so hard I was dizzy. My vision was blurry and I started to feel weak. I felt myself fading out, but I fought like hell to stay awake. I was terrified of what he would do to me if I lost consciousness.

"Stop it Chass!" He called out suddenly. "You used to love it when I made love to you like this!" EL continued to thrust in and out of me as he whispered repeatedly "You know you want it."

As I moved my head from side to side struggling to get his hands off of my mouth, one of his fingers slipped between my teeth. I closed my eyes and bit down on his finger as hard as I could.

"AAAHHH SHIT! WHAT THE...!" he called out painfully as his blood seeped into my mouth. He quickly jerked his hand away and jumped off of me then he ran to the bathroom to clean his wound.

I grabbed my pants and hurried into them as fast as I could, but it seemed like I was moving in slow motion. I prayed that EL would stay in that bathroom long enough for me to slip out the door. When I heard the water turn off I knew he was on his way back so I grabbed my purse and shoes and with one leg in my pants I unlocked the door and ran into the hall. As soon as the hallway air hit my face it gave me the strength to make it to the stairs. I slipped my other leg into my pants and ran down the stairs barefoot. I didn't even stop to put my shoes on. Out of breath and exhausted I ran from the penthouse all the way to the parking garage without pause.

I couldn't control the tears that were streaming down my face as I drove to the loft. I sped through the busy streets of Manhattan like I was in a race. I guess all the cops were on a donut break. Not that I cared if I got stopped. It wasn't until I got back to the loft that I started to feel safe. I quickly took off my clothes and eased my sore body into the bathtub. I scrubbed my skin raw trying to remove all evidence of EL's darkest hour. I soaked in the tub so long that my skin withered up like a prune. I slipped into a pair of loose fitting pajamas and stared at myself in the bedroom mirror. Other than having a killer headache and the thumping of the right side of my face, there was no visible evidence that I had been raped. EL didn't leave any welts or marks anywhere on my body. It was almost as if he knew what he was doing.

I couldn't sleep.
I still felt his breath on my back.
I still felt his cold hands on my body.
I still felt him inside of me.
I still heard his grunts.
I still heard his moans.
I still heard his whispers.
I couldn't get away from him.

I thought about calling the police, but I didn't want to relive that horrible experience with a bunch of uniformed strangers.

I was ashamed.

I was embarrassed.

I couldn't say a word about what happened to anyone. I definitely couldn't tell Shane. I felt like I brought it on myself. I was humiliated and violated in the worst possible way and the worst part was that the man responsible was EL.

Fall 2007…

35

Rooftop Garden
Chass

A few months had passed since the rape. The memories were so vivid and fresh almost as if no time had passed at all. I tried to put it behind me, but the more I tried the more aggressive the memories became. I was determined not to let it turn me into a victim. I couldn't let that moment define the rest of my life. I did everything I could not to wallow in the pain of what was a true violation of my soul. I refused to give EL that kind of power over me. He had already taken so much from me, I wasn't about to let him take my self-respect as well. I couldn't bring myself to tell anyone—not even Shane—especially Shane. I was afraid that if Shane found out that I was raped, he would start to look at me differently. Maybe even his feelings for me would change. Besides I knew that if I told Shane, I would be signing EL's death certificate. Although EL deserved whatever he had coming to him, I couldn't live with a man's death on my conscious—not even EL's.

I spent the next few months increasing my clientele and helping Shane prepare for the opening of the dealership. He had finally fulfilled his dream of opening a car dealership that would only carry custom made cars. The dealerships grand opening celebration was being held at Manhattan's *Rooftop Garden*.

I was sitting at the vanity styling my hair when Shane walked into our master bedroom suite. I caught a glimpse of him in the vanity mirror. He looked like a million bucks in his tailored-made *Armani* suit.

The man just gets better with age, I thought as I studied his mirrored image. Shane looks beyond good on a normal day, but he looked especially handsome tonight. For the first time in my life, I felt like I wouldn't measure up.

"You look so handsome Baby!" I turned in the chair to face him. "All eyes will definitely be on you tonight."

Reaching for his Rolex he smiled and said in the way that only he could, "The only eyes I care about are yours."

Shane always had a way of making me feel special.

"You almost ready?" he asked, noticing that I still wasn't dressed.

"Mmm hmm just give me a couple minutes. I just gotta slip into my dress."

I placed the final bobby pin in my hair then I walked over to the bed where my dress was spread out.

"A'ight Baby, I'll wait for you downstairs." He picked up his keys from the dresser and walked out of our bedroom.

I splashed on my *Dolce & Gabbana Light Blue*, and slipped into my *Roberto Cavalli* dress. I glanced in the mirror one last time before heading downstairs. When I walked into the family room Shane's mouth hung open.

"Damn Baby! I'm not sure I should let you out lookin' like that. You got a nigga wantin' to take you back upstairs."

I winked at him. "Come on let's go. We don't wanna be late."

** ** ** **

The Penthouse Lounge was large, but intimate. The atmosphere had a very sexy vibe. The décor was plush mahogany velvet reminding me of a throw back from way back in the day. The lounge was encased by floor to ceiling glass windows and beveled peach mirrors with breathtaking panoramic views of the Manhattan skyline, the Empire State, Chrysler, and the purple crowned Met Life Buildings. If you had a good eye, you could even catch a glimpse of the Statue of Liberty all the way in the background. Shane and I walked upstairs to the beautifully landscaped rooftop garden. Lit up like Times Square, surrounded by palm trees and lighted fountains, and filled with umbrella covered wood crafted tables. With the help of the city lights the rooftop restaurant and penthouse lounge bar was absolutely magnificent.

The guest list consisted of the cities most elite. There were lawyers from some of the most prestigious law firms in the country. CEO's of major conglomerates, hotel managers, nightclub owners, investment bankers, and the list goes on and on. Even the Channel 7 Eyewitness News team was in attendance, microphone in hand, and reporting live. Shane stood by my side showing me off like I was his most prized possession. We sipped on the most expensive champagne while eating hors d'oeuvres admiring the spectacular view of Manhattan from the rooftop, which was the highlight of the evening.

"I'm so happy for you. You made this happen," I said, admiring Shane's tenacity and determination.

"Baby, none of this would mean shit if I didn't have you by my side."

PK walked up, his face filled with respect and admiration for Shane. "You did it man!"

"Yo man, I'm feelin' this dawg." Cedric walked up behind PK giving Shane a pat and a pound. That's when I noticed the bulges protruding from the sides of their suit jackets. When they walked away I looked at Shane and asked, "Why are they strapped?"

"Baby, niggas don't wanna see you get out the business. They expect you to stay in the game until they put you in the ground. If you do happen to get out, you gotta stay on top of your game because if not you can catch it from all sides."

I looked at him confused. "Come on Shane you don't really think that anything is gonna happen here do you? This place is filled with nothing but corporate top dogs. The only thing on their mind is probably some corporate raid. It's not even that type of crowd in here."

Shane smirked, looking at me like I could never understand.

"Well Baby it's like this...a man will carry condoms even if he doesn't need them. It's just force of habit. I'd rather have it and not need it, then need it and not have it."

Classical music played softly as the city's most sophisticated got on the floor and showed their stuff. When Shane was called away to meet and greet, I walked around the party drinking and mingling. I was approached by a few modeling representatives asking if I ever thought about a career in modeling. One of them even offered me a modeling contract right there on the spot.

"Your bone structure is to die for," one of the agents admired watching me like I was a delicate flower.

"Would you check out her skin texture...those dimples... the color of her eyes—simply gorgeous," the agent said to the photographer that was glued to his side.

I politely excused myself when I spotted the twins slowly making their way up the lit up staircase. I stood at the top of the stairs grinning.

"Well damn, it sure took y'all long enough." I teased as they reached the top.

"Guuurrl... I wasn't tryna bust my ass in these damn things," Aleyma laughed, referring to the six-inch heels she was sporting.

"Chass that shit you got on is banging girl! I know Shane is somewhere around here drooling," Alayna admired.

"Thanks girl. Y'all killing it in those designs too."

"Damn there ain't nothing but money in here!" Alyema looked around at all the well-dressed people wearing enough jewelry to put Jacob out of business.

"Your man is really doing big things girl. His own dealership...Wow! That's huge Chass," Aleyma said.

"I know you're proud of him," Alayna added.

"Of course I am. This dealership is all he used to talk about back in the day. I am so happy that he made his dream come true because he worked hard for it."

"Speak of the devil," Aleyma motioned for me to look to my left as Shane was approaching us.

"Hey ladies," Shane greeted the twins as he walked up.

"Congratulations Shane!" Aleyma excitedly said.

"Thank you. I appreciate you and your sister coming."

"You don't have to thank us. As soon as I get my money up, I'm coming to see you. Hook me up with something lovely," Aleyma said, sipping on her Mulholland 25.

"No doubt Ma. I got you."

He looked at me. "Baby I got some people I want you to meet."

Shane led me to a table where a group of men who looked like movie doubles for Harrison Ford, Sean Connery, Pierce Bronsnan, and Tom Selleck were seated.

"Gentlemen," Shane greeted them as we approached their table. All four men stood up.

"I'd like you to meet my fiancé, Chassidy." Shane said, flaunting me in front of them.

The men greeted me with a smile. "You certainly are one lucky man Mr. Williamson," Sean Connery's double complimented.

"I second that," Harrison Ford's double added.

Shane looked down at me and smiled. "That I am."

I sat at their table as they talked business. That was the first time I had ever seen Shane transform from straight hood to straight corporate, and those men were eating it up. By the way their eyes lit up when Shane spoke; it was obvious how impressed they were with his knowledge of the automobile industry and his ability to fill their pockets full of cash. Shane built his drug empire from nothing to a several hundred million dollar business. Shane knew how to make money, there was no question about it and they were looking forward to adding several more millions to their vast fortunes.

When Akon and T-Pain's *Bartender* played followed by Omarion's *Entourage,* I was glad that the cycle of boring classical music and Russian Ballads had been broken. Just as I thought nothing could spoil my mood—EL walked in. My heart sank to my knees. I felt like somebody just kicked me in the stomach. I knew that I would eventually have to see EL, so coming face to face with him was inevitable; however I still wasn't prepared for it. It was ironic that the man who was responsible for my pain, was also party responsible for Shane's success. Before EL found out about Shane and me, he was the one who assisted Vince in brokering the deal. EL's firm is one of the dealerships largest investors.

EL walked into the party sporting that chick Mia on his arm like she was an MVP trophy while two big gruesome looking guys paced closely behind them. I never liked Mia. I always thought she was pretty damn pathetic. She shared my feelings so there wasn't exactly any love lost. Though pathetic Mia may be, ugly she is not. Sporting her rich chocolate complexion like a jet magazine model, Mia walked around the party acting like she'd just discovered the cure for AIDS. She was sexy and confident, and EL was soaking that shit up like a sponge. I was kind of surprised to see Mia at the party. Word on the street was that Mia stole money from the firm, and she was fired, pending a police investigation. Last I heard she was in jail. Guess she made bail. How stupid can you be? Stealing money from a company whose specialty is money management.

I avoided EL, and he reciprocated. He stayed on one side of the room and I stayed on the other. It didn't stop him from staring though. Every time I glanced across the crowded party I caught him looking at me. I wasn't about to let EL ruin my night or Shane's, so I did my best to ignore him. I walked over to the buffet table where the twins were standing. As soon as I stepped up to the table a woman bumped right into me spilling her full glass of red wine all over my dress.

"Oh my! I'm so sorry darling!" the middle-aged Caucasian woman who could pass for Hilary Clinton said. She reached into her cute little hand bag and pulled out a hanker chef. "Just dab a little club soda on it and that stain will come right out."

I snatched the handkerchief from her hand and looked down at my dress pissed.

Great! Red fucking wine on my cream colored dress! I thought as I sucked my teeth and walked off leaving her clumsy-ass standing there apologizing. I rushed into the bathroom and turned on the warm water. I scrubbed the dress until all traces of the red wine were gone.

36

Hell Hath No Fury...

Chass

"Well...well...well...what do we have here?" EL stepped out from the shadows just as I was exiting the ladies room. "You look like a million bucks in that sexy-ass dress Chass."

I exhaled then sucked my teeth. "Did you follow me out here?"

"Now why would I need to follow you? I came out here to use the restroom same as you."

"Whatever EL. You shouldn't be here anyway!"

"I have every right to be here. My firm is one of the dealerships leading investors."

"But you don't need to be here EL. You just came to make me uncomfortable. You could have sent somebody in your place."

"I'm the one who worked my ass off for months on this deal. Why would I send someone else to celebrate my success?"

"Excuse me, I'm gonna go find my fiancé," I sarcastically said, cutting the conversation short as I happily brushed past him.

He tightened his jaw and his eyes grew real wide. "Your Fiancé!" He suddenly became upset, remembering that Shane and I were engaged.

"Yeah that's right my fiancé!"

"Oh so after you hoed around on me, now you want to flaunt it in my face that you're marrying that muthafucka!" His voice got louder.

"Why are you in my face anyway? What the hell do you want EL? It's not like we have a damn thing to say to each other."

"What do I want? Hummm...let me see...What do I want? What I want is you. It's kind of hard to keep it together looking at you tonight Chass. That's some real skimpy shit you got on. You got me wanting to run up in you right quick."

Oh no the fuck he didn't!

His comment immediately made me uncomfortable. I couldn't believe that EL had the audacity to say that to me after what happened. There was something about the way EL looked at me that made me very uneasy. Even his smile was disturbing. Like there was something wicked living beneath his grin. I wasn't comfortable being face to face with him, but at least those feelings I could identify with, but this was something else. My instincts were screaming at

231

me to get the hell away from him, but I couldn't have EL thinking that he could intimidate me—not this time.

I needed to show him that I wasn't his victim.

I needed to show him that he didn't break me.

Attempting to take back some of the power that he took from me that night, I stepped up in his face and that's when I smelled the alcohol on his breath.

"What the fuck you say with your drunk-ass! You better back the fuck up before you get dealt with muthafucka!" I spat in his face.

"Before I get dealt with?" he repeated, mocking me. "Is that right? Well let me ask you this Chass...Just who is it that is going to deal with me? Huh Chass? You...your *so-called* fiancé...I don't think so," he taunted.

"Oh you don't think so huh? All I gotta do is tell Shane what you did to me and its lights out for you, you fucking bastard!"

"What I did to you?" he repeated, like he had no idea what I was referring to. "What the fuck are you talking about bitch!?"

"Who you calling a bitch nigga? The only bitch here is you!"

"What did you say to me?" He stepped closer to me.

"You heard me muthafucka! It must be that *liquid courage* that got you feeling yourself tonight. That's the only time you grow some damn balls! Now all of a sudden you got amnesia! You know what you did to me you sick bastard! I can't believe I actually cared about you! Did it make you feel like a man? Huh EL! Did you get off on raping me? You disgusting piece of shit!" I yelled, waving my hands in his face.

He tightened his jaw and flared his nostrils as the veins in his forehead came out of hiding.

"Rape! What the fuck are you talking about? I didn't rape you! You loved every minute of it!"

That did it. That was the one thing that I couldn't take. I could take being around EL for hours at a party. Hell, I could even take him being in my face exchanging insults, but the one thing I couldn't take was for him to say that I wanted what he did to me. As if I invited him to violate me that way. For months I told myself that I wasn't his victim, but in actuality, I was. I unleashed all of the feelings that I had been holding onto since that night. It was as if someone flipped a switch.

"Oh now you don't remember raping me muthafucka! You are one sick son-of-a-bitch EL!"

"Back at you," he said with a wink. Judging by the way EL was acting; it was obvious that he was way past drunk.

"Fuck you EL! You got the nerve to talk shit! I hope you go to sleep tonight and don't wake up tomorrow muthafucka!" I walked off. Just as I was about to step back into the party, he pulled me into the hallway and started choking me.

"Get the fuck off me!" I screamed trying to pry his hands from around my throat. There was no mistaking the fire in his eyes. EL looked crazed.

"Nooooooo! EL stop it! Get your hands off of her!" Mia screamed as she ran into the hall. Her screams were simultaneous with mine. Mia tried to pull EL off of me, but the harder she pulled the tighter he squeezed.

"Stop it EL! She can't breathe! You're gonna kill her!" Mia screamed again.

"Get off of me Mia!" He pushed her to the floor. "I will kill her before I ever let her marry another man!"

Mia looked terrified. I don't think she knew what EL was capable of until tonight. She quickly got up from the floor and ran back into the party.

"Get... off... me!" I struggled with him. My breathing was getting shallower by the second. The hallway lights started to dim like a night light. I felt myself losing consciousness. The music seemed faint, like it was miles away. I was slowly drifting off. Like I had been given anesthesia and a nurse was standing over me telling me to count backwards from ten. The next thing I heard was someone yelling for EL to release me.

"Unhand the woman now sir!" The voice was so faint it could pass for a whisper.

EL ignored their direct commands and continued squeezing my throat. I was on my way. I could feel him cutting off my air supply. I didn't feel the pain of his grip around my throat anymore. It was like my neck was numb. Suddenly bright images started to flash through my head. I was back at camp and Sara was there. We were playing hopscotch...Another flash of Sara and I on the swings arguing over who could swing the highest...Suddenly there was a small burst of air flowing back into my lungs. EL's hands were being pried off my throat. I coughed as the air started to make its way through my body.

Aleyma ran up to me.

"Oh my God! You alright Chass? EL done lost his fucking mind! I can't believe that muthafucka put his hands on you!"

Alayna came running right behind her sister.

"I sent somebody to get Shane."

The twins stood on both sides of me helping me to stand while I struggled to catch my breath. My breathing was shallow, but the air was slowly making its way through my lungs, and I was starting to get my strength back.

EL was tussling with both of the security guards who had him restrained. "I said let me go man!"

When I looked up at EL, I just saw red. I charged at him, punching and kicking like I was programmed to attack.

"This time you gonna pay muthafucka! Shane is gonna deal with your punk-ass!"

"Ok calm down Miss. I don't think you should be out here. Let me take you back inside," the taller security guard said releasing one of EL's arms as he walked over to me. The guard was about to escort me back into the party when EL broke away from the other security guard and started running towards me. Shane interceded and knocked EL into the bar. EL pulled himself up and swung on Shane, but Shane was too quick for EL, ducking his punches. EL threw another punch, but Shane blocked it and hit EL so hard that he flew into one of the wooden tables knocking over the food and beverages that were on it. Just as PK and Cedric ran up, Shane ran over to me.

"You a'ight Baby? Did that nigga hurt you?" he asked, examining me with his eyes.

The next thing we heard were gunshots... Shane threw himself on top of me and I hit the ground so hard that I blacked out.

**   **   **   **

When I opened my eyes Shane was lying on top of me unconscious. I tried to shake him, but he didn't wake up. I flipped out and started screaming.

"HELP! OH MY GOD! HELP ME! HE WON'T WAKE UP! PLEASE HELP ME!"

The place was total chaos. People were scattered everywhere. There were sirens and police scanners adding to all the screams and cries while the guests were running through the crowd trying to locate their entourage. A couple of EMT attendants heard my screams and rushed to my aide. They slowly pulled Shane off of me, and that's when I suddenly felt soaking wet. I looked down at my dress and it was covered in blood. I panicked—For real.

"NOOOOOOOOO...NO...NOOOOOOOOO...SHANE!   OH   MY GOD! NOOOOO...WAKE UP SHANE!"

"Calm down Miss please," the Caucasian heavy set EMT worker said, as he helped lift Shane onto the gurney.

"Is he gonna be Ok? Please tell me he's gonna be Ok!"

"Well he's lost a lot of blood ma'am, but we will do everything we can for him," another attendant tried to reassure me as they rolled Shane into the elevator. I held Shane's hand and cried on the elevator ride down to the lobby.

"I'm sorry Ma'am, but you can't come inside. This ambulance is for patients only," the grey hair Caucasian attendant said, as he stepped out of the ambulance so they could load Shane in.

"Either I'm riding in here with him, or I'm riding on the fucking roof! Your choice!" I barked, watching one of the attendants cover Shane's face with the oxygen mask while another started an IV.

That man didn't say another word. He just moved his ass over and made room for me to sit down. When we pulled into the emergency entrance at New York Presbyterian Hospital, I really started to panic. Shane had lost so much blood and nobody was telling me what his chances were.

"I need to be with him!" I cried swatting the nurses' hand away as she tried to stop me from entering the operating room.

"Please let me come inside! I know he can feel my presence! I have to stay with him, PLEASE!" I begged.

"Ma'am you have to let us do our job. You need to stay here. Our primary focus has to be on saving Mr. Williamson's life. We can't have any distractions…please Ma'am just wait here. "

I could see the seriousness of Shane's situation when I looked into her eyes. Just then I backed away from the doors realizing that I had to do what she said so they could save his life. I cried hysterically unable to pull myself together. Shane was all I could think about. He was my whole world and I couldn't be without him—not for anything. The tears rolled down my face as I watched Shane being rolled away from me and into a surgery that I wasn't sure he would survive.

I sat in the waiting room with my hands cupping my chin, rocking back and forth praying for Shane's life. The twins sat on each side of me rubbing my shoulders and my back as I cried.

The police were in and out of the hospital taking statements from anyone who was at the party. A red headed, stocky Caucasian detective walked up to the Aleyma, Alayna and I and started asking questions. After the twins gave their statements, the cop started to question me, but I was in no frame of mind to answer any of his questions. I was still in shock.

"Officer she's not in any condition to give a statement." Aleyma was rubbing my back and wiping my tears with her finger. "Her fiancé is in surgery, and she is too emotional to be of any help to you. Can you get her statement another time?" she kindly requested.

"Yes, I can take her statement later," the officer replied, handing her his card. "Have her give me a call within 24 hours. I'd like to speak with her while the events are still fresh in her mind. The smallest detail could make a big difference," he said, scribbling something on his note pad before walking away.

I couldn't stop crying. I was a wreck. I just couldn't wrap my mind around the fact that Shane could die. I stared at my engagement ring as I twirled it around my finger. Looking at the ring brought me back to The Grand Cayman Islands where Shane proposed. Thinking about how happy we were just made me cry more.

"I can't be in this world without Shane. I just…I just can't," I sobbed.

Alayna hugged me. "You won't be Chass. Don't worry girl. Shane is not gonna die. He is not leaving you. Not as long as it took him to get you. I have known Shane for years and I have never seen him act like this with nobody else before. He is in love with you girl. Best believe that. Shane's a fighter Chass. He will fight to get back to you. He is not going to let a couple bullets take him away from you," she said, rubbing the back of my head.

From the moment that Shane was rolled into surgery, I didn't have a good feeling about it. Even before the ambulance arrived at the hospital, I kept envisioning black everywhere. I saw more black cars on the road than I'd ever seen before. It seemed as though everyone in the hospital waiting room was dressed in black. Since black represents funerals—I was terrified. My fears and my nerves were competing for my attention.

Alyema placed her hand on my back as I rocked back and forth. My tear filled eyes looked up at her with no response. It had been more than twelve hours and Shane was still in surgery. The longer it took, the more worried I was. I felt Shane slipping further and further away from me. It was like being trapped in a dark tunnel with no way out and no oxygen. My mind was scattered, I was anxious and nervous at the same time. My physical appearance was a complete mess. Eyes filled with tears, blood-stained dress, and I couldn't even remember the last time I ate because food and my body weren't on speaking terms. I had to be surviving off of pure adrenalin. That was the only explanation for why I didn't pass out from exhaustion. I was just about to step out to the ladies room to sprinkle some water on my face when an Indian Doctor walked into the waiting area requesting to speak with the family of Shane Williamson.

37

The Price of Obsession

Chass

I had no idea what the doctor was going to say, but I sure hoped like hell that it wasn't bad news. I couldn't handle it if Shane didn't pull through. My life would never be the same without him. The doctor didn't look confident that Shane would be Ok—which made me worry even more.

"I'm his fiancé," I called out, as I rose from my chair and walked over to where the doctor was standing. "Is my fiancé gonna be Ok?" I asked, trying to pull myself together.

"Yes, he is going to be fine. We successfully removed both bullets; one from his chest, and the other from his left leg. It was touch and go for a moment. He went into cardiac arrest, but we were able to revive him. He is one very strong and very determined young man. His will to live is incredible."

"Cardiac arrest?" I repeated, in a panic.

"His heart stopped and he flat lined on the table, but we were able to revive him. Mr. Williamson is one very lucky man."

"So he's really gonna be Ok?" I needed to hear him say that again.

"Yes, Ma'am he is expected to make a full recovery."

I took a moment and cried the happy cry. I was never so happy to hear anything in my life. It felt like ten years had just been taken off my life. Before the doctor came out, I was making all sorts of deals with God. I never considered myself the religious type, but I found myself begging for God's company then. I prayed to anyone who would listen not to take Shane away from me. I would have sold my soul to the devil if it meant that Shane would live.

"See, I told you that he wasn't leaving you girl," Aleyma walked up behind me holding her arms out for a hug. I hugged Aleyma so tight I left my body imprint on her clothing. My system hadn't recovered from the shock and my body was still shaking.

"I can't believe it Leyma. He's gonna make it!"

"Girl I told you he would. I can see Shane now going head up with anybody who tried to take him from you."

"God answered my prayers. He really did listen to me when I begged him to spare Shane's life."

"That and the fact that Shane got the strength of ten men. I'm sure he helped God out a lot in that operating room."

237

"Yes, I'm sure he did," I said, as I cried tears of relief. "Can I see him?" I asked interrupting the conversation the doctor was having with one of the nurses.

"Mr. Williamson will be moved to a private room shortly. You can see him then. His visits will be limited so that he doesn't overexert himself."

When I walked in Shane's room I felt like someone who had just been given a second chance at life. Looking at Shane lying in that bed so still brought more tears to my eyes. After the doctor told me that he flat lined in the operating room, I kept feeling his chest just to make sure that his heart was still beating.

"Baby I'm right here. Open your eyes... please...I need to see those gorgeous green eyes of yours," I whimpered, as the tears fell from my eyes. I kept a close eye on the monitors even though I didn't have a clue how to read them. I knew enough to know that when they start making those loud strange noises—you better call a damn doctor!

I'd fallen asleep in the chair next to Shane's bed, when the next thing I knew I was being awakened by one of the nurses who suggested I go home and get some rest.

"No...I can't leave him! Even if I did go home I would never be able to get any rest." I felt like I had to stay glued to his side. Even though the doctors assured me that Shane was going to make a full recovery, I still couldn't shake that uneasy feeling.

"You should at least go home and get changed. If there is any change in his condition I will call you personally," the kind nurse offered.

I looked down at my dress and reluctantly agreed to go. I rubbed Shane's hand and kissed his warm cheek. Then I exited his room and walked up to the nurses' station.

"Excuse me," I called out, grabbing the attention of one of the nurses as she finished up her phone call. "I'm going to go home and change and I'll be right back. I shouldn't be longer than an hour, maybe two. If there is any change in his condition, I can be reached at this number." I handed her the tiny piece of paper that I'd written my cell number on. "Definitely call me if he wakes up, I don't care if I've only been gone for ten minutes."

I walked back into the waiting area where Aleyma and Alayna had fallen asleep. I honestly didn't know what I would have done without the twins. They were my rock. Taking turns comforting me and making sure I was Ok. They never left my side. I tapped them both on the shoulder at the same time.

"Hey girl? How's Shane doing?" Aleyma stretched both hands above her head and yawned.

"He's still unconscious, but the nurse is in there with him now. I have some clothes at the loft so I'm gonna run there and change."

"PK and Cedric just got here. We saw them a little while ago," Alayna said.

238

"Where they been?" I asked, surprised by their absence.

"PK said they were at the police station all night or they would have been here," Alayna answered.

"Police station? Why?"

"They didn't tell us. I'm guessing it had something to do with the shooting," Aleyma said.

"Cedric and PK didn't shoot Shane so why would the police hold them."

"Here comes PK now," Aleyma pointed as PK stepped off the elevator and started walking towards us.

"How's Shane?" PK asked as he approached us.

"He's still unconscious but he made it through surgery. The' Doctor's say he's gonna be Ok."

"You a'ight. You need anything? What about Shane? He straight?"

"Yeah, he's Ok. Where's Cedric?"

"He had to make a call. You can't use your cell in here so he had to step outside."

"I was just on my way to the loft to change my clothes. I don't want Shane to wake up and see me in this bloody dress. "

"You need a ride?" he offered.

"Oh yeah thanks. I was just about to call a cab because I rode in the ambulance with Shane last night."

As PK, the twins, and I were leaving the hospital we passed through a small waiting area where I noticed a family looking just as distraught as I was just a few hours ago. They were cuddled together in prayer like they were expecting bad news. As we got closer I recognized them as being EL's sisters, and his mother. Mrs. Wiggins was rocking back and forth, praying and clutching a cross; while Liz, Elaine and Amelia huddled over her, trying to comfort their mother. I turned toward PK and the twins and asked, "Why is EL's family here?"

**   **   **   **

After PK and the twins filled me in on what happened at the party after I blacked out, I couldn't believe it. EL tried to shoot me and Shane saved my life. Shane took two bullets that were meant for me. Then Ced fired two shots into EL and PK put two into one of those dudes that EL was with. I hated EL for being the reason that Shane was fighting for his life. I contemplated whether or not to offer my support to EL's mother and sisters, who were like family to me. I was sure that they probably heard about my part in what happened to EL, but I didn't care. My urge to be there for them superseded anything else. Mrs. Wiggins was like a mother to me. I had to make sure she was alright. Aleyma grabbed me by the arm before I could make my way to where they were seated.

"Are you sure about this Chass? EL did try to shoot you. If it wasn't for Shane we would be visiting you in here."

"EL's family doesn't have anything to do with what he did."

"Anybody could see that EL was drunk out of his damn mind. All this happened because he couldn't hold his liquor!" Alayna said, still upset by what happened.

PK interrupted. "I'ma go sit with Shane. I ain't fuckin' with that niggas family. When you ready to bounce, come get me."

I didn't want to leave without seeing Mrs. Wiggins and EL's sisters so I asked the twins to go to the loft to pick up a change of clothes for me. I handed them the keys and walked into the small waiting area where Mrs. Wiggins and her three daughters were seated. She looked up at me with a frightened look on her face as I stood before her.

"Darling are you Ok?" she asked, staring at my blood-stained dress. "Where are you hurt?"

I put my hand on her shoulder and leaned in to kiss her frail cheek.

"I'm fine. This isn't my blood." I sat down next to her. "I just heard about EL. How are you holding up?"

"We're waiting to hear now," Elizabeth interrupted. "But, Chassidy... it doesn't look good," she struggled to say as she wiped the tears from her eyes.

Mrs. Wiggins started to reminisce about EL. A wide smile spread across her face as she reflected back to when EL was a baby.

"I remember like it was yesterday," she started to tell us the story. "I was on the phone with a member from my church when Eldorus suddenly got real cranky. I always spelled words out rather than saying them aloud when referring to Eldorus because he was just that smart that he knew what each word meant. I told my girlfriend that I would call her back after I F – E - E - D my baby, and put him to S - L - E - E - P. As soon as I hung up the phone, Eldorus ran up to me and to my surprise he said, "Mommy, I'm not sleepy, but I am hungry."

"It was the funniest thing I'd ever heard and I thought it was the cutest too." She dotted each of her eyes with a crisp white hanker chef then continued. "That's when I knew that my boy was going to be something special."

Mrs. Wiggins' eyes teared up more with each word she spoke. Yet, she still managed to hold onto a smile as she reminisced about EL's childhood years. Suddenly her eyes drooped down and the tears started to roll off her cheek and onto her blouse. She looked over at her three daughters and sobbed.

"I can't lose Eldorus too. I can't lose another son! I just can't!" she cried. I won't survive it."

"Ma it's gonna be alright," Elaine rubbed her mother's shoulder and patted her back. Eldorus is gonna pull through this. You know how strong he is."

Just as Mrs. Wiggins was beginning to calm down, a red-headed Caucasian Doctor stepped into the waiting room and walked over to where we were sitting. His presence commanded everyone's attention.

"Is my son Ok?" Mrs. Wiggins asked rising from her chair.

The Doctor didn't say a word. He didn't have to. His face said it all. We all saw it.

"Please tell me he's alive. Please God tell me my son is alive!"

The look of sympathy covered his face. He was having a hard time making eye contact with Mrs. Wiggins and he played with the pen that hung from his scrubs. Then suddenly his words stumbled out—the words that would undoubtedly destroy Mrs. Wiggins.

"I'm so sorry... but, one of the bullets hit a major artery and...he bled out. He was losing blood quicker than we could restore it. I'm so sorry...we lost him."

"*NO, NO, NO, NO, NO,* this can't be! My son can't be gone! OH MY GOD! LORD NO!" Mrs. Wiggins was so distraught she had to be sedated.

I was in complete shock. I couldn't move from where I was seated. All this time I kept thinking that Shane was gonna die. All along EL's death is what was haunting me. Relief is what I thought I would feel, and although I felt several different emotions—relief was not one of them. I couldn't understand how I could grieve for a man who had done so many things to hurt me. Suddenly all the good times between EL and I had resurfaced in my memory. Everything that was good between us at one time came rushing back to me so fresh like it was yesterday.

Once the twins returned with my clothes, I got cleaned up and sat with Shane, willing him to wake up. Knowing that EL was dead and thinking how easily that could have been Shane brought on the tears again.

"Chass...Baby... I'm right here. I ain't leavin' you. They ain't built shit strong enough to keep me away from you," Shane spoke softly. He was still so weak. I pressed the call button to inform the staff that he'd woken up.

"Awww Baby, I'm so glad that you're awake. How are you feeling?"

"I've had better days," he said watching the nurse change his IV bag after taking a blood sample. "I think they go to school just to learn how to stick that needle right in the spot where it is the most uncomfortable."

"I know exactly what you mean. Are you really Ok?" I asked staring into his eyes. Shane had a way of downplaying things so I wouldn't worry.

"Besides a little pain when I breathe, I'm a'ight. I can't feel a thing in my right leg though. It's numb."

"Those are the pain killers Mr. Williamson. They have that effect. You will regain the feeling as soon as the medication wears off," the doctor explained as she walked into the room.

"Miss I'm going to have to ask you to step outside while I examine him," she politely asked, as she flipped through his chart making several notations in it.

I was sitting in the hall outside of Shane's room when Liz walked up.

"I was hoping I'd find you here," she said, like she knew exactly where to look. "My brother's belongings were just released to me. When I went through them I came across this envelope. It is addressed to you." She handed it to me. It had my name written across it in EL's handwriting.

I pushed the envelope back at her. "Liz...I...can't take this."

"Chassidy please take it. He had it on him so he must have planned on giving it to you last night."

"I don't want it Liz, I'm sorry."

"I'm just going to put it in here then." She pushed the letter into my opened purse. "Just in case you change your mind."

I closed my purse with a sigh.

"How are you feeling?" she asked, noticing the worried look I carried in my eyes.

"Liz..." I paused as I looked at her. "I know you mean well, but I don't think I should be discussing how I'm feeling with you considering your brother is the reason why my fiancé is in here."

"I can't say that I blame you Chassidy, but my brother is dead and your fiancé is still alive. I really hope you don't waste your time hating my brother when he is no longer on this earth to receive that hate." She gave me a hug and said, "I better get back to my family. I just wanted to give that to you."

I stopped her before she walked off. "How is Mrs. Wiggins?"

"She's taking this really hard as I'm sure you can imagine."

The Doctor walked out of Shane's room just as Liz was leaving.

"You can go back in now. He's asking for you."

"Is everything Ok?" I asked rushing past her to get inside.

"Yes, everything is fine. No need to worry. The examination was strictly routine. I do ask that you try to limit your visits so that you don't tire him out. He does need his rest."

"I have never been so happy to see anybody in my life!" I said, walking back into Shane's room.

"Back at'chu Baby." He smiled at me.

"When we get home, I'm taking care of you. I'm not letting you do a damn thing."

"I won't fight you I promise."

"You better not."

In an instant my mind flashed back to when I woke up to find Shane lying on top of me unconscious and bleeding.

His body still.

His blood soaked my dress.

Shane jumped in front of bullets for me. Talk about some ride or die shit. My man spoke that shit with his blood. I didn't even think it was possible for me to love him anymore than I did, but I was wrong.

I caressed his hand. "You saved my life Shane. I will never forget what you did for me."

"Chass, don't you know by now that I would die for you."

"You almost did Shane. I have never been so scared in my life." I kissed his forehead, "Don't ever scare me like that again. I don't know what I would do if I lost you. I love you so much."

He winked at me and smiled, "Ditto Baby."

I waited until Shane drifted off and then I left for the loft. I walked in and hung my pocketbook on the door. Now that I knew Shane was going to be Ok my appetite was back in full force. I threw some lettuce, tomatoes, and cucumbers into a large bowl with crotons and chicken bites making myself a tossed salad. Then I plopped down on the couch and turned on the TV. *Four Brothers* was playing on Starz & Encore. Since I've always been a huge Mark Walberg fan, I made myself comfortable preparing to get my grub on.

After the movie went off, I walked into the kitchen to refill my glass of Raspberry Iced tea. When I walked back into the living room, I glanced at my bag and remembered the letter that Liz put inside of it. I wasn't going to read it, but my curiosity got the better of me. I had intended on throwing the letter away at the hospital, but I never got around to it. There must have been a reason why I didn't.

Chass,

If you're reading this then that means I finally got up the nerve to give it to you. This thing has been burning a hole in my pocket for weeks. I'm still not sure why I decided to pick up this pen, as if you'd want to hear anything I had to say. But, I had to give it a try. What do I have to lose? It's not like you can hate me anymore than you do right now. I never meant to hurt you Chass. When you told me you were leaving me for Shane, it ripped my heart out. I just couldn't let that happen. I know what I did was pathetic and desperate, but I wasn't thinking clearly. I guess I just lost it. I can look back and see how irrational I was being, but I didn't know that then. All I knew was that I couldn't let you go and in a lot of ways, I still can't. I ended up losing you anyway and a bit of my sanity at the same time. I know I should have told you the minute I regained feeling in my legs, but by that time you had already decided to stand by me and I couldn't risk you going back to Shane. I wanted to hurt you as much as you hurt me and I knew that I would achieve that if I slept with Sara. I knew how you felt about her and I played on that. It was fucked up...I know...but like I said...I wasn't thinking straight.

After you left me, I tried to move on and just when I thought I'd finally gotten over you, I saw you at the airport, and realized that I was nowhere near over you. I should have fought harder for you Chass. I gave up too quick. When I found out that you and Shane were getting married, I snapped. I'd be lying if I said that didn't fuck my head up. I couldn't eat, I couldn't sleep, I couldn't do shit. I didn't even want to leave the penthouse half the time. Depressed didn't even come close to what I was feeling.

Then I decided that I was going to get you back and I let myself believe that it was possible. I went so far as to convince myself that it was what you wanted. I thought that I could get you to see that you belonged with me. I convinced myself that you were making a huge mistake by being with him and you just couldn't see it. It was wishful thinking, I know, but that's all I was left with was hope. Once I finally got you to come to the penthouse I was nervous as shit. I didn't know what to say to you. When I saw that ring I can't even put into words what I was feeling. I just lost it. I was consumed with jealousy and rage. But there wasn't anything I could say that could explain what I did to you. I would rather cut off my arm than hurt you, and it kills me to know that is exactly what I did. I will regret what happened for the rest of my life. I don't expect you to forgive me because what I did was unforgivable. I can only hope you remember that I love you and I always will.

EL

I folded the letter up and stuck it back in my purse. I'd be lying if I said that EL's words didn't affect me. What made the letter even more profound was that EL was no longer alive. A strange feeling came over me as I was reading it. It was almost as if EL was speaking to me from the grave. The letter certainly didn't excuse his behavior, but it explained it. If only I'd known what he was going through I would have handled the situation differently. I was the one who pushed EL to the point of no return. I was the one who made EL lose his grip on reality. I thought back to the man that EL was before the accident. The kind, considerate, hard working man who I argued with non-stop about neglecting me, but who I knew would do just about anything to make me happy. That man died long before those bullets took his life. When EL woke up after the accident he wasn't the same man that he was before.

38

The Dirt Nap

Chass

When I met EL he had everything going for him. His future knew no limits. He was a shark in the corporate world. His resume was beyond impressive and he was well respected among his peers. His razor sharp mind and keen business sense would make even Bill Gates stand up and take notice. His fierce determination and drive were the key elements to his success. EL graduated from high school at sixteen. A year after graduating from Harvard with a Masters in Finance, he landed a position at one of the most prestigious investment firms in the country. As the years went on EL made millions for Miller, Goldstein & Brock and made partner—all before he turned twenty-eight. When most people were figuring out what they wanted out of life, EL already knew. He figured it out early. He accomplished more than most do in a lifetime, and he didn't even live to see thirty. EL didn't have a criminal record. He'd never even been arrested. EL was one of the good guys—until he had a breakdown.

The night that EL raped me was the worst night of my life. I saw a side of him that I never even knew existed. As bad as things were between us, I didn't want him dead. I didn't expect for his death to hit me as hard as it did. Contemplating whether or not to attend EL's funeral had me tossing and turning all night. My head was telling me not to go anywhere near the service, but I was listening to something much more powerful—my conscious. Still, I had no intentions on attending the funeral. In fact, I planned on staying as far away from the service as possible. The strange thing was, I woke up the morning of the funeral and suddenly realized that I had to be there. I needed to make peace with EL. There were too many wounds exposed. I had to let go of everything that happened between us and move on. Put the past behind me—for good.

I was hoping to pay my respects without being surrounded by all of the gossip and bullshit. I knew that the rumor mill was in full swing and I would be the main topic of conversation. I had already anticipated the smart-ass comments and judgments by people who only knew half the story, and I was willing to bet that even that half wasn't accurate. When I stepped inside the church all three of EL's sisters were standing in a row like bridesmaids; greeting the guest as they walked into the service.

"Hello Chassidy." Liz embraced me as soon as I walked in. I could feel her sweaty palms through those soft white gloves.

"Thank you for coming," she continued. "I know my brother would have wanted you here," she said giving me a kiss on the cheek just before stepping back to greet the other guests that were spreading all over the church like spilled water.

I was just about to take a seat when Amelia walked up to me. Her eyes were red and swollen. She looked like she had been crying for weeks.

"Just so you know...I'm not as forgiving as my sister. You got a lot of nerve showing up here after what you did to my brother!"

Elaine stepped in-between us before I had a chance to respond. "Amelia do not do this here. Please remember where you are."

"Oh I know exactly where I am!" she grunted. "Chassidy is the one who's lost." Amelia said, pointing at me with her crooked finger.

"Chassidy my sister doesn't mean what she is saying." Elaine's words were kind and gentle. "She is understandably distraught over our brother's death. Please take a seat. The service is about to begin."

Before I could walk away, Amelia stepped back in my face.

"Trust me, I meant every word I said. I just want you to know that it's only out of respect for my brother's memory that I don't pull your hair out strand by strand!"

Oh yeah...well I'd love to see you try. I DARE YOU.

Amelia had crossed the line. The only reason why I was giving her a free pass was because I knew she was grieving. But the buck stops at insults. She was sadly mistaken if she thought even for a second that I would let her get away with putting her hands on me. Funeral or no funeral—let's not get it twisted.

"Despite what you may think I didn't come here to cause a scene. I know you wanna blame me, but you don't know what happened between me and your brother. Nobody does."

"Oh believe me I have an idea. I guess my brother was too educated and successful for you so you had to go out and get yourself a street thug!" Amelia shouted, as a handful of nosey guest began to crowd around us.

"Ok Amelia that's enough! Both of you come with me!" Elaine led Amelia and I into an empty room in the basement of the church.

Amelia sucked her teeth and shook her head. "You and your phony concern. Where was this 'so called' concern when my brother was alive?"

"Amelia listen to me," Elaine turned her sister in her direction. "Whatever your problem is with Chassidy this is not the place for you to air it out. You know how Eldorus felt about her. He wouldn't approve of you ripping into her like this."

"Then get her out of my sight! She shouldn't be here! She is the one who took Eldorus away from us!"

"That's not true Amelia." Liz walked in and closed the door. "Chassidy didn't take Eldorus away from us."

No, not physically, but mentally she did. Those bullets broke his body down, but she broke his heart and his spirit long before that."

I interrupted. "You wanna blame me for what happened to EL, I can't stop you. But, I'm not the one who brought a loaded gun into a party and started shooting. That was your brother—he did that."

"My brother had a gun, so what? I'm sure he bought it for his own protection because he knew that thug you call your fiancé and his gang of hoodlums would be there. Eldorus would have never done anything like that. Eldorus was strong. He was a fighter. He could have pulled through this, but he gave up. He didn't fight for his life. You hurt him so bad that he didn't want to live in all that pain. My brother loved you and you destroyed him! You are the one who has to live with that and I hope the guilt eats you alive! Get her out of my sight before I bury her ass right beside him!" Amelia sobbed as she fell to the floor in tears. Liz and Elaine each took turns comforting Amelia as she looked up from the floor crying.

"We lost another brother! How could this happen again? How could we lose another brother?" she repeated over and over as the tears poured from her eyes.

"I'm sorry. I should have never come here. This was a mistake." I walked towards the door.

"Wait a minute Chassidy." Liz reached for my arm. "Let's just all calm down. Please do not forget why we're here today."

"I'm not welcome here Liz and I can't say that I blame Amelia for the way she feels. I think it's best if I leave. I'm not doing any good here."

"Chassidy my sister is hurting and she is taking it out on you, for that I am sorry. You came to say goodbye to Eldorus. Please don't leave until you have done that."

I tried to put up a brave front, and pretend that what Amelia said didn't affect me, but it did. As much I wanted to, I could not dispute a word she said. I was responsible for what happened to EL. It didn't matter that I wasn't the one who pulled the trigger. EL was not the same man after our breakup. I broke his heart reducing him to unspeakable acts of desperation. The man who raped me was not the same man I fell in love with years ago.

I took a seat in the fifth row a few minutes after the service started. On the seat next to me was a funeral program. I picked it up.

Eldorus Stanley Wiggins. Damn that's an ugly-ass name. No wonder he went by EL, I thought as I skimmed through the small pamphlet that represented EL's life. There were pictures from EL's childhood through adulthood; capturing his happiest times and proudest moments. I clutched the funeral program with one hand, and held onto the bible; which I carefully tucked EL's obituary in that I cut out of the newspaper just days before with the other.

It was a few minutes into the service when two men wearing all white wheeled Mrs. Wiggins in. They stood on each side of her watching her closely like they were ready to sedate her at the first sign of trouble. Everyone in the church stared at her like she was some sort of freak. They looked like they were holding their breath waiting for her to lose it. Mrs. Wiggins just sat in the wheelchair propped up like a pillow with no emotion. She looked like she was so out of touch with reality that I don't even think she knew what day it was let alone her son's funeral. Meanwhile, EL's father spent the majority of the service questioning God, demanding to know why he didn't spare his son's life and claim his instead. Mr. Wiggins was in such unspeakable pain that it broke my heart just to watch him crying over EL's casket. At least Mrs. Wiggins had the benefit of medication. I hid in my own silent pain while watching EL's family stew in theirs.

Mia was seated two rows from the front and she had a couple kids with her. Even a few of EL's old girlfriends showed up. As soon as they walked in and saw me they started running their mouths. Reinforcing the rumor mill that spreads further from the truth the more the story is told. No one knew what went down the night EL died. I wouldn't tell any of them nosey bitches if they paid me, and EL...well he damn sure ain't talking now. I remained seated and tried my best to keep my head down and get through the service without another incident. I already had to deal with Amelia's rampage and I certainly wasn't about to expose myself to some more bullshit. I ignored all the slick, snide remarks reminding myself that not one person in the church had a clue what it took for me to be there—not one.

All three of EL's sisters and a couple of his business associates made speeches in EL's honor. Once they were done there wasn't a dry eye in the church. However, there was one person who didn't seem to display any emotion. He was dressed in jeans with a hoodie and shades. I couldn't see his face because the shades and hoodie did a good job of shielding his identity.

The service was wrapping up, and the funeral director had instructed the staff to close the casket, but I still hadn't viewed EL's body. I kept putting it off during the entire viewing segment and throughout the service. Just as the suited gentlemen prepared to close the casket, I stood up.

"Not yet please. Not Yet."

I walked what seemed like miles, but were only a few feet to the casket where EL was resting peaceful. I was overwhelmed by EL's presence. His scent was everywhere. It was as if someone emptied his favorite cologne all over the carpet, onto the seats and splashing it against the walls. The closer I got to the casket the stronger EL's presence became. Suddenly images of him flashed in my head like a movie trailer pausing on the highlights.

The day we met in the offices at Teen Sleek Magazine...

"The way you ran out on me earlier, I thought the building was on fire."

The day he picked me up to take me to the Mary J. Blige concert...

"Oh you ain't decent? My day just gets better and better."
The incident with the toll booth clerk …
"Everything shouldn't be a fight. Why you always ready for war girl?"
The Amityville Horror house…
"I didn't think there was anything that could scare big bad Chass."…
The images kept coming at me. It seemed like every moment I ever spent with EL flashed before my eyes. Then the memories of the night he raped me hit me like a ton of bricks.
When he caught me trying to leave the penthouse…
"Where do you think you're going?! I'm not finished with you yet!"
The moment I realized he'd lost it …
"Nothing is going to stop me from having you. Not Shane… not anybody."
Right before he forced himself on me…
"My strength far exceeds yours and I am very motivated to get what I want and right now what I want is you."
When I reached EL's casket my palms were soaked with sweat. I had to hold my legs just to stop them from shaking. I was afraid that if I let them go I would lose my balance and fall to the floor. I was more nervous than a defendant at a felony hearing waiting to be sentenced. I felt like I couldn't breathe. I found myself crying over the casket of a man who not only raped me, but tried to end my life. I couldn't understand why I felt the way I did. It didn't make sense to me.
EL was very well made up. His make-up was flawless. He was dressed in a white suit, and even his fingernails were nicely manicured.
All this just to be put into the ground. What a waste, I thought as I stared at EL admiring how handsome he still looked knowing that this would be the last time I would ever see him. My nervousness began to subside and my thoughts became clear. As I stood over his casket looking down at him, I didn't see the man who had done so much to hurt me, instead I saw the man who had done so much to love me. It was that moment when I realized that I did the right thing by coming.
"I pray that you are at peace EL." I wondered if what Pastor Davidson said was true about EL being in a better place. I looked at EL as if I expected him to answer, instead all I heard was the thump of air conditioning and the closing of the church doors as people were leaving the service. I cleared my throat, wiped my tear stained face and continued. "I read the letter. I have to be honest; I wasn't going to. I will never forget what you did to me. It haunts me every day. As much as I want to, I can't hold onto this pain and anger anymore. I have to let it go. I have to forgive you so I can move on with my life, and I do. I forgive you. I really did care about you EL. I'm so sorry that your last days were filled with so much pain. I never meant to hurt you. You had your whole life ahead of you. You were too young to die," I spoke softly as I looked down

at him. My eyes filled with tears. Although EL couldn't hear me, I felt like his spirit did and oddly enough that gave me peace.

"God doesn't care how old you are Chile," Sister Margaret said as she quietly walked around the church placing the bibles in the slots behind the seats and picking up the funeral programs that flooded the floor. "He sent for Eldorus for reasons all his own. Take comfort in knowing that Eldorus now lives with God and he is taking excellent care of him."

I listened to Sister Margaret's words as I stood there pretending to understand why some people die so young while others live so long. I do believe that in his own way, EL really did love me. It was love that drove him to do such despicable things. He was just as much my victim as I was his. I regret what went down between us and the events that led to his death. My biggest regret was that we weren't able to make things right before he died. It never occurred to me that we would never get that chance.

As I was leaving the church I noticed some chick sitting on the pew a few feet away from the doors with her head in her lap. I didn't think anything of it until she stood up. It was Sara.

"Satisfied?" she looked at me with hate in her eyes.

I abruptly stopped walking and swung my head around so quick I'm surprised I didn't get whiplash.

"I know you didn't just ask me if I was satisfied." I stepped closer to her.

"I damn sure did! This is what you wanted right? Did you come to make sure that EL was dead Chass?" Her tone was fierce.

Oh no this bitch didn't. That remark alone calls for her ass to get horse whipped. I do still owe her an ass whooping, but because of where we are I won't hurt this bitch today.

"You know I never wanted EL dead," I barked while trying to keep myself from spazzing out on her trifling-ass.

"Your conscious gotta be killing you Chass. Why else would you be here? In case you didn't know, a funeral is not the place to ease your guilty conscious."

"You got a lot of nerve coming at me with this bullshit at EL's funeral of all places. I must have missed the part how me being here is any of your business."

"I'm just saying. It's not like there was any love lost between you and EL."

I laughed her off like she'd just told a joke. "I don't have to explain myself to you Sara. Please...If it was up to you, I would have asked you. Now step outta my face before shit gets ugly," I threatened. I was trying to keep my temper in check, but Sara was really stretching my patience.

"You can get as mad at me as you want Chass. But, I know you. I know this is eating you up. EL is dead. I know he did some questionable shit, but he was good people. You know he was."

"Cut the crap Sara. You think I'm stupid? You think I don't know that you up in my face suddenly tryna flaunt whatever it is you think you and EL had like I care. Whatever it is that you were to him doesn't give you the right to judge or question me. You are the last person who should be in my face! You weren't even there!"

"Oh yes, I *was* there!" She suddenly got defensive. "I guess you forgot about *all* the times I lied for you while you ran around with Shane. I saw what that did to EL. That man loved you Chass, and all you did was break him down. I told you that shit you was doing was foul, but you didn't care."

"And I told you that I'm grown! What I do is my business! I stopped giving a damn about what you think a long time ago. Keeping EL's secrets and sleeping with him behind my back was more important to you than our friendship." I rolled my eyes in disgust. "He just used you to get to me. And when he didn't need you any more, guess what...he kicked your grimey-ass to the curb. What he shoulda did was throw your ass in the gutter with the rest of the shit!"

"FYI...I was never tryna get with EL. We just caught each other at a bad time. Tay had just died and EL was dealing with finding out about you and Shane. We were both in a lot of pain."

"Oh please... You still blaming shit on losing Tay. So I guess he's the reason you're in my face right now?"

"You don't need me to tell you that you being here is disrespectful to EL's memory Chass. You see Amelia didn't like it. And Elaine and Elizabeth were just being nice by not throwing you out on your ass. If your conscious wasn't kicking your ass you wouldn't even be here and you know it. I gotta give it to EL's family, they are forgiving. How would you explain what happened and still expect for anybody to be cool with you being here?" she asked, folding her arms across her chest looking at me like I stole her bike.

"I wouldn't explain it! Not to you anyway!"

"Well you're gonna have to explain it to somebody someday," she preached, like she was preparing to give me the God sees all things speech.

"And when that day comes...I will. Now please excuse my back." I rolled my eyes and walked out of the church making sure the door slammed in her face. I had my finger in my purse on my blade the whole time. The way Sara came at me I was tempted to slice and dice. Out of all the fucked-up shit she did this chick had the nerve to judge me. If I woulda stayed in that church a minute longer they woulda been digging a gravesite for her trifling-back stabbing-ass too.

251

Liz was in the parking lot giving the limousine drivers directions to Woodlawn Cemetery when I walked outside. I waited until she finished talking to the drivers before I approached her.

"Did coming here today bring you the closure you were looking for?" she asked as if she knew my reason for attending the service.

I looked at her strangely.

"Chassidy...I know what happened." Her expression changed. She had a sympathetic look on her face.

"I don't know what you mean Liz."

"I think you do?"

"Excuse me?"

"Chassidy...I know what my brother did to you."

"You do?"

"Yes, I do. Eldorus confided in me. I know what happened between the two of you. I can't imagine how much you suffered. That's why I couldn't let you leave the service before you had a chance to make your peace with him. If no one else knows the courage it took for you to come here today—I do."

Liz knows that EL raped me.

I suddenly felt ashamed and embarrassed. I could barely look Liz in the face. I didn't want anyone to know. I was hoping my secret died with EL.

"He never forgave himself for what he did to you Chassidy that's why he wrote that letter. He knew you would never agree to see him after what happened and who could blame you? He must have planned on giving it to you at the party. That's why he had it with him."

"Then why didn't he give it to me?" I asked unable to understand how EL went from writing me a letter to trying to kill me.

"I don't know. Maybe he lost his nerve or maybe he thought you wouldn't accept it. The doctors confirmed massive amounts of alcohol in his system; it's possible that he forgot all about the letter. I'm not sure what happened, but I know for a fact that Eldorus wanted you to have it. He wanted you to know how much he regretted hurting you. He wanted to tell you how sorry he was. Chassidy, my brother loved you with all of his heart."

Liz told me that at one point EL had gotten so depressed that he wouldn't leave the penthouse. His meals had to be bought to him or he wouldn't eat. He stopped cleaning, or even washing his clothes. He had even stopped going to work regularly. Liz said she watched her brother deteriorate before her eyes.

"He had this look in his eye. It was as if the fight in him was gone," she recalled.

Before EL's breakdown Mrs. Wiggins saw the signs, but failed to do anything about it. Denial is a bitch. She'd already lost one son years ago to a complete psychotic breakdown so she refused to believe that the same thing could happen to EL. Mental illness ran in the Wiggins family and I guess Mrs.

Wiggins thought that EL had escaped it. His actions shortly before his death proved otherwise. Liz mentioned receiving several phone calls from her mother just months before EL died. Mrs. Wiggins knew that something was off, but EL wouldn't talk to her about it so Liz stepped in. EL apparently told Liz everything...putting a hit out on Shane, faking paralysis, sleeping with Sara—and—the rape.

I passed on going to the gravesite. There's just something about cemeteries. That horrible feeling you get when you see someone you know being lowered into the ground is incredibly profound. It's so final. I drove away from the church thinking back to the day that EL stopped me in the street and asked me to come back to the penthouse with him. The place was a mess. I had to kick through bunches of stuff just to walk around. I should have known something was off right then because EL was always such a stickler for neatness. He hated when things were out of place. What really pushed him over the edge was when he saw my engagement ring. Maybe that's when he finally realized that he'd lost me.

39

Revenge is Best Served Sweet

Shane

Clean cut investment banker type cat from Wall Street actually paid ma'fuckas to take me out. I slept on EL. I didn't think the nigga had it in him. Dude had it so bad for Chass that he went crazy when he realized that he lost her to me. My temporary residency at New York Presbyterian gave me more than enough time to set up the plan to take out the hit men that EL hired. They were layin' low after PK shot one of 'em, but we were on their trail. Bein' laid up in a hospital bed meant that I had to fall back and let my peoples handle the details. PK used his pops resources at the church to follow the paper trail, and after layers and layers of bullshit found out that EL set up a dummy account through the firm to transfer money. Never wire large amounts of cash. Shit looks suspicious no matter how you try to cover it.

After realizin' that the two dudes EL came to the party wit' fit Barkim's description, that's when the pieces of the puzzle started to come together. EL's hate and his dough didn't do shit except get Tay killed. If that wasn't enough reason for him to die he had the nerve to try to kill Chass. He deserved to hang on a meat hook just for that shit. His death was too easy. A couple shots to the chest and he died in the hospital. I shoulda been the one to take his life. I woulda sent him off proper. Two bullets—to the head—one way ticket—express trip— no mercy type killin'—straight up—execution style.

I sat up in my hospital bed thinkin' 'bout the promise I made to Tay as I stood over his casket. My words played over and over in my head like a CD on repeat.

I got you Tay. You ain't gotta worry 'bout shit my nigga. I'ma make sure you rest in peace dawg. I'm gon' catch these ma'fuckas Tay. Them nigga's that did you is done. They 'bout to take their last breath dawg. That's my word on everything I love. I got you baby boy.

I was lyin' in my hospital bed flipping through the TV channels when Chass walked in.

"Hey handsome," she greeted me with that sexy-ass smile of hers that always lifts my mood.

"Hey Baby. I'm glad you here."

"You look a lot better. How you doing?"

"I'm doin' a'ight. I'm ready to get up outta here."

"I know you are. I miss you at home. That place isn't the same without you."

"I'ma be home in a couple days." I started exercising my leg.

"Shane you gotta stop tryna do too much before you bust your stitches! I know this may come as a surprise to you, but you're not Superman. You can't rush the healing process. You gotta give your body some time. Isn't that what you told me when I was in the hospital?"

"I know Baby, but I'm mad impatient. I gotta be able to move around. I can't be stuck in this bed. How else am I gonna keep up wit'chu?"

Just then Cedric walked in.

"Listen to ya' chick nigga. She ain't just eye candy dawg. She got some sense in that pretty-ass head of hers. Just chill a'ight. You gon' be ghost in a minute. Ain't shit that important for you to go poppin' your fuckin' stitches after it took them niggas hours sewin' yo ass back up."

"What up man?" I pulled myself upright.

"What's good my nigga! How you feel man?" Cedric extended his hand for a pound.

"I'm a'ight. Gettin' my strength back slowly but surely."

"I'm glad you straight kid. Shit wouldn't a been the same without you man. Got me praying to ma'fuckas I ain't never seen and shit. Fuck wrong wit'chu out here gettin' shot. Don't do that shit again nigga!" He looked at Chass. "My bad Ma. How you doin'? It's nice to see you again."

"Same here, I'm just sorry it's always under such horrible circumstances."

"True, but we gon' fix that. As soon as we get this nigga on his feet we gon' throw y'all the hottest engagement party the hood has ever seen!"

"With the way Shane is going he's gonna mess around and have to stay in here longer."

"Nah, he ain't. Don't worry 'bout it a'ight Ma. I'ma make sure he takes it easy."

"Baby can you give us a minute? I need to holla at Ced."

Chass rose from my bedside. "Sure thing." She leaned in and gave me a kiss. "I'll let y'all have ya'll male bonding time. I have a few things to do before you come home anyway."

"Baby this won't take long so don't go too far a'ight. I ain't tryna look in this niggas face too long. Yours is much easier to look at."

Cedric laughed. "Yeah a'ight nigga, you ain't no picture right now yourself."

"I'll check in on your later." Chass glanced back at me on her way to the door. "Cedric can you please make sure that he stays put? We can't have him busting his stitches."

"No doubt Ma I got you." Cedric replied, as he pulled up a chair and sat down. "Yo man where the fuck did you find her? She blazin' kid!"

"Look at you man you're leakin'. Back up off mine a'ight. That's wifey right there dawg."

"You's a stupid ma'fucka man! I know that's you dawg! You been in here so long you don't recognize a compliment. I'm just admirin' your taste nigga that's all. When you get up outta here I'ma need you to take me to where you got her from. Maybe they still have more left."

"You won't find another chick like Chass. She one of a kind man." I suddenly got serious. "Yo I think I know who did Tay." That remark got his attention.

"Who?" He pulled his chair closer to the bed.

"Kim said it was two real big dudes at the warehouse that night. His description matches those niggas that rolled up in the party with EL."

"So how you wanna handle it?"

"You know what we gotta do."

**　**　**　**　**

The sound of the doorbell knocked me out of my thoughts. I glanced at the security camera; it was Ced. I got out of bed, grabbed my cane, and limped down the stairs hoping he had some good news for me. I was home for a few days when Ced called and told me that he had an update about the dudes EL hired to take me out. After realizin' that they were the same two cats that EL bought to the party wit' him; the rest was easy.

"What up my nigga? What'chu got for me man?" I asked Ced as soon as he stepped inside.

"I just got word that they copped a red Porsche Cayenne, and it's been seen in Brooklyn. It ain't gon' be too hard to find that shit man. Ain't too many ma'fuckas drivin' a bright-ass red Cayenne in the hood dawg."

"A red Cayenne? They might as well hang a fuckin' bright-ass neon sign around their neck sayin' I'm a killer for hire!"

"How you gon' be flashy when you a contract killer?"

Ced suddenly got quiet. Then he looked at me and asked, "Yo Shane where your woman at man? I don't want her to walk in on this conversation."

"Don't worry 'bout her man. She still sleep. You know what to do right?" I asked refocusin' his attention back to what he came for.

"Yeah man. I got it handled."

I had confidence in my cousin. Ced was nice wit' a piece. Just like me Ced could kill a nigga in his sleep. I did hits wit' niggas back in the day when I was makin' a name for myself. A lot of them niggas didn't know shit about the game or how it's played. They talk a good game, but when it was time to put it all on the line, they bitch up and can't do what needs to be done. I pulled Ced into the business when I saw his potential. I didn't give him special treatment because he was family either. Ced earned every ounce of respect and loyalty

256

that I have for him. He would clean up jobs for me. That's how he started. When everybody else fucks up—Ced doesn't. I just needed to make sure that the plan was tight. Snuffin' out ordinary niggas was one thing, but takin' out trained professional killer's was somethin' else.

"A'ight so run it back right quick," I said, switchin' my cane from my left hand to my right.

"Ain't no need for all that man. I said I got it."

"Humor me nigga damn. I know you. You get carried away sometimes. This ain't one of your Lone Ranger killin''s Ced. I want this shit to go down a certain way. I don't want you doin' nuthin' crazy. As soon as you locate them niggas, call me and wait till I get there."

I ain't have the pleasure of killin' EL, but I' was gon' rectify that by takin' out the cats who actually put five in Tay. At least I know one of them pulled the trigger.

"EL was one cocky ma'fucka though. He ain't realize that by bringin' those cats to the party he practically gift wrapped them niggas and handed them right to you." Ced pointed out.

"They lucky they lived this long man. It's only because of those two bullets that they wasn't handled before now."

"And that's what's gonna work in our favor. If they figured out that you know, they gonna think you still recuperatin' so they won't see this comin'."

"Exactly, they probably think I'm not in any condition to retaliate. Just find them ma'fuckas Ced." I was anxious to take them out. Just thinkin' 'bout them ma'fuckas somewhere still breathin' had me tight.

"No doubt man. Two big wrestler-lookin' ma'fuckas drivin' a brand new Porsche Cayenne can't be too hard to find. My peoples say they just picked it up."

"Once you locate that truck you got 'em."

"A'ight man I'ma hit you up as soon as I got somethin'."

I rose up from the stool and limped over to my cane that was leanin' against the island in the middle of the kitchen floor.

"Make sure you call me as soon as you find that truck, even if they ain't in it."

"No doubt. You just be ready to roll when I call man."

I gave Ced a pound and watched him hop into his BMW X6 and peel out of the drive way.

4:15 in the mornin', my cell rang. I didn't bother to look at the caller ID. I knew it was Ced.

He found 'em. Is all I was thinkin'.

My right palm started itchin'. It was that itch like I was about to get some dough, but this was a different type of itch. It was the itch of a life about to be snuffed out—in this case two.

I anxiously picked up the phone. "Tell me what I wanna hear man."

"Yo Shane, I got a tip that they was cruisin' around Flatbush. I tracked 'em to this strip club out in Brooklyn called *House of Pleasure*. I'm lookin' at they ride right now."

"I know the spot. They inside?"

"Yeah man."

"Make sure you keep 'em there Ced."

"Oh we good money dawg. Them niggas ain't goin' nowhere no time soon man. I hit a couple of the dancers off to make sure they keep them occupied for a while.

"Smart move man. Ain't nothin' like pussy to throw a nigga off his game."

Wit' my adrenaline pumpin', the pain from my wounds went numb. I flew out the door, hopped in the Range, and sped out the driveway. I pulled into the parkin' lot right next to Ced's shiny new X6. He got out of his ride as soon as I turned my headlights off.

"It took you long enough man!" he said, climbin' into the Range.

"From Jersey to Brooklyn ain't no hop, skip and a jump nigga. I got here as fast as I could man. So what's up? They still inside?"

"No doubt. Those bitches in there treatin' them niggas like royalty so this might take a while. They might not come out 'til they shut shit down."

It was about 6:30 in the mornin' when they finally walked out of the club. I grabbed my cane and pulled my Glock nine millimeter from my waist. I looked at Ced. "You ready man?"

"No doubt. Let's do this."

As soon as they got in that Cayenne we rolled up on 'em and climbed in the back seat not even givin' them time to lock the doors. The driver reached for his piece, but I already had mine drawn.

"Uh-uh! Fuck you think you doin' nigga?" I pressed my nine against his temple.

"Y'all want money?" he asked, nervous as hell. This nigga was scared shitless. All that weight he was carryin' didn't mean shit when my nine was talkin' to his skull.

"Nah nigga we don't want no fuckin' money! Do we look like some broke-ass ma'fuckas to you?" Cedric had his four fifth hand gun pressin' against the back of the passengers head.

"What y'all want then man?" Dude sittin' in the driver seat asked.

"Remember that warehouse y'all shot up a few months back?"

They both glanced at each other but neither of them responded.

"That dude you killed was like a brother to me. So this is what I want you to do. I want you to give him a message for me." I cocked the nine. "Tell him we sendin' him some company!" I squeezed the trigger twice at close range blowin' two holes threw the drivers brain; then I pointed the nine at his chest and squeezed the trigger two more times. Dude was dead when I released the first bullet to his skull, but I got carried away thinkin' about Tay and how these niggas riddled him with bullets.

Ced popped the dude in the passenger seat with three bullets. Blood splatter was all over the headrest and drippin' onto the butter leather seats. We hopped out the truck and fled the scene.

I was home before Chass woke up. I jumped in the shower and slipped in the bed beside her. Chass was sleepin' like an angel. I leaned in and kissed her butter soft cheek. Her skin felt like silk and she smelled like fresh flowers. Chass never needed perfume. I don't even know why she wore that shit. If she bottled her natural body scent and sold it she would make a killin'. Chass was the one thing in my life that I would do anything for. That I would kill for. That I would die for. She was my one weak spot. Fuck the money, the cars, the cribs, the businesses...None of that meant shit to me without Chass. I snuggled up next to her inhalin' her sweet scent as I closed my eyes and drifted off.

By the mornin' the murders were all over the news.

"Shane! Come here! Hurry up!" Chass yelled sittin' up in the bed with her finger pressin' on the volume to the remote control.

"What's goin' on Baby?" I walked into the bedroom.

"Wasn't those the guys that was at the grand opening party?" She pointed to the TV just as the news report flashed pictures of them dudes.

I looked at the TV. "It look like them niggas."

"They were found dead this morning."

"Word." I pretended to be surprised. "They say what happened?"

"Ssshhh," she put her finger to her lips signalin' for me to be quiet. "They're talking about it now."

"Thirty seven year old Brian Patterson and Thirty four year old Benjamin Patterson were found dead in the front seat of a red 2008 Porsche Cayenne. The vehicle was parked outside The House of Pleasure in Flatbush Brooklyn. The brothers' bodies were discovered at approximately 9:00am this morning. Both men suffered from fatal gunshot wounds to the chest and head fired at close-range. Authorities believe that both men were killed in connection with the deaths of at least a dozen other victims in open homicide cases in which both men were wanted for questioning. I'm Heidi Chong Channel 7 Eyewitness news. Back to you Jim..."

"Damn! Close range—seven times. Somebody really wanted them dead!" Chass said wit' her eyes glued to the TV.

"It looks that way."

Six Months Later...

40

X Marks The Spot

Chass

"Surprise!" The guests screamed while throwing confetti at Shane and me as we entered X Marks the Spot. The occasion: Shane's and my engagement party. The club was filled to capacity. Everybody who was anybody was there. Superstar athletes, sports agents, radio personalities, record producers—you name it—they were there. The four sixty-inch plasma televisions played the latest videos while the DJ spun the hottest tracks. While we made our way through the crowd of congratulatory guests, I felt like Jim Jones—I was flying high.

"Can I get a kahlu'a with milk, vodka, whipped cream, and a couple cherries on top?" I politely asked the waiter that was walking towards me with a tray filled with drinks.

"I will be with you in just one moment," he said hurriedly as he sped passed me.

"C'mon Baby let the waiters take care of our guests." Shane gestured for me to follow him to the bar. "I got you."

The bartender went into a daze as soon as I walked up. He was staring at me so hard it looked like his eyes were stuck. That was until Shane shot him that *'what the fuck are you looking at'* look and he quickly turned his attention elsewhere. Who could blame him for staring? It was damn near impossible to ignore my hot *Jean Paul Gaultier* creation. The stunning dress wrapped around my body like saran wrap exposing more of my skin than it covered making all the brothers add bibs to their drink order. And, let's not forget my banging-ass *Guiseppe Zanotti* stilettos, I was hot like fire. Shane kept me close by, watching me like I was going to disappear.

"Damn, you wearin' the hell out that shit Baby! You got a nigga scared to leave your side," he said, leaning against the bar.

"Now you know you ain't got a damn thing to worry about!" I outlined my entire body with both hands then flashed a sexy smile. "All this is you," I flirted, stroking his ego.

"Yeah...huh...it better be." He reached for his drink. "Don't make me hurt none of these niggas up in here Chass. You lookin' a little too damn good in that dress Baby. Just because it's our engagement party don't mean a nigga can't catch it."

261

My mother walked up to the bar and quickly embraced me.

"Congratulations Chassidy! I can't believe my baby girl is getting married! I'm so happy for you honey!"

"Thanks Ma. I'm so glad you could make it."

"My only child is getting married, where else would I be?" she responded, kissing my cheek.

Aunt Tangy stepped from behind my mother and gave me a hug.

"This is a very nice party Chass. You have really outdone yourself babes. It's not every day that my niece marries a smoking hot millionaire!"

Shane blushed. "I'm glad you both could make it."

"You know damn well I wouldn't miss this! I'm gonna get me another drink." Aunt Tangy called out as she rung her hands in the air trying to get the bartenders attention.

My mother looked at Shane. "I know you'll take good care of my daughter so I'll skip that speech."

"Oh nah, you definitely don't have to worry about that. That's my word. I would lay down my life every day for this woman right here. She is my life!" He winked at me as he raised my hand to his mouth and softly kissed it.

"Well you certainly have proven that. If I had any doubts before, I don't anymore. As long as you continue to love my daughter the way you do me and you won't have a problem. Congratulations again. I am so happy for the two of you. Enjoy the party," she said, stepping back into the crowd.

Shane cracked a smile. "You gotta love your moms Baby. She looks out for you. I like that."

"Yeah, well, don't like it too much. If you disappoint her, she can be your worst enemy."

"It's a good thing that I ain't never gotta worry about that then huh," he said lifting my hand up to his mouth again.

"Congratulations dawg!" Cedric walked up behind us embracing both Shane and me. "Welcome to the fam Chass! This ceremony is just formality 'cause as soon as this nigga slipped that rock on your finger that was all she wrote!"

"Thanks Ced. Now all I have to do is make sure that I don't get the two of ya'll mixed up, and I'll be fine," I joked still amazed by their resemblance. Cedric was almost the spit imagine of Shane just a lighter complexion, and without the green eyes because Cedric's were hazel. Cedric had a head full of thick curly hair just like Shane. It was obvious that they were related, although they looked more like brothers than cousins.

"Oh you won't mix us up Baby trust and believe that," Shane said, wrapping his arms tightly around me.

"You better hope she don't man! Or there might not be a wedding dawg!" Cedric joked. The three of us laughed. "So when's the big day man? Y'all set a date yet?" Cedric asked.

262

"Not yet man. Soon tho'," Shane replied, his attention shifting to the door. "Baby I see some people I need to holla at. I'll be back," he said just before him and Cedric stepped away to greet a few of Shane's business associates that were arriving.

I walked to the bar to get myself another drink. As I was leaving the bar, I overheard the bouncer refuse someone entry. I walked over to the door just as Roshawn and Lawanna were trying to convince the bouncer that they were invited.

No these bitches ain't tryna come up in my party. Somebody must have slipped them some of that grey goose when I wasn't looking.

"This is a private party," I heard the bouncer say. "It is strictly by invitation only. Neither of you have an invitation nor do I see your names on the guest list."

With a wicked smirk on my face I said, "That's because they *weren't* invited." My voice carried outside.

The both looked at me.

"Who the hell are you to tell us what we weren't invited to?!" Roshawn had the nerve to try and get it twisted while Lawanna was co-signing.

"Who me?" I pointed at myself in a sarcastic notion. "Oh, I'm nobody except one half of the couple that this party is for. This is me and Shane's engagement party, and LIKE I SAID you definitely were not invited. Now back away from the entrance so my guest can come in."

They stepped away from the door spouting some bullshit trying to hide the fact that they were embarrassed as hell.

Tell me what it is that I gotta do Baby for you to be my girlfriend... Sean Garrett and Lil' Wayne's *Girlfriend* had the guest swooning around the dance floor. I was dancing my way across the floor when I bumped into one of the guest and almost spilled my drink. I looked up at him and apologized while trying to see behind his mystery. He was wearing a baseball hat pulled down completely covering his face. And, the shades didn't help the situation. He accepted my apology with a nod and walked away without saying a word. As I watched him disappear into the crowd I kept thinking that I'd seen him somewhere before. I didn't even get a look at his face, yet his presence seemed so familiar.

"They gettin' ready to bring out the cake," Shane's voice came up from behind me redirecting my attention.

The guest clapped as four pastry chefs rolled out the massive 6-foot masterpiece. The cake was made of two wine glasses each glass filled with champagne. The bubbles that were seeping from each glass were a nice touch. One glass read *Shane* and the other read *Chass*. Below the glasses was a card also made of cake that read...A toast to happy endings. After a lot of ooh's and ahh's, a few Kodak moments, and a handful of toasts, the guest formed a line in front of the cake waiting for their cut of the magnificent masterpiece.

Chris walked up to me while I was cutting the cake.

"Your man don't do shit halfway do he?" he asked, admiring Shane's style.

"You know how Shane is—if ain't making a statement—Shane don't mess with it."

"True dat, true dat 'cause he went all in with this shit here," he complimented pushing his plate at me. "Cut me a nice big piece cuz. You know how much alcohol increases the appetite."

"Don't worry I got you." Chris knew he was my favorite cousin. I would give him one of my limbs if he needed it. I watched as Chris' attention shifted to Aleyma who was sitting at a table directly across from us nursing her drink.

"Your girl over there...she got a man," he asked as his eyes glowed with interest.

"Ask her."

"C'mon Cuz, she your peoples so I know you know if she got a man or not. Hook me up."

"Now you know I would do anything for you cuz, but match making ain't my thing. If you want the girl then you gonna have to rely on your game to her—not mine."

"A'ight cuz I ain't mad at'chu," he said with a smile. I handed Chris a piece of cake and he walked over to Aleyma's table just as T.I. and Rihanna's *Live Your Life* started to play.

I walked back over to Shane. I knew just by the look on his face who was on his mind.

"Thinking about Tay?" I asked, rubbing his hand.

"Always Baby always. There ain't a day that goes by that he ain't on my mind."

"He's here in sprit Shane. You know Tay is still riding with you."

"I know he is."

Just then a few of Shane's boys walked up. "Congrats! She's beautiful man," One of them said.

"Rael this is Chassidy...Baby this is my boy Rael but we call him Rome," Shane proceeded to introduce us.

"We've met," Rael interrupted.

"You have?" Shane looked puzzled.

"Yeah man we're acquainted. We met a while ago at Ambiance. She told me y'all were engaged."

"You did Baby you never told me that."

"It must have slipped my mind," I said, thinking back.

"Baby, remember that pool party a few years ago in Long Island?" Shane asked.

"Ummm hum I remember," I replied, flashing back to all the drama that went down that day.

"That's my boy Rome's spot," Shane said patting Rome on the back.

"I'm sorry I missed it. I was on the road, but if the rest of the female guest look anything like you then it was certainly my loss," Rome said giving Shane a nod of approval.

Shane smiled. "Watch it man."

Shane and his boys took their conversation to the table where PK and Cedric were sitting, so I walked over to Aleyma.

"What's up with Chris? He got a girl or what?" she asked, before I could sit down.

"Girl don't get me to lying. Shit, I can't keep up with Chris."

"I thought y'all were close."

"We are, but I don't be all in his business like that."

"As fine as he is, I don't understand why he's single."

It's still early. Give him time.

Aleyma noticed the looks that Shane and I were shooting each other from across the club and started grinning.

"Girl…I hate to be the one to tell you this, but you need to be prepared to spend your winter in the house," she said like she knew something I didn't.

"Why you say that?"

"Chass, Shane is not tryna hear shit about you hanging out. Watch what I tell you."

"Girl you buggin'. Shane has never had a problem with me hanging out. He's not gonna all of a sudden try to stop me from hanging with my girls."

"That was before he asked you to marry him Chass. You're getting ready to be his wife girl. The game is about to change—big time. Shane is not tryna hear you do all the stuff you used to do. You see how he's hanging all over you now. He only let you out of his sight for a few minutes at a time. I bet he's starting to get jealous a lot now. Am I right?" she asked watching my expression change. I was surprised with how on point she was. "Girl please, I know the signs. I saw this with my older sister and her man once they got engaged. That nigga used to flip whenever Lanie wanted to go out. My sister said he never used to do that before. He acted like getting engaged meant that she had to give up her life."

"Yeah well Shane is not like that. I mean seriously…Have you seen Shane?!" I joked. "Trust me he ain't got shit to be jealous about!"

"It's not about him girl it's about you. You know your man is spoiled. Shane gon' have you in the house all winter just so you can be up under him. Watch what I tell you."

As Mariah Carey sung *Bye Bye* to lost loved ones Alayna pulled up a chair just in time to catch the tail end of our conversation.

"Well I guess I better soak up your company now girl because it sounds like you're about to hibernate." Alayna laughed with her sister.

"Y'all don't know what y'all talking about."

"Yeah Ok, you keep telling yourself that Chass. Shane can show you better than we can tell you." Aleyma insisted.

As I looked around the party, I caught a glimpse of the guy I bumped into earlier standing at the top of the stairs staring down at me. All of a sudden I got real uncomfortable.

"Y'all know him?" I pointed at the mystery guest.

Their eyes followed my finger.

"Know who Chass?" they asked in unison. "There's like a million people in here. You're gonna have to be a bit more specific."

"Him," I pointed again, but the guy with the baseball cap and shades was gone.

That was odd. He was just standing there.

Shane walked up to the table. "I need to steal my fiancé for a minute ladies." He grabbed me by the hand. "I have a surprise for you."

"What did you do this time Shane?" I asked, unable to contain my excitement.

"Not what...who?" He gestured in the direction of the man walking towards us who I hadn't seen in more than five years—that man was my father.

"Hello Chassidy! How are you doing Sweetheart?" He extended his arms for a hug.

I lit up like a Christmas tree in the middle of Times Square.

"Hey Daddy!" I happily embraced him. "I'm so glad you're here!"

"Congratulations Sweetheart! You're getting married. I couldn't be happier for you!" His smile was contagious.

He shook Shane's hand. "Thanks for inviting me."

"It was my pleasure. Thanks for comin'." Shane looked at me. "Baby I'ma let you and your pops talk while I go and holla at my boys for a sec," he said stepping back into the crowd.

I took my dad upstairs to one of the VIP rooms and we talked for a while before he headed back to Maryland. I didn't want to admit it to myself, but I really missed my father. I didn't care that he wasn't around for the last few years—he was there now. That's what was important to me. My father was there to watch me take one of the most important steps in life—becoming a wife. I was so happy to see him and share my happiness with him. His presence made the night that much more special and I had Shane to thank for that.

"Umm mmm," The DJ cleared his throat into the microphone immediately capturing everyone's attention.

"This song is dedicated to Chass from her future husband Shane."

Luther Vandross and Cheryl Lynn's *If This Word Were Mine* started to play. The DJ followed that up with *Here and Now* another Luther Vandross classic. Everyone watched Shane and I as we danced. When R. Kelly's *Step in the name of Love* played a few of the guest joined us on the floor and everybody started doing the Electric Slide. It reminded me of the scene from the movie *Best Man* at Lance and Mia's wedding reception when the wedding party and several guests did the electric slide to Cameos' classic hit *Candy*.

** ** ** **

The minute Shane and I got home; I walked into our bedroom and slipped out of my stilettos. As banging as the shoes were, they were not nice to my feet. I watched Shane as he undressed. The question was burning a hole in my brain so I had to ask.

"Shane, how'd you get my father to come to the party?"

He winked at me. "It's a man thing Baby...you wouldn't understand."

"Yeah I bet I wouldn't." I smiled at him. "So...how much did you pay him?" I joked.

"Baby, your pops cleaned out all my bank accounts and I still owe his ass," he laughed. "On the real tho Baby, I just called him and told him about the party and he said he would be there."

"Just like that?" I asked, slipping out of my dress.

"Just like that."

"I haven't spoken to my father in years. How'd you know he would come?"

"I had a feelin'. I didn't think he would miss somethin' this important. You know Baby you front like the man don't mean shit to you, but it's obvious that you really love your pops."

Shane was right. Underneath all the anger and resentment, I adored my father. I embraced him and gave him a kiss on the cheek.

"You just keep giving me more and more reasons to love you."

"I can think of plenty more," he teased, looking at me in only my bra and panties.

I picked up the stereo remote and pressed play.

"Awww shit!" I called out as I circled around Shane dancing half naked to Ray J's *Sexy Can I?*

"That's what I'm talkin' 'bout Baby. Do that shit!" Shane called out excitedly as he took a seat at the edge of the bed and watched my performance. After a few minutes he positioned me on his lap and started moving my body to his rhythm. The lips of my pussy clapped against his stiffening dick with every move I made causing him to get harder than the state bar exam. He laid me on the bed and slid his face in-between my legs. His tongue caressed the circumference of my vagina before finding its way to my warm center. As his tongue danced across my clit, I felt my body losing control. I was almost at my peak, but I wanted to prolong the ecstasy.

"No...not yet," I moaned as I rose off the bed and made my way to the floor signaling for him to come to me. Shane circled around me admiring the view of my naked body before bending me over in doggy position. He lifted the cheeks of my ass as he entered me slowly from behind. The sound of his balls slapping against my ass as he thrust in and out of me was music to my ears.

"You like that don't you Baby," he whispered, as he slowed down his strokes trying to stop himself from cuming too quick. I answered with a moan as I threw my pussy back at him contracting my vaginal muscles causing Shane to lose his mind. As his moans grew louder his body bucked, and he started to tremble, then he exploded inside of me. He rolled on his side then snuggled up behind me.

"I hope you enjoyed yourself tonight Baby," he said, as he eased closer to me, his dick pressed against my ass.

"Heck yeah I enjoyed myself! The party, the cake, my Dad...You really pulled out all the stops didn't you Baby."

"I wanted to make it special for you."

I gave him a nice soft kiss on the lips. "And you did."

"Now that the celebration and all that preparation is over; we need to get back to doin' us. It's almost winter time and I need that in-door-activity goin' to keep me warm. He started to kiss the back of my neck.

I'd be damned. Aleyma was right.

"Let me find out you being selfish and tryna keep me in this house," I said, pretending to have a problem with it. I loved the idea of all that attention.

"Oh Baby I'm definitely selfish when it comes to you. You already know. I couldn't wait to get you home lookin' at you all night in that damn dress. I was losin' my fuckin' mind at the party. A nigga was brick all night. I hope you know that you ain't gettin' no sleep tonight," he whispered seductively as his dick swelled against my ass.

"Press play and let me start...fast forward to your favorite part..." Shane whispered the lyrics to Mario's *Music for love* then slid his tongue in my mouth ready for round two.

Epilogue

With EL, Barkim, and the Patterson brothers all dead, Shane finally got his revenge for Tay's death. He still struggles with the fact that Tay died in his place, but at least those responsible are six feet under—exactly where they put Tay. Shane set up a five million dollar trust fund for Tayari Jr. that he will have access to once he turns twenty one. He promised Tay that if anything ever happened to him that his son would never want for anything—he kept that promise.

Shane and I bought a cute little cottage in the Hamptons after we were invited one weekend for a couples retreat and fell in love with the place. It was at the cottage where I ran into EL's sister Amelia who was at the retreat with her new husband. Amelia showed us pictures of her adorable new baby boy whom she named Eldorus after his late uncle. She even calls him EL for short. It was strange hearing Amelia talk about EL. After everything that went down between EL and me, I guess it's understandable. Amelia finally stopped blaming me for EL's death and admitted that the entire family was in denial about the extent of his breakdown. Maybe if they wouldn't have ignored the signs, EL would still be alive.

A few weeks after Mrs. Wiggins was released from the mental hospital, she had another break down and was re-committed. When she isn't hugging a pillow or having conversations with imaginary friends, she is kept heavily sedated. On those rare occasions when she is actually lucid, I try to visit. Liz told me that my visits seem to lift her spirits. Since she knew how much EL cared for me, seeing me makes her feel closer to him.

I retired my mother, and she relocated to Palm Beach, Florida. For as long as I can remember, my mother always talked about retiring in Florida. I set her up with a sizeable bank account but then after a few months she got bored and came out of retirement. She started her own magazine called "Flavor." The magazine keeps her so busy that she barely has time for anything else. My mother loves Florida so much it's like pulling teeth trying to get her to visit. Not long after my mother moved to Palm Beach, Aunt Tangy moved about five minutes away. They met some crazy-ass Jamaican chick name Vera and once they found out that she was a stone cold gambler like them—it was on.

Mia was sentenced to six years for embezzlement with the possibility of parole after three. Her kids were put into foster care and will most likely be adopted. I don't know what that chick was thinking trying to embezzle money from Miller, Goldstein & Brock. They didn't get to be one of the largest investment firms in the country by being stupid. What would their clients think if they knew that the firm they entrusted their money to let one of their

269

employees swindle them out of theirs? Like I said, that chick just wasn't thinking. She will definitely have plenty of time to think in the 6x6 cell that she will be residing in for the next six years. Some folks just have to learn the hard way.

Aleyma and Alayna started dating my cousins Chris and Day-Day. I was never big on family and friends mixing it up, but I learned that you have to take happiness wherever you can find it. Besides, Chris and Day-Day could definitely do a lot worse. The twins are a couple real chicks. We clicked from day one.

I haven't seen Sara since EL's funeral. Word on the street is that she started dating some dealer in Brooklyn and got into some shit with his baby mother, and that chick shot Sara in her back twice; leaving her paralyzed from the waist down. Ain't karma a bitch? Sara was the one who helped EL hide the fact that at he could walk from me. How ironic was it that she would end up paralyzed herself? Come to think of it, I never got around to paying her trifling-ass back for betraying me. What can I say? Other shit took precedence. After a while revenge wasn't important to me anymore so I did what I have never been known to do—I let shit slide. She got what she deserved anyway, and I didn't have to do shit.

WHEN YOU HAVE IT ALL YOU HAVE EVERYTHING TO LOSE!

The Drama Continues...

Another Man's Girl 2

A NOVEL

SYDNEY LYTTLE

An Excerpt From
The Drama Continues...Another Man's Girl 2

The Devil You Know

Chass...

The Yukon Denali was riding my rear bumper. I slowly pressed my foot down on the accelerator increasing the speed of the vehicle from seventy to eighty miles per hour, and they were still on me. My eyes darted back and forth from my rearview mirror to the dark road ahead. After passing a sign that reminded me of the fifty-five miles per hour speed limit, I fixated on the speedometer, which confirmed that I was already driving twenty-five miles over the legal limit. Still, the anxious driver who continued to follow closely behind me wasn't satisfied. His persistence now came in the form of flashing high beams that blared from behind making it difficult for me to see the road ahead.

Oh, see now this muthafucka is buggin'. His stupid-ass could just drive around me, but instead he'd rather waste time pissing me off.

If my BMW 650i convertible wasn't just two days old, I would slam on my breaks so fast not giving a damn if he crashed into me or not. Then after Allstate gets through ripping his ass to shreds, he'd think twice before he pulled this shit on somebody else.

"If I'm driving too slow for you then go around me," I yelled as I rolled my window down and stuck my arm out, signaling for the anxious driver to drive around me. That gesture was ignored. The driver continued to flash those blinding high beams while relentlessly honking that damn horn, resting on it for long blows at a time.

If I didn't know any better I'd think that the idiot was trying to get me to pull over. Of course that was out of the question. Along with any ideas I had of moving into the next lane. Those flew right out of the window as soon as I opened it. After the day I had I was just the right person for him to pull this shit on. At this rate I could easily develop a case of road rage myself and run his ass off the road. That thought was becoming more appealing to me at that point. I always hated aggressive drivers that felt like the road belonged to them and to hell with everyone else. There were two other free lanes that he could have easily moved into, but for some reason, he was determined to ride my ass all the way to where ever the hell he was going. The speed of his vehicle increased, forcing me to increase my speed. I was now driving ninety-five miles per hour in a fifty-five mile per hour zone.

The glare that demanded my eyes to widen was no longer behind me. Believing that he'd finally gotten the message that I wasn't caving into his road ignorance, I eased comfortably back into my seat and focused on the dark road ahead. I flicked on my windshield wipers to clear the drizzle that began making its way across my windshield when suddenly the loud honking resumed and the flashing bright lights quickly followed. That damn Denali was on my ass again.

"What the fuck?!" I said out loud more enraged than before. The flashing high beams and horn blowing were simultaneous like they were both stuck on repeat. Thinking it was a couple of college kids having a laugh at my expense, I figured I'd slow down then they wouldn't have any choice except to slow down as well or drive around me. So I lifted my foot off of the accelerator and the vehicle began to slow down. Suddenly I felt a bump to the back of my car. My head spun around like the exorcist as I rolled my window down and started cursing like a sailor at the wreckless driver who undoubtedly was going to pay for whatever evidence he'd left on my rear bumper. I must have pissed him off with my choice of words because he started to swerve in and out of lanes like he was purposely trying to cause an accident. He followed that bump with another one this time causing my car to swerve into the middle lane just as another car was approaching giving me only seconds to swerve back to avoid a collision.

Spotting a police car parked on the shoulder straight ahead, I quickly drove to the far right lane. I was slowly easing toward the shoulder about to alert the police regarding the hits to my vehicle, when suddenly the police car sped off. The colorful lights and loud sirens chased the idiot driver down the darkened highway.

I watched the chase thinking, *that's what his stupid-ass gets for riding my ass like that; had me doing damn ninety-five when I never drive faster than seventy. What was he gonna do if I got stopped? Pay my ticket too.*

I sucked my teeth wondering what the hell his problem was. I never even got the chance to report the hits to my vehicle to the police. Maybe that's why he sped off like that because he knew I was about to report his ass. Hitting my car is the least of his worries now. Stupid-ass probably got his self into some deep shit by making the police chase him. We know how much they hate that shit.

After the day I had, I was anxious to get home. I was so tired I didn't even bother to check my car for damages. I knew I would inspect it thoroughly once I got home anyway. I straddled the middle lane cruising at sixty miles per hour for the remainder of the drive home while listening to Keyshia Cole's *Heaven Sent* which immediately began to relax me making me forget about the unfortunate incident. I exited the highway then pulled into the left lane, and up to the red light. I glanced in my rear view mirror right before stopping. To my surprise a Yukon Denali was exiting the highway like it was on fire.

It can't be that same idiot, I thought watching the Denali from my rear view mirror.

The light changed and I turned left.

So did the Denali.

The driver was on me, approaching me at an alarmingly high speed. The aggressiveness of his driving was familiar. This was definitely the same Denali that I'd had the unfortunate encounter with not even a half hour ago.

How did he know which exit I would get off at? Or better yet, how in the hell did he catch up to me? I left his ass miles back.

I felt my stomach fly up into my throat. My palms leaked of sweat. I sped in and out of the dark streets trying to lose them, but they were on my ass. By this time I was regretting my decision not to alert the police— especially since it was becoming clear that this was no case of road rage. The driver was clearly targeting me. I ran straight through two red lights praying that I would make it the additional ten minutes it would take to get home.

** ** ** **

I woke up tied and gagged and thrown on the cold dirty ground. I faded in and out of consciousness like I was in the middle of a fog. Every breath I took was like a tug of war with my lungs. It felt like I was being stabbed in the chest repeatedly. The left side of my face throbbed like it had a heartbeat. My stomach was on fire. Like someone was sticking a hot poker directly into my flesh.

The duct tape wrapped around my wrists was so tight it was a tourniquet cutting off my circulation causing my skin to turn every color except my natural shade of caramel brown. I tugged on the tape so hard that my wrist were bleeding. I tried opening my eyes, but my eyelids felt like they weighed a ton. I tried to scream, but all I heard were sounds muffling against the fabric that was stuffed inside my mouth. The gag and my voice were enemies—they wouldn't work together.

Unaware of my surroundings and trying to make sense of my current situation I tried to focus on the last thing I remembered which was getting off the highway. And then...and then...Oh my God somebody ran me off the road forcing me into a tree. The next thing I remember was...my mind froze. I could see the images, but they were distorted. I was disoriented. My memories needed fine-tuning. I remembered a hooded figure approaching my car with something in his hand that looked like a—gun!

I tried to focus, but my blurred vision interrupted my sight. The chill bumps protruding from my skin alerted me that my body temperature was dropping at a rapid pace. I struggled to get free, but my efforts were useless. I tried to stand, but the duct tape that was wrapped around my ankles cutting off my circulation made it almost impossible causing me to fall to the ground. The tape was cutting into my ankles so tight that it would have to be surgically removed. I was so weak it was as if all of my energy was on vacation. I forced my eyes to focus on the tiny object lying on the ground beside me: It was a syringe staring at me from the cold floor. I had been drugged.

The sound of voices forced me awake. Realizing that I wasn't alone, I struggled to pull myself up. The voices disappeared replaced by footsteps. The footsteps were coming closer; piercing my ears demanding my attention. Triple images, were reduced to double images, and then finally a single image. I blinked continuously forcing my vision to fine tune as I tried to focus on the fuzzy figure standing before me. He towered over me watching me for several minutes. He was as still as a statue. Not a sound left his lips. His heavy breaths were the only clear indication of his presence. He was hiding behind a pair of shades and a hoodie that seemed to blend in with the darkness that surrounded us.

I tried to visualize what my abductor looked like behind those shades that I was sure was concealing a pair of cold eyes. I felt his eyes blaring at me through those dark lenses. My body twinged as he stared down at me like he was staring through the barrel of a gun—cold—heartless.

When he removed his hat and his shades my heart froze. I almost passed out again from the shock. My eyes and my mind were not in sync. My body started to tremble. I felt like I was in the middle of a nightmare. Reality seemed to be slipping further and further away from me. I began to question my sanity.

It can't be. No way in hell. How is this possible? Could this be the after effect of the drugs? I worried, praying that I wouldn't suffer any long term effects from whatever was in that syringe.

Wearing a wicked grin he kneeled down beside me and looked me in the eye.

"What's the matter Ms. Fondain...seeing ghosts?"

Made in the USA
Lexington, KY
05 January 2012